One Wilde Ride
Book One

It Might Have Been

LM Foster

This is a work of fiction. Names, characters, places and incidents are products of the author's imagination. Any resemblance to actual events, locales, organizations, or persons, either living or dead, is entirely coincidental.

ISBN-10: 0692388788
ISBN-13: 978-0692388785

Cover
Frenzy of Exultations, 1893
By Polish painter Władysław Podkowiński (1866 - 1895)
Oil on canvas (120 in × 110 in)
National Museum, Kraków, Poland
Design by
Ravenna Young
www.ravennayoung.blogspot.ca

9th Street Press
www.9thstreetpress.com

God pity them both! and pity us all,
Who vainly the dreams of youth recall.

For of all sad words of tongue or pen,
The saddest are these: "It might have been!"

Ah, well! for us all some sweet hope lies
Deeply buried from human eyes;

And, in the hereafter, angels may
Roll the stone from its grave away!

- John Greenleaf Whittier

ONE

"Ah, come on, Daina, come with me," Nadine requested evenly. Patiently. "You'll like it. It's . . . quaint. Maybe you'll find a new man."

Daina smiled. "You're the one that's looking for a replacement."

"I've already found him," Nadine corrected, in that same even tone. "I just thought that maybe you might like to find one also."

"Oh, yeah, that's right. You're afraid to jinx it, so you haven't given me a name or a description." Daina looked curiously at her friend and asked pointedly, "What did *they* say about him?"

Nadine shrugged, noncommittal.

"Reply hazy, try again," Daina said and smiled. Nadine smiled back. "You don't care what they say, this time, do you?"

"I always care what they say," Nadine said in surprise. "They're . . . *They know –"*

"You don't have to listen to them, you know. You don't have to *believe.* I've been telling you that since we were kids."

"It is decidedly so," Nadine replied. "But I do believe. And so do you. I'm not buying any post-adolescent rebellion on your part against their influence."

"But they're not picking my men for me, either."

"They're not picking my men for me."

"You've picked your own, this time." It was a statement.

"Don't you always pick your own?"

Daina shrugged. The men she had picked were transitory. Curiosity, adolescent hungers and needs – these had prompted her choices. This one was cute, that one was smart. But none of her relationships had been meant to last. Though a young woman, Daina had an old woman's capacity to look at her interactions with men as memories, even while they were happening. Memories of the way the light shone through this one's hair for just a moment; that's one's killer smile; the rich, chocolate brown color of that one's eyes. Memories that she figured might keep her warm on cold nights in an unimagined future. Memories that would have to suffice, when she was old and alone, man-less, like *they* were.

Daina might scoff, point up the fact that Nadine didn't have to believe in anything they said, especially if it went against what Nadine wanted to accomplish. But that same belief was a genetic part of Daina, as surely as she had the same light blue eyes as her Aunt Bellona, the same crooked smile as her Aunt Penny. What they said would come to pass. Maybe not today, or tomorrow, or next year. The actors were unknown, but the events would occur. It was as if her aunts were reading a history of things that had already happened; a history which consisted of only pronouns. He would do this, and she would do that, and they would move forward in time and space. But who the precise persons were was often in shadow, unless their magical auguries deigned to name them specifically.

TWO

When she was fourteen years old, Daina saw *The Manchurian Candidate,* and immediately believed that she was in love with Lawrence Harvey. He embodied everything that appealed to the heart and imagination of a child on the verge of young womanhood. Seriousness. Sophistication. Daina longed to be smiled at by someone that smiled like Lawrence Harvey, she longed to be kissed. It was becoming a biological imperative, that unbidden, unsought desire that sometimes kept her up at night with its intensity. She wanted to touch Lawrence Harvey, she wanted him to touch her. And the fact that he was twenty years older than her, a famous actor, didn't deter her love. That it could of course never be gave it another layer of excitement and longing that thrilled her to the bone.

Daina was sitting on the deck to her aunt's house: a small, pretty girl, studying a copy of *Life Magazine,* drinking in a picture of her idol. She sighed after a moment and looked up to see Aunt Bellona looking over her shoulder. Daina resembled her aunt a great deal: she was also small, and their blue eyes and dark hair were the same. Bellona's age was indeterminate; she could be forty or sixty. Gray streaked the once black hair, and crow's feet were at the corners of her always-laughing eyes. But those eyes, so like Daina's, were quick, bright, sparkling, like sapphires underwater. Daina knew that when she was old, she could do far worse than to look just like her Aunt Bellona.

"What holds your interest so, my child?" Bellona asked, her voice and language like a witch in some old-timey fairytale.

Daina sighed again and pointed to Lawrence Harvey's picture. "He's just . . ."

"Ah!" Bellona smiled. "So you have discovered that which makes the world go round? I was not much older than you when I made the same discovery. I remember, it was at the harvest . . . the heat of summer lingered during the day, but the nights were growing colder . . . His name was Simon. He was beautiful, like Adonis . . . a mere boy, as I was naught but a mere girl . . ." Bellona's voice tapered away, and Daina watched her aunt's faraway expression as she recalled her first love. It was at first serene, but then clouded after a moment. For reasons unknown to Daina, Bellona and Simon's love had not endured.

Bellona snapped her gaze back to her niece. "So you fancy this . . .?"

"Lawrence Harvey." Daina looked at the picture again. "Yes. I fancy him very much."

She looked back at her aunt with a hope that came from the circumstances of her upbringing. All her life, she had seen the proof; it was an incontrovertible fact of her existence. If Aunt Bellona or Aunt Penny said, "This will be," then it would be. It was as common and as undeniable to Daina as if they said, "The sun will set today."

Wild hope surged through her. If Aunt Bellona pronounced, "You will have what you fancy," then Daina knew that she would meet Lawrence Harvey, she would touch him, he would kiss her . . .

Bellona read the hope in her niece's eyes, and chuckled. "It is a pleasing distraction to fancy a man, Daina. Sometimes it is more pleasing than the actual possession. Sometimes it is all we will ever encompass."

Daina's hope fled. She sighed again. She had never believed that it could ever happen, not really. Lawrence was older than her, a movie star. He would never be interested in a fourteen-year-old girl. They would never meet . . . she accepted all that. But if Aunt Bellona had said that it *would* be, then she would have accepted that just as certainly.

"Since the spring," Bellona continued, "we have scryed the avenues of companionship that will someday come to you."

Daina looked up with interest, Lawrence Harvey's picture and persona forgotten for a moment. This was real life. Aunt Bellona and Aunt Penny had scryed. What they had seen, what Bellona was going to tell her, would be dim, murky; there would be no details, no timeframes, no names. But what would be foretold would occur.

"There will be one that you will love so much more than you feel that you love this one now," she said and nodded at the magazine. "And he will love you, more than that one ever could. Mr. Harvey's fate is . . . well, his fate will not affect yours."

"So, I'm going to meet Prince Charming and live happily-ever-after?" To an outsider, Daina's response would have seemed flippant. The fortuneteller was pronouncing her divination, and it seemed that Daina was a skeptic. But she was not. If Aunt Bellona pronounced *Prince Charming,* then it would be so.

"No," Bellona said, and that one syllable chilled Daina. Bellona sat down beside her niece, and the expression on her face told Daina that she would not, indeed, live happily-ever-after.

"He will not be Prince Charming, as neither are you Snow White, Cinderella or Sleeping Beauty." Bellona fluttered her hands

4

in annoyance. "You are a young woman of flesh and blood, and your blood now begins to sing to you of the *charms* of that being that is woman's other half. But no man is Prince Charming, Daina. That is a fable, a fairytale." She fluttered her hands again in dismissal. "And as for happily-ever-after . . . ever-after is a very long time, and we must take happily as it comes."

"Better not tell you now," Daina replied, with a little challenging smile.

"You may rely on it," Bellona countered, also smiling. "Heed me: you will share a love, as Romeo and Juliet, as Anthony and Cleopatra, as Napoleon and Josephine. 'I truly loved my Josephine,' Napoleon said, 'but I did not respect her.'"

Daina looked at her aunt sharply at this, but Bellona only shrugged. "Yours will not feel that way about you. There will be no disillusionment in your love for each other, Daina, and that's more than the great lovers of history and fiction could say – the disillusionment or else the tragedy are what makes for a good story."

Here was a point that couldn't be denied, and Bellona smiled at Daina's acceptance of it. Then she sobered. "But still there will be tragedy. Even true lovers do not live in a vacuum – they are subject to the whims, caprices, jealousies and vengeances of other actors. The infinite shades of gray that constitute right and wrong, fair and unfair, are only the perception of the fortunate parties, as well as they are the perceptions of those who see themselves as less fortunate. The circumstances of your love – when, who, how – are unclear. But that love shines through; it will endure. Yet still there is a blot of tragedy. Your son –"

"Enough!" Aunt Penny cried from the doorway. She crossed the deck in long quick strides, and wagged her finger at her sister. "The child is already an old soul, and burdened by her lineage. She has suffered more than her share of tragedy already."

The tragedy to which Aunt Penny referred was the death of Daina's parents in an automobile accident when she was seven years old, half her lifetime ago. Daina remembered them but vaguely, more as pictures in the family album than as people. Sometimes there would be a sound, or a scent, or a play of light that would bring them back to her fully, but the memory was without pain. They had gone on to their reward, and she hadn't known them long enough to miss them too much. Her aunts had raised her afterwards, and she was more than content.

"Don't further burden her with what might be," Penny admonished.

"What *will* be," Daina said softly.

Aunt Penny was lighter in coloring than Bellona; she had brown hair instead of black, gray eyes instead of blue; she was taller than Bellona. In family resemblance, she favored Daina's mother more than her other sister. But like Bellona, she seemed ageless. She was not young be any means, but just how old Penny was remained debatable.

Now the gray eyes blazed. "The future is not an open book, as Bellona would have you believe, my child. There are signs, portents, prophesies –"

"That nevertheless point to an inescapable outcome," Bellona said.

"And you're never wrong," Daina added.

Penny sighed. "What may seem to be monumental love, passion, vengeance, tragedy to your aunt, however, might not seem so to you. We are given the foreknowledge – actions will occur, emotions will be felt, reactions will follow. These things will happen – they swirl around us like dust devils; we can sometimes glimpse them aforehand like a will o' the wisp. But just who will feel the emotions, who will act on them and how . . .

"If we knew that we would drop our coffee in our laps, if we knew we would slip and fall down the stairs . . . why would we ever even bother getting out of bed?"

"Yet we can see that we will be burned or injured . . ." Bellona said darkly.

Penny shook her head. "Yet a burn or injury to me will not affect me as the same would affect you. Your sensitivity to love and tragedy is not the same as Daina's. Don't burden her with an old woman's perceptions, Bell."

"What are your perceptions, Aunt Penny?"

Penny brightened. "The love you will find, that will find you, will be all that you could wish it to be." She looked pointedly at her sister. *"Without a doubt.* To ask for more than that, to read any more into it today, when you are but a child, is *a course of impious stubbornness."*

THREE

But Daina had never been able to completely throw off the shadow of Bellona's predicted tragedy. She and his father's love would endure, but her son . . . and Bellona would not be coaxed into any further prognostications about this some-day child of Daina's. *"Cannot predict now,"* was always the reply if Daina would ask about him.

Inescapably, Daina therefore always looked at the men that attracted her with an eye to their potential fatherhood. She would look twice, of course, if they bore any resemblance to Lawrence Harvey, but she always asked herself: *would I want to bear a child to this one, or that one? No.* Never had any of them stirred her to this most basic of desires. She felt that she would be able to tell when her soulmate entered the list – she felt that it would be as simple a thing as wanting to have his baby. His doomed son.

FOUR

Nadine and Daina had been inseparable friends since the age of nine, when Nadine's parents had bought the house across the road. Daina's aunts' gentle parenting had soothed the loss of her parents, but Nadine's friendship had been instrumental in her becoming a confident, happy adult.

Penny and Bellona had immediately accepted Nadine as a part of the family, imparting their folksy wisdom and archaic lore to her as easily as they had to Daina. Nadine believed in their ability to predict the future as completely as did their niece. There were the little things: brief, unseasonable thunderstorms that came out of a clear blue sky and left as quickly; car accidents on the street down the hill from their house; the deaths, disappearances and appearances of cats – all these events proved prophetic when given mention (albeit cryptically) by Bellona and Penny beforehand.

Like all good witchy women, Penny and Bellona always had three cats; no more, no fewer, at least not for very long. They roamed the woods around the house, were seen all over the neighborhood. They would gather every morning on the railing that surrounded the deck of the ladies' abode, lounging silently, staring implacably at the French doors that opened onto the deck, willing someone within to come out and feed them. Whatever petty or serious kitty squabbles that they might have with one another would be put on hold for the moment, in anticipation of Aunt Penny's homemade cat food.

If there were more than three waiting for their feast, Penny and Bellona would give one of them an extra pat on the head, an extended scratching under the chin. There would be an undercurrent of sadness to it, Nadine always noticed, because, within a day or two, they would inevitably be one cat short, and the status quo of only three would reassert itself.

There had been no newcomers for a long time. Currently, there was Holt, a sleek, young white tom, with one blue eye and one green eye. He was always companionable, and enjoyed a vigorous petting. But he was also moody. Daina and Nadine learned quickly to watch his tail when they were petting him. If it started to twitch, it meant that Holt had grown weary of their affection. Too many more pets, and he would strike out at their friendly hands, all teeth and claws, then dart off the railing, only to return later, bright-eyed and innocent, to tenderly request more *lovies*.

Princess Plush – Bellona was fond of outrageous monikers – was an austere and elegant Siamese that Nadine had discovered in a box on her parents' doorstep one morning, like an abandoned baby at an orphanage. She had been just a playful ball of dark fur and crossed blue eyes then. Nadine's mother had an aversion to cats, so Nadine had presented the kitten to her aunts. The next day, Penny's favorite tom, a long-furred gray tabby named Smokey, was absent from breakfast. Penny sighed. Smokey would be seen no more.

The longest-lived resident of Penny and Bellona's revolving door of felines was an enormous old Maine Coon mama cat named Grimalkin. She had been around for about as long as Nadine could remember, raising litter after litter of kittens, sometimes inside her aunts' house, sometimes in the woods. Holt was one of her babies. The rest had either been given away to friends and acquaintances, or had taken off on their own.

Grimalkin had apparently outlived her fertility, however. She hadn't had a litter of kittens in a few years, and Nadine thought that she missed them. Even though it was Princess Plush that Nadine had first discovered, she was always cold to Nadine. After Smoky was gone, the Siamese had adopted Penny as her own.

But Grimalkin had always loved Nadine best. She liked to sneak into Nadine's parents' house, if a door was left open for too long. Her favorite place to sleep once inside was a little to the left of center on Nadine's bed, just below her pillow. Nadine would've welcomed the cat, despite her mother's objections – Nadine came to think of Grimalkin as her *familiar* – except that the old mama liked to climb onto Nadine's back while she was asleep and commence to *making biscuits*, that strange kneading thing that cats do, claws out. Coming from a cat Grimalkin's size, it was painful; it left marks. If Nadine was asleep on her back, Grimalkin was also fond of attempting to curl up directly under Nadine's chin, on her chest, flouncing her big fluffy tail under Nadine's nose and into her mouth.

Nadine's mother would shriek in alarm whenever she saw Grimalkin in Nadine's room, and shoo her none too gently outside. Grimalkin would twitch her giant tail at the indignity, then run across the street and up the hill to Penny and Bellona's, and sit patiently on the deck railing, hoping for a treat. When Nadine and Daina would return after school, Grimalkin would jump into Nadine's lap and purr contentedly. Nadine was *her* familiar.

But besides the comings and goings of cats, Penny and Bellona also seemed to know about larger happenings, always in advance.

They frequently made short remarks, non-sequitur to the conversation of the moment, which would invariably show themselves to be accurate predictions, at least to Nadine and Daina. The fact that a broad interpretation of the remarks, like Nostradamus' portents, could lend themselves to different situations, did not occur to the girls.

On a chill November evening when she was fifteen, Nadine overheard Bellona say to her sister, "The southern sky will be black with shame by this hour tomorrow."

"Cruel fate, dark whimsy, a young face," Penny replied.

"A pleasant, big-eyed, all-American boy's face," Bellona agreed.

"Hiding a capering, gibbering, unhinged mind."

"The known world will teeter, but only for a moment."

"A history-altering tragedy. The black veil, her lost, tear-stained face . . ." Penny sighed deeply.

The next day, President Kennedy was assassinated in Dallas.

And then there was the time that Nadine arrived to pick up Daina for school on an April morning in 1964. When she knocked, Penny bid her enter, then said, *"For as Jonas was three days and three nights in the whale's belly; so shall the Son of man be three days and three nights in the heart of the earth."*

Though not religious now, Nadine had been a regular church-goer as a child. At almost sixteen, she didn't attend anymore. She was too busy living life to sit in church, and she felt she received all the spirituality she needed from Daina's aunts. Yet she recognized the quotation as a reference to the Resurrection; she realized it was Good Friday.

Nadine did not recognize the verse with which Bellona replied to her sister. *"Therefore I will shake the heavens, and the earth shall remove out of her place, in the wrath of the Lord of hosts, and in the day of his fierce anger."*

The sisters had then looked blankly at Daina and Nadine. Daina shrugged, used to Penny and Bellona's inscrutability. "Happy Pagan Ritual," she said, a reference to Easter tradition. It was an expression that she had picked up from her aunts: the bunnies and chickies and the Resurrection were all just rehashings of ancient, springtime fertility rituals. The aunts only nodded, and the girls went off to school.

It was not until the following evening, when Nadine's father was exclaiming over the news of the devastating earthquake that had struck the day before in Alaska, that Nadine made the connection. Daina's aunts (she really thought of them as *her* aunts, too) were always spouting Bible verses and obscure quotations, and they frequently pronounced odd statements of their own. Sometimes, they seemed to be just words – sometimes nothing portentous could be gleaned from their ramblings. But this! Just like the death of the president, and Jackie's pitiful, hopeless face . . . they had predicted the earthquake. *And the earth shall remove out of her place . . .*

When Nadine said as much to Daina, her friend had just shrugged. "It's entirely possible."

FIVE

There would never be any bittersweet proclamations about true love and doomed children for Nadine from Penny and Bellona, however. At thirteen, Nadine had peeled an apple in one long strip, thrown the peel over her shoulder, hoping to see the initials of a future love. The peel had landed upright, in squiggly rings, like a common spring or a Slinky. No letters could be made from it. *"Ask again later,"* Bellona had suggested with a shrug.

At fifteen, she and Daina had peered into a water-filled basin by candlelight on the 1st of May, hoping to glimpse the face of their future husbands. Daina saw nothing – she claimed not to believe in such silliness, anyway. If was nothing but a superstitious old wives' tale to Daina. But her aunts had told the story, so Nadine wanted to believe. She had been quite disappointed when no face had appeared. She agreed with Daina – it was silly, impossible, just a game . . . But still . . .

Nadine's parents would have perhaps raised their eyebrows had they known of their daughter's implicit belief in Penny and Bellona's supernatural abilities. But they didn't know. Not long after they had moved to the neighborhood, after Daina had gone home after having dinner with her new playmate's family, then nine-year-old Nadine had proclaimed, "Daina's aunts are witches."

Not glancing up from the evening paper, her father had said, "Everybody thinks they're a witch nowadays."

"Mostly just the wild, young girls, Sam," her mother had said.

Her parents had given Nadine that smug, condescending, you're-too-old-to-be-believing-in-fairytales look, and the discussion was closed. Nadine never brought it up again. She had never liked that look from her parents, and the mystical nature of Daina's aunts was really none of her their business, anyway, if they chose not to believe in it.

Penny and Bellona were always just the two kindly old ladies across the street to Nadine's parents, raising their niece in the wake of her parents' tragic death. The only thing that was ever remarked upon was their seemingly independent wealth: Penny and Bellona didn't work, had *no visible means of support,* as her mother had termed it. Yet they owned their little ancient house on the hill, as well as the more modern one at its foot, where Daina had lived with her parents until their tragic demise. They also owned the forested tract of land surrounding these structures. Nadine's father had said the phrase *life insurance,* and had nodded significantly at his wife, again over the evening paper. After this pronouncement, Nadine had never heard any further speculation about Daina's aunts from her parents.

When she was twelve, an older girl at school had made fun of Nadine's brand new dress, then had tripped her on the playground. The dress was soiled, torn, effectively ruined. Daina was unable to comfort her – it was a beautiful dress, her favorite, and now it had been destroyed. After school, steeped in furious tears, Nadine had turned to Penny and Bellona for solace. For revenge.

"Teach me how to curse Rebecca!" Nadine entreated. "I wanna make her hair fall out, her teeth turn black!"

Bellona grinned impishly. "All right," she said, and began pawing through cupboards and drawers for the requisite accoutrements.

"A curse is the weapon of the powerless, Nadine," Aunt Penny said quietly. "The strong person strikes his tormentor head-on."

"But Rebecca is bigger than me!"

Aunt Penny nodded. "All of us feel powerless at some time or another – we cannot always simply call out our enemy. Sometimes our enemy is vastly stronger and we must make an oblique blow. A curse is like a poisoner, and a poisoner is universally reviled. He smiles in his victim's face, all the while secretly, slowly destroying his enemy. A curse is authorless – someone encounters bad fortune, but doesn't know who wished him ill, because the ill-wisher means to stay hidden."

"So cursing someone is cowardly," Daina said.

"Sometimes there is no other way to get satisfaction for the wrongs committed against oneself," Aunt Penny insisted. "Many people will attempt to hurt you in this life, Daina. Some will succeed. Circumstances will dictate that some hurts are unanswerable directly, yet still they must be redressed. Failing to redress an injury is a second injury." Penny looked solemnly at Nadine and Daina. "But because a curse springs from powerlessness, from desperation – if I smack you in the mouth, you know that it was I who struck you. You may strike me back. But if I curse you, because I cannot smack you in the mouth . . . then you cannot strike me back. Because I cannot fight honestly, I give up part of myself with that curse. It takes something from me, as well as its victim.

"Therefore, one should always carefully weigh how much of oneself one is willing to lose in the search for revenge, girls. *Heat*

13

not a furnace for your foe so hot that it do singe yourself. A curse should only be initiated for near-mortal hurts, because once begun, it cannot be stopped. It oft-times takes on a life of its own." Penny glared at her sister. "It is not something to be undertaken to assuage meaningless playground disputes. Besides, 'Deen, if you curse Rebecca, she'll never know that her misfortunes spring from you, and she'll only continue to bully you. A curse is not the solution in this case."

Later that evening, while Penny and Daina were out grocery shopping, Bellona mimicked her sister derisively, *"A curse is not the solution in this case.* What are you supposed to do, fight the good fight?"

"She's bigger than me," Nadine replied gloomily.

"Exactly. And what Penny failed to mention is that it doesn't matter if Rebecca knows that the curse came from you. It doesn't matter if it solves, or even changes, the situation. Sometimes, it's enough to see our enemy look like a fool. A few simple words and signs, and Rebecca will turn her lunch tray over in her lap tomorrow." Bellona and Nadine grinned at each other. "Come, my child, I'll show you how it's done."

Nadine loved her aunts and believed their truths. Sometimes she thought that she loved them and believed them more than Daina did. While Daina simply listened and observed, Nadine eagerly absorbed every aspect of her aunts' philosophy. Curses from Bellona (in secret); herbal medicine and potions from Penny; a thousand tales of magical realms. Their ability to prophesy was a gift, unteachable, unlearnable. But there were other ways to see ahead: Nadine became an adept at reading the Tarot, while it never interested Daina. Like any common dabbler, Daina could read a lay, but couldn't ever see the truths it revealed.

Daina never perceived her upbringing as unusual. While Nadine attached romance and destiny to her aunts' unusual skills, Daina was no more excited by her aunts' potions and portents than is the cattle rancher by the round-up. Yet it could not be denied that both of them believed, in their own fashion.

SIX

Daina never shared with Nadine what Bellona had pronounced to her when she was fourteen, about the future of her love life. It was not a happy prediction to Daina – true love but also tragedy – but Daina accepted it. What her aunts foretold was as inevitable and immutable as the change of the seasons. Because she was still just a child herself, Daina didn't feel the need to mention the prediction about her own doomed child to Nadine. That part was alien to her – the very idea of having a baby at all, nonetheless one destined for . . . Aunt Bellona had never specified what evil would befall her son. She had just uttered that one sentence: *your son . . . a blot of tragedy.*

As she grew older, Daina suspected that Penny had forbidden her younger sister from speaking any more of the dire prophecy to her niece. Daina suspected that Bellona knew details of her boy's fate – her son, then still an unknown twinkle in his unknown father's eye – but she could never coax another word about it from Aunt Bellona. *"My reply is no,"* is all she would ever say when asked if she had any more info. After a while, Daina stopped asking.

As a teenager, Nadine asked her aunts to scry the future of her relations with the opposite sex, also.

"Many lovers," Bellona said with a little giggle.

"As you will choose," Penny added with a mirthless, somewhat stern smile.

This was a disappointingly vague augury to Nadine. But since a definite prediction of a one true love didn't seem to be in the offing, to placate her, Penny and Bellona would henceforth frequently bestow a somewhat more useful and prosaic gift upon their niece. Instead of describing the distant future, they provided her with key info about what would happen in the next few days. It was not an amenity that they provided to Daina.

It began when the girls were sixteen, a few months after high school had begun for the year. Nadine and Daina were sitting at their aunts' kitchen table doing homework. Daina nodded at the chemistry text atop Nadine's other schoolbooks. "You're not taking chemistry," she observed.

"Oh, that's Kevin's. He left it in the car."

Daina rolled her eyes, and Nadine grinned at her. Almost from the first day of school, Kevin had caught a ride home with them. Daina thought he lived close enough to school to walk home; she was convinced that he only asked for a ride because he was sweet on Nadine.

Kevin was on the football team, and he was cute enough, Daina thought: tall and broad-shouldered, with a golden blaze of curly blonde ringlets, like a cherub from a Renaissance painting. He wasn't very bright, however. *Definitely not father material,* a little voice in the back of Daina's head had pronounced. It was just a tiny little voice – it wasn't like Daina was prepared to take the plunge that produced offspring quite yet, anyway. But she knew what it entailed, and knew that she would be up for it someday. She had already kissed a few boys, but had never felt inclined to take it any further than that, despite their entreaties.

She thought about the act, sometimes, late at night, usually when a stray moonbeam struck the picture of Lawrence Harvey that she still had tacked up next to her bed. But Lawrence was unreachable, and besides him . . . Daina wasn't ready. And certainly not with the likes of someone like Kevin. He could be sweet on Nadine, and Nadine could be sweet on him, for all that it affected her.

Daina knew that Nadine liked him, too: she had seen them making out in the car when she had been a little slow getting to the parking lot after class that day. He had probably left his book in the car as an excuse to call Nadine later. Yeah, Nadine liked Kevin. Not as much, Daina suspected, as Kevin liked Nadine, but regardless . . . it really wasn't any of her business.

Curious at Nadine's grin, Aunt Bellona picked up Kevin's textbook, then grinned herself. "Ah!" she cried in glee. "You'll have a lot of fun with this one! Adventure! Passion!"

"Will I . . . with him? Will we . . .?" Nadine blushed furiously.

Penny said, "That is entirely up to you, 'Deen." She took the book from her sister, held it for a moment. *"My sources say no,* however," she concluded.

"I would have to agree," Nadine said. "Kevin is okay, but I don't think that I could ever . . . with him." She blushed again.

"Sometimes okay is enough," Bellona opined.

"Okay for you, old woman," her sister chided. "These girls still seek their first true loves."

SEVEN

And so it went throughout the rest of high school. Daina and Nadine went out with their peers. It was the free-loving 1960s, and neither girl entertained any long-lasting relationships. Daina was always on the lookout for the father for her son – the few that she dallied with were definitely not daddy material, but they were still enjoyable in their own rights.

Nadine would purloin something that belonged to each hopeful, and have her aunts read it before she went out with him too many times. Most produced only shrugs – this one was nice, that one was a gentleman. None were seen to last, but all were deemed safe, harmless, some more fun than others.

All harmless, except for a young man named Adam that Nadine met at a party right before high school graduation.

He seemed shy; he didn't speak to Nadine at first. But she noticed him eyeing her from a corner of the room. Every time she would look in his direction, she found the slight young man with the blazing red hair and the large green eyes studying her solemnly, unwaveringly. His gaze was almost hypnotic, and eventually Nadine spoke to him, because it didn't look like he was going to speak to her. It seemed as though he just wanted to watch her.

Nadine said hi and made small talk, and after stumbling over his words for a moment, Adam asked her if she'd like to go out to the movies the following evening. Nadine hesitated – he seemed so painfully shy. But when Adam plucked a daisy out of a vase on a nearby table and rather humorlessly offered it to her, again reiterating that he would like to go to the movies with her, Nadine found the gesture chivalrous and agreed.

Daina had been occupied somewhere else at the party; she never met Adam. Before she went home, Nadine stopped at her aunts' house and presented them with the now wilted daisy.

When Bellona touched the flower, she started as if slapped. Her smile withered. She silently handed it to Penny.

Penny took it, twisted the stem between her fingers. "Dangerous," she said after a moment.

Daina elbowed her best friend, wiggled her eyebrows, grinned. "Dangerous can be fun."

"But he seems so shy," Nadine protested. "Not fun at all. Not at all dangerous."

"Not fun!" Bellona cried in alarm, her normal eloquence deserting her. "Tell them, Penn!"

"A very bad boy," Aunt Penny pronounced gravely. When Daina continued to grin, she added, "But not the type of bad boy that you youngsters like. This one is no slayer of mastodons."

Daina laughed heartily, and Nadine couldn't help but think that her friend was laughing at her.

It was her aunts' theory that the inescapable fact that young women liked bad boys went back to cavemen times.

"There was the hunt," Aunt Bellona would say, blue eyes aglow. "There were the brave ones, the fearless ones, first with their spears, headless of the danger. They would feed the tribe or they would die in the effort!"

"And then there were the shy ones, the civilized ones, the ones that would hang back," Aunt Penny would add, with a rare smile. "They would help clean the carcass, maybe even help to cook it. But while the hunt was underway, they would stay in the background and wait until the kill was achieved. Safer that way.

"But the women wanted the fearless ones – they would produce strong sons, as fearless as themselves; masterful, wise daughters . . . so the women sought these men out, even if they might not make it home from the next hunt."

"You still seek those mastodon slayers," Aunt Bellona said. "It's in your blood, your genes, your imagination. The idea of a fearless man stirs you . . ."

"Except there are no more mastodons," Aunt Penny added, her customary sternness returning. "The forces of nature have been tamed; the modern mastodon-slayer rebels against the wind; he is rudderless. You can buy your own steaks at the grocery store." When the young women smiled, she said, "You might be better to resist the bad boys, my girls – there are no more mastodons for them to slay. You might be better off with a nice guy, an accountant, perhaps . . ."

Daina and Nadine had wrinkled their noses at that pronouncement. An accountant? *How boring.*

But it seemed as though Nadine had picked an accountant this time, and Daina was laughing at her about it. "So Adam is just a nice, dull boy, then?" Nadine asked. "No mastodon-slayer, but –"

"No!" Bellona cried in alarm. "Not nice!"

Penny dropped the daisy into the kitchen trash can as if it was a filthy thing. She turned and washed her fingers at the sink. "This one *is* a bad boy, 'Deen. A very bad boy indeed. But not in the way you would like. He is –"

"A slayer!" Bellona hissed.

"But not of mastodons." Penny dried her hands and turned somber gray eyes upon the girls. "Your aunt is overly dramatic. This young man has slain nothing yet . . . but he seethes. He has death in him. It would do well for you to avoid him."

When Adam called the following day, in anticipation of their movie date, Nadine told him that she was sorry, but an old boyfriend of hers had just moved back to town. A large, jealous, football-player boyfriend. A slayer of mastodons. Nadine would not be able to accompany Adam to the movies, or anywhere else. Ever.

EIGHT

Right after they started college in the fall of 1966, Daina saw an episode of *Star Trek* called *The Menagerie,* and decided that she was in love with Jeffrey Hunter. She joined his fan club, received an autographed picture of him through the mail. Lawrence Harvey's image was placed without ceremony into the bottom drawer of the nightstand beside her bed, and Jeffrey took his place.

"Why do you moon over these movie stars when there are so many real men in the world?" Nadine said derisively. "Why, just the other day, I talked to one that looked just like this guy. The same blue eyes –"

"No one in this town looks like him," Daina sighed.

"Ah, close enough!" Nadine countered. "And he was real and asked me out. I borrowed a pencil from him –"

"And what did they say about him?"

"Outlook not so good." Nadine shrugged. "Bellona asked me to describe him. She said she was not getting a clear picture. I told her that he was thin, with big blue eyes and sandy-colored hair . . ."

"Jeff has dark hair."

"I know. You like those dark-haired ones. The ones that look like they could almost be your brother." Nadine smiled. "Anyway, Bellona said that Glen – that was his name – Glen was not like other men. Glen likes . . . other men."

Daina blinked. "Why did he ask you out then?"

Again Nadine shrugged. "That Bellona couldn't say. 'It would be so much easier if you had pictures, 'Deen,' she told me. 'I can get quite a clear reading from a photograph.' So, look what I got!" Nadine showed her friend a 35mm camera. "It's a Yashica. I told Daddy I wanted a camera, so he gave me this one."

"It looks complicated," Daina said.

"A little bit," Nadine agreed. "But he showed me how to use it. Smile." She snapped a picture of her friend.

Through their first three years of college, Nadine's would-be beaux would have to wait until after she got their pictures developed and Bellona and Penny made their assessments, before she would go out with them. Win, lose, or draw, Nadine stuck their photographs on the wall beside her bed.

At first, the young men in the photographs each had a rather surprised look on his face, but after a while, Nadine became quite a skilled photographer, and the portraits looked more natural; some even a trifle arty. By the time she and Daina turned twenty-one, she had hundreds of pictures. Some were of men to whom she had only spoken a few words; some she had dated; some she had been intimate with. None had lasted for very long – Nadine felt herself in love with none of them. None of them qualified as that ideal for which all young women search.

Conversely, Daina had just the one picture on her wall. Her ideal was Jeffrey Hunter. Like her friend, Daina talked and dated and was intimate with a few young men during college, but none of them struck anything in her either, past the possibility of a few enjoyable moments. And none of them looked anything like Jeffrey Hunter.

On the last Thursday in May, 1969, Nadine hurried over to see Daina. She had not been at the English class they shared; Nadine had not seen her at school all day.

Bellona smiled when she opened the door. "You have a new picture for me." It was a statement, not even a question. Nor was Nadine surprised.

"Yes, but –"

"You have known him for about two weeks. *Them,* actually."

Fascinated as always with the tiny witch and her abilities, Nadine forgot about her concern for Daina for a moment. "Yes. I met them on the commons. They look a little bit like –"

"Let me see!" Bellona said gleefully.

Nadine showed her aunt the picture she had taken of Will and Rob Wilde. They were twins, a year older than her. They were medical students.

"Ah, yes! Brilliant, beautiful boys! One for each of you! Twins! How exciting! It will be a whirlwind!"

"They invited us to the river this weekend. A little pre-end of term celebration. I'm sure Daina would like them. They look just like – where is Daina, anyway? She wasn't at school today."

Nadine was worried. Daina couldn't afford to be cutting English. The class bored her monumentally, she hated studying for it, and therefore, she wasn't going to get a good grade.

"Daina is in seclusion," Aunt Penny said sadly.

She handed a folded-over copy of the *Los Angeles Times* to Nadine, pointed at the headline. *Actor Jeffrey Hunter Dies of Injuries; Fall Believed Cause.* Daina's idol had slipped down a flight of steps at his Hollywood home. He'd been rushed to the hospital, but tragically, he had succumbed. An autopsy revealed that he had died of head injuries.

The death of a minor Hollywood star meant nothing to Nadine, but she felt a sharp pang of grief for her friend. She knocked softly on Daina's door. As Daina told her to come in, Bellona handed the picture of Will and Rob back to Nadine.

"See to it that she goes with you," Bellona whispered. "This mourning for someone she didn't even know is unhealthy. She needs to get out and live."

Nadine nodded and went into Daina's room.

Daina was curled up on her bed, staring out the window. Her face was puffy, tear-stained; a wad of damp tissues was clutched in her hand. She was indeed the picture of grief.

"I'm so sorry," Nadine began, sitting beside her friend on the bed.

"He was so young, 'Deen!" Daina sobbed. "He was only forty-two!" She buried her face in her pillow and sobbed anew.

Nadine frowned. Forty-two wasn't young. It was twice their age. She could never understand her friend's fascination with these movie stars. First, it had been Lawrence Harvey – Daina had taken her to see *The Manchurian Candidate* when it had shown again at the drive-in. Nadine had felt silly sitting in the car, dateless, while Daina gushed over this dull, stiff, foreign-seeming actor, in this talky, confusing movie.

And then this other one – Daina had made her sit through some bad western about Custer in which he had appeared. He was attractive enough . . . but still. Nadine just couldn't get all worked up about actors the way Daina did. There were too many real men around, men to talk to and laugh with, men to go out with . . . like Will and Rob.

"I'm sorry," Nadine repeated. "But I have a surprise for you."

Daina did not remove her face from her pillow. What could any surprise of Nadine's possibly matter, when Jeffrey Hunter was dead?

Nadine sighed in annoyance. This was really too much. She nudged Daina's shoulder, none too gently. "Look, damn it." At last Daina turned her sorrowful face toward her friend. Nadine held up the black and white picture. "This is Rob and Will. That's Rob . . ." She looked at the picture for a moment. "Or maybe that's Rob." She shrugged and held it up for Daina again. "I'm not sure. They're twins, obviously. They're not Jeffrey Hunter, but they do look something like him, don't you think?"

Daina sat up and took the picture from Nadine, then glanced at poor, dead Jeffrey's photo, still tacked to the wall. She looked back at Nadine, expectantly.

"They look a little bit like him, and they're not dead," Nadine continued, and Daina winced at her friend's cruelty. Nadine didn't care. Daina was just being ridiculous. "They're med students. Their parents have a little place on the Colorado River; they've got a boat. They invited us to go up there with them for the weekend."

Daina's eyes widened a little bit. "I don't even know them –"

"Rob assures me that there's an extra room; it's not like we have to sleep with them. I didn't give them the impression – they don't think we're like that, Daina. They're nice guys. Gentlemen." Nadine grinned. "But we could be like that . . . Bellona says it'll be a *whirlwind.* Come on, Daina. It'll be fun. I don't want to go by myself. You gotta go with me. Do it for . . . Jeffrey's memory."

Daina glanced at the color picture on the wall, then back at the black and white one in her hand. The twins did bear a striking resemblance . . . big, clear eyes, identical dark crew-cuts. "All right. I'll go with you."

Nadine leapt over and hugged her friend. "That's what I'm talking about! It'll be fun!"

Daina smiled weakly. "I could use a little fun, especially after this . . ." She looked at the picture on the wall again.

"We cannot dwell on tragedy," Nadine said solemnly. She arose, and before Daina could protest, she took the thumbtack out of the deceased actor's picture, and stuck Will and Rob's photo in its place. She consigned Jeffrey Hunter to the same drawer as Lawrence Harvey, shut it decisively. "I'm sure you'll never forget him. But we're young, Daina. It's time for us to live; not just in our imaginations, with movie stars, but it real life. With real people. Like them."

NINE

The weekend would prove a turning point.

In person, Daina found the twins' resemblance to her dead idol not as striking as in the photo that Nadine had given to her. Nadine had become quite a good photographer, and Daina suspected that her friend had somehow set up the picture to play up the resemblance. In person, Will and Rob's hair was not quite as dark, their eyes a pale green, rather than Jeffrey's light, sky blue. But Daina liked them, nonetheless.

The brothers towed their boat behind an ancient Cadillac, and on the drive to Parker, Arizona – their destination on the Colorado River – the four of them sang songs and drank beer and generally got to know each other. The girls discovered that Will and Rob Wilde were damn near indistinguishable; the only way that they could tell the young men apart was by their Chucks. Rob wore black ones and Will wore red ones. Once they got to the river even this marker was lost; they both went barefoot.

Their parents' place was a nice three-bedroom house, right on the water. When they first came outside and walked down to the little dock, Daina and Nadine were at a bit of a loss – which was which? The boat sat six: two bucket seats in front and a curving bench behind that could hold another four people. One of the boys got in the front and held his hand out to help Nadine into the boat – this one had to be her date, Rob. Both girls noted that, like their shoes, Rob wore black trunks and Will, red. They smiled at each other and wondered how many times during the weekend they would have to make this distinction.

They spent the afternoon on the water, and when the sun went down, there was a big party at the little house. Daina recognized some people from school, but overall the party-goers were strangers to her. Nadine recognized no one.

It was hot and loud inside the house, and Daina didn't hesitate when Will asked her if she wanted to take a little after-hours cruise. He was polite and gentlemanly, erudite . . . perhaps a little shy, definitely a trifle boring. He either talked too much about uninteresting things, or didn't talk at all.

The night air on the water was a little cooler than inside, but not much. Will landed the boat in a secluded cove not far from the house; the music and laughter drifted over to them, like sounds from a dream. Will suggested a swim, and they waded into the water, hand in hand.

They paddled around beside the boat for a few minutes, made small talk, playfully splashed each other. Daina waited, suddenly wishing that this shy boy would make some kind of a move. She discovered that she was physically attracted to him very much, despite his rather tenuous resemblance to Jeffrey Hunter. Daina also discovered that she was quickly forgetting Jeffrey, her unknown dream, now unknown forever, in favor of this flesh and blood reality. It was just as Nadine had said. It was time to live.

When Daina swam teasingly close to him, Will ceased to hesitate. He reached for her, drawing her against his chest and kissing her. To her delight, Daina found out that he was not shy at all, once she gave him the signal that she was willing. She liked the way he kissed, she liked the feel of his hands on her body beneath the blood-warm water. One thing led to another; they made love, standing up in the river, then again on the bow of the boat, with only the moonlight, a few leaping fish, and the whoops of their friends down the beach as witnesses.

They snuck into the house through a side door, avoiding the party that still raged. They quickly achieved Will's room, locked the door, doused the lights. They went at each other like animals, until just before dawn, when they fell asleep, spent, exhausted.

TEN

Nadine laid out plates and silverware for brunch on a picnic table under an awning outside the house. When Daina emerged, Nadine met her friend's tousled appearance and languid expression with a raised eyebrow. While Will and Rob cooked inside, out of earshot, Daina said, "You are *so right,* my friend. A real man is much better than an imaginary one. And this one is definitely a real man."

"His brother, too," Nadine agreed and they giggled girlishly. "Are we in love?"

Daina considered the identical twins through the sliding glass patio door. Her few couplings in the past had been born out of curiosity, the heat of the moment. They had been bittersweet to her, because she knew that they had not been destined to last. When these adventurers had called back, Daina had almost invariably turned them down. Occasionally she went back for seconds, but rarely thirds. She didn't want to hurt anyone, didn't want them to fall in love with her when she knew she wouldn't reciprocate it. She had never felt anything for them but a momentary interest.

Now Daina saw this all as maudlin sentimentality, as childish and melodramatic as her unrequited yearnings for Hollywood actors. What difference did it make if she loved them, or even if they loved her? What difference did it make what kind of fathers they might be?

Daina *was no longer doubtful of what she was livin' for* – just like Aretha said. Will made her *feel like a natural woman.* She *wanted to be close to him, he made her feel so alive.* So what if she didn't love him, if he was as boring as cornflakes when he talked? She loved what he did behind closed doors, more than she ever had with anyone else before. That was love enough.

"I don't know if we're in love," she told Nadine. But she did know, at least for herself. Will was a diversion; he would not be the father of her son, would not share that mysterious, *tragic blot* with her.

Daina decided on the spot to thenceforth give up even considering the whole father angle. It was irrelevant. Will was temporary. She had not met her son's father yet, would not even think about him anymore. But in the meantime . . .

"Whatever you want to call this, it'll do for now."

The girls didn't have any trouble telling their dates apart now – not because they were any more distinguishable, despite the fact that

Nadine and Daina knew them so much better – but because each had watched hers don that day's attire. Will wore a pair of maroon trunks, and Rob a dark gray pair.

Nadine staring fixedly at the brothers through the glass. Daina asked her friend what she was looking at.

"I've just had a thought. I don't know whether to be insulted, flattered, or both." She looked at the brothers for another heartbeat, then turned to Daina. "Did Will get up, leave your room last night, oh, about two or so?"

Daina considered. "He got up a couple of times, actually. I don't know what time it was. He made us a sandwich once, after everything was quiet."

Nadine looked over at them again. "You don't suppose . . . I just got the idea that maybe they switched on us. In the middle of the night. I mean, they look *so much alike* . . ."

"You mean?" Now Daina considered them anew. She grinned. "No! Really? You think they . . ."

Nadine was surprised at her friend's reaction. "You're not mad?"

Daina shrugged. "Two for the price of one." She felt herself blush at her own audacity.

Now Nadine grinned, too. "I don't know for sure. Rob told me that Will went to his Government class for him, one time when he was sick, and seeing them together in there . . ."

"How could we find out?"

Now Nadine frowned. "I don't know how we're gonna be finding anything out anymore. You live with the witches, and I live with my parents. It's gonna be tough enough to get them alone, nonetheless, alone, together, in the same place, like this. But . . . you'd be okay with it?"

"Would you be okay with it?"

Nadine looked at them again, shook her head a little, considering. Eventually she nodded. "Why the hell not?"

"If they do switch on us . . . They'd think they'd be fooling us, but . . . We'd really be fooling them."

Evidence would show that Rob and Will had not played the ol' twin switcheroo on them in Parker, nor would they ever attempt it. But it had been fun for Nadine and Daina to consider for a moment.

The two couples spent the day on the water again, and as night fell, the Wilde brothers' friends again started showing up in twos and threes, and another party was thrown. Will and Daina again disappeared early.

In the middle of the loud party, Nadine sat at a table close to the wall and read the Tarot for anyone who showed an interest. Nadine had oftentimes seen tragic events when she read the cards for her school chums: sudden deaths, infidelity, alcoholism, suicide, wasted lives; but when it was bad, she never revealed what she had seen to the smiling, eager faces sitting across from her.

Why should she kill the mood with sad visions, when these people were not believers, anyway? It was just a game to them. As with her aunts' fortunetelling, there were seldom any concrete details, yet Nadine knew that what she saw would come to pass, regardless. But she didn't feel that it was necessary or even useful to pronounce dire events if she foresaw them in the cards – it was not like anything she said to the sitters could alter what would befall them. Even though the details were often hazy, what would be would be – the future was as immutable as the past.

And Nadine found that if she concentrated on only the immediate future as she read, just the next couple of days, the weekend – then she rarely saw anything tragic. Her sitters were all young, healthy, in the prime of their lives. The darkness wouldn't arrive until later.

And it was all good for the slightly drunken girl that sat across from Nadine at Rob and Will's party tonight. She asked if her relationship with the young man she had met at the previous night's party would last. Nadine saw nothing but joy and mutual satisfaction between them, at least through the end of the summer, which was as far as she cared to look. The girl clapped happily at Nadine's prediction, and thanked her, then wandered off to locate her new beau.

Nadine smiled and shuffled the cards. *How long will Daina and Will's thing last, now going so strong that they can't even make an appearance at the party?* The cards told her that by Hallowe'en, Will would be nothing but a fond memory for her friend. Nadine sighed, asked the same question about herself and Rob – they were twins after all, and if it was to end between her friend and Rob's brother . . .

Rob was sitting on the couch, a short distance away. A bookcase blocked one end of the couch and the little hall to the kitchen from Nadine's view. She glanced over at him as she began to deal the cards and he smiled. "What does my future hold?" he asked her.

"A long and happy life," Nadine said automatically. She looked at the cards and frowned slightly. It seemed that Rob's life, long, happy or otherwise, would not be known to Nadine. The cups and pentacles told her that he would not be around in *her* life any longer than Will would be in Daina's.

Nadine sighed. Oh, well. It didn't matter, not really. She had only been kidding when she'd asked Daina if they were in love. The question was sprung from Nadine's reaction to Daina's obviously enjoyed use of someone she'd just met. Nadine knew that she wasn't in love with Rob, and she knew that Daina wasn't even looking for love.

Nadine firmly believed that there was someone for everyone, *the other half that made one whole,* as her aunts had always put it. The fact that they could never name him for Nadine, nor even so much as point in the direction from which he was to arrive, did not deter her from the belief that he was out there, and she would find him. It was the purpose of existence, Nadine believed in her poetic soul – to find your true love and to live happily ever after with him, just like in a fairy tale.

Nadine liked men – Bellona's prediction that she would have many lovers had already started to come to pass. While she was never able to see a future with any of them, she was not thereby unwilling to share a present. How would she ever meet that special one if she stayed home all the time like Daina did, mooning over movie stars?

There had always been a blank spot in Nadine and Daina's friendship when it came to men and relationships: the future was something they never discussed. Girl talk was always confined to giggling descriptions of the current one, but serious or wistful musings about true love and what might be never took place. Nadine was unaware that a monumental love was predicted for Daina, marred by tragedy. All Nadine knew was that her friend was picky, far pickier than she was. And all the ones that she had picked in the past had been found lacking. There had been very few second dates for Daina.

But she liked Will; that was obvious. It was not love, by any means, and the cards had told Nadine that they would not see the year out together. *It's not her heart,* Nadine thought with a grin – but Will had touched something in Daina. He was not the one for her, but he was the one that had showed her how much fun her other half could be, even if he was not to make that whole with her forever.

Nadine looked at her Tarot lay. Cute and fun, Will and Rob were not to outlast the last few months of this turbulent decade with them. By the time 1970 dawned, they would be nothing but a charming memory.

What does the future hold for me?

Nadine dealt again, suddenly brightened. The swords and wands, the arcana, major and minor, revealed that a new man would enter her life, and soon. A fire of anticipation seized her as she looked at the cards. This one would be extraordinary, flawless. He would have an immediate, profound and lifelong effect on her. She would want no other . . . one interpretation of the Tarot lay would even call him the love of her life, her *soulmate* . . .

As if snapping out of a trance, Nadine glanced over at Rob, but he wasn't looking at her. He was looking down the hall, behind the bookcase, toward the kitchen. As she watched, he smiled expansively and said to someone, "And how are things with you and Marta?"

"Like one, that on a lonesome road, doth walk in fear and dread, and having once turned round walks on, and turns no more his head; because he knows a frightful fiend doth close behind him tread."

Nadine blinked in astonishment. The voice was deep, melodious, crammed with a humor that did not befit Coleridge's words.

"So all's well, then?" Rob said to the unseen owner of the wonderful voice. There was no audible answer, but Rob's grin widened. "Does her daddy's fine boat still run?"

"Like an Elgin watch."

"Did you bring it?"

"Neither it nor her," the voice rumbled merrily. "Marta tripped over a tree root in their spacious backyard yesterday. She held out her arms to break her fall and instead broke both wrists."

"Clumsy," Rob commented, his smile not dimming. Apparently he was not too fond of this Marta person.

"That's why I'm just getting here now. I sat in the emergency room with her —"

"Daddy didn't summon their personal physician?"

"Daddy's out of town," the smooth voice replied.

"So you're here with no boat?" Rob asked incredulously.

There was a chuckle; it put Nadine in mind of molasses, dark and sweet. "I brought my skis. You've got a boat. I thought you might help a brutha out."

Rob shook his head. "Oh, no. I'm not wasting my last day on the water dragging you. That's Marta's job."

"Not all day, Rob. I promise," the voice wheedled. "Just for a while. In the morning."

"Why didn't you bring your boat?"

"It's in the shop for a little overhaul. It's been sitting in the driveway since I met Marta, so I thought I'd take it in. We've always used Daddy's." There was a pause, another rueful chuckle. "I couldn't exactly leave her there, all busted up, and bring Daddy's boat up here, could I?"

Nadine watched Rob shrug. "You could. The weekend's already shot. You sat with her at the hospital – why couldn't you borrow the boat for a day without her?"

"It was hard enough to get away as it was. She thought I was gonna sit around on the veranda with her all weekend, hold her casted-up hand. She didn't even plan on going out on the lake. So, here I am, without a boat, without a driver, without a friend in the world. Here I am, all alone, just me and my skis, friendless, unloved, unwanted.

"I drove all the way up here, because the hot waters of the Colorado summoned me. 'Forget that stagnant green lake,' they said. 'The court is at Parker for the weekend. Go see Rob. He won't leave you stranded on the riverbank like an orphan . . .'"

Rob rolled his eyes. "Oh, all right. Christ, how you do go on. But just for a little while, in the morning. I'm not staying out there with you all day. We're having a barbeque tomorrow."

"How many barbeques have you been to?" the voice challenged. "You're gonna want to stay out there and ski."

"I'm not as addicted to it as you are."

"Anymore," the voice retorted.

"I've had to study harder this semester," Rob said defensively. "I can't be spending every single weekend at the lake with you. There's more to life . . .

"You're full of shit, Roberto. What more is there to life?"

"There's school."

"Fuck school," the voice said heartily, and Nadine blinked at the profanity. "Not everybody wants to be a doctor."

31

"All right," Rob grinned. "There's the future and love and marriage and . . . you and Marta . . ."

There was a laugh then, and the voice said, "And then you woke up. And then *she* woke up –"

"Some other girl then. You're never going to meet any girls if you never get back in the boat."

There was a pause, then the voice asked, "Have I ever had a problem with that? What's the one thing I can't do in the dark?"

Rob grinned. "Ski?"

"Exactly. Ski during the day, girls at night . . . Tell me I'm wrong. It's the perfect life. And you used to agree with me." The voice paused again, waiting for a reply, and when Rob didn't answer, he said challengingly, "I bet you skied today."

"No. Will's got a girl – you know how he hates anything to do with skiing, anyway. He wanted to entertain this girl, so I didn't ski today. Or yesterday. We just cruised –"

"Pointlessly. Will doesn't ski, but he'll ride back and forth up the river all day. *So boring.* There is absolutely nothing to see here. *If time be of all things the most precious, wasting time must be the greatest prodigality.*"

"Will thinks skiing is wasting time."

"That's because Will needs all the hours in a day to pick up girls." The voice paused a third time, then asked, "Was his chick impressed with the scenery? Why didn't you just ski behind their boat ride?"

"Will didn't want to be bothered with it, like I told you. Besides, I've also met a girl . . ." Rob turned and looked at Nadine. Unable to hide the fact that she had been eavesdropping, she just smiled at him. Rob smiled back, said her name, then, "I'd like you to meet my cousin, Ian."

Nadine stood up as the owner of the mellifluous voice stepped from behind the bookcase. He wasn't as tall as Rob, but he was broader, more muscular. He had dark brown hair, cut in a shoulder-length shag; the bangs hung over his eyebrows and in front of his eyes. He had a large nose and apple cheeks, and a prominent dimple in his chin. He smiled at Nadine, grasped her hand firmly, warmly. *"Enchante,"* he said, and Rob rolled his eyes. Nadine noticed a slight gap between his front teeth.

Nadine shook his hand, and mumbled something about it being nice to meet him. It was so much more than nice to meet him. He was not classically beautiful, like the twin, Jeffrey Hunter-looking

32

Dr. Kildares, she thought. His nose was a little too large for that, and he seemed to squint perpetually, like someone who spent a lot of time out in the sun without benefit of sunglasses. But his gap-toothed smile was the friendliest Nadine had ever encountered, and that deep, silky voice . . . He was adorable.

She glanced over for a moment at her Tarot lay, then back at Ian. He was still smiling at her. "Waterski, do you, Nadine?"

Nadine, trapped by the cobalt blue of Ian's eyes, nonetheless caught Rob rolling his own pale green ones again. "He's addicted to it."

Ian grinned at Nadine, nodded.

Nadine knew nothing about waterskiing. She recalled that Rob had pointed at a pair of skis hanging in the garage the previous day, when they were getting the boat ready, but Will had shook his head firmly. "No one wants to ski."

"But –"

"No one wants to ski," Will had insisted. Rob had shrugged, given up. The subject was closed, and Nadine had paid little attention to the skiers they had passed on the river. It was an activity that had not even remotely interested her, not in the least. Until now.

"I've never . . . I would . . . I'd like to learn," Nadine said at last.

"Maybe Rob should teach you, then." Ian looked at his cousin. "Maybe first thing in the morning?"

"How do I get sucked into these things?" Rob asked. "I was going to sleep in tomorrow. The barbeque –"

"Your girlfriend wants to learn to ski," Ian said and looked back at Nadine. "I try to never deny a beautiful woman."

The words were right, and the words were enough: Ian's voice made Nadine feel weak. But the tone was light, innocent. Ian wasn't flirting with her, with his dark, syrupy voice. He was just being nice, still trying to finagle a ride out of Rob in the morning.

Rob knew his cousin wasn't hitting on Nadine. He knew Ian's motivation; he just wanted to ski. Rob said, *"You* can teach her. I'm going to the barbeque."

Ian turned to Rob. "But who's gonna pull me?"

"Teach her how to do that, too. Besides, Sissy's here."

Ian glanced furtively around the room, then ducked behind the bookcase again. Quite without realizing that she had done so, Nadine took a step forward, so that she could still see him. "Who's Sissy?" she asked.

"Sissy's daddy owns the local ski shop," Rob explained. "She knows how to ski, how to pull a skier; I think she can overhaul an outboard, too." He grinned at Ian. "Why didn't you bring your boat up here to Sissy for that overhaul, Cuz? I'm sure she would've done it for free." Ian peeped around the bookcase at the crowd again and didn't respond. "Sissy's got a little bit of a crush on Ian," Rob told Nadine.

"She seems perfect for you," Nadine said. She was glad that he seemed unwilling to run into this girl. It didn't seem to matter that she knew about waterskiing as much as he did; he was trying to hide from her. *She must be horribly ugly,* Nadine thought.

"Sissy is sixteen," Ian said. "She thinks she's perfect for me, too. I met her last summer. I went into her dad's shop –"

"To buy skis," Rob said. This seemed obvious to Nadine, and she felt a pang of irritation at him for interrupting Ian's story, creating a jangled break. She wanted to listen to Ian's voice, to his words. She wished Rob would just shut up.

"Exactly," Ian agreed. "I was looking for . . . I didn't want . . ."

"She started following us around in the store," Rob said. "Not us, actually. Just him."

"Why would you let her come to your party?" Ian asked incredulously. "Her dad –"

"Anytime we light the home fires, she shows up, Cuz. Every time we're in town, she knocks on the door. 'Is Ian here?' she asks. Like a little kid looking for her playmate."

"I'm not her playmate, for Christ's sake!" Ian hissed.

"She was here yesterday, and when I told her you hadn't showed up yet, she left."

"But she's here now?"

Rob shrugged. "She was."

Nadine failed to understand why Ian was so distressed at the possible presence of one teenaged girl, a local, a skier like he was. "What's wrong with her?"

"I already told you," Ian said. "She's sixteen. And her dad –"

"It went like this." Again Rob interrupted, and again Nadine wished that he would shut up and let Ian tell the story. But Ian was again looking around nervously; he let his cousin speak. "Sissy followed Ian around in her dad's shop, making goo-goo eyes at him; she sold him a pair of very expensive skis."

"They're worth it," Ian said defensively.

"It's a *hobby,*" Rob said, "You spend every dime you get –"

"It's a lifestyle," Ian countered. He grinned a trifle earnestly at Nadine, and she thought for a moment that her heart stopped. "It's what I do."

"It's all he does," Rob said. A feminine voice tittered across the room, and Ian peeked nervously around the bookcase. Rob continued. "So Dad observed all this, his daughter following two tourists around, making this big sale. We chatted with Sissy for a few minutes; and when we went up to the counter to pay, Dad asked Ian casually, 'Would you like to get our newsletter?'

"Ian is not the smartest guy I know." He grinned at his cousin and his cousin grinned sheepishly back. "How does that saying go? *Never trust anybody over thirty.* I never sign anything in this town. I'm just here on the weekends. I prefer anonymity.

"But not my Cuz, here. He fills out a little card with his name and address on it, so he can be on this little Podunk ski shop's mailing list. While Dad rings us up, Sissy giggles and says, 'I'll see you guys out there!' and skips out of the store.

"Ian and I exchange a look. Dad clears his throat. He says, 'My daughter has been around boats and skiers her whole life. Locals. Not just rich boys up for the weekend with Daddy's runabout.'"

And that's exactly what you are, Nadine thought. She knew that the twins came from money; they had this weekend hideaway; they were going to medical school; they both drove nice cars. In fact, she had been surprised when Rob had asked her to accompany them to the river for the weekend – he and his brother were obviously a little higher up on the socio-economic ladder than she was. *Perhaps they're slumming,* Nadine thought suddenly.

"The ol' man paused for a moment," Rob continued. "We didn't say anything. Then he went on. 'This is the very first time I've ever seen her even remotely impressed. But she's definitely impressed with you.' He looked pointedly at Ian. 'Sure, there've been boys come sniffing around already. But like I say, Sissy was never interested before.'"

"I saw Dad's point. He didn't want any college boys taking advantage of his innocent little girl. But what were we supposed to do about it? It's a free country. 'We can't keep her off the launch,' I told him.

"'No, I wouldn't expect you to do that,' Dad says. 'I wouldn't even expect you to keep her off your boat. That would hurt her feelings. Even though she's only fifteen,' – at this point Ian regretted even *talking* to her – 'she knows how to take care of herself. She'd

35

never get herself into a situation that she couldn't get herself out of. She's not unaware of what you boys come up here for.'

"'Sir, we would never –' Ian begins.

"'Of course you wouldn't,' Dad says, cutting him off. 'I expect that educated boys such as yourselves are gentlemen. If you run into Sissy, you have my permission to take her for a ride. It would hurt her feelings if you didn't. I'm sure she skis better than both of you.' Nonchalantly, Dad reaches under the counter, and just as nonchalantly places a sawed-off shotgun next to the cash register. He picks up the little piece of paper that Smart-Fella has just filled out. 'Just remember,' he says, and smiles at Ian. 'My Sissy is only fifteen. And I know where you live.'

"Ian just stares at him, open-mouthed, until he says, 'Have a nice day, boys. Enjoy those skis,' and puts the shotgun back under the counter. I nudged Ian. He picked up his skis and we left."

Nadine studied Ian for a moment. She could see why a sixteen-year-old townie would find him irresistible. Hell, she was far more grown-up then some high school kid, and she found him irresistible, standing right there beside Rob, her supposed *boyfriend*. There was just something about him; he exuded confidence, intelligence. She said, "Did you take her for a ride?"

"She was waiting by my truck when we came out," Ian said simply.

"I thought of Dad, with that big gun, telling us not to hurt her feelings," Rob added. He slapped Ian on the back. "Why not take her for a ride? Her jailbait-ass hadn't imprinted on me."

"So you took her for a ride." Nadine smiled faintly at Ian.

"Not the kind of ride she wanted, but yeah," Rob said. "Like you said, Nadine, they're perfect for each other."

"Jesus Christ, Rob! Quit saying that we're perfect for each other! She's just a kid!"

"She likes to ski as much as he does, and she knows how to pull a skier, which is not something your average sixteen-year-old girl knows how to do. Long after the rest of us are tired, and want to go have a beer, sit on the beach, get something to eat – do *anything else* – Sissy will stay out there and ski with Ian."

"And so . . . you let her." Again Nadine smiled faintly at him.

"Let her what?"

"Ski with you."

"All day long and three times on Sundays," Rob said.

"There's always someone else with us," Ian protested.

36

"You need three people to be safe," Rob explained.

"Best safety lies in fear," Ian said and grinned at Nadine. She grinned back.

"One to ski, one to watch when the skier falls, and one to drive," Rob continued. "So it's not like they were ever alone. That's probably why he's still alive."

There was a squeal from the kitchen. Then all Nadine saw was a flash of blonde hair and a blur of tanned skin as a tiny young woman scampered down the hall and leapt into Ian's arms. He had no choice but to catch her. She wrapped her legs around him and hugged him tightly. Ian set her down immediately; but she remained pressed against him, her arms wrapped possessively around his neck. She gazed up at him adoringly. "Let me go, Sissy," he said in exasperation.

Reluctantly, the girl obeyed. "Goin' skiin' in the morning, Ian?" she asked eagerly. He nodded. "Takin' Rob's boat? I didn't see yours." Sissy glanced at Rob and they smiled at each other. It occurred to Nadine that Rob enjoyed his cousin's predicament. "Goin' with us, Rob?"

Rob shook his head. "I'm having a barbeque."

Sissy was barely over five foot tall; she was pixie-cute, with lovely blue eyes, a mass of sun-bleached, frizzy blonde hair, and a dark, desert tan. Now she smiled hopefully. "What, no chaperone?" Sissy went to put her arms around Ian's neck again, but he shook his head, and she withdrew them.

"Nadine's going with us." Ian nodded at Nadine and she introduced herself to Sissy. "I'm gonna teach her to ski."

Sissy looked Nadine up and down and frowned. "That might take all day."

Ian rolled his eyes. "Take it or leave it, Sis. I've only got the boat until . . .?"

"At least noon," Rob replied. "If Will doesn't want to use it, you can have it all day."

"Where is Will?" Ian asked.

Ron wiggled his eyebrows and grinned. "I doubt if he'll be wanting the boat."

"Great!" Sissy said. "We can ski all day, then!" She looked dubiously at Nadine. "You might want to bring a hat, honey. And maybe a long-sleeved shirt. Wouldn't want you to get sunburned. Ian's not one for sitting on the beach, and there's no shade on the water." She looked adoringly at him again. "Say, six?"

37

"You're not gonna be up at six," Rob said dismissively.

Nadine looked at him in surprise. Sissy would be up at six to go waterskiing with Ian; she would be up at four if he asked her to be. That was as plain as the button nose on her face. Young Sissy *loved* Ian. She would do anything he asked – her greatest disappointment was clearly that he wouldn't ask. Not for what she wanted.

Nadine didn't love Ian, not yet. She glanced over at the Tarot deck on the table. She'd forgotten it, but only momentarily. She gathered up her cards and stuck them in the back pocket of her shorts. Like an electricity in the air, she could already feel the change. The cards had told her that Rob would be gone by Hallowe'en, and his brother with him.

This was the tipping point, right here. She felt a little sorry for Daina now; she had misread how it would go. Will was not going to be the initiator; it was not going to be him that broke up with Daina. Hell, he and Daina couldn't get enough of each other – why would he leave her?

Nadine saw now that it was going to be the other way around. Nadine had already lost interest in Rob; like water on a hot griddle, it had instantly evaporated the moment she had heard Ian's voice recite Coleridge. She longed to hear him speak again. She thought she could listen to Ian talk forever.

Nadine could now put a corrected progression to what the cards had hinted: she would break up with Rob, in favor of his cousin. The awkwardness of the whole situation would force Will to also leave Daina. *It'll be sad for a minute,* Nadine thought, *but one cannot escape one's fate. Daina will find someone else. The cards never lie. I've found the one they called my soulmate.*

Ian.

"I'll be here at six," Sissy insisted. "Actually, I could sleep on the couch. Aren't you staying in the spare room, Ian?"

"You're not staying here, Sissy," Ian said. "Your dad would kill me."

Sissy stomped her foot. "It's not fair! She gets to stay here!"

Nadine blinked at the little girl in surprise. Why should Sissy care where Nadine stayed? Then it occurred to her that Sissy thought that *Nadine was with Ian,* and that it was perfectly fine with Ian (and Rob as well) that Sissy thought so. Ian just wanted to ski; he needed someone to drive the boat. If Sissy thought that Nadine was his girlfriend, maybe she wouldn't be trying to climb into his lap all day.

"My daddy knows where am I, and with whom," Nadine said smugly. "Does yours?" It wasn't entirely the truth, but close enough. It was 1969, she was twenty-one, and she didn't have to answer to her dad about every detail of her life anymore. He had accepted her liberation, and as long as she did well in school, wasn't on drugs, and came home when she said she was going to, he accepted that she was an adult.

Sissy hesitated, and Ian rolled his eyes. "I swear to *Christ,* Sissy! You're gonna get me killed! If you didn't know your way around a boat –"

"But I do," Sissy said, and Nadine could tell that she longed to touch Ian again, to wrap herself around his arm. But she had some propriety. She wouldn't do so in front of Ian's *girlfriend.* "And I ski better than anyone you know."

"Come on," he said, ignoring what was apparently the truth. Sissy skied better than anyone Ian knew, and more importantly, she was willing to do it all day, just like he was. "I'm gonna take you home. You're gonna get us all arrested."

ELEVEN

When Daina and Will arose at mid-morning, they discovered Rob sitting outside at the picnic table, alone. He was reading a textbook. Daina glanced curiously at him; school was practically out for the summer, yet here he was, still studying.

"Where's Nadine?" she asked.

Rob looked up and smiled, snapped the book shut. "Nadine is learning to waterski." He looked at his brother. "With Cousin Ian."

"Son of a bitch," Will muttered under his breath, and stepped back into the house. He returned after a moment with a pair of binoculars, and scanned the river, mostly empty at this time on a Sunday morning. "It's a good thing you weren't interested in a ride this morning," he said to Daina. "I can't believe you gave Ian the goddamn boat, Rob! We won't see it again 'til sunset."

"Relax. I told him to come back by noon." Rob held out his hand, and Will handed him the binoculars. "I'm sure Nadine will be tired of being dragged through the chop by then."

"Maybe she will, maybe she won't," Will said, as his brother handed the binoculars to Daina. She scanned, but all the boats looked pretty much the same to her.

"Nadine doesn't strike me as the type to instantly take to skiing," Rob rejoined. "I think she was just being polite."

"You're about a dumb ass, you know that?" Will said, and slapped his brother on the back of the head.

"What are you talking about?"

"Cousin Ian gets more ass than a toilet seat. Why would you let your girlfriend go out with him all alone?"

Daina looked over at Will in surprise. Did he really think of Nadine and her as their girlfriends? Already? *I guess that's all right,* she thought and went back to looking at the river. She still couldn't pick out the twins' boat. But she pretended to look, because she wanted to hear what Rob was going to say next.

"You're just jealous because he got to Marta before you did."

Will frowned at his brother, silently saying, *Why would you mention Marta in front of this new girl?* To recover, he stammered, "Well . . . I've got Daina now."

He put his arm around her shoulder possessively, and she thought, *Do you really believe that? After just one weekend?* Daina put her arm around his waist. It was okay for him to think that. He was a lot of fun.

Sensing that there was no jealousy in Daina, Will murmured, "I'll never understand what Marta sees in him." Now Daina glanced at him in surprise: he sounded like a jilted sorority girl.

Rob winked at her. "Perhaps Cousin Ian got a little more of the Wilde charm. We got a little more of the Wilde brains."

"It doesn't take the legendary Wilde brains to figure out what he sees in Marta, however," Will said. He looked at his brother and they said in unison, "Daddy's boat."

Rob reached for the binoculars and Daina handed them to him. "And he's not gonna do anything to mess that up. Besides, he'd never hit on someone else's girlfriend . . ."

"Unless her daddy's got a nice boat," Will opined tersely.

"He'd never hit on *my* girlfriend. I trust him. He's not gonna mess up what he's got with Marta."

"He's not gonna mess up what he's got with Marta's daddy's boat —"

"At least not before the end of the summer. And besides, they're not alone. Sissy's with them."

Now Will grinned. "You don't say. I hope she doesn't drown Nadine."

TWELVE

Learning to waterski was a bust for Nadine, although she did enjoy it when Ian touched her: on the sides of her hips to help her balance in the water, on her knees to help her try to keep the skis straight. But whenever she thought she was ready, and Ian would signal Sissy to pull her up, she never made it out of the water. Nadine thought Sissy was doing it on purpose – too slowly and it seemed like the weight of the whole river was across her; two quickly and the handle was either jerked out of her hand, or she was jerked out of the skis and dragged. Each time, Nadine could hear Sissy's distant laughter.

After about an hour of this, Nadine sensed that Ian was losing interest in trying to teach her how to ski. "Maybe I'll pick it up next time," she told him.

"Next weekend," he agreed.

"I can't drive all the way up here next weekend," Nadine said, although she would, if he requested it.

"Not here. Lake Elsinore. The water's not as nice as this, but it's not all the way out here, either."

Ian was inviting her to go skiing with him next weekend. She didn't care for skiing herself; of that she was already quite assured. But like their underage companion, Nadine was just as sure, already, that she would do anything Ian asked.

Sissy brought the boat up alongside them and shut it off. Nadine climbed up the little rope ladder over the stern. She rather collapsed into the back seat, and took off her ski vest. Yeah. This was exhausting, and it wasn't for her. But she discovered that she was looking forward to watching Ian do it.

He grinned over the stern of the boat for a moment, wiggled his eyebrows at them. "As the poet says, ladies, *Now is it time to ski: come, shall we about it?*"

"I think that's, *Now is it time to arm,*" Nadine corrected him gleefully.

Ian's grin widened. "I'm 4-F. No arming for me." His eyes flickered over to Sissy. "Do me, baby," he said in that dark, honeyed voice, and pushed off the stern of the boat with the skis and the towline.

"You won't let me!" Sissy called after him. She moved the boat out ahead slowly, spooling the rope behind it. Then she put it into neutral and waited for Ian to give her the signal.

While Ian put his skis on, Sissy glanced over at Nadine and asked curiously, "Does he talk to you like that?" When Nadine blinked in surprise – she had just been thinking, *I wish he'd talk to me like that* – Sissy hurried on. "I mean, I don't know how long you've been going with him . . . but, we've been friends since last summer. He only talks to me like that when he's in the water. 'Do me, baby.' He'd never say that if I was in a position to actually . . . I'm sorry. I guess I'm rude. He and I, we've never . . . but I knew him before you did!"

There was that childish petulance again, Nadine observed. But she couldn't blame Sissy; she couldn't help being only sixteen. She couldn't help wanting Ian. Nadine understood that completely.

Nadine couldn't carry on this charade; it was cruel. Ian was using this little girl, and not at all in the way she wanted to be used. "I'm not going with him, Sissy. I just met him last night."

"And you already . . .?"

Nadine's eyes widened. "No, Sissy! I'm not *with him* at all. I'm with Rob."

"I want to be with him," she admitted, gazing out at Ian in the water.

You're not the only one, little girl, Nadine thought. *But I'm pretty damned sure I'm gonna beat you to it.*

As if answering her smug, unspoken thought, Sissy said, "I won't be sixteen forever. Hold on to something." She powered the boat up quickly and after a moment, Ian was bouncing along behind them. Even at the distance, Nadine could see that he was grinning.

Remembering Ian's words, she shouted over the roar of the outboard, "This is what he does, huh?"

"This is *all* he does," Sissy yelled back, echoing Rob. "At least during the daytime."

Sissy dragged Ian behind them for some distance, for a long time; when he finally fell, she slowed the boat, and brought it around so that the rope would pass within his grasp. She continued her thought to Nadine, as if no time had passed. "He won't let me hang out with him after dark, at Rob and Will's. He says he's afraid of my dad . . . I think he doesn't want me to see him with all the other girls." Sissy eyed Nadine apprehensively for a minute, as if she'd said too much. Then she shrugged. "You're not his girlfriend, so it's not like I'm hurting your feelings.

"I met him Memorial Day weekend, last year. He went home and was gone all of June, but then he was here for the rest of the summer. Rob likes to ski, but not like Ian does. A lot of days, it was just the three of us. But other days, Rob would sleep in, and then Ian would bring some girl along . . . *to teach her to ski.* Right. I'm not stupid. I know what he'd been teaching her the night before, or what he planned on teaching her once the sun went down. That's why I thought that you were one of them."

Ian signaled that he was again ready, and Sissy pushed the throttle down.

"It wasn't a different girl every day," Sissy shouted, "but almost. I don't know where he picks them all up, but when they figure out that he's gonna ski all day – he isn't gonna sit on the beach and hold their hands and whisper sweet nothings into their ears – they take off."

"And then he just finds another one?" Nadine shouted.

Sissy nodded, then yelled, "Oh, don't think I'm saying he's a choir boy. Like I say, it's not like he isn't sleeping with all of them." Sissy pouted prettily, glanced over her shoulder. "Damn him," she said to herself; the wind took her words and Nadine didn't hear them.

Nadine considered Ian curiously. She didn't know why she was surprised; she'd heard him say it: *Ski during the day, girls at night . . . It's the perfect life.*

Sissy wound the boat up a little higher, and shouted, "He lets them stick around as long as they want – one of them stayed with him for four whole days. I think she thought she was gonna be Mrs. Ian Wilde." She grinned at Nadine. "Surprise! Boy was she disappointed. Ian doesn't want a wife. He wants to ski. Sure, he'll accommodate them, but they're interchangeable to him."

Ian fell again, and Sissy brought the boat around, reduced speed. Nadine could again speak to Sissy in almost a normal voice. "But there's only one you," she said with a smile.

Sissy smiled back. "No one he knows – no other *girl,* anyway, knows how to do this." She brought the rope in front of Ian: he barely had to reach out for it.

"What time is it?" he shouted to them.

Sissy consulted the clock on the boat's dashboard and signed to Ian that it was eleven-thirty. He gestured to Sissy: *Do you want to ski?* Sissy shook her head. "I ski every day, Tourist," she said aloud, even though she knew he couldn't hear her. Ian gave her the thumbs up.

"I'm gonna show up on his doorstep, the day I turn eighteen," Sissy told Nadine. "He won't turn me down then. We're simpatico.

Who else will stay out here with him, sunup to sundown? Not even his cousin."

I'd stay out here with him all day, Nadine thought, *as long as I got to go home with him at night. As long as I could listen to his voice, his words . . . As long as I got to hear him say, "Do me, baby."*

Before she hit the throttle again, Nadine said to Sissy, "You're right. Not too many girls would stay out here with him all day. But about that showing up on his doorstep when you turn eighteen? You might want to call first."

He won't be alone, if I have anything to say about it. Nadine grinned to herself as Sissy throttled the boat forward and pulled Ian up on his skis again.

THIRTEEN

Ian returned Rob and Will's boat to the dock promptly at noon. In a playful mood, he picked up a giggling and squealing Sissy and threw her over the stern. He hopped out of the boat and offered his hand to Nadine; she shivered at his touch and quickly stepped out onto the dock. He hauled Sissy out of the water by one arm, then threw her in again.

"Take a swim with me, Ian!"

He glanced at Nadine. Her expression told him that she thought it was the least he could do, after the love-struck teenager had dragged him all over the river all morning. Ian agreed and leapt off the end of the dock. He picked Sissy up and threw her into the air a few times.

Nadine knew that it wasn't what Sissy wanted, but she knew it was better than nothing. Nadine dwelt for a moment on how much she would like to be in the little girl's place, to feel his hands on her hips . . .

In fact, Nadine decided that if she watched them for much longer, she might just go ahead and jump in there with them, and it wouldn't be seemly, now would it, for his cousin's *girlfriend* to be swimming up next to Ian, for her to be wrapping her arms around his neck, to be kissing him, to be . . . Nadine turned to go.

Sissy called to her. "Will you go ask Will if he wants to use the boat?" Sissy had the same idea as Nadine: she was trying to swim as close to Ian as possible, but he was literally holding her at arm's length. "We'll wait here."

Nadine nodded and walked toward the house. *Good luck, Sissy,* she thought. *You're finally alone with him, unchaperoned. Make the most of it.*

Nadine found Rob manning the grill, surrounded by the same people that had been at his house all weekend. He gave her a hug and a kiss – Nadine discovered that she was no longer even vaguely moved, not even to affection, by it. She was amazed at how utterly her attraction to Rob had evaporated, but then remembered that the cards didn't lie. She had met the one she wanted, the one she *would have.* Rob's ship had sailed, for all intents and purposes, the moment Nadine had heard his cousin's voice. It was all over but the formalities of ending it between her and Rob. And then her conquest of Ian could commence.

"Where's Will? Sissy sent me up here to ask him if he wanted to use the boat."

Rob grinned. "You left them alone?"

"Ian was being nice. Taking a swim with her. He's safe for a minute, I think."

Rob shielded his eyes with the hand that held the spatula and peered toward the dock. Ian was sitting on the side of the boat with his legs dangling over the side, and Sissy had a hold of his foot and was trying to pull him back into the water. "Don't be so sure. She's very insistent."

Nadine asked, "What does he tell her?"

Rob looked down at the grill, flipped over a burger. "He tells her the truth. That she's too young, that her dad would kill him."

"That's not the whole truth, though, is it?" As Nadine watched, Ian allowed Sissy to pull him into the water, to duck his head under. But when he came back up and she tried to put her arms around his neck, he gently pushed her away and vaulted back onto the boat. Sissy, undaunted, started pulling on his foot again.

"No," Rob agreed. "Even if she wasn't underage – Cousin Ian likes 'em a little more sophisticated than a river rat townie who's probably never been out of the desert. Someone with such an obvious crush on him. No matter how well she can ski."

Ah, what a shame for young Sissy, Nadine thought. *But I'm neither an underage townie, nor will I let him see that I also have a crush on him.* Nadine was confident of her looks, her wits. She had already heard Ian quote Coleridge and Shakespeare – she had no doubt that after a few after-sundown conversations – after he was done skiing – he would see that they were destined for each other.

When Nadine didn't reply, Rob said, "Go tell them they can take the boat back out. Will's done for the weekend. He's more interested in Daina."

Ah, poor Daina! It would probably be sticky when Nadine told Rob that she didn't want to see him anymore, stickier still when she started dating his cousin. Will would probably dump Daina as a show of solidarity to his jilted brother. Daina would get over it. It wasn't like she was in love with Will; that was clear to Nadine. It wasn't like she would miss him, like he was her *soulmate . . .*

Nadine realized that her friend would laugh at her if she used that word. "Some guy you just met? Your *soulmate?*" Daina would say, and she would laugh. Nadine hated it when Daina laughed at the beliefs, beliefs she had learned at the knees of Bellona and Penny.

Nadine knew that Daina believed as completely as she did, but somehow, Daina lacked the same sense of destiny about it that Nadine had. The future could be seen or at least an educated guess could be made, but to Daina, there was no sense in getting all dreamy-eyed about it.

So Nadine decided on the spot not to gush to her friend about Ian, about their being soulmates. At least not until she had him safely in her hip pocket.

"Well, if I'm going back out with them, I'm gonna take some pictures," Nadine said, and stepped toward the house.

Will was coming outside at the same moment, and he said, "Maybe you can send them to one of those waterskiing rags." He held up his hands to form a caption. "Ian Wilde, Amateur. Legend in his own mind."

FOURTEEN

As Nadine approached, she noted that Sissy was sitting in the boat, arms crossed, failing to disguise her annoyance. She was annoyed because Ian was on the dock, talking to two girls, refugees from the party. He was leaning back casually, both hands on the top rung of the railing, one bare foot on the bottom rung. The girls stood across from him, leaning against the other railing. Nadine paused, found him in the viewfinder of the Yashica, and called his name. When he looked in her direction, she snapped his picture.

"Rob says you can take the boat back out," Nadine told him. "Will's more interested in his date than the water." Nadine wasn't sure why she didn't refer to Will's date by name, why she more or less glossed over her best friend's existence. It didn't matter. Daina would get to meet him, and Ian would get to meet her, as soon as he was hers . . .

"Oh, take us for a ride, Ian!" the blonde gushed.

"Yes!" the dark-haired one agreed with a coquettish smile.

Ian opened his mouth to speak, but Sissy cut him off. "You guys waterski?"

Nadine looked at the two girls: they were made up and coiffed for a party. Sure, they were wearing swim suits, but it was obvious that they weren't planning to get in the water: getting wet would completely mess up their looks. Nadine imagined the gouts of mascara running blackly down their faces. No, they weren't even going swimming, nonetheless skiing.

Just a boat ride would mess up their hair-dos, but it was worth the risk to them to take it with Ian. Their eyes glowed when they looked at him, just like Sissy's. Nadine, on the other hand, was careful to veil her appreciation when she looked at him. It would not do for her to be making eyes at her *boyfriend's* cousin. Not yet.

The girls regarded Sissy as if one of the seat cushions on Rob and Will's boat had suddenly addressed them. They took in the tan, the cut off shorts and bikini top, the sun-frizzled hair, the lack of make-up – *put a little lipstick on her, and you wouldn't know she was only sixteen,* Nadine thought – but bare-faced, she looked like a kid. The two girls dismissed Sissy as of no consequence, as no competition. They didn't know why she was in the boat, but they knew that she could not possibly compete with them for Ian's attention.

"Your kid sister?" the dark-haired one asked him derisively.

Maybe it was the girl's cutting tone, or maybe it was the fact that Ian didn't reply quickly enough, didn't speak up, didn't at least say that they were friends, that she was there because she was the best skier he knew. Sissy waited a heartbeat, then said, "Oh, fuck this."

She hopped out of the boat and tossed the keys at Ian, so that he had to abandon his pose on the railing and reach to catch them. She started walking away toward shore. "Come back and get me when you want to ski, Ian, when you're done trying to get your –"

"Sissy!" he said sharply.

She turned around, put her hands on her hips. "What? Are you gonna ski or are you gonna play tourist?" Sissy looked through the girls as if they weren't even there. When Ian hesitated again, she said, "That's what I thought. You don't need me then. I'm just the driver. I'll see you later." She turned and walked up the dock.

Ian shrugged helplessly at Nadine. "I did want to ski . . . But I'm not going to beg her. Do you want to go back out?"

Nadine considered the other girls for a moment: the blonde met her eyes with a poorly disguised sneer, and the brunette's expression was not exactly welcoming either. Then the two of them tossed their heads and climbed into the boat as if they owned it, and from where she stood on the dock, Nadine couldn't see them behind the windshield.

Nadine looked over her shoulder at Sissy, walking dejectedly away – Ian was cruel, picking up these girls in front of her – how did he expect her to react? It wasn't like the four of them were going to bond over watching Ian waterski. But on the other hand, he really couldn't be expected to take Sissy's feelings into consideration, now could he? She was just a townie kid.

And it wasn't like Nadine was going to take her feelings into consideration, either. She aimed to take Ian away from Sissy – and that made her more conniving than these girls, who didn't know what he meant to her.

But it wasn't going to happen today. Nadine was his cousin's girlfriend; she wasn't on Ian's radar any more than the young townie was, at the moment. Regardless of what the future would bring – Nadine was quite sure that it would be her and Ian together, because the cards didn't lie – in the meantime, she didn't want to watch him flirt with these girls any more than Sissy did.

So she shook her head. "I'll see you later."

Ian looked over his shoulder at the girls, then back. He said, "If I *don't* see you later, have a safe trip home. Have Rob call me about skiing next weekend at the lake. I'm sure you'll get the hang of it."

One of the girls rudely blew the boat's horn, and they both giggled.

"I'll do that," Nadine called as Ian climbed in the boat. He smiled at the girls and waved absently at Nadine. She was of no interest to him at the moment, but she was confident that that situation would change very soon. The cards never lied.

Nadine quickly caught up with Sissy. She put her arm around the girl's shoulder, gave her a little squeeze of consolation. Sissy looked up, and wiped away the tears that threatened to fall. "I hate him," she hissed. "I thought he wanted to ski today."

"He skied all morning."

Sissy laughed bitterly. "Now it's time to nail sluts."

Sissy had quite the mouth on her, Nadine observed. She decided to be stern. "Don't you think you're overreacting a little? I mean, there are two of them. It's not like he's going to . . ."

But the look of *Are you kidding?* on Sissy's face stopped this line of reasoning.

Nadine tried again. "But you're his friend. That'll last longer than some romp on the beach with . . ."

Again Sissy's expression stopped her.

Nadine looked back at the water, but she couldn't pick the boat out. Two at a time? Really? Ian was cute enough, sexy, even. But that was all secondary to Nadine. She liked his voice, the way he spoke; she liked the things he said, his confidence. She aimed to get around to what Sissy wanted, and what those other girls wanted, because she was just as attracted to Ian as they were, if not more so. But her attraction to him was more than just the quickie physical kind. He was cute enough, but she had known a deeper truth the moment she'd heard his voice. The cards were never wrong. Ian Wilde was her soulmate.

FIFTEEN

The twins decided that they would leave the boat at the house for the summer.

Rob felt sorry for Sissy, also – he assigned her the responsibility of telling Ian to stow the boat and lock up the house before he left. She grinned and thanked Rob. She now had a legitimate reason to be hanging around when Ian showed up with his conquests, and Nadine could see that she hoped to break up Ian's little party. Nadine thought it would be futile; he would just drive her home, then come back and do whatever it was he planned to do with the two girls.

Nadine sat in the backseat of the Caddy with Daina; the boys sat in front and switched off driving a couple of times as they traveled back to Riverside. They were all tired, but on the surface the weekend had been a success for the four of them. New relationships had been cemented, or so it seemed.

When they stopped for gas, Daina let Nadine know that apparently the brothers saw them as their girlfriends, already. Nadine said, "Of course they do. We're spectacular," and smiled at her friend. "Do you consider Will your boyfriend?"

Daina sighed. "If that's what he wants. He'll do for the moment. And Rob?"

Nadine shrugged. "It's just like you say. He'll do until something better comes along." *He'll do until I can get Ian alone and explain things to him,* she thought.

For his part, Rob was happy enough. He'd had fun this weekend, and he liked Nadine. She would be nice to have around. The pressures of med school would only continue to increase, he knew that, and Nadine didn't add to them, because she wasn't a sorority girl, wouldn't insist that he take her to all the important parties, to see and be seen. She was unaware of, or at least unfamiliar with, the Greek world, and that was fine with Rob. He might have use for those sorority types later, but for the time being, Nadine would be all right for a girlfriend.

Will grinned at Daina in the rearview mirror and she grinned back. She was a wildcat, and he liked that in a woman. He supported all the feminism and liberation that was spilling out of college campuses across the country. Ever since he was a freshman, he'd noticed that their liberation frequently manifested itself in sex: not only was no one going to tell them that they should be good girls and not do it, no one was going to tell them who they weren't going to do it with, or how frequently, either. He was more than willing to listen to their rhetoric, agree with their travails, because he'd discovered that it seldom failed to land them in bed with him.

Daina isn't a feminist, but she fucks like one, Will thought with a grin. Like them, she had none of the shy bashfulness of the rest of the girls. Daina liked what she liked, and wasn't afraid to do it, to ask for it, he'd discovered to his delight. They didn't really have a lot in common, hadn't really talked a whole lot over the weekend, but that was because they had spent most of it in bed. And that was fine with him. Will didn't need a woman for an intellectual foil – he had a twin brother for that.

He and Rob planned to go into practice together eventually; and eventually, Will knew, they would have to stop slumming and find women that came from the same ranks of power and privilege that they did. As their father said, it was just as easy to marry a rich girl as it was a poor one, and there were plenty of them around . . .

Like Marta.

Will frowned at the road ahead of him. *Goddamned Ian.*

Over the Memorial Day weekend the previous year, Will and Rob had thrown a party similar to the one they'd had this weekend. They knew that it was better to bypass the holiday – every factory worker within two hundred miles dragged his boat to Parker on Memorial Day weekend – but every couple of years they liked to mingle in the crowds and festive atmosphere. It wasn't like they had to wallow too much – they still had their own house and a private launch. It was fun, but only every so often. They hadn't arrived at the river until after the holiday had passed, this year. Two years in a row would have been too much.

Will had a few classes with Marta, and they'd had had lunch together a few times over the semester; they'd gone out to dinner once. She was curvy, with sleek, dark auburn hair and haughty, flashing brown eyes. Her mouth was large, the lips full and pouty. Will thought he would walk across the desert barefoot for her, if she would just allow him a little access to that mouth.

He was surprised when she said she'd accompany him for the weekend, even if he did tell her that there was a spare bedroom that she could use. Will believed that Marta knew that he was just being polite: if she agreed to come with him, it was understood that she would be *with him,* so he was pleasantly surprised when she smiled and nodded. Marta wasn't the type to sleep with some guy just because he'd invited her to the river for the weekend. She was too rich, too sophisticated for that. But Will knew that he wasn't just any guy, and was confident that he would be experiencing Marta's soft, red mouth before the weekend was out.

They'd left Thursday night. That way they would beat the crowds, and it was always better to drive through the desert at night, if it could be arranged. It was easier on the old Caddy. It had been just the three of them: Will and Marta and Rob. Rob didn't have a girl last year, because Rob had been still completely addicted to waterskiing, just like worthless Cousin Ian. Will could ski, was even fairly good at it. But it wasn't the most exciting thing in the world to him. He preferred snow skiing. It was summertime, and he would much rather spend his time entertaining the ladies.

When they arrived at the house on the river, it was late, everyone was tired. There had been little opportunity for Will to apply his inestimable charm on the ride up – as with most girls, Marta had been fascinated with the identicalness of Will and his twin. She had spent as much time smiling and laughing with Rob and she had with Will. When it was time to retire and Will raised an eyebrow hopefully at her, Marta just giggled and closed the door to the spare bedroom.

That was okay. There were still strangers. Plenty of weekend left to get to know each other.

At first light on Friday morning, Ian arrived, and he and Rob immediately disappeared, to try to get as much skiing in as they could before the holiday weekend glut of boaters got out on the water.

Will would later find out that they hadn't gone out on the water immediately, however. Cousin Ian had wanted to buy new skis. This was the day that they'd met that mangy river rat, Sissy.

Will could never understand why Ian didn't just give her what she wanted. It seemed to go without saying, it seemed only logical, that the girl would keep her mouth shut – her father would never have to find out, would never have cause to put that shotgun to any use. It was 1968, for Christ's sake! Was anyone really still so Victorian?

Maybe Ian really was scared of the ol' man. The idea that Ian was a chickenshit fit in well with Will's opinion of him anyway.

SIXTEEN

Ian's father and the twins' father were brothers. Jameson, Ian's dad, was an English professor at UCR, and Will and Rob's dad, Doctor Felix Wilde, was a successful surgeon. Ian was one year his cousins' senior; the boys had grown up together.

Rob had always had an affinity for Ian, and if he admitted it to himself, Will had always been a little bit jealous of that. Whenever the three of them were together, it always seemed to Will that Rob forgot that they were twins, that he treated Ian as if he wished that Ian was his brother instead of Will. Ian and Rob were best friends. Since he always considered his brother to be *his* best friend, whenever the three of them were together, Will always felt left out.

And then The Incident occurred.

Ian's dad was a snob. From the ivory towers of academe, Professor Wilde looked down on his fellow man and found them to be mostly ignorant and brutish. The politics of the world stage bored him, as did faculty politics. Like a throwback to another era, along with his wife and son, he enjoyed the opera and the symphony and the theatre, as well as the classic literature that he taught. But despite his aristocratic air, Jameson Wilde loved baseball.

Generally, his uncle made Will feel ignorant and unschooled. When he was a kid, his uncle frequently chastised him if he used a word incorrectly or used improper grammar, to the point that Will became nervous and reticent to even open his mouth in front of him. Rob had no such problem – he was always laughing and at his ease around Uncle Jameson, just as he was with Ian. Like Ian's, Rob's grammar was flawless. It was another source of resentment to Will.

But unlike Rob, there was one thing that Will could always discuss with his uncle, something he enjoyed and understood as well as Jameson. Baseball. When they were talking about baseball, Will felt comfortable with his uncle. Jameson didn't correct his adverbs when they talked about Ty Cobb and Joe DiMaggio.

One afternoon, when Ian was ten and the twins were nine, Uncle Jameson had promised to take them to the Dodgers game. They were at Dr. Wilde's house. The boys were energetic and excited, and the twins' mom had shooed them outside to burn off some of their energy while the elder Wilde brothers talked for a while. At odds for something to do while they waited to go to the game, the three boys wandered around the large grounds, and eventually wound up at the gardener's shed.

While they sat in the shade of the shed's eaves, Ian began to tell them the story of King Arthur and the Knights of the Round Table. He told them about how they were always going on quests and crusades, always riding their massive war chargers into battle. Rob was rapt – he loved Ian's fanciful stories – it was one of the reasons he got along so well with Ian, and with Uncle Jameson, as well. Rob always had the imagination to follow such adventuresome tales, and enjoyed it even more if Ian read such stories in verse.

Will thought the stories were stupid and the verse girlish, but he didn't want to be left out. On this occasion, he reluctantly asked Ian about the only part of the story that interested him. "When the knights would go to battle, what kind of weapons did they use?"

Ian considered. "Swords and daggers, I guess. And staves, probably."

"What's a stave?"

"A staff," Rob corrected.

Will glared at him, then looked expectantly at Ian.

"It's just a big stick, really."

"A stick? Like a branch from a tree?"

"No. A straight, thick piece of wood." Ian ducked into the gardener's shed. "Like this."

Now Will thought that his cousin was pulling his leg. Ian was holding two garden spades. "Those are shovels," he said.

"Actually, those are spades," his know-it-all twin said. "A shovel has a flat end. A spade comes to a point."

Will ignored him. "The knights fought with shovels," he said to Ian. It was ridiculous.

Ian tossed one of the spades to his cousin. "Forget about the blade part. Just pretend it isn't there." Ian was good at pretending, Will thought sourly, much better than he was. "I'll show you."

Ian proceeded to show Will how to fight with a staff, at least in the manner that Ian imagined that it must have been done. They smacked the shovel handles against each other; the loud clacks reverberated in the still afternoon air. Rob looked on, and Will couldn't help but get the impression that he was cheering more for Ian than he was for his own flesh and blood, for his brother, his *twin*.

This idea enraged Will, and he fought back harder, sloppier. It was all just a game to Ian; when Will stumbled backwards, Ian lightly brought the shovel handle down on Will's upraised handle, then turned to grin at Rob.

Will saw an opportunity. He planned to drive the spade into the ground a little to the right of Ian's foot and then quickly move the handle in front of Ian's shin. When his cousin moved forward, he would collide with the shovel handle and fall. Will threw Ian's handle off of his own and executed his move.

But his aim was off – Will would always swear that it was just that his aim was off, he didn't do it on purpose – and instead of burying the shovel in the soil, he buried it in his cousin's right foot, neatly slicing through the ten-year-old's blue Keds and cleanly severing his baby toe.

There was a rush to the hospital, and even though a colleague of Dr. Wilde's was the attending, and he was one of the best orthopedic surgeons in the county, it was still 1956 and Ian's toe couldn't be saved.

Theatrically, Rob vowed on the spot that he would become an orthopedic surgeon someday, and he would devise methods for reattaching baby toes. He had kept his promise: he was already studying the orthopedic discipline. His brother's interest had influenced Will's choice of a field of study, although Will was more interested in diseases of the bone than pins and plates, breaks and fractures. Or reattaching amputations. But it was all the same area of expertise.

Needless to say, the Dodgers game was missed. In punishment for what he termed his son's *incredible stupidity and appalling violence,* Felix Wilde forbade Will from going to see the Dodgers for the rest of the season. What little bonhomie Will would ever share with his Uncle Jameson was lost.

Ian himself immediately forgave Will. That was perhaps the worst part of The Incident. If Ian would've remained angry or resentful, if he would have railed bitterly about how his own cousin had crippled him, then Will would have been able to angrily defend himself, to protest that it had been only an unfortunate accident. But Ian conceded immediately that it had been just that, and he hobbled around gamely, garnering everyone's sympathy, while the rest of the family just shot Will hard looks and shook their heads at him.

And Will's maiming of his cousin served to help Ian immeasurably in the end. Ian might've avoided the draft because he was in college (his father saw to it), and because he was an only child. But he definitely avoided it because he had a disability, thanks to a pretend game of knights and a very sharp spade and his cousin's poor aim. After a few years, Ian could not remember the time when he'd possessed that toe – he didn't even limp – yet its absence saved him from the having to study too hard in school. Even if he flunked out, even if they decided to start taking only heirs, he was still 4-F; he would never see the jungle.

So it was through this novel set of circumstances that Ian was passed over for the draft. The only thing saving Will and Rob was their grade-point average, their father warned them darkly, frequently. *And our money,* Will thought righteously. But through an avoidable, childhood accident, Ian skated on the curse of their generation.

Will understood that that kind of thing was commonly referred to as *luck.* Cousin Ian didn't feel guilty, was not in the least apologetic about his good fortune in bypassing the draft. It was all part and parcel of how life treated him: Ian had always been lucky. His mother had often told him that 1946, the year of his birth, had been one of the worst years for the polio epidemic. Yet he had escaped that scourge, also.

Ian had always been lucky, and Will had always hated him for it.

SEVENTEEN

The first day of last year's Memorial Day weekend had been great. Rob and Ian had disappeared early – Marta had not even had the dubious pleasure of meeting the twins' cousin – and Will had taken her and another couple out for a nice, sedate boat ride of their own. Waterskiing wasn't even mentioned.

An hour or so before sunset, Will brought them back in, tied up and abandoned the boat. He was done with the water for the day. He wanted to have a conversation that wasn't drowned out by the outboard; he wanted to walk around, smile at Marta, maybe put his arm around her; give her a little kiss, maybe. Remind her why she was there.

Will fired up the barbeque and put on some steaks. Marta sat beside him with a drink in her hand, and smiled and listened attentively, laughed at his jokes. Friends that were in town for the holiday began to show up and the party commenced. Marta remained by his side, didn't look twice at anyone else. Will began to think that she liked him, and he began to believe that maybe she liked him well enough that she might let him sneak into her room a little later on.

Ian and Rob returned not long after sundown, with the newly-met, love-struck Sissy in tow. On this point, if on no other, Ian and Will agreed: neither of them wanted any underage kids hanging around their house, their party. Rob introduced Ian and Sissy to Marta, then Ian immediately drove Sissy home.

A half an hour or so later, Will stepped out of the house to discover that Ian had returned. He was sitting at the picnic table beside Rob, across from Marta. She was smiling at them, and Will thought again about how much he wanted to possess her incredible mouth. He thought about it so thoroughly that he didn't pay any attention to what she was saying. All he heard was, ". . . waterski?"

"To the depth and breadth and height my soul can reach," Ian replied and smiled back at her.

Marta giggled prettily. "That's supposed to be a sentiment about a lover, Ian," she chided. "Not an activity."

"He has a poetic soul," Rob commented drily.

"It's not just an activity. It's a lifestyle. Besides," Ian shrugged and glanced around, "there are no lovers forthwith."

To his dismay, Will thought he caught a little glint in Marta's eye when she said with mock gravity, "What a pity."

Ian shrugged again, smiled faintly. *"Que sera, sera,"* he said, then glanced at Rob, who smirked at him. *"Whatever will be, will be."*

Ian did not look smolderingly into Marta's eyes; he didn't look at her at all, in fact, instead glancing over his shoulder and greeting Will with a hearty smile. "Going skiing with us in the morning, Cuz?"

Will hated it when Ian called him *Cuz*. It was the cutesy appellation that he and Rob used for each other, and more than that, it had roots in the bond of stupid old stories and classical literature they shared. Rob and Ian didn't call each other *Cuz* because their fathers were brothers. Oh, no, that wasn't enough for these poets. It had to be Shakespearean. How many times had Will heard one of them say to the other, *Thou dost not wish more help from England, Cuz?*

To which the other would reply, *God's will, my liege, would you and I alone, without more help, could fight this royal battle!*

And then they would laugh together and look at Will as if he were stupid for neither knowing nor caring about whatever piece of drivel they were quoting.

Will felt as though Ian was patronizing him when he called him *Cuz*, as if Ian knew that Will felt left out of the friendship Ian shared with his brother and was being magnanimous by attempting to include him. Will realized that none of that was true – Ian didn't think about Will enough to worry about whether he felt left out of not – but regardless, he still loathed it when Ian called him *Cuz*.

Will opened his mouth. He was going to say that he had better things to do than ski, and then he was going to smile at Marta. But before he could make a sound, she said, "I'll go with you."

"You don't understand," Will said immediately. "They're not going for a little pleasure cruise, stop on the beach, sit in the sun, that kind of thing. All they do is go back and forth, back and forth –"

"I don't think *you* understand, Will," she replied, with enough of an edge to her voice that his brother glanced at her in surprise. "I know what's involved. My dad keeps a little place not far from Lake Elsinore. I've been waterskiing, on and off, since I was twelve."

"Well, I'll be damned!" Ian said with undiluted appreciation. "I've only been skiing since I was sixteen."

"Constantly," Will threw in.

"That's great, Marta," Ian told her.

She smiled at him then, and Will saw that little glint in her eye again, even if there was not an answering one in Ian's. He was impressed that she could ski, but he wasn't flirting with her. No one realized it more than Marta herself.

Ian was not a flirt. When he spoke to girls, he would be politely complimentary, he would drop a line of verse here and there, but he was never even remotely suggestive. Cousin Ian never wanted for female companionship, Will knew. But he also couldn't remember a single instance when he had heard Ian make the first move. He always offered the façade of innocent nonchalance, as if the idea of getting into some girl's pants was the farthest thing from his mind. The tactic was usually successful. Like Will himself, and Rob, too – wealthy, attractive young men all – Ian rarely went home alone.

It was all a ruse. There was not a single thing innocent about Ian Wilde. The girls would be appalled, Will thought, if they ever overhead how his boyish cousin talked about them in the company of other men.

EIGHTEEN

So there was not a snowball's chance in hell that Will was going to allow his brother and Cousin Ian to take Marta out waterskiing alone. There was not a chance that Will was going to leave her alone with Ian for a moment. For the rest of the evening, he stuck to her side, as if she might disappear like a mist if he lost sight of her.

Will endured an endless conversation about waterskiing that looped back on itself to cover boats, outboards and direct drives, then the Colorado and Lake Elsinore and other bodies of water they had sampled, then more about skiing. Marta kept up with Rob and Ian, and they were more than impressed with her knowledge. Will was bored with the discussion. He liked to boat and he could ski, but he could take or leave both. He would've wandered off to talk to someone else after the first five minutes, if it hadn't been for the enjoyment he took from watching Marta's mouth when she spoke, regardless of what she was talking about.

At one point, he had to use the facilities, and when he came back out, the thing he feared most had occurred: the picnic table was deserted. "Goddamn," he murmured under his breath in disbelief. He had only been gone for a minute, and could not believe that Ian could spirit Marta away so quickly. But Ian didn't know that Will wanted her, unless Rob had told him. *It wouldn't matter to him anyway,* Will thought, *the son of a bitch.* And Marta . . . He wouldn't have believed that she would just so cavalierly disappear with his cousin, in front of a houseful of people. What kind of tramp was she, anyway?

But then Will heard Marta's high, girlish giggle. He looked back into the house, expecting to see her all cuddled up on Ian's lap, laughing and whispering. They wouldn't be talking about boats and skiing any more, Will thought morosely. But he still had to see, had to punish himself by looking. He had to see how his lucky cousin had succeeded again.

Marta was sitting on the couch next to a pretty blonde girl; a skinny redhead was perched on the arm on her other side. They had their heads close together, whispering. When the blonde saw Will looking at them, she stopped speaking. It was evidently girl talk, and she didn't want Will to overhear.

Marta smiled at Will, nodded in the direction of the kitchen. "They're playing cards."

It was a little disconcerting to Will that she thought he was looking for his relatives instead of her. He saw Ian at the kitchen table with a beer in his hand. Someone spoke and he shrugged, grinned, and looked down the hall. His grin widened when he saw Will.

What a bastard he is! Will thought. *He was looking over here to see what Marta's doing, and when he sees me he still has the nerve to smile!*

Ian nodded an invitation to join them in the kitchen. Will shook his head and turned back to Marta. "Do you want to take a walk?" he asked. "Get out of this stuffy house?"

Marta had the good grace not to look in Ian's direction, but still she demurred. "We haven't seen each other in while," she said, indicating her sorority sisters. "We're kind of catching up."

"But . . ." Will stopped. He sounded like a schoolboy to himself, and Marta was a grown woman, smart, sophisticated. Sexy. He wasn't going to get anywhere by wheedling. Besides, tomorrow was another day, and tomorrow night he would have another chance. If he played aloof, he thought he might even get a chance tonight.

"We'll have plenty of time to talk tomorrow. While we're skiing," she said. There was that glint in Marta's eye again, but still she didn't look past him at Ian. Maybe it wasn't his cousin at all that was putting that little twinkle there. Maybe she was just really looking forward to waterskiing. Maybe Will still had a chance.

"Okay." Will smiled and Marta returned his smile warmly. He hesitated for another heartbeat – he obviously couldn't stay here with them and interrupt their girl talk, their reunion. But he wasn't going to let Ian out of his sight, either. Ian wouldn't have any problem joining three women whispering together. He would just smile guilelessly at them, and they would go ahead and invite him to sit with them. Will had no trouble whatsoever picking up girls, but Ian had a knack for talking to them that never failed to amaze him. And tonight his cousin's effortless charm exasperated Will, because the girl he wanted was clearly already interested in goddamned Ian.

Will sauntered down the hall, paused in the doorway. Ian and Rob and another guy were playing poker. Will sighed. The only thing he disliked more than skiing all day was playing cards all night. And this looked like it was tuning up to be a long game. But if he joined them, he could keep an eye on lucky Cousin Ian. He didn't think that Marta would just come in and jump in Ian's lap with Will sitting right there. That would just be gauche. She might not want to take a walk with Will, but he didn't think she'd flaunt her interest in his cousin blatantly in front of him. That would be rude. It had been Will, after all, who had invited her.

His brother and cousin smiled at him in welcome when he sat down; they immediately dealt him in. Rob introduced him to the other player, a slight, dark-eyed young man named Carmine.

"I hear you're a Dodgers fan," he said.

Now here was a subject Will could warm up to. No more boring talk about skis and fiberglass hulls, cavitation and two-strokes versus four-strokes. America's pastime. Baseball. Will could talk about baseball and forget that he was only playing cards with his cousin to keep him away from the girl he wanted.

"Gonna go all the way this year," Will said automatically. He looked down at his cards and was pleasantly surprised to see that he'd been dealt a full house.

"Is that what you think, or is that what you want?" Ian asked. He threw a dollar into the pot.

Rob folded. Rob was an absolutely gutless poker player, Will reflected. If he didn't have at least a pair, he didn't even draw. Carmine threw in his buck, as did Will.

Ian took three cards. Carmine took two. Will of course took none.

Ian bet a dollar. Carmine saw his bet. Will threw in a buck and raised another one. "It's what I want *and* what I think," he said.

Ian saw Will's raise and raised again, two dollars this time. "*The race is not always to the swift, nor the battle to the strong, but that's the way to bet,*" he said. "It doesn't matter what you want, only what they can do."

"You don't think they can do it?" Carmine asked, a little testily. He folded.

Will saw Ian's raise and called. His cousin was bluffing; he was sure of it.

Ian turned over his hand. He had three sixes. Will smiled, turned over his cards and raked the pot toward him. His smugness was dimmed a little when Ian again looked down the hall at Marta. He said, "I was just making conversation, gentlemen. Baseball's not really my thing."

"Nor poker either, apparently," Rob observed.

"*Whenever a man does a thoroughly stupid thing, it is always from the noblest motives,*" Ian replied and winked at his cousin.

Will considered. Was Ian saying that he'd just let him win? Will was fine with that. Ian's money was green.

"I don't know about you UCR English majors," Carmine said, "but where I come from, we say, 'Shut up and deal.'"

The game continued. Will thought it might drag out to the last trump. He drank too much; it was his only defense against the staggering boredom he felt, even though he was taking everybody's money. Carmine drank too much because he was losing. The blonde that had been talking to Marta earlier came into the kitchen once and kissed him; she was his girlfriend.

Seeing their happiness added to Will's bad mood. He should be off somewhere kissing Marta instead of sitting here playing cards with Ian, to make sure that *he* wasn't off somewhere kissing Marta.

Rob and Ian didn't drink too much. It wasn't that they weren't drinkers – Will had seen them both blotto enough times, at wintertime parties. But it was summer, and they were going skiing in the morning. Didn't want to oversleep and miss that. When Will recalled that he was going with them, he frowned and drained his drink. He looked down the hall: Marta and Carmine's girlfriend and the skinny redhead were still in conversation.

Why am I in here with these assholes instead of out there with them? With her? Will asked himself. *Because I missed my chance today.* He looked down at the pile of money in front of him and smiled. *Tomorrow is another day. I might not be getting any tonight, but either is Cousin Ian. And I've got all his money.*

"*The urge to gamble is so universal and its practice so pleasurable, that I assume it must be evil,*" Rob said as he dealt. Carmine rolled his eyes.

"*Gambling is the son of avarice and the father of despair,*" Ian replied with a grin. "Rob, your brother is a hustler. If I was not a gentleman, I would challenge him to a duel."

"No one likes a sore loser, *Cuz.*" Will grinned with a shade a malice.

Ian returned his grin, showing all his teeth. "I'm not familiar with losing enough to be sore, Will. Call me simply a surprised loser. An old horseracing proverb goes, *'Eat your betting money, but don't bet your eating money.'*" He looked at his cards and folded. "I would amend that to say, *'Don't bet your gas-for-the-outboard money.'* I will see you winners in the morning." Ian stood up, stretched.

A sudden panic sliced through Will's smug buzz. "Where are you sleeping tonight, Ian?" He usually stayed in the spare bedroom, but Marta was staying in the spare bedroom . . .

"On my boat."

Ian's pride and joy was a fifteen foot Raysoncraft called *One Wilde Ride*. It seated only four in back-to-back bucket seats. There was barely enough room to stow life jackets and a pair of skis in it.

"There's no place to sleep on the boat," Will stated. It was like they were kids again, and Ian was pulling his leg. *There's never a shovel around when you need one,* he thought darkly.

Rob arose with Ian. "He's sleeping on the bow," he said, and held his arms and legs out in an *X* shape. He grinned at his cousin. *"A good soft pillow for that good white head were better than a churlish turf of France."*

Ian supplied the next line. *"Not so, my liege: this lodging likes me better, since I may say, 'Now lie I like a king.'"* Again, Carmine rolled his eyes. Ian said to Will, "Thanks for your concern, Cuz. But I have a pillow and a blanket." He glanced down the hall for another split second, then continued. "No honeys to keep me warm, but I'll manage." He smiled at his cousins. "Maybe we'll all have better luck tomorrow night, eh?'

"Fuck that," Rob said. "It's the shank of the evening." He walked down the hall and greeted the three ladies, paying special attention to the skinny redhead.

Ian shook his head. "I guess that just leaves you and me stag, huh, Cuz?" He clapped Will on the shoulder. Will flinched. He didn't want Ian to touch him, didn't want to be in any type of commiseration with him at all. There was a houseful of eligible girls, and as the night was waning, it wouldn't be too difficult to pick any one of them up. Ian didn't have to sleep alone on the bow of his boat. But Will believed that Ian was biding his time, waiting for his opportunity to get at Marta, just like he was. It infuriated him.

"There's always that townie," Will said. Rob had told him the tale, while Ian had gone to take the minor home. He thought that a scrawny river rat was just the type of girl for Ian. They could ski themselves into oblivion until one of them drowned, and leave the grown-ups to more pleasurable pursuits ashore.

Will was pleased to see Ian's smile evaporate. "Her daddy doesn't like college boys." But then Cousin Ian's killer smile crept back. "Besides, she a little young for me. What would we talk about?"

"How about waterskiing?" Will said immediately. Then he immediately regretted it.

Ian glanced down the hall and smiled at Marta. To Will's dismay – but he was not surprised – she smiled back. Waved. Ian said, "I don't have to scare up high school girls for that."

Will was going to say something then – he felt like he was perfectly in his rights. He had been the one that had discovered Marta and her flawless mouth; he had been the one that had invited her up here for the weekend. He was going to tell Ian all this, tell him to back off. Marta was Will's girl. She was here for him.

But Will didn't say anything. Marta wasn't his girl, not yet, and he wouldn't give Ian the satisfaction of knowing that they were in competition for her. He wasn't completely sure that Ian was even interested in Marta; he and Rob were here to ski this weekend. But Will was convinced that if Ian knew that Will was interested in her, he'd go out of his way to make a play for her. That was the tack Will would take, if their situations were reversed.

"I'll see you in the morning, Cuz," Ian said and walked down the hall.

Will watched him say a few words to Rob and the ladies, and then take his leave. Will couldn't help but notice that Marta looked after him wistfully. *Goddamned Ian.*

But she did not get up and follow him. Will thanked God for small favors and walked down the hall toward them. He was drunk and in a bad mood, but his charm was more or less intact. It might serve him yet.

NINETEEN

Will had a hangover. It was not the worst one he'd ever experienced, but the thought of going out in the glare, the thought of the noise and vibration of the boat – *the things I don't put myself through for a piece of ass,* he thought. The thought didn't cheer him.

He had simply waited Marta out the night before, simply outlasted her. Carmine and the blonde left first, then after a while, Rob and the redhead had gone for a walk, and had no doubt snuck back in the house via the side door and went to Rob's room.

Will had sat beside Marta on the couch, chatted her up, and continued to drink. He had resigned himself that he wasn't going to get anywhere tonight. Like Rob and his contemptible cousin, Marta wasn't drinking, to be all the more fit to ski in the morning. So her inhibitions were up like a barricade; she giggled good-naturedly at Will's suggestion that they retire to his room to view his etchings, but she didn't make so much as a glance in that direction.

Around one in the morning, she yawned expansively, genuinely. Everyone had decamped – there were a few hangers-on passed out in a chair here, or against the wall on the floor there – but the party was long over. "I've got to get some sleep, Will," she said and arose from the couch.

Will got unsteadily to his feet, slurred, "I could –"

Marta held up her hands in a little warding-off gesture. "I'll see you in a few hours. I've got to get some sleep right now. Goodnight." To his surprise and delight, she brushed her sexy lips lightly against his cheek. "Thanks so much for inviting me." Then she turned and made her way to her room. Will distinctly heard the lock turn.

But that was okay. She hadn't told him *no;* she had only told him *not now.* He grinned. Tomorrow was another day. Once this waterskiing ordeal was out of the way . . . Then he would make his move. Will staggered to his room and passed out on his bed with the door open.

TWENTY

But this waterskiing ordeal was going to be brutal, Will realized as they trooped down to the dock at the god awful hour of seven am. Marta was bright-eyed and bushy-tailed; she talked enthusiastically in her high-pitched, little-girl's voice. Will discovered that he liked her voice almost as much as he liked her mouth. It was the only thing that didn't seem to grate on his senses this morning.

"I'm so excited!" she said and squeezed his arm. "This will be my first time out this season. I usually go with my brother Sid –"

"Sid Codder?" Rob asked.

"Yes. He's my brother."

"I know Sid," Rob said absently. *It's a small world after all.*

"We've usually been out on the lake by now, but he's been so busy with school . . ." Marta gave a little shake, like a shiver. She looked at Ian. "Let's do this thing!"

Ian gave her a little half smile, as if he was surprised by the double-entendre that could be read into her words. Will wasn't surprised. *Goddamned Ian.*

Ian glanced at Rob, who was helping Allie, the redhead from the night before, into the boat. She seemed a little uncertain, but Rob gave her a quick kiss once she was seated and she smiled up at him. She wore a giant, floppy straw hat. It was tied on with a red string, jauntily, off to one side of her jawline. "You better hold on to that hat, Red," Ian told her. *You're still gonna fry,* he thought.

The desert sun was ruthless, and she was just as white-skinned as a lily. An open boat on the Colorado River was no place for someone so fair-complexioned. Rob had tried to tell her so, tried to tell her that he would see her this evening, but she had pouted and told him that she wanted to go, that she'd been sunburned before.

Not like this, Ian thought. Simpatico as always with Rob, they shared a glance that said that Rob wasn't going to be touching Allie tonight, unless it was to be putting milk compresses on her hot, angry red skin.

Will frowned behind his black shades as he stepped rather stiffly into the boat. His head hurt. He wouldn't undergo this for anything but a chance at Marta and her glorious mouth. The sun, the noise, the chop – it was going to be like the tortures of the damned. He held out his hand and helped Marta into the boat, although it was obvious that she didn't need any help.

Ian cast off, hopped in the boat, and Rob took them out.

TWENTY-ONE

Ian sat beside Rob in the other front bucket seat. Will liked that just fine; the farther he was away from Marta, the better. Will sat between Allie and Marta on the curved bench seat. Will studied Allie, noted that she seemed exceptionally nervous. She held onto her hat with one hand and onto the edge of the seat with the other.

Rob motored out to the middle of the river and killed the engine. Will watched as Allie tensed further, glancing fearfully over the side at the swirling water. Rob was oblivious. He grinned and said to Marta and Ian, "Who's first?"

"We usually Roshambo for it," Marta said. When they all looked at her blankly, she added, "Rock, paper, scissors."

"All right," Ian said. He and Marta played the child's game. Will winced when Marta covered his fist with her hand; did she let it linger there? Her paper beat Ian's rock.

She turned to Rob. The first time was a draw: two rocks. The second time, Marta's repeated rock beat Rob's scissors. She stood up and belted on one of the ski vests that was stowed along the side of the boat, then without further ado, she dove overboard.

Will's appreciation for Marta didn't extend to helping her waterski. Once she was in the water, he didn't move to assist her. Ian could do it. It wasn't like he could touch her from inside the boat.

Ian vaulted gracefully over the seat and threw the tow line to her. "We've got a staggering *three* sets of skis," he shouted to her. "There's a pair of trainers."

Those were painted pink, Will knew. Rob called them his *teaching the ladies to ski* set.

"We've got Will's Highbridges, and my brand new Maherajahs."

Marta smiled. Will thought she looked very young and girlish with her hair wet. "Give me the Highbridges."

"Not the trainers?"

"I don't think so." Will was appalled to see Marta wink at him.

The Highbridges were constructed of alternating light and dark strips of wood; Ian leaned over the stern and gently shot one and then the other of the striped skis to her.

Ian stood up, turned, and was about to say something to Rob when he noticed Allie practically cowering in her seat. She seemed almost frightened now that Marta wasn't in the boat with her. "Can you swim, Allie?" Ian asked.

She looked up at him with big, round blue eyes. "Not very well."

Ian shot an annoyed glance at Rob. Rob made an exaggerated, *How the hell was I supposed to know?* shrug. Ian extracted another ski vest from the side of the boat. "Here, honey, stand up." Allie slowly complied, and Ian put the vest on her. "Someone has to be thinking of boating safety around here," he said, shooting another irritated glance at Rob. Will noticed that Ian did not touch Allie in any way that could be misconstrued as inappropriate, although it would've been easy for him to do so as he snugged up the straps on the vest. "There. Now you'll be fine. As safe as in your mother's arms."

If her mother is a mermaid, Will said to himself.

Allie smiled gratefully at Ian and sat back down, considerably more at ease. *Always a way with the ladies,* Will thought. *Goddamn him.*

TWENTY-TWO

When Rob initially pulled Marta up out of the water, Ian studied her technique curiously for some time. To show off, she took one hand of the handle and waved at him. Ian waved back, and shouted over his shoulder to Rob, "She's good. Not as good as Sissy, but she's still very good."

Rob shouted back, "Should we go by the marina and pick Sissy up? I'm sure she'd love to see you with another girl that knows how to ski!" Ian shook his head.

Will glared at his brother over his sunglasses. *She is most assuredly not* with *him,* the look said.

Again, Rob shrugged, grinned. *Not yet,* was his silent reply.

Will flipped his brother off. Ian and Allie didn't notice; they were watching Marta.

When Rob skied, Will sat next to Ian in the other bucket seat, to prevent Marta from doing so. She sat at the end of the curved back seat with Allie, who was no longer frightened in the least. They giggled and whispered into each other's ears like schoolgirls.

Allie's telling her all about her thrilling night with my brother, Will decided. When Marta whispered back, he hoped she was asking for details, perhaps thinking that whatever Rob had, Will would also have. Allie blushed – her already pinkening skin flushed a deeper red – and then she whispered in Marta's ear again and they both giggled gleefully.

Will smiled to himself. Allie's glowing report couldn't do anything but reflect well on him. He and Rob were twins, after all.

Will's smug confidence that Marta was now anticipating spending the night with him evaporated when he observed the girls when Ian skied, however. Will didn't think Ian was any better at it than Rob; hell, he didn't think Ian was any better at it than Will was himself. But Ian was built for it. Will and his brother were taller than their cousin, thinner. They looked gangly on skis. *Like skinny herons,* someone had once noted unkindly.

Ian, on the other hand, was sturdily built, with a broad chest and muscled shoulders and arms. His thighs were also thickly muscled. He wasn't anything special when he was dressed, but once he was barefoot, in swim trunks – Will had watched girls turn around and stare at Ian when he walked by them on the public launch. No, Will didn't think Ian skied any better than he or his brother; but Will had to admit, however grudgingly, that he *looked better* doing it.

And he could see that Marta thought so, and Allie, too. The girlish giggling had ceased. The two of them stared at Ian over the stern of the boat, awestruck, almost open-mouthed. He waved, and both of them slowly lifted their hands and waved back.

Goddamned Ian! Will thought, disgusted at their amazed, rapt expressions. *So what if he looks good on a set of skis?* He wanted to scream at them. *He's an idiot! He's a fucking* English *major! Do you sorority bitches even know that? What kind of a job is he going to get with that? A professorship, like his snooty dad? Hell, he doesn't even have the ambition for that! He spends every spare minute he has getting dragged behind a boat, and yet you people are looking at him like he's on the menu! I'm going to be a doctor, for Christ's sake!*

This weekend is not going the way I planned, Will said to himself, his anger draining away to resigned resentment. *And it's all goddamned Ian's fault.*

TWENTY-THREE

The fact that the girl Will had handpicked to spend the weekend with him was going to wind up with his despised cousin was a forgone conclusion to Will by the time they returned to the house. Ian, ever magnanimous, had cut the day's skiing short, because by four o'clock, Allie was just as toasted as she could be, as red as a boiled lobster. She would've stayed out there with them all day – she was Marta's friend, her sorority sister, and she was sweet on Rob – but Ian insisted that she'd had enough and bade them come back long before dark, his usual quitting time.

Marta had become quiet. She stared solemnly at Ian, that sparkle in her dark eyes now a permanent fixture. The only time it left was when she spoke to Will or Rob. It remained when she spoke to Allie, because Allie was no doubt aware of her desires. Will was now convinced that the earlier giggling and blushing hadn't been about Rob, and it certainly hadn't been about himself. They'd been whispering about Ian.

Rob again fired up the grill, and Marta and Allie, like dutiful housewives, brought out steaks from the kitchen. Will thought the coup de grace, the last nail in his coffin of certainty, was when Marta fixed Ian a plate and brought it to him. Will was left to feed himself.

Instead, he went into the house and returned with the bottle of gin that he'd kept hidden from the rapacious crew of party-goers the night before; they were once again arriving in twos and threes. He figured that since he wasn't gonna get laid, he might as well get drunk.

By nine-thirty, Will was quite a bit more than half in the bag. He was surprised when Marta retired to her room with Allie, to help her apply those milk compresses that Ian had suggested. Ian and Rob were oblivious to girls' absence; they had found another kid to play poker with them and were again sitting at the kitchen table.

Will sat on the couch in the living room, nursing his bottle of gin, angrily mulling over the fact that this weekend was turning into a total bust. Maybe Marta was not as hot for Ian as he had first assumed; he had expected her to hang on his cousin all evening, from the way she had looked at him during dinner, but she had not emerged from her room. Regardless, it didn't look like Will was gonna get any either.

He was in such a foul state of mind that it took him several minutes to recognize that the chubby, dark-haired girl that had plopped down next to him on the couch and started talking to him was actually flirting with him, and rather straight-forwardly.

"I so like a tall, green-eyed boy," she was saying. She lowered her lashes coquettishly.

She was pretty, what his mother called *pleasingly plump.* Her mouth wasn't as scintillating as Marta's, but it was nice enough, and she was perceptibly showing him interest, something Marta had not done for more than a few moments. *Until she met Ian,* he thought sourly.

"What's your name?" he asked.

"Catherine," she said with the slightest of slurs.

As he introduced himself, Will realized that Catherine was almost as drunk as he was. He decided it was time to cut his losses. "Would you like to take a walk?" he asked. "Get out of this stuffy house?"

"I thought you'd never ask."

TWENTY-FOUR

Will awakened with a start. He looked at the clock on the nightstand: it was one-fifteen in the morning. The house was quiet, and he slowly recalled the events of the evening. In the darkness, he could just make out Catherine's sleeping outline beside him. He smiled. She had been okay, compliant and eager to please. Not a haughty bitch like Marta. The weekend hadn't been a total loss, after all.

Will realized that he was ravenously hungry. He hadn't eaten anything at the barbeque, disgusted as he had been with watching Marta wait on his cousin like a scullery maid. He slid gingerly out of bed, not wishing to wake up Catherine, and found his trunks on the floor. *What a sight I must've been,* he thought – he hadn't even changed out of them after coming back from the disastrous day on the water. He'd just sat down and commenced to drink. *But Catherine didn't mind.*

He cracked the door to his room and looked out cautiously. The little house was set up so that all the bedrooms opened directly onto the living room. Will's room was across from Marta's; Rob's was in the opposite wall, across from the patio. The bathroom was next to his room.

Will peeked out into the living room. He didn't want to interrupt anyone that might have decided to have a quickie on the couch after the party. It had happened before.

He didn't see anyone on the couch, but he noticed that the door to Marta's room was open. The light from the bedside table was on, bathing the room in a dim, cozy yellow glow. Will couldn't help but look. What was she doing up at this hour?

There was a man sitting on the edge of Marta's bed, shirtless, facing away from Will. From the muscled shoulders and shaggy dark hair, he knew it could only be one person – *goddamned Ian.* Suddenly, Marta glided across the living room from the hall to Will's left. She was wearing a short, black lace teddy and a flowing, black, satin robe. *She brought that to wear for me,* Will said to himself. She was coming from the kitchen, carrying two glasses of ice water.

Jesus, Will thought, *I almost ran right into her. How awkward would that have been?*

Ian turned and grinned at her when she entered the room, and Will noticed that he had the bed sheet wrapped around his waist. *How did I fail to notice that before?* Will asked himself. So it had all already happened. This was the lull before Round Two. He also noticed that all trace of his cousin's trademark innocent indifference was gone. He leered at Marta now.

No need to feign disinterest anymore, Will thought bitterly. *It had worked, hadn't it?*

Marta closed the door with her foot. Will stood there for another moment, still stunned at how this opportunity had slipped through his fingers. Then he could've sworn he heard Marta moan, but it might've just been his imagination tormenting him.

"Where ya goin', Willie?" Catherine called softly from across the room.

God, that was awful: *Willie.* It was almost as bad as *Cuz.*

Will stared across the room at Marta's closed door for another moment, then, in one fell swoop, he threw off the ridiculous black cloud of jealousy he'd been functioning under all weekend. *Fuck her,* he thought. *She wants worthless Cousin Ian? She can have him.*

It wasn't like she was Elizabeth Taylor; she was just another sorority girl with a nice mouth. There were plenty more where she came from. There was one in his bed right now.

"I'm not going anywhere," he said and returned to her.

As Catherine eagerly wrapped her arms around his neck, Will again thought, *The hell with Marta. This one's just as good. It's all the same in the dark, anyway.*

But still he seethed with hatred toward his lucky cousin Ian. *His luck is gonna run out someday,* Will thought, biting Catherine on the neck until she squealed in delight. *I just hope I'm there to see it.*

TWENTY-FIVE

Will woke up at seven. It was impossibly early after the night he had just spent, but he couldn't help it. He had to go to the bathroom. He peeked out of his door again. He certainly didn't want to run into either Ian or Marta. He sprinted quickly across the living room, wondering how they were going to play the whole thing off for the rest of the weekend. Would they hold hands? Or would they just pretend that nothing was going on between them?

Will got his answer when he returned to his room. There was an envelope on the floor with his name on it, just inside. It must've been slipped under the door sometime during the night and he had missed it in his haste to get to the bathroom.

It was from Marta. *Surprise!* Will thought.

Dear Will,

Thanks so much for inviting me. I'm so sorry that I have to leave, but I got a phone call last night that there's been a death in the family. It's my aunt. I knocked on your door, but you didn't answer, so your cousin said he'd run me home. Thanks again, I had a wonderful time. See you at school.

Will would not have thought it possible that so many lies could be crammed into such a short epistle. There had been no phone call, no death in the family, no knock on his door. He doubted that he would see her at school, either. The only truth the note contained was that she was gone and that she'd had a wonderful time. *With Ian.*

Will balled up the note and threw it in the waste basket. He let Catherine sleep and went out to the kitchen to fix himself something to eat.

The kitchen door was open and his brother was standing just outside, drinking a cup of coffee and looking at the water.

"Why are you up so early?" Will asked him.

Rob looked at him in surprise. "Why else? I'm going skiing."

"I don't think so. Ian's gone."

Rob looked into his coffee cup. A shade of guilt crossed his face. "I know."

Will let his brother's guilty look slide. It wasn't his fault that Marta was a slut and their cousin was an asshole. But Rob *was* friends with him . . .

"Then who are you going skiing with?"

Rob grinned. "Guess who knocked on my window about a half an hour ago, looking for Ian?"

"That mangy townie?" Rob nodded, grinned. "Christ, what nerve!" Will marveled.

"If thou remember'st not the slightest folly that ever love did make thee run into, thou hast not loved."

Will rolled his eyes, ignored Rob's poetry, like he always did. "Just the two of you?"

Rob looked dubiously at his brother. "Why not? She's not in love with me."

"But you need three people –"

"I'm sure we'll find someone else."

"Red's not going with you?"

"Not if I can help it. Another day in the sun, and she won't have any skin left at all." Rob grinned. "She's all yours, my brutha. When she wakes up, tell her you're me."

A ghost of a grin touched the corner of Will's mouth. "That hasn't worked since high school. Not when they already know there's two of us. Besides, I've already got one."

Rob's eyebrows went up. To hide his surprise, he sipped his coffee again. At last he said, "Good for you."

"Where's the townie now?" Will asked, to change the subject.

"I sent her to get gas. I had to have a cup of coffee first. I'm not fifteen."

"Goddamn it, Rob! You can't just be giving the boat to strangers!"

"She's not a stranger. I'm thinking of adopting her as sort of a mascot. We can call her *Ian's Parker Wife.*" Rob grinned into his cup. "Besides, she handles a boat as well as you. And she knows where to get gas this early in the morning."

TWENTY-SIX

The twins didn't see their cousin for the entire month of June; they didn't even hear from him. Nor did Will see Marta at school, past a wave in the classes they shared. But Ian was back in Parker for the 4th of July.

The 4th was on a Thursday in 1968, making for another long holiday weekend. As always, Ian walked in the house like he owned the place, early, just as the twins were sitting down to breakfast. Will had brought Catherine with him, because she was nice enough. She would do for a summer girlfriend. He knew why she was plump: she was a great cook.

When Ian walked into the kitchen, shirtless as always, Catherine stared at him, open-mouthed. *Goddamned Ian!* Will thought. *What is it about him that makes them look at him like that?* He decided that if Catherine suddenly developed an interest in waterskiing, he would have to drown them both.

Past a nod of greeting, Ian ignored her, and Will as well. He said gleefully to Rob, "You've gotta see what I've got, Cuz."

"What is it?"

Ian shook his head. "A picture is worth a thousand words, and words won't do it justice. You've gotta *see* it!" He nodded outside, turned and went back out the door.

Rob set his fork down and followed his cousin. Will, curious against his will, went next; Catherine turned off the stove and brought up the rear.

"Ta-fucking-da!" Ian said. Attached to the tow-hitch of his beat-up old truck was a spectacular wooden Chris Craft. With a flourish, Ian removed the cover from it. The mahogany gleamed mellowly in the early morning sun.

"It's a 1940 Barrelback. One hundred and thirty glorious horses, Cuz. Direct drive, "M" engine."

"Hot damn!" Rob cried. He stretched the words out, pronouncing them *hod day-um*. It was his ultimate expression of appreciation. "Where did you –"

"It's Marta's. Her daddy's, actually."

"Marta's with you?" Will asked incredulously.

Although he wouldn't have thought it possible, Will saw Ian's grin widen. "Marta's in Rome. Or Venice, or somewhere over there. On vacation with her family. She wanted me to go with 'em, but I don't think you can ski in those canals. They won't be back 'til school starts in September. We've got this stupendous piece of Americana for the whole summer, Rob!"

To Will's eternal annoyance, lucky Cousin Ian stayed with them in Parker for the whole summer, impressing townies and tourists alike with his fine, borrowed Chris-Craft. The boat was called the *Ooh-La-La,* and like a soldier on leave in France, partly through his charm and partly by way of the gorgeous boat, like Sissy would tell Nadine the following summer, Ian brought a different girl back to the house practically every night.

Will thought about writing to Marta in Europe somehow, letting her know that Ian was cheating on her, and prodigiously. But it would be a catty, womanish thing to do, and Will believed she deserved it, anyway. That's what she got for picking someone like Ian over him. That's what she got for lending someone like Ian such an incomparable boat.

TWENTY-SEVEN

As Will drove back to Riverside with his brother and their new girlfriends this year, he speculated about how Marta and Ian's relationship might be faring. Ian had shown up late this weekend, boat-less, Marta-less. Rob told him that she had just broken both her wrists – Will knew that she was therefore in a lot of pain, and probably hadn't want to make the long drive up to Parker. It wasn't like she could waterski now. But why hadn't she lent Daddy's boat to Ian this time?

She'd only known him for six weeks last year, but she'd already been enamored with him enough to give the *Ooh-La-La* to him for the whole summer, while she was out of the country. Why not now, for just the weekend? Will grinned in grim satisfaction. Perhaps the honeymoon was over.

Lucky Ian had still succeeded in his pursuits this weekend, even without Marta's boat, without his little Raysoncraft. Rob had lent him their boat, and he'd gotten to ski, and had managed to secure himself a girl – maybe two – for the evening. Maybe Marta had discovered that he was a cheating son of a bitch. Maybe that's why she'd refused to give him her boat.

Ian's a cheating son of a bitch. Will glanced in the rearview mirror and studied Nadine's expression for a moment. She had a thoughtful, musing look on her face; a slight, dreamy smile curved her mouth. He had seen that look before, on dozens of girls, on Catherine, now long forgotten; on Allie, on Sissy, who was too young and ignorant to even attempt to hide it. On Marta.

He glanced over at his brother for a moment. *I tried to warn you, Rob,* he thought. *Only a complete idiot allows lucky Cousin Ian to be alone with his woman, even if they're only waterskiing, even if they have a love-struck townie river rat for a chaperone. There's just something about him . . . they don't care that he's worthless, futureless, practically penniless. All they know is that they want to do the stocky, squinty-eyed water-skier, and at the first opportunity. You have made a big mistake, my brutha . . .*

TWENTY-EIGHT

When Daina and Nadine returned home from school the day after their trip to the river, their aunts had a surprise waiting for them. They had opened up the house at the bottom of the lot, where Daina had grown up. After her parents had died, her aunts had shuttered the house. Daina had afterwards lived in the house on top of the hill with them.

"You're a grown woman now," Bellona said, with an impish twinkle in her blue eyes. "You need your privacy. You can't be cooped up with your old aunts anymore. You need a place of your own. There's a room for you, too, Nadine. If your parents will allow it."

Nadine blinked in astonishment – how great would it be to live with Daina? They grinned at each other.

"You're going to need some furniture," Penny said, with a rare smile. Nadine looked on in amazement as she handed Daina a thick wad of bills, held together with a rubber band. "We got rid of what was in there after your parents moved on. We didn't want you to dwell sadly on what was past."

The house was cozy, practically brand new in architectural terms: Bellona and Penny had caused it to be built as a wedding present for their sister. Daina barely remembered its layout; walking around inside of it was as much of an adventure to her as it was to Nadine.

There was a nice-sized kitchen with a cheery breakfast nook. The living room was paneled in dark wood and featured a brick fireplace with a raised hearth where people could sit. There was a master bedroom with its own half-bathroom; a spacious full bathroom, tiled in green; and a second bedroom. A cavernous, detached, two-car garage.

The interior of the house had been freshly painted. Standing in the second bedroom, which had been hers as a child, Daina discovered that she couldn't summon up a single memory of it. She couldn't even remember what color it had once been. "How did you get it all painted so quickly?" she asked.

"We had been planning on giving it to you for a while," Bellona replied. "We were just waiting for your little trip, so we could surprise you."

Of course, Daina thought. *This is just another stage in my life, one that they've already seen.* Against her will, the thoughts swam through her mind: *Will I live here with my one true love? Will my son be born here? Will tragedy befall him here?*

Daina and Nadine hugged their aunts in overjoyed gratitude.

"It's time," Bellona said. She smiled, but snuffled back a tear. "You're grown women now."

Daina and Nadine moved into the house that evening, sleeping on the living room floor in sleeping bags. Nadine's parents had a few misgivings – their daughter was only twenty-one, far too young to be out on her own.

"I'm not on my own," Nadine countered gently. She didn't want to get into a fight with them – they still gave her an allowance, were paying her way through college. She didn't want to lose any of that, but she wanted to be free, have her own private space. Just like Bellona had said, she was a grown woman. "I'm with Daina. And it's just across the street. And it's free. Daina's aunts are paying all the bills." Her parents had no argument for that, so reluctantly they let her go.

The twins were thrilled with the news, and came over to help Nadine move her bedroom furniture into the house the next day. Daina would have to buy a new set. Her furnishings at the house at the top of the hill had once belonged to her departed mother; her aunts didn't want to part with them.

Rob and Will still lived at home, but it was in similar circumstances to what the girls now had: they lived in a guest house on their parents' ample estate. Mom and Dad had to make a special trip to see them; the guesthouse was not visible from the main house.

Such was not the case for Nadine – her parents simply had to look down the street to keep an eye on her. She fretted for a minute about what they would say when Daina and Nadine entertained callers overnight. But then she reasoned that they wouldn't say anything – they had recognized her adulthood the day she turned twenty-one.

Daina and Nadine planned to go furniture shopping the following Saturday, but on Wednesday evening, Nadine suggested that they go Thursday and Friday after school instead. She told Daina that she was really excited about buying couches and dinettes, lamps and end tables, and didn't want to wait all the way until Saturday. Daina agreed. It was all the same to her. They went to Sears and Montgomery Ward and spent all the money that their aunts had provided. Everything was due to be delivered on Sunday.

Nadine was glad to have the furniture selection and purchase out of the way by Friday night, because the truth was that Ian had called and asked Rob if he and Nadine wanted to go skiing on Saturday. When Rob casually mentioned it to her at school on Wednesday, all thought of furniture shopping vanished. All thought of Rob vanished. All thought of everything vanished until only one thought remained: she was going to get to see Ian again.

TWENTY-NINE

Rob and Nadine tiptoed quietly out of the house at six o'clock on Saturday morning, so as not to wake Daina and Will. The night before had been the first time that the twins had stayed at the girls' new digs; Daina and Will had camped out in her room, because the furniture had not yet arrived.

Nadine had lain awake since four am, staring up into the darkness, listening to Rob's even breathing beside her. She thought about Ian; whenever she was in bed, she thought about Ian. Sometimes she went into her bedroom, sometimes long before bedtime, specifically so she could *think about Ian.* She played through her mind all the different scenarios that might occur to bring them together, what poetic things he would say, what she would say in response, how he would reach out and touch her on the shoulder, or lightly on the cheek. And then it would begin.

When Ian would cross her mind during the day, Nadine thought mostly about how much she loved him for his mind, for his knowledge and recitations of the classics. But when she was all alone in bed, she fantasized about how he would kiss her, tenderly at first, then with more ardor. She thought about how completely excited she would be, how utterly she would give herself to him. Nadine would have sex with Ian in her mind, and when one scenario concluded, she would dream up another, to the point of intense arousal.

From the moment that she'd seen Ian, Rob had become only a tool to slake the lust for his cousin produced by Nadine's imagination. Rob enjoyed her intensity, never imagining that Nadine had only been making love to *him* the first night that they'd been together. She'd met Ian the next day, and afterwards she had always dreamt, always pretended, that Rob was Ian. Every single time.

And today, Nadine was going to see Ian again. Eventually, the ceiling began to become visible as the sky lightened in the east. She got up then and made coffee, just for something to do, again being carefully quiet, so as not to wake Daina and Will.

It wasn't as if she thought that they'd want to come along. Will had made it clear in Parker that waterskiing was not his thing. Nadine's reason for not wanting to wake them, on the outside chance that they *would* want to come along, was that Nadine didn't want Daina to see her around Ian. As far as Nadine knew, Daina didn't even know that the twins had a cousin. Nadine had never even mentioned him to her best friend.

Nadine was sure that if Daina watched her interact with Ian, she would *know*. She would know that Nadine was through with Rob, she would know that she was just keeping him around until she could seduce his cousin. Nadine wasn't worried that Daina would see her as a bad person for stringing Rob along because of this ulterior motive; Daina wouldn't judge her in any way. The twins were not permanent to either of them.

But Nadine was concerned that Daina would laugh at her for expending all this energy in the pursuit of some guy. They were interchangeable; why waste time scheming to get a particular one?

At last Rob woke up, took a shower, got dressed. He and the hands on the clock moved so slowly that Nadine wanted to scream. She calmed herself by thinking about Ian's deep voice, the poetic way he spoke. She was up and awake, out of bed now; her thoughts were no longer about his body and how much she wanted to touch him. *If wishes were horses, then beggars would ride,* she thought. The time wouldn't pass any quicker for her wishing it to. She just had to be patient.

THIRTY

Rob parked, and they walked down to the end of the public launch on Lake Elsinore. It was deserted at this time of the morning, although there were a few boats on the lake already. Rob waved his arms, then cocked his hand to his ear theatrically. After a moment, she heard a low rumbling and saw a dark wooden boat approaching.

Ian put the boat in neutral and slid up beside the dock without tying up. Nadine and Rob boarded quickly, and Rob pushed off. Ian engaged the motor again, turned the craft sharply, and roared back off toward the center of the lake, causing the shallow shoreside water to slosh and splash against the dock.

"Too much wake," Rob commented over the burble of the motor.

"Fuck 'em," Ian said with a grin. "There's nobody launching right now." Rob just shook his head.

Nadine's mind was a riot of emotions. She was breathlessly, speechlessly thrilled to see Ian again. She was glad for the moment that conversation was unlikely, because she didn't know what she would say to him. She was astonished by Ian's polished wooden craft; it was the most beautiful boat she'd ever seen.

These good feelings warred gamely to combat an almost hysterical feeling of crushing disappointment. Beside Ian in his beautiful boat sat a beautiful woman. She was wearing large sunglasses and a kerchief around her dark-red hair. She didn't smile. But even with a neutral expression and her face obscured by these accoutrements, still Nadine could tell she was beautiful.

Once out in the middle of the lake, Ian killed the engine and turned to greet them. The girl continued to look straight ahead, until Rob made introductions. "Marta, this is Nadine." At the sound of her name, the beautiful girl looked over her shoulder and smiled faintly. "Nadine, this is Ian's girlfriend, Marta."

Ian's. Girlfriend. Marta.

The beautiful woman spoke. She had a musical, little girl's voice. "So nice to meet you, Nadine. You'll pardon me if I don't shake hands." She held them up: her thumbs and fingers peeked out from casts that went to the middle of her forearms.

Ian's. Girlfriend. Marta.

Where had Nadine heard that name before? She concentrated for a second, trying to remember. At last, it came back to her: the conversation she had overheard in Parker. What had Rob said?

Nadine remembered only Ian's mellifluous voice, his quotation from *The Rime of the Ancient Mariner.*

Nadine realized it was her turn to speak. "Nice to meet you, too." She nodded at Marta's casts. "I'm so sorry. Does it hurt terribly?"

"Only if I forget to take my pills." Marta reached gingerly into her bag on the floor of the boat, and came back with a prescription bottle. She shook it weakly and then handed it to Ian.

He frowned. "You just took one –"

"It's been long enough."

Nadine watched Ian and Rob exchange a glance; Rob rolled his eyes. Nadine again tried to remember what Rob had said in Parker – she knew that she'd heard this girl's name come out of his mouth when he was talking to Ian; before she'd even *seen* Ian. What had he said?

As Ian took a pill out of the bottle and handed in to his girlfriend, the conversation came back to Nadine.

"And how are things with you and Marta?"

"Like one, that on a lonesome road, doth walk in fear and dread, and having once turned round walks on, and turns no more his head; because he knows a frightful fiend doth close behind him tread."

Nadine blinked in astonishment. Ian had said that unkind thing about this beautiful woman. She also remembered how she had last seen Ian, smiling at two other girls as he prepared to take them for a boat ride. He hadn't been too concerned about his *girlfriend* then . . .

Marta had a bottle of Coke on the floor beside her bag, and she took a swig to wash down the pill. "All better. Now, Nadine. Tell me about you."

Nadine wanted to hate her; she wanted to hate her more than anyone in the world. She wanted to throw a curse upon her that would erase her beauty, her lyrical voice. It would be a simple enough spell. But Nadine discovered to her dismay that she couldn't hate Marta, couldn't curse her: she was so pleasant, so friendly, so pretty. And Ian had referred to her as a *fearsome fiend*, had made time with one, perhaps even two girls, just last weekend. Maybe things weren't so good between them . . . Nadine dared to hope.

"You girls talk. I'm gonna ski." Ian stood up and dove over the side. Rob arose to give him his skis and feed him the tow line.

"This is the most beautiful boat I've ever seen," Nadine commented to Marta, mostly just for something to say. "Ian must be –"

"Thank you," Marta replied. "My dad has two of them. He keeps the other one at Tahoe."

That's right! Nadine thought. She heard Rob's words in her head again. "Does her daddy's fine boat still run?"

"Like an Elgin watch," Ian had replied.

This wasn't Ian's boat at all! It was hers! No wonder she was his girlfriend!

Rob plopped behind the steering wheel and fired the exquisite wooden boat to life. He looked over his shoulder and when Ian gave him the signal he quickly throttled forward.

Nadine was by no means a watercraft aficionado. She'd never even been on a boat before the previous weekend, but the difference between this sleek, lovely, *enclosed* thing, with its inlaid wooden stripes, its green leather bench seats, its hidden engine – and Rob and Will's open fiberglass ski boat, with its cheap-looking vinyl seats and its rattling, screaming outboard . . . There was simply no comparison.

Nadine looked at Ian; waved. He grinned, waved back. *This is what he does,* Nadine thought. *And with a boat like this . . . I bet Sissy would be his girlfriend, too, if she had a boat like this.*

Nadine glanced at Marta again. She was looking over her shoulder, watching Ian ski. But after a moment, she lost interest. She turned and looked ahead. Nadine was amazed. Could it be that Marta was *bored with Ian?*

Nadine glanced back at him again. She wouldn't ever be bored with him; he was too clever, too poetic. She knew what it was that Marta and Sissy and those other girls saw in him, what they wanted from him. Ian was so strong, so utterly masculine; just looking at him made a girl want to throw herself at him, if only for the night. When darkness reigned, Nadine thought about it, too, over and over and over again.

But Nadine wanted him for more than just one night; she wanted him for more than just what she imagined he could do in the dark. She wanted to listen to him talk, to converse with him until they were both old and gray, until he didn't look like a million bucks, tax-free, anymore. She wanted to be beside him when the day came that he could no longer waterski.

Nadine didn't care about his looks – he was her soulmate. She didn't care about Sissy, wasn't jealous of the beautiful girl sitting in front of her. They were only temporary. Ian would be hers soon enough, before the year was out. The cards never lied. She was patient. It was only a matter of time.

THIRTY-ONE

For the next two Saturdays, Rob and Nadine went waterskiing with Ian and Marta on Lake Elsinore. More precisely, Rob and Ian skied. Marta could not, because of her broken wrists, and since neither Rob nor Ian had again asked Nadine if she wanted to learn how to ski, she hadn't brought it up herself. She was more than happy just being around Ian: watching him, listening to him, talking to him. Learning to ski was unnecessary.

When the sun set, each week Nadine and Rob had dinner with Ian and Marta at the tiny vacation house that Marta's family kept in the City of Lake Elsinore. They talked and laughed, just two happy college couples. But Nadine noticed that Ian spent an inordinate amount of time in the garage with Rob, before as well as after dinner, looking at the immaculate engine of the wooden boat, or just standing around talking. It seemed as if Ian tried to spend as little time with his *girlfriend* as possible.

This left Marta and Nadine alone for long stretches. Nadine longed to coax Marta into a little girl talk: what was Ian like, what did he do, what did he say? Was he romantic? Was he tender, or was he brutal?

But Nadine dared not ask. Ian was attractive: Marta might become suspicious of such intimate questions. She didn't know Marta very well, and these kinds of curiosities about each other's men were something that only close girlfriends would dare to ask each other. Daina had heard all about Rob, and Nadine had heard all about Will. They had compared notes, coming to the conclusion that, for twins, their techniques were surprisingly dissimilar. They had shared a good giggle about that.

But Marta was not her lifelong friend as Daina was, so Nadine kept a rein on her inquisitiveness. She was convinced that she would be finding out everything she wanted to know about Marta's boyfriend soon enough, anyway.

When she wasn't watching Ian by himself, Nadine watched him interact with Marta. There was some physical contact between them – he would touch her shoulder, or her back, or her knee; they exchanged perfunctory kisses. But there seemed to be no tenderness, and certainly no passion, and they sometimes snapped at each other like an old married couple. It was obvious to Nadine that Ian didn't love Marta; at times, it seemed like he didn't even *like her* very much.

Marta seemed to be fond of him – she would also sometimes touch him on the shoulder, or affectionately brush his hair out of his eyes with the fingers of her casted up hand. But if he didn't smile at her or respond the way she expected to these tenders, Marta would become immediately, visibly angry with him.

Yep, Nadine thought gleefully, *there are some definite cracks in this relationship.*

Nadine wondered what the final straw would be. She knew it was coming: the cards never lied. She knew that she and Daina would be free of Rob and Will by Hallowe'en. She wondered if the cause of it would be her revelation of her love to Ian, and his acceptance of it, or if her opportunity to proclaim her love would only come after his union with Marta had dissolved on its own. It didn't really matter what the catalyst turned out to be. *The readiness is all,* Nadine thought. She was certainly ready; she was only waiting for the correct moment to present itself.

THIRTY-TWO

On the evening of Friday, the 27th of June, 1969, Rob came down with a tummy ache, not long after he and Nadine had eaten dinner at their favorite hole-in-the-wall seafood place. As the night wore on, it became clear to Nadine that he was going to be in no shape to go skiing in the morning. He was going to be in no shape to do anything much more than gulp Pepto-Bismol and be miserable.

Nadine felt sorry for him, truly she did, but she couldn't miss seeing Ian. That she just couldn't do. She only got to see him once a week as it was, and never alone, never how she wanted to see him. She lived for it, meager and unfulfilling as it was, and she wasn't going to miss it just because Rob had indigestion.

So at ten o'clock on Friday night, Nadine insisted that Rob get in the car so she could drive him home – his father was a doctor, wasn't he? What if there was something more seriously wrong with him that just simple upset stomach? What if he was having an appendicitis or something? She wanted Rob's dad to have a look at him, just to be safe. Rob went along meekly; he wasn't in the mood for company, anyway. Nadine dropped him at the door to the guesthouse, kissed him on the cheek, and told him to call her just as soon as he was feeling better.

She arrived at Marta's house the next morning at six am sharp, and parked her car on the street. No more waiting around for Rob to get his ass in gear, so that they would have to meet his cousin at the launch. Nadine circumvented all that by leaving early and going directly to the house instead of the lake.

Nadine knocked on the door. A stranger opened it; he was a little bit older than Nadine, and had dark-red hair and surly brown eyes. He looked at her suspiciously for a moment, and when she just stared back at him in surprise, he growled, "Yes? Can I help you?"

Nadine found her voice. "Is Ian . . . Is Marta here?"

The redhead looked at her neutrally for another second, and Nadine thought that she must have come to the wrong house. Finally he opened the door the rest of the way and said, "Come on in. Ian and Marta are in the shower. He's gotta help her, 'cause of her wrists."

He leered at Nadine, letting her know that whatever Ian and Marta were doing in the shower, he didn't believe it had anything to do with bathing. Nadine blushed, because she immediately thought of what she'd like to be doing with Ian in the shower. She didn't begrudge Marta her time with him, because she knew that her own time was coming, and that it would last forever.

The guy that had opened the door caught her blush and leered further; Nadine looked down at the floor to avoid his eyes. "Hi," he said, and stuck his hand out. "I'm Sid. Marta's brother."

Nadine looked up at him again. Now she could see the family resemblance: he had the same auburn hair, the same brown eyes, the same large mouth as his sister. But they combined to make her beautiful. Sid just looked like a lout to Nadine. Maybe it was the leer.

"And you are?" Sid said.

"I'm sorry, where have my manners gone?" Nadine said. *Away from this guy,* she thought as she introduced herself.

Sid politely shook her hand and said it was nice to meet her. His smirking expression now changed to one of courteous interest. "Are you going out on the boat with us today?"

Nadine nodded. She was about to open her mouth and make small talk, ask brother Sid if he waterskied – it seemed unlikely, as he had said *Are you going out on the boat with us today?* instead of *Are you going skiing with us today?* Then Ian stepped into the living room, draped from the waist to just below the knees in a light blue towel.

He blinked at her in surprise and ducked quickly back out of the room. "Hell, Nadine! What are you doing here?" He stuck his head out of the door and said angrily, "Why didn't you tell me someone was here, Sid?"

Sid shrugged. "Sorry, man."

Nadine found Ian's modesty adorable. When he emerged a moment later in his swim trunks, he was technically wearing less than when he'd come out in the towel. She could see his knees now, and his strong thighs . . .

Nadine looked up from considering Ian's thighs and met his eyes. He still looked mortified that she'd caught him in a state of undress, even if he was more covered then than he was now. It was just the idea of it, that his cousin's girlfriend had seen him in nothing but a towel, a towel that might've just fallen off at any moment . . .

Nadine couldn't suppress a smile at that idea, and Ian repeated, "What are you doing here?"

"Rob's sick."

"I know Rob's sick. He called me last night. I didn't expect . . ." Ian smiled at her then, and Nadine's heart melted. "I'm sorry. I'm just surprised to see you. But I'm glad you're here. Have you met Sid?"

Nadine nodded. Ian was uncomfortable; he apparently didn't like to be seen in this scene of domestic bliss. This impression was underlined when Marta, wearing a robe, came up behind him and put her arms around his waist. She squeezed him tightly, possessively, *languidly* across the belly with her casted-up wrists.

"We've got company," he said tersely.

Marta looked around him in surprise. "Oh, hi, Nadine!" she said in her open, friendly manner. She didn't release Ian and now he took her hands from around his waist in irritation, and stepped out of her embrace. "What the hell's wrong with you?" she asked in annoyance.

Ian ignored her. "Come on, Sid. Let's get this show on the road." Ignoring Nadine also, Ian went out the back door. Sid followed.

"Rob's sick," Nadine said to Marta. As usual, she said it just for something to say. Marta's relationship with Ian was definitely showing some strain, and standing there in stunned silence would only play this up.

"I heard," Marta replied. "That's why Sid's here. Can't miss skiing." She sounded more annoyed than bitter, but Nadine thought that bitterness might be waiting right there in the wings. Then Marta smiled. "I'm so glad you could come, though. At least I'll have someone to talk to, so the day won't be a total waste!"

THIRTY-THREE

Sid and Ian put the *Ooh-La-La* in the water, then Ian went to park the truck. Marta sat in her usual place in the front. She wouldn't move from there all day, Nadine knew. She had her bag and her pills and her Coke. It was all she needed.

Ian hopped in the boat and Sid took them out. Nadine was delighted to have him sit next to her on the back bench seat. She watched the annoyance fall away from his features as he put on his vest – he was going to ski, and Marta and their troubles were the farthest thing from his mind then.

Sid killed the motor in the middle of the deserted lake and Ian dove overboard. Sid looked at Nadine expectantly: his sister was crippled, and he was only along for the ride. It was going to be up to Nadine to hand out the tow line and send Ian his skis. That was fine with Nadine; it was an honor, in fact.

Ian had only been skiing for about twenty minutes when Marta began to search frantically in her bag. Sid looked over at her curiously, and she just shook her head. Then she looked behind her and made a throat-cutting gesture at Ian. He shook his head; Marta made the throat-cutting gesture again. Again, Ian shook his head. Marta shouted for Sid to kill the boat.

"I can't just kill it," he said matter-of-factly. "We'll swamp. You know that."

"I don't care!" she shouted. "Ian has to get in the boat. I have to go back to the house."

Sid shrugged and throttled slowly back; Ian lost momentum and sunk into the water. Sid killed the engine.

"Bring the line in, will you, Nadine?" Marta wasn't looking at her, but out at her boyfriend. Ian was staring back, confused and pissed off, and she shouted at him, "We have to go back to the house!"

"Why?" he shouted back.

Marta tossed the rope ladder over the side. "Get back in the boat, Ian!"

Ian swam over to the boat. As he handed his skis up to Nadine, she could see that he was livid. He climbed back in the boat and glared at Marta. "What's going on?"

"We have to go back to the house."

"We just got here!"

"I can't find my pills. I must've left them at home."

"Oh, for Christ's sake, Marta! You just took one!"

"My wrists hurt!" Marta wailed.

"They're almost healed!"

"I don't care," she said, a tinge of hysteria in her voice. "I need a pill. Take us back, Sid."

Sid looked at Ian, waiting for him to sit down. He did so with an angry sigh, and Sid took them back to the launch.

Ian held the boat off of the dock until Marta climbed out. When he jumped out, she was already on her way up to the truck.

"Should I tie up and wait?" Sid asked.

A family with an ugly, faded red fiberglass boat had arrived, and were backing it toward the launch. The father stopped and looked questioningly behind him at Sid.

"This guy wants to put in," Ian said. "Why don't you just take a couple spins around the lake? We should be back in twenty minutes. A half hour, tops."

Nadine thought she saw that leer flare in Sid's eyes for a split second. "You're the boss." Ian frowned at that, and Sid looked at his watch. "We'll come back for you in a half hour." Ian nodded absently; he didn't even look at them again. He sighed and walked up the dock toward the parking lot. Nadine heard Marta lay on the horn in Ian's truck.

Sid grinned at Nadine and backed the boat out. He brought it about and opened the throttle, but she barely had time to enjoy the smooth, fast ride of the marvelous, powerful wooden boat before Sid slowed it down again, then abruptly killed the burbling engine. The stern rose and pushed them forward as the wake caught up with them. After that, the lake was like glass. It was early, it was a little overcast, and there was not another boat in sight.

"I don't know how to ski, Sid," Nadine told him.

"I don't wanna ski," he said with a little chuckle. "Why don't you come over here and sit on my lap, so I can get to know you a little better?" Sid slid away from the steering wheel and closer to Nadine, until she was almost pinned against the side of the boat. He put his arm around her shoulders and attempted to tug her toward him. "How 'bout a little kiss?"

"I'm very flattered, Sid." What she was, actually, was more than a little outraged. *Who the hell does he think he is?* Nadine put both hands on his chest and tried to gently push him away. But he still had his arm around her and didn't budge. "But I don't think my boyfriend would appreciate this very much."

"Who's your boyfriend?" Sid glanced over his shoulder, toward shore. "You and Ian got a little something going on the side? Don't worry, I won't tell him. Or Marta." He tried to pull her closer to him again, leaned in and attempted to kiss her on the cheek.

"Not Ian," she said and pushed against his chest again. Nadine realized that she wasn't very good at fighting men off, because she had always been careful in the past to never get herself into a situation like this. Nadine was not a tease; if she allowed a man to be alone with her, it was because she liked him and wasn't going to tell him no if he asked. If there was ever any doubt, she made sure they had chaperones. For Sid, she would've preferred perhaps a stadium full of people.

"Ian's cousin's my boyfriend. Rob Wilde."

"Oh. I know Rob." Sid stopped trying to pull her toward him, but didn't immediately take his arm from around her shoulders. He eyed her suspiciously. "Why isn't he here?"

"He's sick. He's got food poisoning."

Still Sid studied her. "I just thought, when you said *your boyfriend* . . . Ian's a hound from way back, and the way you look at him . . . Marta surely doesn't look at him like that anymore."

"What?" Nadine was confident that she didn't *look at Ian.* She took great pains to hide her feelings, but here was this oaf saying that he could tell, that he could see through her painstakingly constructed façade of indifference. "I'm sure I have no idea what you're talking about."

"It doesn't matter, either way." Sid continued to stare at her hungrily for another moment, and Nadine experienced a moment of stark fear. They were alone, in the middle of the deserted lake. If Sid decided to force himself on her, no one could hear her scream. It wasn't like she could jump overboard and just swim away.

He continued to stare at her, until finally, she spoke up. "Since you're friends with Rob, I won't tell him that you . . . I won't tell him about this, Sid. No need to stir up any upset like that. I won't tell anyone. Like I say, I'm flattered. But you need to take me back now."

Sid narrowed his eyes for a split second; again Nadine was afraid. Then he shrugged. He took his arm from around her shoulders and slid back across the seat. Without another word, he fired up the boat and took them back to shore.

Nadine was surprised to see that Ian had the trailer in the water. Sid idled the boat slowly onto it without comment. Ian winched it up securely, then got back in the truck and pulled it out of the water. Sid jumped over the side onto the concrete of the ramp. As if Nadine had ceased to exist, he didn't offer to help her out of the boat, but just walked around the front of the truck and got into the passenger side.

I'm dead to him now, Nadine thought with a little grin. *Thank Christ.*

"What the hell, Sid?" she heard Ian say. He got out of the truck and slammed the door, his face clouded with anger and annoyance. He picked Nadine up over the side of the boat, and she reveled in the feel of his hands on her hips. She wanted to wrap her arms around his neck and squeeze him to her as he set her down . . . But there was no time to think about all that. Ian was pissed.

Nadine waited patiently for an explanation.

"No more skiing today." He put his hand on the polished bow of the boat for a moment, almost like a caress. Then he sighed. "Marta can't find her pills. She's hysterical. I was hoping that maybe you could talk to her . . . Maybe calm her down."

"Me? I don't really even know her, Ian."

He sighed again. "Well, she won't listen to me. I told her, they've gotta be there somewhere. She just had them. I told her to just retrace her steps . . . But she's just sitting there crying."

Ian indicated for Nadine to slide into the truck, and he got in beside her. She was glad to be sitting next to him, instead of pinned between Sid and the door. They drove the short distance to the house in a rather grim silence. Ian let them out of the truck and then proceeded to back the boat into the garage; it was obvious that he was in no hurry to check up on his girlfriend.

Today's skiing had been truncated, and Ian was anxious to unhook his truck from the *Ooh-La-La,* the better to make a quick escape if necessary. Ian was only with Marta because he coveted her daddy's expensive wooden boat – beyond that, she was just annoying to him. All of this was suddenly so evident to Nadine that it was just downright embarrassing.

She almost felt sorry for Marta, but only almost. Nadine didn't think that Marta was in love with Ian any more than Ian was in love with her. Ian liked to ski and Marta had access to a fantastic boat. Ian had a fantastic body, and Marta no doubt liked to . . .

Nadine grinned to herself. No wonder he seemed so disconcerted this morning. He had been caught. It was different when they were all having dinner together, as friends, as equals. But from the precious scene of the embarrassed water-skier wrapped only in a towel and the sorority girl with her arms laced tightly around his belly, it was clear, beyond a shadow of a doubt, that Ian Wilde had whored himself out to a rich girl with a nice boat, and he was horrified that Nadine could see it for exactly what it was. Apparently it wasn't as cushy a gig as it would at first appear to be.

Nadine and Sid went into the house. Marta was no longer hysterical, but it was obvious that she had been: dried mascara traced down her cheeks in two black lines, making her look like a harlequin. Sid asked if she'd found her pills; Marta shook her head.

Sid echoed Ian. "They've gotta be here somewhere, Mart. You had them before we left."

"I've looked everywhere." Her voice trembled. "The one I took this morning has already worn off. It hurts, Sid. What am I going to do?"

Sid shrugged. Nadine didn't sense a whole lot of sympathy for his sister coming off of Sid. *He's kind of an all-around ass,* she marveled.

Ian came in as another black tear ran down Marta's cheek. He rolled his eyes in irritation. "You're supposed to get the casts off in what, ten days? It shouldn't hurt that much anymore. I think it's all in your head."

Marta glared at his insensitivity, then narrowed her eyes in concentration; to Nadine, she looked just like her brother for a moment. Of all the syllables in the English language, Nadine never could've predicted the next one out of her mouth. She said, "Will," and brightened a little bit. "He's a med student. His dad's a doctor. He might be able to get me something for the pain."

Again Ian rolled his eyes. "For Christ's sake, Marta," he said wearily. "You sound like some kind of hophead."

"You don't understand, Ian. You're not in pain. Both of your wrists aren't broken. If they were, then you wouldn't be able to ski, would you? Then your whole life would be over, wouldn't it?" She glared at him again, then softened, wheedling in her little girl's voice, "Will you call your cousin for me?"

Ian was exasperated. "My cousin and I aren't exactly the best of friends, Marta. No one knows that better than you." Sid grinned, and Nadine wondered what the undercurrent there was. "We don't hang out together too much. I don't have his number."

Marta turned away from Ian in disgust and said to Nadine, "Could you call Rob and see if he can get in touch with Will for me?"

Nadine didn't have to call Rob: Will was probably still at her house with Daina. She didn't feel like explaining all of this, however, so she just nodded.

"Thanks so much," Marta said and tried a smile. It was weak. "I really appreciate it. There's a phone in the kitchen."

Daina answered on the second ring. Nadine said, "I know this is gonna sound strange . . ."

Daina chuckled. "Go on."

A wellspring of love bubbled up in Nadine for her friend. They had always been like sisters; Nadine had never been close with other girls, because Daina had been all she'd needed. Nadine reconsidered then: maybe she *would* reveal her interest in their boyfriends' cousin to Daina. Maybe she would confess her love for Ian, admit that she wasn't really as cavalier as she had once been about the opposite sex. Surely, they had all been interchangeable before, just warm bodies. But not anymore.

Nadine would good-naturedly submit to her friend's laughter, but then she would explain. She would preach; she would *testify*. The cards didn't lie. The adorable, squinty-eyed water-skier with the space between his front teeth, with the cleft in his chin, with the sexy, muscled body – he was her soulmate. She would go on to tell Daina how none of these physical things about Ian – the things that appealed so thoroughly to other girls – mattered to her. She wouldn't mention her feverish fantasies. She loved Ian for his words, his wit; she wanted to listen to him talk for the rest of her life. *Old age, that ill layer up of beauty,* would not dim Nadine's love.

"I know he's cute," Nadine would tell her best friend, "and I know all the girls want him. But all that's *just in moment's sunlight, fading in the grass. If you hear the song I sing, you will understand, Daina. Ian Wilde is my other half.*"

And maybe if Nadine was solemn enough, and earnest enough, Daina *would* understand. Daina had always been laissez-faire about men: she never sought them out, always allowing them to come to her. Nadine had never understood – she'd say, "Don't you believe that there's someone for everyone?"

Daina would nod in her aunts' direction. "So I've been told."

"Well, if you believe it, why aren't you out looking for him, then?"

"Here's what I believe, Nadine." And Daina's grin would fade. "I believe that my one true love, whoever he is, wherever he is, whenever it will happen – he'll find me. So I'm not wasting my time looking for him."

That's all well and good for her, Nadine thought, *and I hope it doesn't take a lifetime for him to find her. But the next stage of my life is set to begin. I've found my partner. And maybe I'll tell her about him when I get home today, and endure her laughter – because it won't take long for her to see I'm right. Once Ian and I start our life together, it's going to be glorious . . .*

But Nadine had to deal with this wounded-debutante fiasco at the moment. There'd be plenty of time, a lifetime, in fact, to regale Daina with Ian's wonderfulness. Right now she had to assist him in handling the situation in which he'd placed himself. All so he could use a nice boat.

"I'll let Will fill you in on the details, after I speak to him," Nadine said to Daina.

"You wanna talk to Will?" Daina was surprised. She didn't think that her friend had said two hundred words to Will in all the time they'd known each other. Will wasn't a big talker, and when he did speak, Daina found his thoughts to be as boring as watching the grass grow. Nadine thought so, too, and had never had much to say to him. The girls often giggled and made jokes about Will's dreariness. But Daina thought Will was a lot of fun, at least for the moment.

"Yes, if he's there."

Will's voice, equally surprised, said, "Hello?"

"Ian's girlfriend was wondering if you might be able to get her some painkillers. She's got two broken wrists, and –"

"Ian's girlfriend?" Pause. *"Marta?"*

Daina remembered hearing Rob say the unusual name when they were in Parker. It had been in connection with their cousin – yes, they'd said their cousin's name was Ian. This cousin had been out on the water teaching Nadine to ski, but he hadn't returned with her, so Daina hadn't met him. Nadine had come back to the house with some skinny girl, who'd just sat at the picnic table, scanning the river with Will's binoculars. Daina recalled some mention of *Daddy's boat,* and something about Ian's getting to Marta first. It was then that Will had made it clear that he thought of her as his girlfriend, already.

"Well . . . I've got Daina now," he'd said, and at the time, Daina had been in too much of a hurry to tell Nadine about that development to remember to ask about the cousin.

Will was saying irritably, "Just calm down, Marta, for Christ's sake! I'll take care of it. What did they give you?" He paused. "No, I don't know why – when do the casts come off?" Another pause. "It shouldn't still hurt. You didn't try to ski in the casts or anything, did you?" Now he grinned at Daina. There was a wail from the phone. "Okay, just calm down."

Will gestured for Daina to get him a pen and paper; he quickly scribbled down an address. *He's already got a doctor's terrible handwriting,* she observed.

"I'll be there as soon as I can." There was a burst of gratitude from the other end of the line. "You're welcome. See you soon."

Will hung up the phone and drummed his fingers on the receiver thoughtfully for a moment. Then he grinned at Daina and said, "My cousin's girlfriend thinks I'm Doctor Feelgood."

Daina's eyebrows went up. "Are you?"

"She's got two broken wrists, but the casts are supposed to come off soon. It can't possibly still hurt that much. She's been taking something for the pain – she couldn't tell me what it is, because she can't find the bottle. She's wigging out a little bit about that. I think it's all in her head. But I've got some stuff I can give her."

"So you *are* Dr. Feelgood."

"Not quite yet." Will winked. He paused again, thinking. Daina just had time to wonder what kind of a pill stash the medical-student son of a successful physician might possess, when he said, "If nothing else, I have some Valiums. That'll at least calm her down. I have to stop by my house first." It seemed to Daina that he hesitated just a microsecond before asking her, "Do you want to go with me? They're in Lake Elsinore."

Daina frowned. Lake Elsinore was quite a little drive away, and she would have to listen to Will talk all the way there, perhaps a description of setting wrist breaks, or perhaps a treatise on painkillers and Valium. Or perhaps he wouldn't talk at all. That was no way to spend a Saturday.

"I'll stay here." She squeezed his arm. "I don't want to horn in on your very first house call."

Daina thought that Will might try to talk her into it – it *was* a long drive, after all. Be he did not. "Okay. I'll be back as soon as I can."

They shared a hug and a kiss. Will was just pulling out of the driveway when it occurred to Daina to wonder what Nadine was doing in Lake Elsinore with Will's cousin and his girlfriend. She knew Rob was feeling under the weather; she had watched Nadine hustle him out of there the night before, and then she had been gone when she and Will got up this morning. Daina had assumed that her friend had gone to sit up with Rob, but apparently not.

Will had said something about waterskiing to the girl on the phone: *You didn't try to ski in the casts or anything did you?* Daina knew that Rob liked to ski, and perhaps that one lesson that his cousin had given to Nadine in Parker had hooked her, too.

Daina shrugged mentally. She would find out all the details soon enough.

THIRTY-FOUR

Ian absented himself from the house again: he fled to the garage, and took his time putting the cover on the *Ooh-La-La.* Nadine had longed to go with him, but that just wouldn't have looked right. Instead she sat beside Marta on the couch and tried to comfort her, reminding her that Will would be there soon with something for her pain. Sid sat on Nadine's other side, closer than she liked. They watched TV in silence, and Nadine thought that they would look like See-No-Evil, Speak-No-Evil, and Hear-No-Evil to Will, if he ever showed up to take Marta and her pain and her whining off of Nadine's hands.

When Will arrived, Ian walked out of the garage to meet him. He smiled and said, "Thanks for coming out to help her, Cuz."

"Why are you taking her out skiing with two broken wrists?" Will demanded angrily.

Ian raised his eyebrows at his cousin's tone. "She's a big girl. All she does is sit and ride anyway. She's never complained before."

Will stalked into the house without making a reply.

After a moment, Ian walked in behind him. *"If thou couldst, doctor, cast the water of my land, find her disease,"* he began, but then stopped.

They all glared at him for a moment, unamused. Ian decided that there were just too many people crowded into the tiny living room, none of whom seemed too happy with him: Sid, whom he could take or leave on the best of days; Marta, who was telling Will how Ian had *made* her take the boat out damn near every weekend since her accident; Dr. Kildare himself, whom – it was clear to Ian – had not yet gotten over losing Marta to the better man; and Rob's girlfriend, who just looked uncomfortable.

It was as if they believed that Marta's distress was his fault. They all seemed to have forgotten that she was a skier, too. Because they both liked to ski, Marta had switched horses in the middle of the stream last Memorial Day, so to speak. Ian hadn't found out that she was there as Will's guest until she told him that she didn't want to see Will in the morning, that they had to leave, like thieves in the middle of the night. Rob had confirmed it when Ian knocked on his door to tell him that he was about to disappear.

"Jesus Christ, Rob," Ian had whispered, "why didn't you tell me that she was Will's chick?"

Rob shrugged, whispered back, "I'm not my brother's keeper, Cuz. Him nor his women. Apparently she's not Will's chick, now is she? She's your chick now."

Now, looking at Marta, Ian thought, *It's not like we have one other thing in common besides skiing.* And nobody had twisted either of her damaged arms to *make* her go, not today or any of the other Saturdays since she'd tripped over her own clumsy feet and practically ruined the whole summer, for both of them.

Nadine noted that everyone was ignoring Ian. *"Throw physic to the dogs; I'll none of it,"* she said and smiled sympathetically at him.

He grinned at her and said to his casted-up girlfriend, "Well, you seem to be in capable hands. I'm going to run over to The Lookout and get something to eat. You want to go with me, Sid?" Sid shook his head and gestured at the TV. "Nadine?" Nadine was on her feet before she quite realized it. "You guys want us to pick something up for you?"

Sid shook his head again. Marta said she wasn't hungry. Will, examining Marta's casts, said he'd already eaten. *The hell with all of you then,* Ian thought, and without saying another word, he turned and left the house, with Nadine following.

The silence continued as Ian drove around the lake and up the long curvy hill that was the Ortega Highway, to The Lookout Roadhouse. It was his favorite place to dine in Lake Elsinore, a little honky-tonk with a huge parking lot and an unparalleled view. It was popular with tourists and locals alike. Ian wasn't a local, but the staff knew him by name, anyway, because he'd been skiing the lake almost every weekend since he was sixteen.

Ian and Nadine ordered burgers, then Ian called after the waitress and requested a beer, although it wasn't barely one o'clock in the afternoon.

They continued to sit in silence, even after the waitress brought Ian his beer. Distracted, bored, annoyed, he picked absently at the corner of the label on the bottle and gazed out at the spectacular view.

Nadine wanted to listen to him talk. Silent Ian was no fun at all. "How long have you been going with Marta?" she asked, trying to sound off-hand.

Ian sighed and put his head down on his arms on the table for a moment. "It seems like forever." Then he looked up at Nadine, a trifle embarrassed at his meanness. "It was a year Memorial Day."

But Nadine, feeling a little gleefully mean herself at any sign of discord in their relationship, said, "I get the impression that you don't love Marta *to the depth and breadth and height your soul can reach.*"

He smiled ruefully. "Not even *to the level of every day's most quiet need.*" The waitress brought their burgers. "It's funny you should mention Browning, though. When I first met Marta, she said that Rob had told her that I liked to ski, and I said just that: *To the depth and breadth and height my soul can reach.*" Ian smiled at her and Nadine thought she might stop breathing.

But it was only for a split-second. Despite what Sid thought he'd observed, Nadine was confident that Ian didn't know that she was in love with him, because she believed that she hid it expertly. Ian was cute, but it wasn't his looks that made her love him, so she had no problem pretending to be unimpressed with just the thing that impressed all the other girls. To Nadine, the way he looked wasn't the most impressive thing about him.

And except for the momentary shock of speechlessness that always came when she beheld him after not having seen him all week, Nadine had no trouble talking and joking with Ian, had no trouble kidding him a little bit. He was just a man after all, even if they were destined to be together; Nadine had never had the slightest trouble talking to men.

Now she said, "How charming you are, Ian! What girl doesn't dig a little love poetry?"

Ian shrugged, not self-conscious in the least. "It's a seminal piece, don't you think? Some of the most famous lines in the English language – some of the most beautiful. She sings of her one and only, her soulmate . . ."

When Ian said that word, the same one that the cards had foretold, Nadine's eyes brightened. "Do you believe we all have a soulmate, Ian?"

Now he looked at her awkwardly – maybe it wasn't appropriate to be discussing love poetry with his cousin's girlfriend. Nadine found his respect for her position endearing. But he didn't evade the question. "I'd like to think so, yes." He knew that it was what girls liked to hear. Why not say it to this one, too?

Nadine had never actually witnessed a Tarot lay's prediction as it came true – she had heard of endings and beginnings after the fact, of course, but not like this, in real time, as it was happening. So sure was Nadine that Ian would soon be hers, and forever, that she allowed herself a little smug cattiness, allowed herself to kid him again. "Is Marta your soulmate?"

She wanted Ian to gaze into her eyes then, and ask her if Rob was her soulmate, and when she said no, she wanted him to reach across the table and take her hand, and thus would their lives together begin. But that was a little over the top, even for Nadine's romantic imagination, so she wasn't disappointed when it didn't occur. Ian just guffawed in surprise and said, "Not hardly." That was validation enough for Nadine. The cards never lied.

She smiled at him, without a visible trace of the longing she actually felt. Just a friendly smile, the kind one would innocently give to one's boyfriend's cousin. "Recite it for me, Ian. I can never remember all the lines."

He looked surprised for a moment, but then said, "All right." It wasn't like Nadine was Sissy, or some other girl he didn't want at the moment, that was trying to pick him up in a bar. This was Rob's girlfriend, and she appreciated Browning. It would be all right to speak the sonnet to her; they were friends. She wouldn't construe it to mean that he was making a pass at her.

Nadine had to use all her willpower not to close her eyes in pleasure as Ian's deep, dark voice said the famous words.

"How do I love thee? Let me count the ways.
. . . I love thee with the breath,
Smiles, tears, of all my life; and, if God choose,
I shall but love thee better after death."

"That was great," Nadine told him softly, and then picked up her burger. She was in complete control, secure in the knowledge that Ian would be hers. *Maybe not today. Maybe not tomorrow, but soon and for the rest of my life.*

THIRTY-FIVE

The 4th of July weekend began for Rob Wilde at sundown on Thursday, the third. He packed up his enthusiastic girlfriend and jumped into the big, heavy Caddy. His boat was already at their place in Parker. All he had to do was get there.

The pressures of school had stolen a little bit of Rob's love of waterskiing the past semester. Like he had told Ian, he had to study; he couldn't be spending every single weekend at the lake with his cousin. He'd told Ian that there was more to life than just skiing. There were girls.

But now his passion had returned and was once again almost equal to his cousin's. Sure, there were girls. But when the one you picked like to ride in an open boat – why not ski? She had no desire to ski herself, which made it even better – not only did Rob not have to waste time teaching her, he didn't have to waste time dragging her after she learned. But she sure did like boating. They'd been on the water every Saturday with Ian and Marta since their initial weekend together in Parker; she'd even gone to Elsinore once without him. She was thrilled to go back to the river for the 4th of July.

Rob congratulated himself on his choice of girlfriends. He couldn't say he was in love with Nadine – Rob wasn't sure that he'd ever been in love – but just like Ian and Marta, they did have this one thing in common. And just like Ian and Marta, they had that other thing, too. Rob grinned to himself.

They didn't talk about big plans for the future; they didn't talk much at all, really. But Nadine never turned him down if he reached for her, even if she did keep her eyes tightly closed the whole time. And she liked to ride in the boat while he skied. Just like his cousin had said, "Ski during the day, girls at night." It had been a great summer, so far.

Rob heard Cousin Ian's truck in the driveway bright and early on Friday morning, and he and Nadine walked outside to meet him. Rob was surprised to see *One Wilde Ride* behind Ian's truck.

"Where's the Chris?" he said by way of greeting.

"Marta doesn't get her casts off 'til next week, so she stayed at home. My boat was out of the shop, so here I am." Ian grinned. "You should be thanking me. I could've just shown up and commandeered your boat, like the last time we were here. Now, we don't even have to worry about inconveniencing your brother. He can use your boat to cruise, and we can use my boat to ski."

"We can switch off. Will's not here."

"Really?" Ian said in amazement. "The Wilde twins, separated on the 4th of July? That's gotta be a first. What's he doing?"

Rob shrugged. "He didn't say. He didn't say anything at all until we were getting ready to go, then he just told me he was staying home. Said he had other fish to fry this weekend."

Nadine had also been surprised; she thought that the holiday weekend at the river was a foregone conclusion for the twins: Rob had told her that it was something they did every year. She figured that as soon as they had loaded up the Caddy, they were going back to her house to pick up Daina. She went into the guesthouse and called her friend. "I didn't know you and Will weren't going to the river with us."

"I didn't know we were," Daina replied. "He didn't say anything about it to me one way or another. You know he doesn't talk a lot."

"Or he talks too much," Nadine said. Daina chuckled. "Do you want to go anyway? With Rob and me?"

Nadine could hear the smile in her friend's voice. "I'm not the boater that you've turned out to be, 'Deen. You guys have fun."

In the driveway of his cousin's pad in Parker, Ian said, "The less Will, the more skiing." He smiled at Rob's girlfriend; as always, her heart skipped. "Are you ready for *One Wilde Ride*, Nadine?" He indicated the covered craft behind his truck.

She nodded, because it always took a moment to recover her voice when she first saw him. *The readiness is all,* she thought again.

Ian grinned at Rob. "What are we waiting for then?"

Rob grinned back. "Not a goddamned thing."

Ian hopped into the truck and took the boat down to the dock to put it in the water. Rob and Nadine paused in the house for a moment, to pick up sunglasses and Coppertone. By the time they walked outside, Ian already had the boat launched and the truck stowed.

Rob helped Nadine into the little boat, then paused on the dock to listen to the Raysoncraft's Evinrude outboard. It was a lot louder than the Mercury on his boat. Ian gave it a little rev for his cousin's benefit and shouted, *"Hark, how our steeds for present service neigh!* For Christ's sake, get in the boat, Rob! Before Sissy shows up!"

Rob grinned at that thought. He untied the bow line and boarded. He shouted at his cousin. "You're right. She would've been here before ya know it. Sometimes I think she can smell you!"

And so the first day's skiing commenced.

THIRTY-SIX

The house was dark and deserted when they came back, just after sunset. There was no party, because Will wasn't there to invite people. Rob was back in his groove: all he wanted to do was ski. They sat on the patio, called for a pizza, cracked a couple of beers, watched the fireworks. That was enough of a party for them.

Will said, "I'm sorry there's no honeys here for ya, Cuz. I could call Sissy –"

Ian rolled his eyes. "Since I've reached adulthood, I've found it prudent to forgo high school honeys. Especially Sissy." He sipped his beer. "All I want to do is ski this weekend, and we've got crew enough for that." Ian winked at Nadine. "Besides, the last girl I met here has proved to be more trouble than she's worth." Ian grinned. "The burnt child fears the fire."

Rob was confused. "Hell, Cuz I don't even remember the last girl you met here. I'm surprised that you do." Then realization hit him. "Oh. You mean Marta." Ian nodded. "Everything's not *Ooh-La-La* in Chris-Craft paradise?"

"There are more things in heaven and earth than are dreamt of in that *philosophy.* Even with one hundred and thirty direct-driven horses."

"You pays your money and you takes your chances, Cuz."

Ian looked out at the dark water for a moment. "Yep," he finally said. "That Chris is fine. No arguing with that. It's got everything. But you know the one thing that it has, in abundance, that I don't miss at all on mine?"

"The bitching?" Rob said.

Ian grinned. "I was actually thinking of the whining, but that's another thing. My boat is smaller, but it is absolutely bitch and whine-free."

Rob and Ian clinked beer bottles. Nadine smiled to herself in the darkness. *It won't be long now,* she thought hopefully.

THIRTY-SEVEN

When they went to leave the dock on Saturday morning, Ian's boat wouldn't start. The battery was turning over, but the motor just wouldn't catch.

"No gas, no spark, no start," Rob said. "You got spark. Check the fuel line."

Ian unlatched the ponderous gray and white cover from the outboard and set it on the dock. There was no room for it in the boat. "Fuel line looks good," he said. He fiddled around for another moment, then said, "Shit."

"What?" Rob asked.

"Float bowl's cracked. Look." He pointed to a tiny, clear, delicate-looking piece of glass, smaller than a shot glass, attached by a metal keeper to the side of the motor. It was indeed cracked.

"We split, we split! Farewell, my wife and children!" Rob grinned ruefully. "Shit."

Nadine wondered how such a little thing could have any effect whatsoever on floating – they were floating fine. They just weren't *starting.*

THIRTY-EIGHT

Ian was appalled and more than a little pissed off that a) there was only one boat shop open in Parker on the 4th of July weekend, and b) that one shop didn't carry something so vital as a float bowl for the carburetor of a 1962, seventy-five horsepower, four-stroke Evinrude outboard. In desperation, Ian even called Sissy's dad at the ski shop, just to see if he might have some kind of townie inside track to where they might locate a replacement for this suddenly irreplaceable part. He did not.

"Let's just take my boat," Rob suggested as they drove back to the house.

Ian glanced at his cousin thoughtfully for a moment. They had left Nadine back at the house while they undertook this fruitless quest. Ian said, "How long are you are guys staying?"

"'Til Wednesday or so. Or maybe through next weekend. It depends on my mood. The other shops'll be open on Monday, Cuz. I'm sure somebody's got one."

"Maybe. Maybe not. This stupid town . . . The killing thing is, I've got an extra one. It's sitting in my tool box in the garage in Lake Elsinore."

"Let's just take my boat," Rob repeated.

But Ian hadn't dragged his Raysoncraft all the way to Parker to leave it on the trailer and use Rob's boat. *One Wilde Ride* had a race-boat hull; it was smaller and sleeker and faster than his cousin's big six-seater. He'd like to put a direct-drive in it someday, but even with a clunky outboard that featured a *glass* float bowl, Ian much preferred skiing behind it, instead of Rob's runabout.

"I'll tell ya what I'm gonna do, Cuz. I've been third-wheeling you guys all weekend. Time you had a little romantic evening all alone. *When Love speaks, the voice of all the gods makes heaven drowsy with the harmony.* I'm gonna drive back and get the part –"

"It's a four hour drive, Ian."

"That's what I'm saying – it'll give you guys a night alone. I'll drive back, catch a few hours' sleep maybe, then I'll see you in the morning."

"If that's what you want to do."

"I haven't had her out on the river in more than a year, Rob. Just these two days haven't been enough."

THIRTY-NINE

The sun was starting to set when Ian pulled up in front of Marta's vacation house in Lake Elsinore. The gate was closed, so he parked on the street. He was surprised to see her car in the driveway. What was she doing out here if they weren't going skiing? What was she doing out here all by herself?

Ian thought back over the year they'd been together – he couldn't quite bring himself to call it a relationship. That first month had been great: they skied, they screwed. They didn't do much else but that, but it was enough for the first month. Then she told him that she loved him and took off overseas for the rest of the summer, leaving him with Daddy's boat.

And for the rest of the summer, he'd used it to his heart's content, and almost forgot that Marta even existed. He was flattered that she thought she loved him, but just like Rob, Ian didn't know what love felt like. He was sure that what he and Marta shared wasn't it.

When Marta returned from her European holiday, Ian learned that there was to be a great deal more to the care and feeding of what she called love than just skiing and screwing. She expected him to entertain her. Ian was game at first; he read poetry to her, he took her to the theatre.

But these pursuits bored Marta. She was a sorority girl, and during the winter months, she dragged Ian to parties that he didn't want to attend, introduced him to people that he didn't want to meet. He didn't mind too much because there was that flawless Chris-Craft in Elsinore, just waiting for the weather to warm up again.

Ian overlooked a lot of annoying things about Marta because of that boat, like the frequent times when there was absolutely no pleasing her. At those times, the very fact that he was standing there breathing was just wrong. When Marta couldn't make up her mind what she wanted to do on a Saturday night, her inability to make a decision on how to amuse herself suddenly became Ian's fault. She'd find reasons to disagree with him, meaningless things. She'd sulk and pout.

Ian stayed with her, though, because there was that fine boat, and sometimes he felt a little twinge of guilt when the idea would cross his mind that maybe he was taking advantage of her. Marta lived on a palatial estate, larger even then his cousins', and she, too, had a little cozy bungalow out beyond the pool and tennis court, all to herself. Ian had spent most nights there for the past year. It was nice to get out from under his dad's nose – he was almost twenty-four years old and still lived at home – so any night away was a treat.

And of course there was the *Ooh-La-La.*

And there was the fact that he quit his job almost the moment Marta came back from Europe, at her insistence. Because he was in school, his dad gave him walking-around money, but if he wanted to put gas in the truck and the outboard – and those Maherajahs hadn't come cheap – Ian needed to augment his income. So he'd had a little bartending job at night. But Marta wanted him with her at night, and since she paid for the gas for the truck and for the *Ooh-La-La,* since she paid for dinner whenever they went to The Lookout, Ian quit. Anything Marta wanted, she paid for it.

But just about the time that Ian felt like he was taking advantage of her affections – because he knew he surely didn't love her – Marta would make it clear that she wasn't a victim of his charm, after all. She would mention the house or the boat to him, or point out who had just paid for dinner, and then she'd make some thoroughly blue remark about *trade,* and laugh heartily. Marta make it clear to Ian that *love* was not the basis of their relationship.

Ian didn't dwell on their situation if he could help it. It depressed him. Marta was moody, and if her mood had been mostly sarcastic and unpleasant since she'd broken her wrists and couldn't ski, he would just have to endure it. It wasn't like he was trapped with her – the minute something better came along, he'd be gone – that's what he told himself, anyway. But she was all right in the meantime. The whole deal wasn't untenable. It was just a little irritating. Maybe her mood had always been sarcastic and unpleasant, and he just hadn't noticed it before, because he was either dragging her behind the boat or she was dragging him, or they were dragging each other into bed.

Ian walked quietly past Marta's car to the garage and flipped on the lights. He checked his toolbox to make sure the float bowl was there – he would feel about stupid if he drove all the way back to Parker without looking first, only to discover that it wasn't where he thought he'd put it. But there it was. He picked up his toolbox, shut off the lights and left the garage.

Ian paused in front of the door to the house. His first inclination was to just jump back into the truck and head back to the desert. If he went in and talked to Marta, she might decide that she wanted to go back with him, and he discovered that he really, *sincerely,* didn't want her to go. He was having a good time with Rob and his chick – it was pleasant to not have worry about whether his own was having a good time or not. Marta coming back with him would put a wet blanket on all that.

There were no lights on in the house; maybe she was sleeping. She'd gotten her prescription refilled the past Monday, and the pills always made her sleepy. And bitchy.

Ian thought that he could just go, and she'd never even know that he'd been there. But then he recalled that her casts were coming off on Tuesday, so Marta wouldn't want to accompany him back to Parker. He was planning on staying there until Rob left on Wednesday, or maybe even until the following Monday. Marta had to stay in town to get her casts off. She wouldn't want to go back with him, so he decided that it would only be polite to stop in and say hi. Maybe he'd let her show him how much she'd missed him over the past two days. He set the toolbox on the front porch and opened the unlocked front door.

The living room was dim; there was not a single light on there or in the kitchen. The bedroom door was open, and a faint glow spilled out into the hall from the bedside lamp. Ian thought he would just peek in; if Marta was asleep, he wouldn't wake her – she could be a bear when she just woke up. If she was asleep, he'd just tiptoe back out of the house and drive back to the river.

But Marta wasn't asleep. She was kneeling on the bed with her naked back to him, the sheet gathered up around her hips, her casted-up arms raised above her head. For a moment, Ian thought she was practicing one of her yoga exercises; then he saw a man's foot poking out from under the sheet. Not only wasn't Marta asleep, she wasn't alone. And apparently she hadn't missed him at all.

Ian blinked in surprise. He discovered in a split-second that he wasn't jealous or angry. In a flash he realized that here was the out he'd been searching for, ever since Marta had broken her wrists and couldn't ski, ever since he had discovered what an utterly whiny bitch she really was. He found that he was amused, curious. She'd always gone out of her way to tell him what a whore he was, and how much she liked it – so whom had Marta chosen to do behind his back, while he was safely out of town?

Ian rapped sharply on the doorframe. "Sorry to interrupt, kids . . ." Marta glanced over her shoulder and her partner moved a little to his left and looked around her. "Ah, Cuz. I should've known."

Marta blinked in dumb shock, but Will grinned smugly. He wasn't ashamed or afraid. Marta had at last seen her mistake. The day after he had given her enough Valium to make her forget about what he was sure was a pain that existed only in her mind, she had called to thank him, and the conversation had devolved into how unhappy she was with Cousin Ian. Marta had cried piteously to Will, begging him to forgive her for being so cruel, for abandoning him, for behaving like a slut and taking off with his worthless cousin last year.

Will had been forgiving her all weekend.

He was glad Ian had caught them. Marta had called him the moment Ian had left to go to the river, late Thursday night. She had been waiting here in bed for him, and they hadn't left it too much since. But despite her eagerness to betray his cousin, Will had a suspicion that Marta was going to want to keep it a secret from Ian. She was going to try to play both of them, to have her cake and eat it, too, so to speak.

It might've gone on for months like that; it might have gone on indefinitely. Ian was far too self-centered to be very observant, and he certainly never would've suspected that anything was going on between his girlfriend and his cousin. Will would've objected to Marta staying with Ian and having him on the side . . . Maybe. He'd discovered that he'd become addicted to her mouth in a very short time, just like he'd always known that he would, and if she had said that she'd wanted to keep their affair a secret from Ian, he wasn't completely sure that he would've been able to refuse her. She would've turned him into a whore just like she had his despised cousin, and he would've let her.

But the cat was out of the bag now, and If Ian wanted to fight about it, Will was more than happy to hop right on out of Marta's bed and whip his ass for him. Will suddenly tasted his lifelong loathing for his cousin: he didn't like Ian; he had *never liked Ian.* Will discovered that he no longer wanted to pretend a friendship that he'd never really felt. Will wasn't very good at pretending. What better occasion to demonstrate his dislike, than after getting caught *in flagrante delicto* with Ian's woman?

But as always, his cousin stymied him. Ian didn't want to fight. "She's all yours, Will. I cannot tell a lie – I'm gonna miss that sweet Chris, but her . . ." He shook his head. "No one's ever done me a bigger favor than you have here today, Cuz, and I thank you from the bottom of my heart. I just stopped by to pick up my toolbox." Ian glanced around the room. "If I've left anything else here . . . Mail it to me. I'll be seeing ya."

FORTY

Ian was back in Parker not long before midnight. He was a little surprised to find Rob sitting outside at the picnic table, drinking a glass of milk. He thought his cousin would be inside taking advantage of the solitude with Nadine, but since he had other news that he couldn't wait to tell, Ian was glad Rob was awake. "Guess where I found your brother," he said without preamble.

"I have no idea."

"Ah, come on, Cuz." Ian grinned and clapped him on the shoulder. "Humor me. Guess."

Rob shook his head. "I have not a clue."

"I found my toolbox in the garage at Marta's, and made sure the float bowl was in there. I was surprised to see her car there – what was she doing in Elsinore if we weren't going skiing? I thought about just sneaking out past her car, not going in the house to see her at all. She wouldn't even need to know I'd been there. But I decided that would be a chickenshit thing to do.

"So I thought I'd stop in for a moment and say hi to the woman who's been a lodestone, an albatross around my neck, almost from the first moment she invited me into her room." Ian jerked his thumb over his shoulder. "But I've stayed with her, all this time –"

Rob grinned. "Because of that Chris."

Ian endeavored to look sheepish. "Yeah, well . . ."

"And you haven't been exactly *faithful* to her . . ."

Ian shrugged. "I kept it out of town. We're not married. And as it turns out, turnabout, as the poet says, is fair play. I walked into the house, looked in the bedroom, and what to my wondering eyes should appear but *my supposed girlfriend* riding some guy like a borrowed donkey."

"No way!" Rob paused with the glass of milk halfway to his mouth.

"It was Will."

"No way!" Rob set the glass down on the table and stared at his cousin in astonishment for a heartbeat. Ian grinned back at him.

Will and Rob were brothers, twins; but Ian and Rob had always been copasetic, simpatico. Like Shakespearean actors, they quoted poetry to each other without a shade of reticence, and didn't care what anybody thought about it. They were closer than mere brothers.

Ian knew that Rob was ignorant of what Will had been up to, and even if there had been a shadow of a doubt in his mind, Rob's gobsmacked expression proved that Will hadn't confided his nefarious intentions to his twin. Of course he hadn't. There was no way he could. Will knew where Rob's loyalties resided: firmly with Cousin Ian. And he hated Ian for it.

"What did you say?"

"I said that while it was true that I was gonna miss the *Ooh-La-La,* I wasn't gonna miss her. I told Will that he was welcome to her."

"Jesus!" Rob exclaimed in disbelief.

"He saw her first, Cuz, but she made him wait his turn." Ian giggled. "I do believe they call that *sloppy seconds.*"

Rob wrinkled his nose at the vulgarity. "Did they say anything to you?"

Ian shook his head. "I didn't really give them the chance. I'm so goddamned glad to get rid of her that all I could feel was relief, Rob. But if either one of them would've spoke up, my masculine pride might've also had to speak up. I might've had to smack one of them in the mouth." Again Ian giggled. "But probably not. Will just grinned like he'd won the Irish Sweepstakes. He'll find out soon enough. She's not all roses and lollipops. Not by a long stretch."

"I can't believe this, Ian. Marta maybe, but Will? Jesus! What about –"

"What about Daina?" They turned to see Nadine standing in the doorway, wearing an over-sized t-shirt for pajamas, carrying her own glass of milk. She frowned deeply.

"Who?" Ian asked.

"Daina. Will's girlfriend. My best friend."

Ian looked at Rob in confusion. *"Will's got a girlfriend?"*

"Yeah. She was here with him the last time we were here. At the end of May. She and Nadine live together. I told you that he'd found a girl. I don't know how you didn't meet her."

"So not only did Will fuck me, he fucked his girlfriend, too? *For Marta?* His taste is in his mouth." Ian paused, shook his head. "You told me he took some chick for a cruise. I didn't know that made her his girlfriend."

Nadine stomped back into the house. She put her glass of milk down on the coffee table, then sat on the couch and picked up the phone.

"He's not gonna have a girlfriend for much longer, probably." Rob winked at Ian. "On the other hand, now he's got yours. Maybe you might want to take a look at his. She's cute."

Ian shook his head. "I think I'm gonna swear off women, Cuz. At least for the rest of the summer. At least the ones that want to stick around and monopolize my time."

"No more *girlfriends?*"

Ian nodded. "Too much effort."

"All that effort guarantees a continuously available warm when a guy gets home at night."

Ian laughed. *"A continuously available warm?* Is that how you think of them?"

"A rose by any other name . . ." Rob considered his cousin. "Isn't that how you think of them?" When Ian didn't immediately reply, he said, *"Go to your bosom: Knock there, and ask your heart what it doth know.* Besides Marta, when have you ever wasted a second thought on a girl, Cuz? Beyond today's boat ride and tonight's roll in the hay?"

Ian attempted to look contrite. "I've always endeavored to *love all, trust a few, do wrong to none."*

Philosophically, Ian was familiar with all the lofty ideals of true love. It was unavoidable: his father taught classical literature and poetry; he's been raised on it, and like his cousin, enjoyed it thoroughly. A couplet, whispered breathily into some chick's ear, had rarely failed him. So Ian was quite familiar with the *idea* of soulmates and love everlasting; he'd just never bothered looking for them.

Ian didn't have to look, anyway: women always came to him. His seemingly innocent indifference was intrinsic to his charm. A man that didn't chase a girl was refreshing – even past his good looks, Ian intrigued them.

So he never wanted for a date. Sometimes he attracted too many, ones he didn't want, like Sissy. Ian had never dwelt on the prospect of an eternal, once-in-a-lifetime romance, because the kind of romance that never failed to come his way, while temporary, was quite good enough for him. Bach said, *It's easy to play any musical instrument: all you have to do is touch the right key at the right time and the instrument will play itself.* That's how Ian looked at girls: a smile, a bit of poetry, and they played themselves right into his bed. It never failed to secretly amaze him, actually, how easy it all was. Still, he didn't look down on them for their eagerness. He had just never sought out that mythical soulmate, because there were just *so many women;* like his cousins, they were identical to him.

"But we're not talking about me," he said to Rob. "We're talking about you." One corner of Ian's mouth quirked up curiously. "Did you not tell me just a little while ago that there was more to life than skiing?"

"I've reevaluated that idea," Rob protested.

"'There's the future,' you said, 'love and marriage. I've met *a* girl,' you told me, like there was something special about her, like you don't meet new ones every day. I was under the impression that you were in love and all that." Ian nodded in at Nadine. "Have your happily-ever-after illusions been shattered already?"

"You were under the wrong impression about my illusions, with this one, Cuz. We aren't a match made in heaven. We don't really talk a lot. Mostly it's just dinner and bed and skiing –"

"Danger, Will Robinson." Ian's grin widened. "I just got out of a scene like that." He consulted an imaginary watch on his wrist. "Just a couple of hours ago. If you're not careful, she's liable to wind up in the sack with your brother."

Rob smiled wickedly. "It wouldn't be the first time that's happened. But usually they didn't know it."

"You're a very bad boy, my royal cousin."

Rob smiled and waved at Nadine through the patio door. She neither smiled nor waved back, but only looked straight ahead, still frowning. He sighed and said to Ian, "Your other royal cousin may have just ruined everybody's good time."

"How so?"

"I may have just become a sad reminder of her best friend's broken heart. Not only is the cheating bastard my brother, he's my *twin* brother."

"But like a Boy Scout, you're thrifty, clean, reverent and true. You'd never cheat on your girlfriend."

"Any more than you would."

Ian shrugged, reiterated, "I kept it out of town." He looked in through the patio door at Nadine. She had the phone to her ear, but wasn't saying anything. "Do you really think she'd be through with you simply because Will's through with her friend?"

Rob shrugged. *"Whatever will be, will be.* If it happens, then I'll be back out on the boulevard with you."

Nadine hung up and crossed the living room, still frowning. As she stepped out onto the patio, Ian said to Rob, "Speaking of the boulevard, I think I'm gonna get my old job back when school starts.

Maybe even before that. Dad's been whining about my lack of ambition again."

"At the bar?" Ian nodded. "The return of the Blue-eyed Bartender?"

Ian looked embarrassed, and Nadine's expression neutrally asked for explanation, with perhaps a little bit of irritation thrown in. She wasn't too happy with their gender at the moment – at least that was the emotion that she wished to communicate to them, until she could be alone and *think* for a minute.

"Before he met Marta, Ian was a bartender for a while," Rob said.

He has an uncanny knack for stating the obvious, Nadine thought, her irritation expanding a notch. *Why doesn't he ever just let Ian tell the story?*

"The evil twin and I . . ." Rob tried for a smile with that one, but Nadine remained unamused. "We used to hang out at his bar most nights and watch Ian sling watered-down beer and talk to the ladies.

"One day, this chick comes up to me after class, trailed by three of her girlfriends. She says, 'I hear you know the Blue-eyed Bartender.'

"I said, 'I know a lot of bartenders, honey. I can't say I've ever noticed the color of their eyes.' I didn't have a clue who she was talking about. I *do* know a lot of bartenders." Rob grinned.

"She said, 'I saw you talking to him last night, so I figured that you knew him, but . . .' She started to walk away, taking her friends with her. Then it hit me that she had to be talking about Ian, so I said, 'Is he about this tall? Squinty-eyed? Dumpy-looking?'" Rob clapped Ian on the back and he smiled. He was squinty, but there was not one single thing dumpty-looking about him, and he knew it.

"She nodded and I said, 'Yeah. I know him. He's my cousin.'

"She handed me a folded-up piece of paper, and said, 'Will you give this to him for me?' I nodded and she said thanks, then walked away. The next one handed me a similar piece of paper, and said, 'Me, too?' I nodded. Then the third one did the same thing. The last one hesitated, and I said, 'Do want to give your number to the Blue-eyed Bartender, too?'

"She smiled and took my arm. 'No,' she said. 'I want to give my number to *you.*'" Rob laughed and slapped Ian on the back again.

"He loves to tell that story," Ian said.

It was an amusing enough anecdote, but Nadine was still in Outraged Womanhood mode, so she remained unmoved. "And how did all that turn out for you?" she asked coldly.

Rob's grin evaporated. "Ah, we went out a few times. It was a long time ago, way before I met you . . ." Ian looked at him in surprise. Was he really apologizing? Rob couldn't believe the words that were coming out of his mouth, either, so he shut up.

Silence reigned for an uncomfortable heartbeat, then Ian smiled, as if a thought had just struck him. "What did your friend say? About Will's . . ." He looked at Rob in mock horror for a moment, searching for a gentle word. "About Will's . . . infidelity?"

Ian then tried to hide his smile, but failed. He realized that this was a sad and serious situation for Nadine's friend: betrayal can be heartrending, blah, blah, blah. But it wasn't the case for him – the other injured party – and he just couldn't pretend that he was anything but happy about it. Marta had meant less than nothing to him, and he was glad to be free of her. He'd been spared the drama of dumping her himself. One of the reasons he'd stuck around as long as he did was the desire to avoid that big break-up scene.

Besides, it was 1969, they were young: this kind of thing happened every day. Ian had been a party to it enough times himself, as had Rob: the single girls they picked up weren't always completely single. But neither of them had ever been caught like Will had been. His cousin's treachery, Marta's disloyalty, had freed Ian, and not soon enough – he had not a single hard feeling about it.

Nadine looked disdainfully at them for a moment, her expression effectively communicating, *There's a lot of dog in a man.* "She didn't answer. She's asleep, I'm sure. I'm going to go in and try again, myself. Goodnight, gentlemen."

After Nadine was gone, Ian said, "Try what again?"

"To sleep. That's why we're up at midnight drinking warm milk. She said she was having trouble getting to sleep, so I said I would warm her up some –"

"Did you try –?"

"Yeah." Rob grinned. "But it didn't work this time. She still couldn't sleep."

Ian paused for a moment and then said, "Are you gonna call Will? I'll give you the number."

Rob was surprised. "I wouldn't've thought that you would care –"

"I *don't* care, Cuz. But some of these girls can be nuts. Hysterical. *Violent.*" Ian winked. "His girlfriend's gonna find out, sooner instead of later. Your chick's chomping at the bit to tell her. I wouldn't let my worst enemy walk into that unprepared." He grinned expansively. "It's the least I can do. I opened my big mouth and let Nadine overhear it. You be sure to let Will know that was unintentional. But the least you can do is warn him. It's a bad situation any way you look at it, but it would surely be better if she heard it from him rather than from Nadine, don't you think?"

Rob agreed. Ian gave him the number and he called Marta's vacation house.

FORTY-ONE

Nadine had not been able to sleep earlier – even after Rob's romantic ministrations – because Ian was gone. Sex with Rob was satisfying enough, because she simply pretended he was Ian. It would not be that way forever, of course; already, little things he did, both in and out of the bedroom, had begun to irritate her. She knew that she wouldn't be able to keep up this charade with Rob for much longer.

But between the end of his attentions and the onslaught of sleep she always thought about Ian again, and it usually worked. She had no trouble drifting off.

But not tonight. Ian was gone back home to pick up another one of those glass floater things for his boat. What if he decided not to come back? Then she would be stuck out on the water with Rob. He had convinced himself that she just loved to sit in the boat in the blazing sun, to bounce around in the chop, and *watch him ski.* Now he would need a third to help him, if Ian didn't come back – so he'd probably call Sissy. Nadine knew that Sissy was a barrelful of monkeys in her own right, addicted to skiing just like Ian and Rob. There would be no rest at all if her boyfriend summoned Sissy. Nadine wanted to get off the water if Ian wasn't there, but Sissy would just want to drown her desire for him by staying on it.

It was coming up on Sunday morning, and Rob wanted to stay until at least Wednesday. Four more days of absolutely *not* fun-in-the-sun, if Ian wasn't there. *For there is nothing either good or bad, but thinking makes it so,* and it never ceased to amaze Nadine how much the same scenario didn't bother her at all, was quite wonderful in fact, if Ian was going to be there.

She had fretted about whether or not he was going to come back, and her nice boyfriend had seen her inability to sleep and had nicely volunteered to fix her some warm milk, of all god-awful things. And then this other bomb had exploded in her face.

It was a little frightening to grasp the relentlessness of fate. One could guess at the actions that would produce the predicted outcomes – and be utterly mistaken, as in this case. Who would've thought that beautiful Marta would've thrown Ian over – *oh, sweet Jesus, Ian is single again* – for boring, skinny Will? But the pieces were falling into place. *Will will be out of Daina's life, as soon as I tell her about this,* Nadine thought, *just as the cards have foretold. She doesn't care for him that much anyway, and there are way too many fish in the sea not to throw back a cheater.*

And Will was taking Marta away, too, out of Ian's life. Two birds killed with one adulterous stone. All Nadine had to do now was get rid of Rob, and the path to her soulmate and the rest of her life would be clear.

FORTY-TWO

Will came back to Daina's house at first light, looking sleep-deprived and more than a little hangdog. He calmly laid it out for Daina: he had run into an old girlfriend. They'd had a heart-to-heart. The upshot was, he'd come to the decision that he had to get back together with her. They were meant for each other. He said he was sorry, said that he'd never forget her. Then, non sequitur: "I thought it would be better if you heard it from me."

Daina was speechless; not from heartbreak or even anger, but from surprise. This was the first time any of them had ever broken up with her first. After a moment, she recovered. "I'm sure it's for the best." It was a ridiculous, nonsensical phrase, but not one other thing came to her mind.

Will seemed inordinately relieved. *He was prepared for a scene,* Daina realized. *We've barely known each other for six weeks, but he thought I was going to be hysterical. The ego of a man!*

He said he was sorry again, then solemnly intoned, "Goodbye, Daina."

"Goodbye, Will. It was fun."

Will nodded, and Daina suddenly had the urge to laugh in his face; she barely kept it under control while he hastily left the house without a backward glance. It was a laugh of relief, of looking forward to the excitement of a new man: one always came along soon enough. Another temporary way to spend a weekend. But Will wouldn't have interpreted her laughter that way. He would have seen it as bitterness, hysterics. That thought made her laugh all the harder.

Daina was still giggling and wiping away tears of mirth when her best friend called. With deadly seriousness, Nadine said, "I don't know how to tell you this, so I'm just gonna straight out tell you. I overheard Rob's cousin telling him that he . . . *saw* Will with someone else last night."

"Oh, no!" Daina could not keep the amusement out of her tone. "Not with someone else!"

Nadine said softly, "I'm not kidding, Daina."

"Oh, no! You're not kidding!"

"What's wrong with you?"

Slowly, sadly, sounding startlingly like Brenda Lee, Daina sang, *"Break it to me gently, let me down the eeeeasy way . . ."* Then she laughed lightly. "I already know, 'Deen. Will just left. He told me he's decided to get back together with some old girlfriend. We are officially . . . how you say? *Finito.* "

That not exactly accurate, Nadine thought. *Will's decided to get together with* someone else's *girlfriend.* "So you're . . . You're okay with it?"

"Yes, I'm okay with it. He's not exactly Prince Charming, is he? And we're not exactly engaged, are we? I'm not going to miss him." Daina giggled. "Well . . . I might miss parts of him . . ."

Nadine replied with Brenda Lee's other plaintive lament: *"I'm sorry, sooo sorry, that I was such a fool. I didn't know love could be so cruel . . ."* Then they both laughed.

"Wait a minute," Daina said. "How do *you* know about it? What did you say about Rob's cousin? Where are you, anyway?"

Nadine hesitated, then spoke too quickly; perhaps there was a shade of defensiveness. "I'm in Parker. With Rob. I told you we were going to the river for the 4th of July."

"And his cousin's there with you?"

"Yes."

"And Will was there? With this girl?"

"No. Ian saw Will with this girl in Elsinore, and told Rob about it when he showed up here last night. I overheard. I tried to call you right then, but you didn't answer. It was late."

Nadine waited for Daina to ask for specifics. What did this girl look like? What exactly did Rob's cousin see them doing together? But Daina truly didn't care, not even enough to be curious. The six or seven weeks that she had dated Will had been the longest she'd ever spent with anyone before, but that didn't mean she wasn't glad it was over. Or if not glad, at least not upset. She didn't love Will; outside of the bedroom, he bored her.

Nadine was relieved that she didn't have to draw her friend a picture of all the sordid events that had occurred, didn't have to explain how she had come to be a party to them. Daina knew that she'd been skiing with Rob and his cousin the past couple of weeks, but she hadn't asked for details, and Nadine hadn't offered any. She'd never gotten around to describing Rob's cousin. Nadine rarely even referred to him by his Christian name. She had not confessed her love for Ian to Daina – there had never been a good time. Neither had Nadine mentioned Ian's pretty, whiny, injured girlfriend, nor her impressive boat or cozy, lakeside love-nest.

So since Daina asked for no further particulars, Nadine felt no need to explain that Rob's cousin had caught his *own girlfriend* in the kip with Will, that it should've been as much of a betrayal to him as it should've been to Daina, except that Ian wasn't taking it any harder than Daina was. There was no need to burden her friend with extraneous details, such as the fact that Nadine actually *knew* this adulteress; that it was the same girl with whom she and Rob had been skiing every weekend, that it had occurred at the same house where they'd dined every Saturday night.

It was also once again not the time to tell Daina about her love for Ian, either. Nadine and Rob were going together; it was not the time to mention that she was having adulterous thoughts of her own. That she, like Will, intended on acting on them at the soonest opportunity.

Will had left her for someone else, and Daina was fine with it. No need to bother her with the Byzantine connections between these people – she'd hopefully never see Will again, she'd never meet Marta, and she hadn't met Ian yet. Really, all Daina needed to know was that Will was gone. *Simplest is best,* Nadine told herself.

"I'll be home as soon as I can," Nadine promised.

"It's really okay, 'Deen," Daina assured her friend. "You have fun. I'm fine."

"But I want to see you, anyway. To tell you the truth, this happening might turn out to be a good thing for both of us. Rob is becoming kind of . . . tiresome." All at once, Nadine began to warm up to the idea of using Will's infidelity as an excuse to jettison Rob and get at Ian. Once Rob was gone, her own motivations wouldn't seem so illicit. She would be in the market for another man, just like Daina was now.

"And you know what they say, right? If it walks like a duck and quacks like a duck . . . And Rob certainly looks just like this other, cheating son of a bitch of a duck, doesn't he?"

"Oh, Nadine, that's not really fair. Just because they're twins . . ." *Did Will actually cheat on me?* Daina wondered. No physical culmination had been mentioned, but on the other hand, how would he have phrased all that? Will had only said that *he'd come to the decision that he had to get back together with* this old girlfriend. Had he come to something else before he'd come to that decision? Daina smiled wryly to herself. Now his other statement made more sense: "I thought it would be better if you heard it from me."

"The concept is still valid," Nadine was saying. "Does this one duck not walk and quack and look astonishingly like this other?"

132

Daina giggled. "Remember when we couldn't tell them apart?"

"I still can't tell them apart!" Nadine exclaimed gleefully. "Are they not birds of a feather?"

Daina abandoned mature argument, giving in to her friend's childishly unkind game. "Possibly!"

"It's inescapable. I must come home and meditate on their similarities."

"If you must."

"I'll be there as soon as I can."

"I love you, 'Deen!"

"I love you, too, Daina! See you soon!"

FORTY-THREE

Nadine walked down to Rob's private dock, where he and Ian already had *One Wilde Ride,* carburetor newly restored, launched and ready to go. Though she didn't feel it, she again assumed an austere look of displeasure: her friend had been betrayed, dishonored, and this was no time for fun and games. Sincerely, it was no time for the frivolity of waterskiing.

She would dearly love to spend more time with Ian, but she wasn't in the mood to watch him pick up chicks. She was still the good twin's girlfriend to him; that perception would have to change, and quickly. She'd like to stay and look at him, but the groundwork had to be laid. If she left now, she'd be *having* him all the sooner, instead of just looking at him, instead of watching other girls get him.

She stood on the dock silently, until they stopped talking and looked at her. "Rob, I have to go home."

Ian grinned. "Did you lose your pills?"

He was making an inside joke, and Nadine allowed herself a quick smile, but then immediately reined it in in favor of gravity again. "My friend . . ." Why could she never say her friend's name in front of Ian? She forced it out. "Daina's just had a shock. I should be with her."

Anger clouded Rob's pale green eyes. He said to his cousin, "What did I tell ya? Goddamned Will. He ruins everything." He stood up and jumped out of the boat.

"Wait a second, Cuz," Ian said. "Nadine said *she* had to go back. She didn't say anything about you."

Nadine's heart leapt to her throat. Ian was volunteering to take her home! She pictured the long drive: she would snuggle up next to him in the truck. She would have all the time in the world to tell him everything. She would regale him with the tale of the fateful Tarot lay, how it had shown her that they were destined to be together. She would point to the proof – the game was already afoot – Will taking off with Marta was only the beginning. She would confess her love for him, perhaps shyly suggest that they pull over into some secluded spot so she could demonstrate it . . .

Ian said, "I'm sure Donna isn't in the mood to see anybody that looks like you right at the moment." Rob grinned.

"Daina," Nadine corrected.

Ian shook his head, dismissing his error. "Why don't you let Nadine take the Caddy back home, Rob?" Aiding his cousin's girlfriend in her quest to soothe her friend's ruffled ego had not even crossed Ian's mind – not when there were four more days of skiing at hand. Maybe a whole 'nother week!

Ian looked hopefully at Nadine, as if it was the best possible solution. *Hot damn, ain't I clever?* his expression said. Inarguably, the best possible solution to this thorny matter of the heart was for Nadine to go back to Riverside by herself.

"That way, poor . . .?"

"Daina," Rob supplied.

"Right. Poor Daina doesn't have to be reminded of Will; I don't have to be left here all alone to sadly ruminate on the betrayal I have suffered at the hands of my own flesh and blood." He attempted an expression of sadness, but could only maintain it for a moment. Then that killer, Ian Wilde smile broke through again. "And you don't have to get pissed at Will for pulling this high school bullshit on the 4th of July and ruining the weekend for everybody. What do you say, Nadine? You don't really need Rob to go with you, do ya?" Regardless, he was making it clear that *he* wasn't going to go with her. "You can drive the Caddy, right?"

Rob looked uncertain for a moment. He knew that he was being insensitive if he stayed behind. Daina was his friend, too – sort of – and he should go, if for no other reason than to make an apology on behalf of his evil twin. By staying behind with Ian, the statement that he was making was that even though Daina was in pain, he'd rather ski.

Nadine said, "Yeah, I can drive the Caddy." It was okay. This would work. Rob's cavalier disregard for Daina's hurt was just one more thing Nadine could cite later as a reason for breaking up with him, if it came to that.

"Great!" Ian said. "I'll see you in a couple of days, when I bring Rob to pick up his car. You drive safely now!"

Nadine nodded at Ian, but he was no longer looking at her. She turned back toward the house. Even after this rather curt dismissal, it was *so* difficult to leave him. But it was necessary in order to ensure their future together. By the time Rob showed up to pick up his car, enough time would've elapsed, so that Nadine could tell him how she'd been doing a great deal of soul-searching, and she had come to the conclusion that things weren't working out between them . . .

135

Back inside the house, while Rob scared up the keys to the Caddy, he offered to go back to Riverside with Nadine, if she really needed his support. "It won't take Ian long to find Sissy to ski with him, if he has to," he said.

But Nadine told Rob that it was okay. Ian was right. It was true that Daina wouldn't be too glad to see Will's twin brother right then, and there was no sense in him and Ian missing out on skiing because of this little bump in the road.

Nadine didn't communicate any anger to Rob regarding his decision to stay and have fun. She made it sound like it was a perfectly reasonable thing to do. Nadine realized that she was going to have to let Rob *down the eeeeasy way*. He was Ian's best friend, and she was bound to see him again, once she and Ian started their life together. It wouldn't do for her to end it on an acrimonious note. This stuff just happened; things sometimes didn't work out between people. They were ships that had passed in the night and all that. No reason not to remain friends . . .

Nadine even gave him a big kiss and a loving squeeze goodbye. She planned on it being the last one.

When he got back to the dock, Rob said in amazement, "You are a piece of work, my friend."

Ian grinned. *"Thou dost not wish more help from England, Cuz?"*

"God's will, my liege, would you and I alone, without more help, could fight this royal battle!"

"Now is it time to ski: come, shall we about it?"

"Lay on, Macduff," Rob said conversationally. He untied the bowline and hopped into the boat.

Ian fired it up. *"And damn'd be him that first cries, 'Hold, enough!'"*

FORTY-FOUR

Rob and Ian decided to stay on in Parker until the following Sunday night, and during the week, Nadine rehearsed her big break-up speech. "Things just haven't been working out," it would go. "But I'll always care about you, and I hope we can be friends."

There was really no place to park the truck and boat on the narrow, alley-like street that ran in front of Daina and Nadine's house, so Ian didn't even bother to get out and say hi. He just dropped Rob off at the mouth of the street and went on his way.

Rob had talked to his brother at length on the phone while he was still in Parker, then he made Will and Ian have a conversation. Ian admitted fault in his initial swoop on Marta, swearing that he hadn't known Will wanted her, and therefore, he said, he couldn't really have any hard feelings whatsoever because his cousin had swooped her back.

Will didn't apologize in turn. Although he'd hoped for an argument, a way to have a final break with his cousin, he had to agree with Ian's point. There was no reason for discord between them. And because Will agreed, he realized that he would have to remain "friends" with his cousin.

Thus, through Rob's intervention, Will and Ian were reconciled back to at least their former level of – well, he couldn't really call it *friendship* – they were not enemies, no matter how much Will thought he would've enjoyed that. Ian and Will couldn't argue with Rob's basic premise: the two of them were childhood friends, *family* – such a bond couldn't be severed, nay, not even strained, by something as transitory as a woman.

Ian also listened to his former girlfriend's penitent apology about the way she had gone about breaking up with him, and he said everything was cool with him on that score. They, too, would remain friends.

Rob took a deep breath before knocking on the door to his, for lack of a better word, *girlfriend's* house. He had restored the status quo between his twin brother and his cousin, his best friend. Now he had a few things to discuss with Nadine, and he knew that he held their immediate future in the balance. Things could go either way with Nadine after what he had to tell her, and he felt a little bit guilty that he hoped they would tip towards an ending.

Nadine opened the door and gave him a rather desultory hug and a kiss on the cheek in greeting; she wouldn't meet his eye for more than a moment. She offered him a seat on the couch, sighed, and shot over his bow the opening salvo of every break-up battle since time immemorial. "Rob, we have to talk."

He echoed her sigh. "Indeed."

Nadine felt a fondness for Rob at that moment. He was really as poetic as Ian, though sadly, he lacked Ian's joie de vivre, his cleverness, his *aliveness;* at least he lacked these qualities to Nadine. Rob would've sufficed, perhaps indefinitely, at least through the end of college, if fate hadn't intervened and shown her the true path to happiness. She and Rob were destined to be only friends, acquaintances, in-laws, someday. The cards didn't lie. Ian was the one for her.

But before she had a chance to open her mouth and recite the fateful clichés, Rob said, "I'm going to Europe for the rest of the summer. With Marta and Will." He let that sink in for a moment, then continued. "You're more than welcome to come with me . . . if you really want to."

Ah, the relentlessness of destiny! There was no fighting it, no bargaining. What would be, would be, and the fates were smiling on Nadine now. She was not going to have to let Rob down, easy or otherwise, after all.

"I'm very flattered by the offer, but I couldn't in good conscience do that, now could I?"

Relief flooded Rob's mind. "No, I don't suppose you could."

"It would be a slap in the face to my best friend. Taking off overseas with you and her ex-boyfriend and his new girlfriend? It would be reprehensible."

"I understand where you're coming from." Everything was working out as Rob had hoped it would.

On the phone, Will had pointed out to him that the time was perhaps past due for them to stop slumming. It seemed like an ancient and archaic maxim, but it was no less true for that: they needed to start dating their own kind. No more pretty, playful, poor girls.

Marta was surely pretty and playful enough, and she had a host of friends from which Rob could choose, whose fathers' were just as rich and powerful as Marta's. Girls who could foot their own bills on the continent. Alliances with girls from their own social strata could only benefit them in the future, Will told him, and Rob knew it was true.

"And also," Nadine was saying. "I don't think it would be fair to you, to be over there, seeing all those exotic, foreign women . . . And having to be saddled with a commitment back home." *I'm gonna put it all on him,* she thought. *He could be loyal, but now, he doesn't have to be . . .* "Maybe we can talk again when school starts, when you come back . . . But in the meantime, let's just part as friends."

Rob paused for a heartbeat. He didn't want to seem too eager, didn't want to upset the delicate balance of things going exactly the way he wanted them to, by saying, *Well, hot damn, Nadine, I'll see ya in a few months, then! Maybe, but probably not!*

"If that's the way you want it," he said. That made it her decision.

"I think it's for the best."

Rob counted to ten before he stood up. Nadine also stood and they shared a hug. Rob said goodbye, then, forcing himself to walk slowly, he fled.

Daina peeked around the corner from the hallway. "So much for twins," she said with a grin. "What's that saying? Men are like buses. If you miss one, another one will be along in a few minutes."

"I've already met the next one," Nadine said with a conspiratorial grin.

"Really? Is this guy the reason why you were so eager to get rid of Rob? Do tell!"

"Be innocent of the knowledge, dearest chuck, till thou applaud the deed."

Daina frowned. She found Nadine's odd phrases annoying sometimes, just like Will *(my ex-boyfriend,* she thought with a little grin) did, when his brother would spout the same rubbish.

Daina saw Nadine's tiresome poesy as a part of her overly romantic nature; it seemed sometimes that her friend lived in a dream world, concerning herself far too much with rhyme and verse, with magic and curses and predestination.

Magic existed, Daina knew, just as she knew that it was possible to predict the future. But the predictions were always murky, unclear, open to broad interpretation. One such claim had colored her entire life, caused a bittersweet pall to hang over the time she'd spent with each man she'd ever met. Daina failed to see the same romance in augury that Nadine did.

Nadine caught her friend's frown and rephrased. "I haven't approached him yet. I don't want to jinx it by telling you about it."

Daina shrugged. Jinxes and charms ruled her friend's life. She was certain she'd meet Nadine's new man soon enough.

FORTY-FIVE

It was not long after Rob left that Nadine realized that she'd made a major error. She had no way to get in touch with Ian. Consulting the *Pacific Bell White Pages,* Nadine found that there was no listing for an *Ian Wilde.* She had the number to the house in Lake Elsinore, but that wasn't going to help. She doubted seriously that Marta would be lending the *Ooh-La-La* out to Ian ever again, and it wasn't like Nadine could be buddying up to the homewrecker that had stolen her best friend's boyfriend, so that she could find out Marta's ex-boyfriend's phone number, now could she? Such actions would give everyone pause, and Nadine didn't want that.

Nadine didn't know where Ian lived, either, though she knew he still lived at home. *That's why there's no phone number listed for him,* she deduced. She knew that his father was an English professor at UCR; as a freshman, she'd taken one of his classes. Nadine looked up *Jameson Wilde* in the phone book, called the number and shyly asked for Ian. He was out of town, the polite voice on the phone informed her; was there a message?

Nadine panicked. She had not thought up a reason why she'd be calling her ex-boyfriend's cousin, and so soon after their break-up, so she quickly said, "No message, thank you," and hung up.

She went to the library and looked up Professor Wilde's address in the Thomas Guide, then drove past a large, white columned house not too far from the twins' estate. *The professor isn't as wealthy as his brother the doctor, but he's doing okay,* Nadine thought. The driveway curved around to the back of the house, so she couldn't see Ian's truck or his boat, even if he was home.

For the rest of July, Nadine was frantic. She simply could not think of what she would say to Ian. No words came to her usually quick and inventive mind. The day of reckoning was at hand, but the normal ease with which she could converse with Ian failed her. The only thing that she could think to say to him – *I love you* – was simply too abrupt.

FORTY-SIX

As the summer wore on, Daina didn't go out on the town looking for a new male distraction, any more than Nadine did. While Nadine's mind was filled with coming up with just the perfect words to say to Ian, Daina busied herself with wallpapering the kitchen, and trying to get the grass in their front yard to grow. She also bought cookbooks and taught herself new recipes, at last paying attention to her aunts' instructions on all the herbs that they grew in a little box garden in their window. Daina started one of her own, but never quite got the knack of being a good cook.

Daina also resumed a hobby she and Nadine had loved as children: making candles with their aunts. There was a gas-fed pyre a short distance from the house, surmounted by a metal gantry with a chain and cauldron. When the wax was hot enough, the pot could be swung out from the flames and tilted, allowing the wax to flow into molds. They also made fancy dipped candles. Their creations included tapers and anatomically correct figures of men and women – Nadine and Daina had giggled at the little naked people when they were kids.

Penny and Bellona sold the candles to a woman named Lily, who ran an occult bookstore called Mohini's House of Magic, in downtown Riverside. Lily was an old friend of the family from way back, and like Penny and Bellona, she seemed ageless. Sometimes, the black outstripped the gray in her long, curly hair – sometimes, it seemed to the girls, that it disappeared completely. Sometimes her large, striking green eyes would twinkle and sparkle like a schoolgirl's. At other times, Lily would seem once again to be their aunts' peer, maybe forty, perhaps sixty. In later years, this effect seemed diminished to Daina and Nadine, when they realized that Aunt Lily probably dyed her long locks on occasion, sometimes just utilized a few more cosmetics than did Penny and Bellona.

From Mohini's House of Magic, Lily sold the candles and all manner of other occult supplies to local hippies, Satanists, and self-proclaimed witches. Daina and Nadine had often heard their aunts and Lily laugh uproariously about these customers, whom they referred to as the *Dawning of the Age of Aquarius* devotees.

FORTY-SEVEN

On the first Saturday morning in August, as they drove downtown to drop off the latest batch of candles to Mohini's House of Magic, Nadine wondered wistfully where Ian would be waterskiing today, and with whom. Was he out on Lake Elsinore, or was he out of town again, in Parker with adoring Sissy? Nadine still hadn't been able to come up with a legitimate-sounding reason to call him.

A few days before, Nadine had finally gotten around to dropping off the rolls of film that she'd shot in Parker, the pictures from their first weekend with Will and Rob. Getting them printed had been low on Nadine's to-do list; there existed no wistful desire in her to relive party scenes with ex-boyfriends and a bunch of people she didn't know. But it was just one more errand that needed to be accomplished, one more little thing that had to be done in this, the most boring, the most exciting summer of her life. One more item to be crossed off, while she tried to organize her thoughts and decide on the perfect thing to say to Ian. And maybe Daina might like to see them, although Nadine doubted it.

They picked up the pictures and Nadine stuck them into her purse without looking at them. They went on to Mohini's to see their "Aunt" Lily.

On this hot morning, Lily appeared to be a well-rested, handsome woman of about fifty. Nadine and Daina shared a glance. Time for the old gal to break out the Maybelline again.

Lily was overjoyed to see them; she stowed the candles in the back room, then grinned. "Beholding your shining young faces makes me realize that I haven't been enough in the world, lately. I feel like playing hooky today. Do you think your aunts would be offended it I imposed on them for brunch?"

Daina grinned. "They certainly wouldn't be offended. I'll call and let them know we're coming."

Bellona and Penny had brunch waiting, complete with grapefruit halves and mimosas. The five ladies sat, and as it always did, the conversation turned to Lily's business and the state of modern spirituality, witchcraft and magic.

Tongue firmly in cheek, Bellona said, "It seems that nowadays, there has come a flowering of the old ways. Young women are not afraid to call themselves witches." She winked at the young women present and Nadine grinned. *We could be called witches, I guess,* she thought, because of the lore and traditions upon which they'd been raised. *But we'd never call ourselves that. It's not something we do; it's simply what we are.*

Lily sighed. "The girls that come into the shop . . . I think that they use the rituals mostly as an excuse for all this free love."

"But hasn't love always been free?" Bellona's grin included Daina and Nadine. "Haven't you always found it so, ladies? A whole world of men from which to choose." She giggled. "What other purpose do they serve other than for our pleasure?"

Lily stared at her friend with faux embarrassment, then smiled slyly and sipped her mimosa.

"For people like us, that's been their purpose," Penny observed drily. "But it's a man's world, and for most women there's always been the shame that men have tried to impose upon us. Are we not their property? Do not our bodies and desires belong solely to them? How dare we share ourselves with whomever we choose?"

All four of her companions smiled at the ridiculousness of those concepts. "Lily's right. Today's young women use mysticism and the unseen world as an excuse," Penny continued. "They throw off the patriarchal shame by calling it liberation, free love, a return to nature. They call it *Wicca,* and slavishly follow either Mr. Cardell or Mr. Gardner's precepts." The older women rolled their eyes at that. "They fail to grasp the responsibility that comes with embracing all this freedom that they've discovered."

"Responsibility?" Nadine said in surprise.

"Yes," Penny said. "If you don't feel as though you are in love with the partner you've chosen, if only for the night . . ."

Bellona rose and selected a volume from a nearby bookshelf. She paged through it for a moment, then read, *"She taught him that after a celebration of love the lovers should not part without admiring each other, without being conquered or having conquered, so that neither is bleak or glutted or has the bad feeling of being used or misused."*

"Many of today's girls regret their liberated indulgences the next day," Penny said. "They indeed feel used."

Nadine and Daina exchanged a guilty look. Lily caught it and said, "I don't think our young friends here have ever felt bleak or misused, Penny. I think they feel themselves to be the users."

"That's because they are naturally free," Penny replied. "They don't feel compelled to clothe their inclinations in rituals best reserved for other things, like some of our young *Wiccans* do."

144

Again the three older women laughed, and Daina and Nadine smiled. Lily and Penny and Bellona were seers, clairvoyants. It was second nature to them that there was but a gossamer veil between this world and things unseen, but not untouchable. That there were powers that could be wielded for one's own satisfaction was not some new, outlandish idea to them – it was life and breath, just the way the universe ran.

The magical tradition was the fabric of their lives, so they had nothing but disdain for new age converts and self-proclaimed witches and warlocks, who used modern takes on ancient traditions as nothing more than an excuse for anonymous romps in the woods on Sabbats. Nadine and Daina also laughed at the idea that some of their peers thought it was necessary to affect robes and stilted speech in order to be witches, that they felt they had to invoke forces beyond their ken to guiltlessly enjoy a one night stand.

But these new pagans' money was green, and Lily did a land office business selling candles and pentacles and robes to this generation of self-enlightened, self-recognized adepts.

After brunch, Lily said she had to return to the store, and said her goodbyes. While Daina and Bellona and Penny lazed on the deck in the sun for a while, Nadine returned to the house at the bottom of the hill and started a load of laundry. While it agitated, she sat on the couch and flipped through the first envelope of the black and white pictures she'd taken in Parker.

There was a shot of the river from the back patio; Will and Rob by the barbecue; three or four people Nadine didn't even remember; Will and Daina, Daina and Rob, more people she didn't recognize. Nadine sighed and threw the envelope full of boring pictures into a drawer in the desk in her room. The second roll was more of the same: party pictures, partygoers, Will and Rob, Will and Daina, Daina and Rob. Nadine sighed. It was a waste of money getting stuff like this developed. She was about to throw the other set of prints into the drawer with the first when she came upon the very last picture in the roll.

It was the shot she'd taken of Ian, standing on the dock, when he had been talking to the two girls from the party. Seeing him in black and white was almost as much of a shock to Nadine as it would've been had he appeared unbidden on her doorstep in the flesh, because it was completely unexpected. Nadine had forgotten all about this one picture she'd taken of him.

She ran her finger lightly over the small, glossy print. Knee bent, Ian had one foot up on the bottom of the metal railing to the dock, and both hands braced casually behind his back on the top rail, as if he might be about to hop up backwards and sit on it. He was shirtless, barefoot, wearing the same pair of off-white trunks with green piping and a green waistband that he always wore. Thinking back, Nadine couldn't remember seeing him in anything else but those white trunks, rarely with the addition of a carelessly thrown-on shirt. Except for the first night, when he'd been wearing bell-bottoms and a dark-blue, three-buttoned, collared shirt. The night when the forces of the universe, through the medium of the Tarot, had revealed to her that he was her soulmate.

Nadine studied the picture. Ian looked squinty, as always, and the expression on his face was probably a smile, but there seemed like there might be just the tiniest trace of annoyance to it, too. Nadine had called his name, taking his attention away from the two girls that he was in the middle of picking up, after all. He looked perfect, the very archetype of virile, powerful, shaggy-haired, late 1960s manhood. It made Nadine weak, just looking at this picture that she'd taken.

While it was true that she told herself that she loved Ian for his mind, his wit, Nadine could no more deny his physical charm than Sissy could – after all, she couldn't hear his voice from looking at this picture.

Nadine took a thumbtack and hung Ian up beside all the scores of other photos of men on the wall beside her bed. She realized that his would be the last one in the collection. There was no longer any need to take pictures of strangers for Aunt Bellona to read; Nadine had found her soulmate. After a moment, she took the picture down and put it in the night table drawer instead. That way it would be easier for her to take it out and look at it, to fantasize about him before she fell asleep at night.

With the delightful discovery that she had a photograph of Ian, a sudden calmness and clarity descended upon Nadine. All her worries about the perfect thing to say disappeared. She would call and simply ask him what he'd been up to all summer, ask him if he'd like to have lunch, or a cup of coffee, or a drink. The idea that he might consider such a suggestion to be odd or suspicious fled. They were friends. They had boated together for much of the summer, laughed and talked. There was not one thing unnatural in her contacting him, rekindling their friendship. Maybe they could even take his boat out again.

But the fates decided to withhold fruition from Nadine for the moment. Throughout August, whenever she would call Ian's house, he was absent. Once, the polite voice on the other end of the phone had told her that she'd just missed him. Emboldened, Nadine had at last left her name and number. There was nothing untoward or even forward about it. They were old friends. Nadine waited patiently by the phone for the rest of the evening for a return call. When no call came, she'd didn't feel snubbed. Ol' tomcat Ian was probably out for the night. Nadine was sure he would return her call at his earliest convenience. They were pals.

But Ian didn't call her back. Nadine left a couple of more messages the first week of September – perhaps the anonymous voice on the other end of the line wasn't giving his messages to him. School started and Nadine assured herself that she was bound to run into Ian on campus sometime.

To make doubly sure, she added Professor Wilde's class, entitled *Three Kings – Contrasting Macbeth, Richard III, and Henry V,* to her schedule. Nadine thought she might buddy-up to pretentious Professor Wilde, tell him that she was friends with his son. Perhaps ask him to tell Ian to drop by the house and visit her some time, so they might renew their friendship.

But that kind of moment never presented itself. Jameson Wilde was quite imposing; his persona did not lend itself to small talk after class, especially not about something as off-topic as his son. Nadine told herself that there was nothing wrong with her trying to look Ian up again, to resume their friendship. But she felt that perhaps his dad wouldn't see it the same way.

As the sun set on the second Friday in October, Nadine paused for a moment, taking a seat in UCR's exquisite botanical gardens. She sighed. She would never doubt that she and Ian were meant for each other, but her patience with the powers-that-be was wearing thin at the moment. She had been unsuccessful in finding him, and the longing to see him again was starting to keep her up at night.

Before taking out a textbook for a moment's study, she scanned the faces of the other students strolling by, as she always did, on the off-chance she might run into him. To her horrified surprise, she spied Rob, Will, Marta and some other girl, laughing and smiling, now only yards away from her. She quickly ducked behind a tree, until they passed by, oblivious.

Nadine had not heard from Rob – for all she knew, he and his brother and Marta had decided to go to school in Venice or Heidelberg, or some other European seat of higher learning. She had not thought of them once all summer, and she surely didn't want to chat them up now.

"I see you, Nadine," a voice said.

Nadine peeped around the tree, hope swelling in her. Was it? Could it be?

But it was only Chuck Markis, who insisted on sitting next to her in math class. "Who are you hiding from?" he asked.

"An old boyfriend," she said truthfully. Nadine heaved a mighty sigh of disappointment and stepped back onto the sidewalk.

"What you need is a new boyfriend," Chuck said cheerfully, and smiled at her. Chuck reminded Nadine of a boy named Kevin that she'd known in high school, all dimples and blonde curls and obvious affection for her.

"I'm kinda seeing someone, Chuck," she lied, hoping that it would persuade him to move along about his business.

Chuck glanced around, as if Nadine's imaginary beau would materialize from behind another tree. "He's not very smart to leave his girlfriend here all alone when it's getting dark. The Big Bad Wolf might get you." Again, the dimpled smile. "Maybe I should wait here with you 'til he shows up. Make sure you're okay. After what happened in LA, a girl shouldn't be walking around alone in the dark. Who knows, whoever did it might've come out here to hide."

Jesus Christ on a crutch! Nadine thought furiously. *It's 1969, and I don't need a blonde choirboy to look after me! After what happened in LA . . . That's just an excuse for you to hang around and pester me.*

There had yet to be a break in the case of the gruesome murders that had occurred in Los Angeles in early August. Such horrific tragedies were a million miles away from Nadine's perception; she concentrated most of her waking thought and all of her dreams on that ever-hoped-for reunion with Ian. But in reality, LA was only sixty miles away, and Nadine's dad read the paper every day. There had been an argument – Mr. and Mrs. Germaine had insisted that their only child move back home immediately, where she would be safe.

"Two young girls living all alone is just an invitation to those kind of crazies," her father had intoned. There had been men as well as women brutally slaughtered, Nadine knew, and their presence had not stopped it. She doubted if the crazies were on the way to Riverside, looking for two young girls living all alone to slay next; they were probably a thousand miles away by now.

But Nadine didn't offer any of these logical arguments to her worried parents. She insisted on staying with her friend – if she moved back home, then Daina would be *all* alone – and allowed her father to install beefier locks on their doors and windows to assuage his worry.

Now Chuck was volunteering to protect her from that same band of roving murderers, at least until her non-existent boyfriend arrived.

"I'm not waiting here for him," she told eager Chuck. Although that wasn't really the truth, was it? She was always waiting for him. She had been waiting for him since that night in Parker, when the Tarot had told her –

"Come have a beer with me, then," Chuck suggested gamely. "I won't bite you. I'm sure your boyfriend won't mind."

Damned right, you won't bite me, Nadine thought with another flare of anger. But since Chuck didn't look like he was going to leave her to the imaginary dangers of the night, and since there was no fictional boyfriend coming, she said, "Ok, but just one."

Chuck said nothing about a car, so they walked across the grounds and settled on the first bar they came to, immediately off-campus. It was dim and beery-smelling inside, a little run-down, just another college dive.

But the moment Nadine walked in, she smiled, and an involuntary shiver enveloped her, shook her from the ends of her hair to the tips of her toes. Chuck's choice of watering holes featured a bartender with blue eyes. Nadine had found Ian at last.

FORTY-EIGHT

Nadine stood patiently at the bar, with Chuck beside her, waiting for Ian to look in her direction. At last he did, and a smile bloomed across his face. "Well, hot damn!" Ian put both palms flat on the bar and vaulted over it, then enveloped Nadine in a big bear hug. Her knees went weak at the unanticipated surprise, the glory of it. Ian had never hugged her before. She had never been close enough to smell him; in the past, he would've probably smelled like river water anyway. But he smelled great now; Nadine felt immediately, completely intoxicated.

Over Ian's shoulder, Chuck frowned and said, "Is this him?"

Nadine, eagerly, gleefully hugging Ian back, nodded and said, "I'm afraid so." It was just a small lie, a fib of timing. The next time she and Ian saw Chuck, Ian *would* be her boyfriend. The cards didn't lie.

Chuck's frown deepened for a moment. "Well, I guess I'll be seeing you then." He looked around the bar, hailed some of his friends, and walked away.

Ian was smiling at her, and it was as if Chuck had never existed. "It's so great to see you, Nadine!" Then his smile faltered a little bit. "I was sorry to hear about you and Rob."

Nadine shrugged. "These things happen. It wasn't meant to be." She couldn't help but grin. Ian was right there in front of her, smiling at her, after so long. "I like being single again."

Ian walked back around the bar, and tapped two beers for a couple of frat boys that signaled him. He took their money, then said to Nadine, "I'm glad to hear that."

Nadine's heart leapt; he was glad to hear that she was single! *Let it work,* she thought. "So what time do you get off, Ian?" *My darling, my one and only!* "We need to catch up."

"My shift ends at ten." Nadine watched Ian's eyes slide over to a table full of girls in the corner. One of them waved and he reluctantly waved back. "I've got some stuff to do tonight . . ." His blue eyes snapped back to Nadine. "But, yeah . . . We have to get together. Catch up."

An atomic inspiration exploded in Nadine's mind, climbing up through her cortex like a mushroom cloud. "I'm having a Hallowe'en party at my house. The Sabbat falls. . ." Nadine lowered her eyes self-consciously and then began again. "Hallowe'en falls on a Friday this year, so we get to have the party on the actual day." Ian didn't seem impressed with this fact, so Nadine added, "It's always more fun to have a Hallowe'en party on the actual day, don't you think?"

"Of course," he agreed, mostly for something to say. A party was a party, whatever day it was held –

"It's a costume party . . ."

"Of course," Ian repeated. Now he saw her point. A Hallowe'en costume party should be held on Hallowe'en.

Nadine crossed her fingers and her toes and said the fateful words, fraught with more meaning, more destiny, than Ian could ever know. "Would you like to come? My aunts live in a little house at the top of the hill, next-door to my house, and I'm sure we could get away for a moment there . . . to catch up."

If Ian read anything into Nadine's thinly veiled proposition to *catch up*, it didn't show on his face. His tone was only that of someone seeing an old friend for the first time in months. "That sounds like a lot of fun, Nadine. I'd love to come."

Nadine felt as though she would stop breathing; but she realized that she had to set the hook. She tilted her head and asked coyly, "You're not just saying that are you? It's not going to be a very big deal, because most of the people I know are going out of town . . . Just a little costume party. So it would really mean a lot to me if you showed up."

"My calendar is empty for Hallowe'en. I promise, Nadine. I'll be there."

Nadine watched him look at the table full of girls again; she went out on a limb. "Are you . . . seeing anyone right now, Ian?"

Ian looked back at her in mild surprise. "No. I'm single, too, right now, like you. All alone in the big, cold world."

Nadine said quickly, "So you'll come to the party . . . alone, then? So we can get a chance to . . . catch up?"

By his expression, Ian again failed to grasp the subtle come-on inherent in Nadine's words. He blinked guilelessly at her. "Sure. I'll come stag, if that's what you want."

Oh, Ian, you cannot imagine what it is I want, Nadine thought. *But I aim to show you.*

"Yes, it's been too long. I'd like to have you all to myself for once." Nadine dared to wink at him.

She found a pen and a scrap of paper in her purse, and like that trio of girls of whom Rob had told tale, she wrote down her phone number and her address. As an afterthought, she also wrote down her name. She was not unaware of Ian's attractiveness; she knew he probably received scores of phone numbers, each and every night.

Nadine handed the piece of paper to the Blue-eyed Bartender. Ian stuck it into his shirt pocket. He said, "I'll be there."

"Promise?" Nadine said with a generous helping of faux hope, designed to disguise the real hope that she felt.

"Promise," he repeated. "Scout's honor." Ian made the Boy Scout hand gesture, and smiled at her again. "It's really great to see you again, Nadine. But these people are thirsty." Ian nodded behind her.

Nadine looked over her shoulder to see a group of patrons frowning at her, unimpressed with her and Ian's joyful reunion. They wanted to drink, hopeful new beginnings be damned.

"Oh!" She stepped out of their way, so they could give Ian their drink orders. "Call me any time, Ian! I'm looking forward to talking to you again!"

Ian nodded at the first guy standing in front of him, and went to tap him a beer. "I'll be sure to do that, Nadine. Sorry I'm so busy right now. I'll talk to you soon."

Nadine thought that she would like to sit at the bar, or at a little table in the corner, and just watch Ian all night. It seemed like it had been forever since she'd seen him, and she wanted to just look at him again. But she couldn't do that. He would notice her rapt attention and perhaps wonder at it. She'd approached him as an old friend and didn't want to get caught making goo-goo eyes at him, like the group of girls sitting across the room. There would be time enough to reveal her true feelings for him, once she got him alone. At her Hallowe'en party.

Now all she had to do was go home and talk Daina into throwing a Hallowe'en party.

FORTY-NINE

But Daina didn't need any convincing. She was thrilled with the idea. "I've lived like a nun all summer," she told Nadine. "What better night to cut loose than the Sabbat?"

"Maybe we'll become Wiccans," Nadine replied and the two of them dissolved into gales of laughter.

The Friday before Hallowe'en, Nadine decided that she wanted to drop into Ian's bar, just to remind him about the party. She hadn't gone back there in the interim, had not called him, nor had he called her. Nadine was patient. The hook was set, all she would have to do was reel in her prize on All Hallow's Eve.

Nadine asked Daina if she wanted to go to the bar with her. Daina shook her head.

"Ah, come on, Daina, come with me," Nadine requested evenly. Patiently. "You'll like it. It's . . . quaint. Maybe you'll find a new man."

Daina smiled. "You're the one that's looking for a replacement –"

"I've already found him," Nadine corrected, in that same even tone. "I just thought that maybe you might like to find one also –"

"Oh, yeah, that's right. You're afraid to jinx it, so you haven't given me a name or a description . . . What did *they* say about him?" Daina asked pointedly.

Nadine shrugged, noncommittal, and did not answer. *"Reply hazy, try again,"* Daina said and smiled. Nadine smiled back. "You don't care what they say, this time, do you?"

"I always care what they say," Nadine said in surprise. "They're . . . *They know –"*

"You don't have to listen to them, you know. You don't have to *believe.* I've been telling you that since we were kids."

"It is decidedly so," Nadine replied. "But I do believe. And so do you. I'm not buying any post-adolescent rebellion on your part against their influence."

"But they're not picking my men for me, either."

"They're not picking my men for me."

"You've picked your own, this time." It was a statement.

"Don't you always pick your own?" Daina nodded, so Nadine said, "Why not come and see if you'd like to pick one from the bar? It's a nice enough crowd. Then you'll have one all lined up for the party."

"Maybe I'll meet one *at* the party."

Contrary to what Nadine had told Ian, this Hallowe'en party promised to swing like a pendulum do. They had invited everyone they knew, and nearly everyone had said that they'd be there. Penny and Bellona had even signed on with gusto, promising to dress up, tell fortunes, and make their special punch.

"It's an aphrodisiac," Aunt Bellona confided. "Its influence helped convince your father to propose to your mother," she told Daina with a giggle.

Penny shook her head. "*Very doubtful,* Daina. Your father needed no paltry potion to propose."

Nadine grinned at her aunt's alliteration. "*No eye of newt and toe of frog, wool of bat and tongue of dog?*"

Penny shook her head again. "Daina's father loved Denise from the moment he saw her."

"Oh, Denise, my little Deino, how I miss her sometimes!" Bellona said softly.

After a moment, Daina stated, *"You may rely on it* – I'm not so sure about this love at first sight business. It's never happened to me. Unless he's a movie star."

Penny, Bellona, and Nadine looked at her as if she had stated flatly that she didn't believe in evolution, or gravity. "Yet, *it is decidedly so* – it comes when it comes," Penny said.

"In the best of worlds," Bellona said sadly. "For some, it never comes."

It's already arrived for me, Nadine thought and smiled to herself.

FIFTY

As Nadine drove downtown toward campus, toward the bar where Ian worked, she recalled Daina's words. "What did *they* say about him?"

Neither Penny nor Bellona had offered any opinion about Ian; that was because Nadine had not mentioned him to her aunts. She had not purloined a piece of his property for Penny to read, nor showed Aunt Bellona his picture so she could study it. Nadine felt a little guilty about the omission; she was failing to utilize her aunts' vast knowledge and ability for augury. But Nadine figured that she was a big girl, and she could read her own Tarot. She had witnessed the great forces at work already, moving to bring her and Ian together. She didn't feel as though she needed her aunts' advice this time, didn't feel as though she needed them *to pick a man for her*. Not anymore.

And in the back of her mind, a little impish thought whispered, *I don't want them to say me nay, to ruin it for me. I don't want them to know about Ian. Not yet. The cards were enough. The cards never lie. Ian and I are soulmates; we are destined to be together.*

But Nadine's soulmate was not tending bar on that Friday night. She wondered where he was and with whom, but she didn't lament. All the girls that had been with Ian would soon have to hold their memories of him dear, because memories of him were all that they would ever again possess – all the memories he would be making in the future would be with her. Nadine smiled at that thought and drove back home.

FIFTY-ONE

Ian didn't call to say that he'd be at the party during the final week, but Nadine was too busy to fret about it. She was in a fever of indecision again, unable to decide on a costume, one that was sure to dazzle him. The imp in her mind suggested that she could dress as a mermaid for him, but another logical part of her brain demurred, pointing out that mermaids inhabited the ocean. She'd heard Ian say once that he didn't have a whole lot of use for the ocean, because he didn't know how to ski on it.

Daina had no trouble at all coming up with a costume. She went to the library and looked up stills from *The Manchurian Candidate;* the part where Jocelyn Jordan wears the Queen of Diamonds costume. Daina made some grainy Xerox copies, then spent the afternoon in conference with the lady from the fabric store. Before long, Daina had created her own handmade Queen of Diamonds costume. It was really just a pair of red tights and a red leotard with a giant Queen of Diamonds playing card, made out of felt cutouts, pinned to it; there was a red cape with gold fringe. Daina looked both adorable and sexy in it.

By Tuesday, Nadine was frantic again. She turned to her aunts for help.

"You could be Lady Macbeth," Penny suggested. "A scarlet gown . . ."

Nadine shook her head. She thought that Ian would appreciate the choice, after she told him who she was, but she didn't want to spend the entire party explaining to everyone the character that her costume represented.

"How about Charlie Chaplin?" Bellona said brightly. "I think I have a hat and a cane around here somewhere."

Again Nadine shook her head. Daina's costume was cute, but it was also sexy, showing off her good legs and her nice shape. Nadine didn't want to appear in baggy men's clothes as the Little Tramp. She knew she would be cute, but also a little frumpy. She remembered beautiful, traitorous Marta; she didn't think Ian would care for frumpy.

"I know!" Bellona enthused. "You could be Pocahontas! Penny, do we still have that frightful buckskin blanket thing – the one that cowboy gave to you once upon a time? We could cut it up – it's got all kinds of fringe on it, Nadine! You could be a cute little Indian girl!"

This idea sounded great to Nadine, and while Daina was putting the finishing touches on her Queen of Diamonds get-up on Friday afternoon, Penny and Bellona were also putting the last leather stitching onto Nadine's adorable, mini-skirted, fringed, tight-fitting Pocahontas costume. She consulted the mirror, and with a young woman's vanity, she saw that she was just as cute as Daina, but a whole lot sexier. She would be irresistible to Ian.

FIFTY-TWO

Eight-thirty arrived. Nadine had not heard from Ian, and now she let despondency reign over her. She sat on her bed, resplendent in her Indian maiden costume, and watched as Daina applied her make-up.

What if he didn't show up as he'd promised? Nadine's evening would be ruined. The party would mean nothing to her. She'd only wanted to throw it so she could see Ian, tell him of their destiny. If he didn't show up tonight . . . Nadine went so far as to blaspheme in her mind: maybe the cards were wrong this time.

"Do you still have that Cherry-Wine lipstick?" Daina asked. "I think it would go perfectly with all these reds."

"Look in the nightstand drawer." Nadine sighed and gestured listlessly beside the bed.

Daina started pawing through the drawer, making clacking noises as she set the contents on top of the nightstand, searching for the lipstick: other cosmetics, an empty perfume bottle, a broken pair of sunglasses, a scratched 45 of *Ode to Billy Joe*. Then suddenly all was silence, and Nadine looked in her direction.

Daina was holding Ian's picture between both thumbs and forefingers. She looked at her friend with an expression of stunned amazement. *"Who is this?"* she demanded, awestruck.

Mixed emotions funneled through Nadine: smug pride, worry again that he wouldn't show up, and some small trepidation that Daina was expressing such naked interest. Smug pride won out. *"That* is Will and Rob's cousin. Ian."

"This is Cousin Ian?" Daina heard Will's voice in her mind. *Cousin Ian gets more ass than a toilet seat. Why would you let your girlfriend go out with him all alone?* She eyed Nadine with interest. "This is the guy that you went skiing with all summer?"

"With Rob, too," Nadine said defensively. She didn't want her friend to know that she had coveted Ian from the moment she'd met him. When she eventually wound up with him, it would therefore just seem like kismet. Fate. Which it was. Not the result of summer-long machinations on her part . . .

"How did you fail to describe *this guy* to me?" Daina studied the picture again, ran her finger over it in much the same way that Nadine frequently did. "Hot damn, 'Deen!" she said in a perfect imitation of Rob, so that it came out *hod day-um.* "Cousin Ian is fine!"

Nadine ignored the little imp in her mind that was suddenly quite alarmed at Daina's appreciation for Ian, instead concentrating again on the self-satisfaction that came from the fact that she knew him, they were friends, he was her soulmate; and Daina had never *even seen him.* "He's supposed to be here tonight."

Daina spied the Cherry-Wine lipstick for which she had searched. She set Ian's picture down on top of the flotsam on the nightstand and grabbed the tube out of the drawer. She turned and looked at herself in the mirror again and told Nadine, "Well, you be sure to let me know when he arrives. He looks like just the kind of king that this queen could use."

He's destined to be my *king,* Nadine said to herself. Then she thought glumly, *If he shows up.*

Lipstick applied, Daina turned and grinned at her friend. "Shall we do this thing?"

FIFTY-THREE

At eight-forty-five, Daina and Nadine's front door stood open to the night, and vampires and ghosts, clowns and pirates milled around, beers in hand, in the front yard, the living room, the kitchen. Daina was off somewhere giving a tour of the house, and Nadine sat on the couch, ignoring everyone, grimly concentrating on peeling the label off of the beer she wasn't drinking, just as she'd watched Ian do a million years before at that restaurant in Elsinore. She was unaware that he had arrived until she heard his deep, silky voice, almost directly in front of her.

"Veni, vidi, vici," he said to a girl dressed as a hobo. "At least the beer, anyway." The girl pointed towards the kitchen; Ian said thanks, and crossed the living room without noticing the Indian maiden seated on the couch.

Speechless, Nadine watched him walk by. He was costumed as a gladiator, and Nadine thought he pulled it off faultlessly; he had just the broad-shouldered, stocky build for it. There were the sandals – studded strips of black leather that covered the front of his legs from the ankles to the knees, held in place by broad bands encircling his feet and solid calves. Just the shoes were almost enough for Nadine. But there was so much more. There was the leather skirt, also black, which fell to just above his sturdy knees; some kind of brilliantly white, pleated under-contrivance peeked out between the strips of leather. This was surmounted by a wide leather belt, almost like a cummerbund, bristling with small buckles and straps. Ian also wore black leather wristlets.

Leather, leather, everywhere, Nadine thought, paraphrasing Coleridge. *I am Spartacus!* But Ian, athletic, probably half of Kirk Douglass's age, put him in the shade. *Hod day-um!* Nadine said to herself in surprise and delight. *Cousin Ian is fine!* She arose and followed him to the kitchen.

Ian also wore some manner of claret-colored toga-cape affair, held in place at his right shoulder by a large golden clasp. The material fell down his back; in front, it covered his left shoulder and his chest, but only partially, essentially leaving nothing of what was underneath to the imagination. For some seconds, Nadine entertained the idea of running her fingers beneath the red garment, across his collarbone, down his arm . . . She suddenly hoped that no one was observing her studying him; she felt the heat of a blush rise on her face.

It wasn't that Ian's costume was immodest in any way. *His modesty is legendary,* she recalled. It was just that he looked *so good* in it, that a girl just couldn't help wanting to divest him of it immediately. Except maybe for those shoes. *Yes,* Nadine said to herself, *he can definitely leave those shoes on.* A branch of plastic laurel leaves mingled with his shaggy hair.

He was breathtaking, and it took Nadine a moment to find her voice. At last, she was able to compose herself and touch his bare shoulder. "I'm so glad you could come!"

He turned. "I told you I'd be here," he replied with a smile.

Nadine didn't hesitate. The time was at last nigh to tell him everything. *Boldness be my friend! Arm me, audacity, from head to foot!* But not here with all these people around. She grabbed his hand and tugged him toward the door. "Come on, Ian. Take a walk with me. We need to talk."

"But I just got here," he protested. "I haven't even got this beer opened yet."

Nadine snatched the beer from him and set it back on the table. "We'll drink later. Come on. Take a walk with me."

Ian allowed himself to be dragged out the front door, across the yard, and through the little gate, out into the narrow street that ran in front of the house. After a moment, Nadine felt a trifle forward holding his hand and let it go. She still walked very close to him, however, as they strolled up the street.

They passed the detached garage to her house; a wooded hill rose beside and behind it. Nadine pointed across the street. "That's my mom and dad's house," she told Ian. The street ended there in a cul-de-sac. Behind the pavement, another hill and more trees curved around to meet the ones that went back toward Nadine and Daina's house.

Nadine had a plan as to where she wanted to take her beloved. She turned to her right and led Ian onto a fairly wide path that curved uphill through the woods. By following this path, eventually they would come to her aunts' house. There she could be alone with him and tell him of their mingled fates.

The path should've been dark, but her aunts had caused it to be hung with electric lights, at least until they reached the summit of the hill. There the path turned to the right again, and after a few feet was lost in the darkness. Even though it was late fall, it was California, and the trees still kept their leaves; the half-moon's light didn't penetrate to the ground. The house was a hundred yards or so through the trees.

"Let's play hide and seek, Ian!" Nadine cried in almost hysterical glee. She couldn't believe that he was really there, looking like a god. It was just the two of them, all alone in the friendly woods on the Sabbat. She skipped ahead of him into the shadows.

"Wait, Nadine! Where are we going?"

Ahead of him, no longer visible, she called back to him. "To my aunts' house. The path goes by there, then back down the hill. It comes out behind my garage. Come on, Ian! Catch me!"

"Wait, Nadine!" he called again with a trace of irritation. This wasn't how he'd planned to spend the evening, chasing Rob's ex-girlfriend through the trees. He slapped a mosquito that had landed on his arm. "I don't want to get lost in the woods, like Hansel and Gretel," he said. "I'm fresh out of breadcrumbs."

There was no reply. The forest was silent. Nadine had frolicked on ahead. Ian sighed; he debated whether he should go back the way they'd come, or go on ahead after her. He figured that the shorter route would be to go forward; he speculated that he was probably about halfway back already, had he been at the bottom of the hill on the street. Ian sighed again, and began gingerly picking his way after Nadine along the dark path.

He stumbled on for a while in the blackness, blindly, not thinking too many kind thoughts about Nadine. He was unsure of her game, what it was *they needed to talk* about. He hoped that she didn't want him to play Cyrano to Rob for her; that ship had sailed.

Rob was already engaged to be engaged to Andrea, the girl that had spent the summer with him in Europe. She was pretty enough, Ian reckoned, but she was cast from the same mold as Marta. Ian felt that their wealth and sense of entitlement made their type pushy, bossy, and ill-mannered – and unless they'd taken up the cause of some downtrodden segment of society that their wealth would never permit them to understand – they were always shallow. *So shallow.*

Although he was more or less from the same social strata as they were, unlike his cousins, Ian didn't care too much for girls of his own kind. His dad wasn't a surgeon, and he wouldn't have bankrolled a boat like the *Ooh-La-La* for Ian, but he would've sent his son to Europe, if he'd asked to go. But after Marta, Ian vowed to himself that he'd never yoke himself to such a girl again, not for all the sleek wooden boats on the *Mare Nostrum*.

Ian had pointed out Andrea's unfortunate characteristics to his cousin, but Rob had just shrugged. Andrea's daddy was the head of some prestigious unit at some expensive hospital, and Rob's alliance with his baby girl could only benefit young Doctor Wilde in the future. Ian, ambitionless, couldn't see how putting up with a bitchy girlfriend now could possibly be worth it at some later time. But Rob was a big boy; he'd put the ring through his own nose, quite voluntarily.

Regardless of Ian's opinion of his cousin's dating practices, the undeniable result was this: Rob wouldn't be reconsidering a reunion with Nadine, and Ian hoped that wasn't what she wanted to discuss with him.

Maybe Nadine was flirting with him, but Ian doubted it. She had never seemed in the least bit impressed with him; she'd always displayed nothing but polite friendliness to him in the past. But she was single again, and Ian knew all about a woman's prerogative. However, if this was how Nadine showed that she had all of a sudden grown an interest, Ian considered it to be a stupid way of letting him in on it.

Ian hoped that a sudden interest in him wasn't what she wanted to talk about, either. He was sure that Nadine was probably a nice girl, certainly nicer than Marta or Andrea, but the idea of dating one of his cousin's cast-offs didn't appeal to him. Had there been something extra special about her – had she been exceptionally beautiful, or if she could ski – he might've tended toward more curiosity about her. But between this adolescent forest foray and the fact that, because of her history with his cousin, she was only marginally attractive to him – Ian was more annoyed than eager. He reflected that he wouldn't turn her down if she suddenly jumped out from behind a tree and dragged him into the bushes; but on the other hand, if he made it back to her house without falling and breaking his neck, he would definitely not be talking her up.

Through the trees, he perceived a dark structure silhouetted in the moonlight. A light suddenly blazed, unexpectedly, making Ian blink. It revealed a clearing in sharp relief and an odd little two story wooden house, painted a dark, brick-red, and o'ertopped with a deck.

From the deck, two figures – middle-aged, Ian could see – peered out into the darkness, into the trees, in his direction. One was dressed as the wicked witch, the stereotype, with pointy hat and high-collared, flowing black habit. The other was all babushkas and colorful skirts, hooped earrings and tinkling necklaces. She was the picture of a gypsy fortuneteller.

Ian paused, allowing his eyes to adjust to the sudden brightness. He knew that it was impossible for them to see him; he was still in the shadows. Yet it seemed as though they looked directly at him, as if they'd turned the lights on especially for him.

The witch grinned and said clearly to the fortuneteller, *"By the pricking of my thumbs, something wicked this way comes."*

The fortuneteller opened her mouth to speak, but the temptation was too great for Ian. He stepped out into the light in order to beat her to it. *"Open, locks, whoever knocks!"* The women smiled, first at each other, then at him. Encouraged, he crossed the narrow clearing and stood at the bottom of the staircase, looking up at them. *"How now, you secret, black, and midnight hags! What is't you do?"*

In character, the witch chortled. *"A deed without a name."*

"Join us, Roman." The fortuneteller gestured for him to climb the stairs.

When Ian hesitated, the witch suggested, "Trick or treat."

"I thought I was supposed to say that to you," Ian replied with a sly smile. Women were women, young or old. His charm was always the same.

The witch put her elbows on the railing and leaned over it a little farther, as if to get a better look at him. She put her chin on her fingertips. "Which would you prefer?"

Ian wiggled his eyebrows. "I guess that depends . . ."

"Come on up," the fortuneteller said. "I'll read your palm."

"Tell your future," the witch added, then said, "Trick or treat," again.

Still Ian hesitated. Sure, he'd like to hang out with these old gals, hear about his future, but there was a whole party full of women his own age at the end of the dark path; maybe even Nadine. "Did you ladies see a girl come through here?"

"There are two girls for you tonight, Roman," the fortuneteller told him. "Come up and we'll tell you all about them."

Now Ian's eyebrows went up in surprise. *"Had I three ears, I'd hear thee."*

Two girls. There was an intriguing idea; it would certainly make up for wandering around in the dark for the last twenty-five minutes. Ian started to climb the stairs. He could spare a few moments to hear about such a thing. It was usually a difficult task to talk two of them into it, requiring all his powers of persuasion; however, he hadn't been entirely unsuccessful in the past. If they were close friends, sometimes they'd surprise him and acquiesce with hardly any qualms at all.

Ian was shocked at the direction his thoughts had taken; he didn't know why he thought that these two mysterious women knew wherein they spoke about two girls for him – he should've been embarrassed at the very suggestion, coming from two little old ladies. But it was Hallowe'en, and they said they'd tell him about his future. If it was to be as wild as his past . . . Or, maybe two girls *at the same time* wasn't what they'd meant at all. But if it was, a little blush wouldn't hurt this witch and this fortuneteller. Ian was sure of it.

He hopped up the last step onto the deck and looked at them expectantly.

The fortuneteller studied him appraisingly for a moment. "Mercy," she said, then looked over at the witch. "I haven't seen such a healthy gladiator since Caesar was an aedile . . ." Ian blinked, not understanding, and she said, "Here, Roman, sit. We'll unfold all for you."

She indicated a bench which overlooked the dark forest, built into a corner of the deck. In front of it was a wooden table and two chairs. Atop the table, the occult ambiance was completed by an iron cauldron suspended from a tripod, over a can of Sterno. While Ian watched, the witch threw something into it; there was a sizzle.

"Scale of dragon?" he asked. *"Tooth of wolf?"*

The witch blinked at him expressionlessly, ignoring his attempt at humor. "It's hot cider, actually. Would you like some?"

The fortuneteller used a ladle and dipped a portion of the tan, frothy liquid into a wooden cup, offered it to him. Ian looked at it, hesitated. The fortuneteller narrowed her eyes and tossed half of it off in a single swig. "We're not going to poison you, Roman."

Ian smiled and sat down on the bench. "I would very much like some, then."

The fortuneteller refilled the cup and gave it to him, taking the opportunity to touch his wrist briefly with her other hand. Both ladies watched him raise the cup to his mouth; their interest made Ian pause for another heartbeat. Then he shrugged. It wasn't the first time that two women had tried to get him drunk, although these were a tad bit older than he was used to. He downed the cider. It was warm and spicy and cinnamony, and blazed an agreeable path to his belly. He set the cup on the table and the fortuneteller immediately refilled it. "Thanks," he told her.

"It is entirely my pleasure," she assured him with a girlish giggle, and sat down in one of the chairs opposite him.

"Tell me about these girls," Ian requested. He was enjoying the carnival atmosphere, suddenly pregnant with possibilities: a witch and a fortuneteller, here at his disposal, to reveal the future to him, something about two girls. He wondered if they'd been hired to work the party, and would tell anyone's fortune, if they wandered up the hill. Ian doubted it. The path through the woods hadn't been easy to follow; he still didn't know exactly how to get back to Nadine's house. So it wasn't likely that anyone would just wander up here from down there on their own.

Ian realized that he might've stumbled around in the trees for some time had these ladies not turned on the floodlights at just the right moment. It was as if they'd known he was out there, and had wanted to welcome him. He had no trouble convincing himself that they were just what they appeared to be – a witch and a fortuneteller, placed there by fate for his benefit, to tell him the events which impended in his life . . . Perhaps two girls at once. It was a pleasing concept to him; suspension of disbelief was easy for Ian.

The fortuneteller held out her hand, and he held out his. She grasped his hand firmly, and turned it over; her thumb pressed lightly into his palm. Then she laid his hand gently on the table; she place two fingers on his wrist, as if feeling for his pulse. With her other hand, she ran her thumb slowly, sinuously acrost wrist, then palm, then up his index finger.

To his surprise, Ian suppressed a shiver. As the fortuneteller went to trace his palm again, the witch slapped her hand. "Stop touching him, Bellona. You're just being theatrical. You don't need to actually read his palm."

The fortuneteller pouted at Ian for a moment, and he smiled guilelessly back at her and withdrew his hand. The witch sat down in the other chair and said, "You stand at a crossroads tonight, young man."

"Miss Bellona mentioned something about two girls?" Miss Bellona's light-blue eyes sparkled in delight, that the stunning Roman had caught her name. He paused, then said, "Greetings and salutations, ladies." He held his hand out again. "My name is –"

"We know your name, Ian Wilde," Penny declared. Bellona went to shake Ian's hand – another opportunity to touch him – and

Penny slapped it away again. She took it in hers instead; Ian noted that her grasp was as firm as steel, vise-like.

When she released it, Ian's own dark-blue eyes matched Bellona's sparkle. Nadine must have mentioned that he would be at the party, described him to them; how else could they know his name? But it was enjoyable to think that the knowledge had come to them by other, more supernatural means.

Ian had always wanted to believe that there were forces beyond his ken, but he'd never quite been able to talk himself into it. A man had walked on the moon scant months ago; the shadowy, archaic ideas of spirits and demons and magic just couldn't stand up to the brilliant daylight of humanity's latest achievements.

"And you are?" Ian asked politely.

"Not schooled in a classical tongue, you would have difficulty pronouncing my name," the witch said imperiously. "So –"

"So you can just call her Penny," Bellona said.

"All right." Ian winked at her. "Now that we've all been properly introduced, tell me about these two girls, Miss Penny. Are they strangers – will I meet them separately? Or will they be known to each other, like Helen, of the *face that launch'd a thousand ships,* and Cassandra, cursed by Apollo to be able to see the future but never to be believed?"

"They are like sisters," Penny confirmed. "One has heard a prophecy and strives to ignore it. The other has read her own prophecy, and in fevered reveries eagerly awaits its . . . *fulfillment.* Which future unfolds depends solely upon you."

Ian's eyebrows went up. "Perhaps I could make their dreams come true for both of them," he said playfully.

"Perhaps," Bellona agreed. "If you asked nicely . . ."

"No!" Penny said, and slammed her fist on the table. The can of Sterno jumped. She softened a little. "You mustn't be greedy, my sweet young friend. You must choose between them."

"But –"

"Have you heard that little tune by those delightful young men from New York City? *Did You Ever Have to Make Up Your Mind?*" Bellona burst into song: *"Did you ever have to finally decide? And say yes to one and let the other one ride?"*

Ian supplied another stanza: *"It's not often easy and not often kind. Did you ever have to make up your mind?"* He grinned. "I wouldn't have thought that would be the kind of music that you ladies –"

167

"What are you saying, Roman?" Bellona asked haughtily. "Are you saying that you think we're not hep? Why, it doesn't pay in this world to let time pass you by. One grows old along that path. All the decades –"

"Bellona has a little transistor radio," Penny told him with a trace of condescension aimed at her sister. "She's very fond of modern music."

"Allow me to fetch it!" In a flurry of multi-colored skirts, Bellona flew into the house, and returned a moment later with a white plastic radio. She turned it on, extended the antenna. She fiddled around with the dial, and after a moment of static, *Undun* blared out. Bellona allowed it to proceed at full volume for a moment: *It's too late, she's gone too far, she's lost the sun, she's come undun.* Penny stared at her until she reluctantly turned it down to a whisper.

Ian sipped his cider, smiled at them over the rim of his cup. "The girls?" He set his cup down and Bellona refilled it. She found another cup behind the cauldron, and filled it for herself. She dipped the ladle in again, paused and looked at her sister questioningly. Penny nodded. "I have to get more mugs, then." Bellona dropped the ladle into the cauldron and went into the house.

"Economics first, *Paegniarius.*" Penny smiled, a trifle mockingly; Ian's Latin was rusty, but he was pretty sure that he'd just been insulted. "One of the young women in question can be termed independently wealthy, although not affluent. Her funds are held in trust; she is propertied. She has never stopped to consider these monetary truths, and thereby, she's never learned to be extravagant. She only knows that all the bills are paid, and thinks no more about it."

"I've never been much for rich girls," Ian said archly. He found it an amusing coincidence that he had been thinking about rich girls only moments before. "They always seem to believe that their money makes up for a certain lack of character."

Penny made no reply.

"The other," Bellona said, returning with three mugs – Ian didn't fail to notice – apparently other guests were expected, maybe even these girls of whom they spoke. "The other comes from a family that is not nearly as old as the first's, and thereby, their savings are modest. They are still comfortable, but she will have to earn a living someday. And you'll have to work to help support her."

"Support her?" Ian sputtered. "I haven't even met her yet! I'm not really in the market to be *supporting* anyone at the moment, Miss Bellona."

"Not even yourself," Penny observed drily.

But Ian wouldn't be baited. He grinned and said, "I'm still in school. As long as I'm in school, my dad said that he would –"

"But school has to end sometime," Penny replied. "And then what will you do?"

Now Ian looked down at the table sheepishly. "I don't know . . ." Then he smiled again, irrepressible as always. "Whatever it takes, I guess."

"A sound plan," Penny returned expressionlessly.

"I'll be sure to break it to the poor girl, before she expects my *support,"* he retorted.

Bellona waved her hand impatiently. "Your heart isn't for sale, *Rudiarius,* that's evident." Ian didn't know this term either, but somehow he liked it better than whatever Penny had called him. *"A book of verses underneath the bough, a jug of wine, a loaf of bread – and thou . . ."*

"All I need!" Ian agreed.

"The worldly hope men set their hearts upon turns ashes – or it prospers . . ." Penny suggested.

"Where is thy conscience now?" Ian countered. *"In the Duke of Gloucester's purse."*

"Enough!" Bellona cried. "He won't be bought!" She smiled fondly at Ian. "No more talk of rich girls and poor girls."

"Tell me of their beauty, then, Miss Bellona. Are they, like Hero, *too low for a high praise, too brown for a fair praise and too little for a great praise?"*

Ian glanced into his cup, again nearly empty. He didn't feel drunk, precisely; but the potion was definitely having an effect on him. Instead of a happy befuddling of his senses, a sloppy slowing of motor function, he felt focused, ebullient, alive. The moon was bright, the air was clean; his mood had improved exponentially since meeting his companions.

His deep wellspring of verse, rhyme, poetry, bubbled. He reflected for a moment on his father, from whom his appreciation for literature had come. His father loved him and was proud of him, despite his lack of ambition, because since boyhood, Ian had devoured the flowering of the English language, and then had effortlessly recited it back to his dad.

In this, he had found a kindred spirit in Rob, and the cousins had spent many a late night constructing conversations from old prose and poetry, just as the witch and the fortuneteller were doing with him now. First as boys, and then when, for whatever reason, they were stag in the world; Ian had never enjoyed such a cerebral pastime with any women, at least not for more than a few minutes.

Fellow female English Lit majors had always talked themselves into an illusion of romance almost immediately. It only took a comparison to a summer's day or mention of the nightingale's complaint, issued in Ian's deep, lyrical voice, and his peers forgot that they already knew these lines by heart. And with little additional effort, they convinced themselves that Ian spoke the charmed words only to them. It was a cakewalk to him.

Whereas, *Would you care to come back to my place to discuss complex inter-related cultural and political trends and then fuck?* would've gotten him slapped – although he'd seen that exact line work for Will once – Ian knew that a whispered, *My love is like a red, red rose, that's newly sprung in June* rarely failed, even, *especially,* with modest English Lit majors who should've known better.

But the witch and the fortuneteller were far too . . . *mature* to believe that Ian had been moved by timeless verse to express a sudden passion for them. It was an intellectual exercise with Penny and Bellona, as it had been with Rob. Yet still were they women, and Ian found it all the more refreshing, thereby, fun, and he mined his brain for further gems to throw out for their perusal.

"Plainness has its peculiar temptations quite as much as beauty," Penny said, one corner of her mouth quirking up. Despite her years, Ian saw that the witch was not nearly as immune to his charm as she would like him to think.

"Are these girls plain?"

"My reply is no." Bellona filled his cup again. "They are fair . . . Though not *the fairest of them all* – she passed on to her reward – what has it been now, Penny? Six years ago?"

"Seven," Penny said sadly.

"Here was a beauty!" Bellona declared. *"When comes such another?"* The two ladies sighed and shook their heads. Then Bellona said to Ian, "The girls of whom we speak are not as fair as Marilyn, but they are fair enough, *both alike in dignity,* intelligence, womanly wiles." She winked at him.

Penny rolled her eyes. "Besides, are you not surrounded by fair women, Roman?" She gestured around her, as if the trees might harbor a host of wood nymphs. "Do you not take your share?"

"For several virtues have I liked several women," Ian admitted.

"You've never delved past their looks. But I'm here to tell you that beauty is only a single, fleeting aspect of womanhood. One of these girls of whom I speak is your destiny; you will call her beloved long after her beauty has faded."

"Even when she is as we are," Bellona said. *"Grow old along with me, the best is yet to be."*

"Either of them will love you with her entire being," Penny concluded. "But by custom, you can have only one."

Ian shrugged, sipped his cider. *"I cannot be confined within the weak list of a country's fashion."*

Bellona grinned in delight. *"If it were so, it was a grievous fault, and grievously hath Caesar answer'd it."*

Penny, impatient, refused to be amused. "Mark me, boy. Before the dawning, you will know. Your life will be complete because of one of them."

Ian was enchanted with this fairy tale of eternal love and provident destiny, with him at its center. While he believed none of it, it was still effortless for him to pretend to himself that he did.

"But if only one of them appeals to me, yet I appeal to both of them . . . *Stronger than lover's love is lover's hate . . .*"

"Incurable, in each, the wounds they make." Bellona fetched a heavy sigh. "Yes. You *will* have to deal with that. *Thy fate is the common fate of all, into each life some rain must fall."*

Penny also sighed. *"Heav'n has no rage, like love to hatred turn'd."*

Ian was surprised and a little disconcerted at their sudden dolor. He tried to lift the mood again. "I guess it's a shame that there's not enough of me to go around, but like a modern poet says, *You can't always get what you wa-ant."* He grinned, reveling in his own arrogance. "I accept this path, ladies. *The motto of chivalry is also the motto of wisdom; to serve all, but love only one."*

Ian didn't believe this any more than he believed that his future had been divined, that it was even divinable. There were just *so many* girls. He'd always been amenable to *serving* them all, or at least the ones that appealed to him. But he was unable to imagine wanting only one to love, one that was not interchangeable with all the others.

There was a slap of a moccasined foot on the stair; the trio turned at the sound. Nadine appeared. She paused, expressionless, for a heartbeat. Then she grinned condescendingly. "What's a'matter, Ian? Are you afraid of the dark? Do you need to be protected from *ghoulies and ghosties and long-legged beasties, and things that go bump in the night?"*

Ian was a little surprised at her derision, so he ignored it. "Please allow me to introduce you to my new friends, Nadine. And what delightful young ladies they are."

Bellona tittered. "You flatter us, Roman. *Young ladies*, indeed." She reached across the table and squeezed his hand.

"If we did not flatter ourselves, the flattery from others would not harm us," Penny remarked drily.

Bellona removed her hand from Ian's, but smiled at the gladiator again. "Mark Twain said, *Age is an issue of mind over matter. If you don't mind, it doesn't matter."* Ian smiled back at her.

"We've met," Nadine said to Ian testily. "Perhaps I should introduce them to *you."* He noted a slight increase in volume, perhaps a little slur, in Nadine's voice. He reckoned that she might've downed a few shots of liquid courage back at the party before returning to fetch him. "This is Pemp – Pemphre –"

"Penny," Bellona supplied. "Easier for the intemperate tongue." She winked at Ian.

Nadine began again. "This is well-clad Penny, bright-coiffed, of the heights, the lost and returned." She put her hand on the witch's shoulder and Penny patted it. "And this is Bellona, saffron-robed, she who works from afar, the fire-eyed maid of maleficium."

"That's of *your* native tongue, Roman," Bellona said. "Latin. It means *mischief."*

Nonplussed, Ian said to Nadine, "Those are some epithets."

She sat beside him on the bench and leaned in close. She started off softly, then her voice rose stridently. "Jest not, Unbeliever. These before you are curse-bringers, spellcasters, necromancers –"

Bellona held her palm above the table, wiggled it in a *comme ci comme ça* gesture. "I've never really been much for necromancy, 'Deen. I find it to be depressing, and –" Penny glanced at her in mild amazement and Bellona fell silent.

"They know what is to come. *Cross them at your peril!"* Nadine whispered sternly, and Ian was sure of it: Nadine was drunk. She glanced at the witch and the fortuneteller, then her ferocity vanished as quickly as it had appeared. She smiled brightly. "So! Have my

172

aunts been revealing your destiny to you, on this All Hallow's Eve, in this Year of Our Lord, 1969?"

"Indeed they have, all about my sunny future. But I'm superstitious, 'Deen. I think that if I tell you what they've told me, then it'll never come true – the same reason why you don't tell what wish you make when you blow out your birthday candles."

"I would never ask you to reveal a prophecy," Nadine replied with as much gravity as she could muster. Then her smile broke free again, and Ian was surprised to detect affection peeping out at him, impishly, from behind her eyes. This happy demon was loosed, no doubt, by the alcohol, he'd wager, because if it had ever been there before, Rob's former flame had always kept it expertly hidden.

Ian speculated that if these ladies – these mysterious benefactors that had saved him from the darkness as if they'd already known that he was out there – were Nadine's aunts, then Nadine had to be one of the girls that they'd talked up to him. He saw that it was all an elaborate set up – Nadine had dragged him up here and abandoned him to her aunts' tender prophecies – then she'd returned on cue, to warn him that they were indeed what they seemed: uncanny and dangerous and prescient.

But who was the other girl? Ian realized that there probably wasn't one – mention of a second party had all been part of the con, so that it didn't seem entirely too obvious that these whimsical beldames were trying to fix him up with their niece. If the poor girl was fictional, he mused that Nadine must be the wealthy one – *propertied,* they had said. She lived in a nice house at the foot of the hill, her aunts at its summit, her parents across the street: Nadine no doubt stood to inherit it all.

Rob had always called her *his poor girl,* but that was only because she didn't go in for the sorority scene. Penny had said that she *had never learned to be extravagant,* nor had Ian ever saw Nadine display a *Daddy will buy me anything* attitude like Marta (with her fine, expensive boat). Maybe that's why Rob thought she was poor. Rob hadn't really known her long enough to delve into her finances, anyway, Ian decided.

Nadine had seemed devoted to Rob when they were dating; she had never so much as looked sideways at him before. But the fact that she'd cooked up this elaborate scenario – whatever her former opinion of him had been – it appeared that she was interested in him now.

Ian considered her, as if seeing her for the first time – he was only human, after all, and discovering that someone likes you tends to make you like them back a little bit – if for nothing else than their good taste. Nadine had lovely light-brown eyes – they matched her straight brown hair, which she wore parted down the middle, simply, as was the fashion. *Rob's type,* he thought. Ian didn't have a type; if he found a girl attractive, he was game, whatever her coloring.

But Rob was a one trick pony: Nadine and Andrea could've been sisters: they had the same hair color, worn in the same style. The same eyes, the same pretty, expressive mouth, although the elitist sneer that usually marred Andrea's was absent from Nadine's. Ian noticed that the Indian princess had beautiful, clear skin, and dimples – quite pretty was Nadine, now that Ian took a good look at her.

A man's voice whispered out of the plastic radio. "Now to sing this lovely ballad, here is . . . Mama Cass."

"Oh, I love this one!" Bellona said and turned it up. Cass Elliot's voice, clear and crisp, began: *Stars shining bright above you; night breezes seem to whisper 'I love you.' Birds singing in the sycamore tree. Dream a little dream of me . . .*

Inspired, Ian said, "Would you like to dance, Nadine?"

FIFTY-FOUR

After snatching Ian out of the house the moment he had arrived, then *leading him over hill, over dale, thorough bush, thorough brier, over park, over pale, thorough flood, thorough fire*, Nadine had run gaily down the hill that ended behind her garage. She'd changed her mind. She didn't want her aunts hovering around on the periphery while she told Ian of her love for him, so while still up on the hill, she'd abandoned the idea of taking him to their house.

Here, in the round, yellow pool of light from the goose-necked fixture above the side door to the garage – this place was secluded enough. And after she revealed all to him, and he smiled his acceptance of it, she would push him up against the rough wall of the garage, out of the light, and kiss him . . .

Breathlessly, Nadine turned around in anticipation. After a heartbeat, then two, she realized that Ian was not behind her. Indecision: should she go back up the trail after him, or should she wait for him to find his way down? She frowned, debating. It might seem a little pushy of her to go back, a little clingy; maybe even forward. She had waited all summer for this – *now that he's under my battlements, there's no reason to play my whole hand all at once.* No reason to rush it. She'd just wait right here for him.

Barely a moment passed before someone came out of the back door to the house and called her name. She turned, and saw Chuck Markis approaching across the narrow side yard. He was dressed as a cowboy, and he exclaimed, "Look! We match! Wanna play cowboys and Indians, Hiawatha?"

Nadine ignored *that* remark, and said tonelessly, "What a coincidence." She looked up the dark path again. Where was Ian?

Chuck followed her gaze and said, "It's seems that I'm always finding you all alone in the dark."

"It seems that you're always finding me while I'm waiting for my boyfriend," she replied, not unkindly. She was too happy to be unkind, not even to can't-seem-to-take-no-for-an-answer-Chuck.

Chuck glanced around, as he had that evening in the botanical gardens, as if the Blue-eyed Bartender (whom he believed to be her boyfriend) was going to suddenly appear out of the thin air. Seeing no one, Chuck asked, "Where is he this time?"

Nadine nodded up the dark path. "He was right behind me." The thought occurred to Nadine that, while it would be of no consequence to Chuck when Ian stepped out into the light to join her, it might seem a little odd to Ian to find her standing out here all alone in the darkness with Chuck. He might get the impression that she was interested in the always-eager blonde cowboy. He might assume that there was something going on between them.

That just wouldn't do. Nadine took Chuck's elbow and turned him back toward the house. "I'm sure he'll be along in a minute. He probably just stopped to use the biffy." When Ian came down the hill and back into the house – hell, Nadine would just take him into her room and tell him. That was the most private place of all.

"The biffy?" Chuck asked as they stepped into the kitchen and the light and the noise of the party.

"The *bathroom in the forest for you,*" Nadine supplied. "Didn't you ever go to summer camp?"

Chuck shook his head.

"Here, try this, 'Deen!" Steve Andre, a tall, skinny, redheaded hippie who was in Professor Wilde's class with her, shoved a paper cup into her hand. He picked another one off the kitchen table and handed it to Chuck.

"What is it?" Nadine asked doubtfully, sniffing it.

"It's fruit punch," Chuck said. "Steve's specialty." He grinned at Steve and Steve grinned back.

"A little lemonade, some orange juice. A packet of Hawaiian Fruit Punch. Fruit," Steve explained. He pointed to an enormous plastic bowl on the table, filled with what appeared to be a slightly red-tinged orange juice. Sliced lemons, oranges, maraschino cherries floated on the surface.

Nadine wondered who had found that bowl, and where. She'd purchased it when they'd first moved into the house, stuck it into a cabinet somewhere, and had forgotten all about it. She marveled how her party had taken on a life of its own, without her: Daina was nowhere in sight, so Steve must've scared up something in which to mix up his punch all on his own.

Nadine didn't know the girl in the hobo costume, the one that had pointed Ian to the beer earlier; she must've been a friend of Daina's. The beers that had lined the table before were gone, replaced by the punch, and now the hobo ladled out the concoction to a line of party-goers.

Steve gestured at Nadine with his own cup. "What d'ya think? It's an old family recipe."

They took hesitant sips. It tasted exactly like its ingredients led Nadine to expect it would: lemony, orangey, sweet.

"Not bad," Chuck said. Nadine nodded in agreement.

"Enjoy!" Steve said and waltzed out of the kitchen.

Nadine drained her cup – she was thirsty from running down the hill – and handed it to the hobo, who refilled it and gave it back to her with a little smile. She and Chuck made small talk; it couldn't have been for more than a few minutes, but it seemed interminable. It wouldn't seem suspicious to Ian if he saw her talking to Chuck here, inside the brightly lit house, with plenty of other people milling around them, laughing and talking, queuing up for Steve's punch, so she decided to further endure talking to him, while she waited for Ian's return.

Nadine was still thirsty; she drained her second cup while Chuck told some inane joke to Betty from her Women's Studies class. The punch was really quite tasty. Nadine kept glancing through the open back door into the darkness. Where was Ian? He had to come through this door, or else walk all the way around to the front of the house in the dark in order to enter that way.

Nadine handed her cup to the hobo again, said thanks when she refilled it. Nadine drank it all down in one long gulp. The hobo looked at her in surprise when she handed her cup back a fourth time.

"It's delicious," Nadine said by way of explanation. The girl shrugged and filled her cup again. Nadine noticed that the bowl was nearly empty – her guests were apparently as thirsty as she was. "Steve's gonna have to come in here and make another batch pretty soon," Nadine remarked to the hobo.

"Yeah, if he's still standing." The hobo filled cups for two more people, then set the ladle against the side of the bowl and stepped out into the living room. "Steve!" she called over the music and conversation. "We need more punch!"

Nadine sipped hers, and noticing there was a cherry in it, she picked it out by the stem and popped it in her mouth.

Chuck was grinning at her. "I bet you can do that thing with your tongue, huh?"

"What?" Had he really just said something about her tongue? *Why did I feel the need to invite* him, *anyway?* she asked herself. *Oh, yeah, that's right. I invited him so I could rub the fact that I have a boyfriend, and it's not him, right in his chauvinistic face.*

Chuck giggled. "That thing. With the cherry stem. I bet you can tie it in a knot with your tongue."

"You know, Chuck . . ." Nadine smiled faintly, lowered her lashes coyly, and took a step closer to him. Then her eyes blazed up at him. "Actually, it's none of your business what I can or can't do with a cherry stem. Or my tongue." She moved even closer to him and he recoiled a step. "In fact, I don't think that's a very nice thing to ask me. I don't think my boyfriend would appreciate –"

"Oh, for Christ's sake, Nadine, I was just kidding. You don't have to get your boyfriend to kick my ass for offending your maidenly honor." Chuck took an exaggerated look around. "Where is he, anyway? I hear that Cindy – the hobo? She really likes bartenders. And what d'ya know, now she's gone, too."

Nadine sipped her punch to give herself time to think up a really cutting remark. When she had one, she again began, "You know, Chuck –"

"Where have you been, Nadine?" Daina stepped into the kitchen. She glanced curiously at Chuck, then back at her friend. "I've been looking all over for you."

Nadine felt a surge of love for Daina – her best friend! She just had to hug her right away! "I've been around. Here and there."

Since Daina had never known her best friend to be a big hugger, she narrowed her eyes suspiciously at Chuck over Nadine's shoulder. He grinned, shrugged, nodded at the punchbowl. Nadine ended the uncharacteristic embrace and grinned crookedly at Daina, her pal, her childhood buddy, her best friend! Daina observed Nadine carefully, nodded at her cup. "How many of those have you had?"

"Four," Chuck supplied, still nursing his first. "In, oh, I'd say about twenty minutes. Half hour, tops."

Daina eyebrows went up. "Jesus, 'Deen!'"

"What? It's only fruit punch."

"A little lemonade, some orange juice. A packet of Hawaiian Fruit Punch. Fruit." Chuck grinned. "And Steve's special ingredient."

Nadine was just about done with Chuck. "And just what would that be, Mr. . . . Mr. . . . ." Her well of insults suddenly dried up. "Mr. *Smartypants?*"

"You're about to find out." Chuck nodded at the door. Nadine whirled around and discovered that the room whirled with her. Steve and Cindy the hobo had returned, laden with paper grocery sacks. Cindy went over to the counter and dumped three oranges and a couple of lemons out of her bag. She removed a can of frozen orange juice, a can of frozen lemonade, a jar of maraschino cherries, and an envelope of red Kool-Aid.

"I always wanted to see how it would come out with Kool-Aid," Steve said to Chuck.

"'Bout the same, I would imagine." Chuck speculated.

Nadine observed Cindy as she began to slice up the citrus, then she turned back, just as Steve was dumping an entire bottle of Everclear into the punch bowl. She looked at Daina in horror.

"The secret ingredient," Daina said wryly. "You wanna come out in the living room and sit down for a minute, 'Deen?"

Nadine nodded slowly, and Daina took her by the hand. Chuck, inquisitive, followed. He wanted to see just what kind of an effect the ingestion of quite a bit of very high octane liquor in an unbelievably short period of time would have on the sexy, uppity Indian maiden.

Chuck contemplated telling Nadine that he'd seen her boyfriend the bartender all cozied up in a corner booth with other girls after his shift ended, more than once. A girl ought to know when her boyfriend was deceiving her, and her squinty-eyed tapster had been paired-up with a different chick every time Chuck went into his bar. In her present state, Nadine might even be inclined to let Chuck comfort her a little bit about that. Edward G. Robinson's voice, from when he'd played Dathan in *The Ten Commandments,* spoke in Chuck's mind: *Where's your boyfriend now?*

Chuck giggled to himself; now *that* was funny. But where the odd thought had come from, he had not a clue, so after a moment, he set his cup of Steve's fruit punch down on the coffee table and left it there.

Nadine was appalled. This couldn't be happening. She couldn't be drunk already! The party had just started. And Ian . . . Where was Ian? Daina was still holding her hand, worry etched on her face, as if she thought that Nadine might just pass out cold at any minute.

I have to think! Nadine said to herself. She found that the effects of the Everclear hit her in waves: she would feel dizzy, giddy, positively *toasted* for a few minutes. Then her steady determination to embrace her fate, *to embrace Ian,* and tonight! would fight back the tide of common drunkenness, and her head would clear for a moment. But only for a moment.

In one of these brief flashes of lucidity, Nadine comprehended two things. The first: Aunt Penny and Aunt Bellona had evidently waylaid Ian. The deck had been dark when she'd flounced past, but

Nadine knew that they were home, busily preparing their spiced cider to bring down for her guests. *Like this party needs anything else to drink,* she thought woozily, as the room tilted.

Ian had discovered the witches' gingerbread house and, lost in the forest as he was, he'd knocked on the door to ask for guidance back to the party. Perhaps he'd even asked after Nadine by name. She grinned, picturing Aunt Bellona's proud smile when she beheld such a handsome young man asking after her (favorite) niece. Nadine imagined that her aunts had offered Ian a little hospitality, invited him up to sit on the deck for a while, so they could tell him all the good things about their clever, intelligent, *single* niece.

Out of politeness, Ian wouldn't refuse. He was still up there with her aunts, and Nadine aimed to go back and get him, just as soon as the next wave of dizziness passed. Now that Aunt Penny and Aunt Bellona had gotten a look at him, perhaps they would glean her intent, and not hover, after all. They would discreetly retire into their house, or perhaps even decide to bring the cider down to the party at that moment. Nadine would be left all alone on the deck with Ian, in the moonlight . . .

The second thing that Nadine realized was that if she tried to leave the house in her perceived state of *toastiness,* either Daina or Chuck, or both, would follow her. They didn't know that she was having momentary sparks of clarity; they *couldn't know* that her resolve to see Ian alone, *and right now!* could not be completely obliterated, not even by a heavy dose of Steve's 190-Proof fruit punch.

Daina would follow her out of concern for her safety, because of her inebriated state. Chuck would follow her in hopes of *compromising* her safety, because of her inebriated state. Regardless, Nadine needed to ditch both of them.

She took a deep breath and announced, "I think I need to go lie down."

"Be sure to lie on your stomach," Chuck counseled, ever the poet.

Nadine ignored him and rose. "I'll be okay," she said to her worried friend, and started toward her room. The living room was crowded: the party was in full swing. When she was opposite the front door – she had to just take a few steps forward down the hall, then turn right down another short hall to her bedroom – Nadine glanced back.

Daina was facing away from her, having a few choice words with Steve. Chuck was talking to a girl in a skin-tight nurse's uniform. If he glanced to his left, he would see Nadine as she made a break for it out the front door. But the nurse was tittering prettily at one of Chuck's stupid jokes, and thereby was his undivided attention absorbed. Like the Indian maiden that she was pretending to be, Nadine stealthily glided out the door and into the seeling night.

She made a concerted effort not to stagger up her own street. Prayers were answered: neither Mr. nor Mrs. Germaine just happened to look out the window and see their buckskin-clad little girl gamely battling a decided blurring of her fine-motor skills. With relief, Nadine turned onto the lighted path and climbed upwards. With more relief, she stepped onto the darkened part of the path and leaned against a helpful tree for a long moment while another wave of dizziness passed. Then she looked up cheerfully, and once again practically skipped down the trail. The closer to Ian, the better Nadine felt.

When she got to the top of the steps, she found the three of them precisely as she had pictured they would be. Nadine considered for a moment – maybe she'd had a vision at last, maybe she had finally *seen* in her mind what was actually to come; maybe her aunts' gifts were rubbing off on her.

Maybe it was the punch. She couldn't really imagine Everclear as an entheogen – but perhaps it had generated the divine within in this particular case, because had she not *seen* her aunts just like this, sitting around on the deck with Ian like it was Old Home Week?

Nadine felt smug in her precognition, so she'd asked him if he was afraid of the dark, because she *knew he had been, because she'd seen it.* Further validation of the veracity of her prediction came when Ian introduced her own aunts to her as his *new friends.*

A desire for vindication had passed through Nadine, not unlike the waves of dizziness produced by the liquor she'd unwittingly consumed. She'd wanted to recognize her aunts for what they were: not silly old women that Ian thought he could flatter by referring to them as *young ladies,* but powerful, awe-inspiring creatures, forces of nature, who *knew things,* who understood, channeled, utilized energies that college boys such as Ian Wilde could not even *imagine,* nonetheless comprehend. So she'd called them out by the ancient monikers, those funny-sounding old words that they'd jokingly recited to her once when she was a child.

181

And Penny and Bellona had smiled at her, pleased that she remembered. And then Nadine recalled the rest of her vision: that her aunts would tell Ian good things about their *favorite niece,* the one that ascribed to, and followed, and *believed in* the powers of the universe in the same manner that they did.

Penny and Bellona must have seen the future, too, just as Nadine had – maybe they'd seen it on the same night that she had dealt that fateful Tarot lay; maybe they'd *always known* her destiny. Nadine felt guilty that she'd been hesitant to discuss what the cards had revealed with them – how could she have ever even *considered* that they wouldn't also see the same shining path that lay ahead for her, that they might somehow have interpreted it differently? They had seen it, just as she had, and they'd described it to Ian. The witch and the fortuneteller had shown him the truth, the inevitability, the *wonderfulness* of it. Nadine knew that they had done so, because Ian smiled fondly at her. Ian asked her to dance.

FIFTY-FIVE

Ian was not much of a dancer; it had never been necessary. He knew a basic box-step and where to put his hands, and of course, how to lead. But Ian never had to emulate Fred twirling Ginger across the ballroom for very long. It might start out that way, but inevitably, Ian and his partner wound up molded together, her arms around his neck, his around her waist, with absolutely no room for Jesus in between. It was just another aspect of women's natures that Ian accepted as how things worked: girls liked to dance close to him, as close as they could get. And as many times as not, a slow dance was really just public foreplay; there was seldom a second dance that wasn't horizontal.

Ian had come of age during the birth throes of a shifting morality, so he'd never heard a whole lot of rhetoric about *good girls don't*. He wouldn't have believed it, anyway. By the time he was sixteen, Ian knew as gospel that *all girls* did, good, bad, or indifferent, beautiful, plain, intelligent, dim, big, tall, and small. And because such a fact was slowly becoming – if not more accepted, then at least more acknowledged – Ian didn't look down on the girls that didn't play hard to get. But the obverse of his accepting that they wanted the same thing that he did, and usually before the night got much older, was that Ian wasn't the most loyal of partners.

He thought his cousin Will had stated it the best. "When you're at a party, they stand in a little circle together, whispering. What are they whispering? 'Eenie, meenie, miney, mo. *You.* I'll take you,' based on whatever arbitrary standard of lust they ascribe to at the moment. And that's fine with us.

"So we've been chosen as a suitable partner. But all of a sudden, by this random, completely arbitrary decision, they think *they own us*. Historically, *we owned them*, but not anymore. They call that *Women's Liberation*, boys. I guess some guys don't mind being owned – they're looking for that one and only, and this next one must be her.

"But we're damn near always *their* one and only. I ask you, are we not? It's expected, unspoken. Some girl heels over, and she believes she owns you, body and soul, *forsaking all others*. I never signed up for that."

"Hear, hear," Rob said, and the brothers clinked beer bottles.

Ian agreed. He knew that faithfulness was expected of him, but unless a girl made him actually agree to a commitment out loud, he

was as unrestricted with his charms as the age and the availability of
a bedroom allowed him to be. And none of them had ever asked him
to swear his fealty, anyway, not in so many words, because they felt
it was unnecessary. Surely, Ian Wilde would be true – had he not just
said that he loved them *freely, as men strive for right; purely, as they
turn from praise?*

But these were Browning's words, not Ian Wilde's. Just as Will
had said, the girls chose him based on arbitrary whim – for his looks,
his turn of phrase – there was no contract inherent in that, no matter
what they believed.

Ian didn't live by the status quo, but he was aware of it, and this
awareness made him discreet. The same was true for Rob, and, up
until that little incident in Lake Elsinore, Will as well. They didn't
want to hurt anybody's feelings. They didn't think less of a girl
because she was willing; nowadays, most of them were. But neither
did it mean that the circle was suddenly to be unbroken. There were
just too many willing girls.

So when Nadine hung on him as they danced, curled the hairs at
the nape of his neck through her fingers, it didn't signify anything
special to Ian. For whatever reason, Rob's pretty ex-girlfriend had
suddenly taken a shine to him. She was drunk, so she was letting it
show. This was all par for the course for Ian. Girls liked him.

He was cautious, however. It was apparent that Nadine might be
a little smarter than most girls. She had cooked up this scheme with
her aunts to ensnare him into monogamy; that had been the gist of
the whole evening, laid on with a trowel throughout. "You mustn't
be greedy, my sweet young friend," Penny had told him. "By
custom, you can have only one." Well, that just wasn't the case, now
was it? He never signed up for that. He could have as many as he
wanted.

Penny had also promised, "Your life will be complete because
of one of them." There were many things in life, Ian had often
reflected, that would be glorious if they were true. A jolly fat man
travelling the globe, rewarding children just because they were
children and deserved reward. *I am the resurrection, and the life: he
that believeth in me, though he were dead, yet shall he live: and
whosoever liveth and believeth in me shall never die.* The concept of
magical realms, signs, portents, fate, predestination – all those
supernatural abilities that Nadine and her aunts claimed to possess
and wield. Wouldn't the world be a fine place, if all that stuff was
real?

Ian knew most women wanted to believe in love eternal. *And this maiden she lived with no other thought than to love and be loved by me.* Ian thought of Sissy. But little kids wanted to believe in Santa Claus, too. It would be nice if there truly was someone for everyone, if it was probable – if it was even *possible* – that his life could be complete because of a woman. But Ian didn't believe in such a completion, any more than he believed in Santa Claus.

And while Nadine was a nice girl, and it was nice that she liked him, and he might even consider *fulfilling* whatever *fevered reveries* she might have about him, at least for the night, the situation in which he found himself at the moment did not make him any more inclined to believe that any girl would ever change his life, least of all her. This whole scene was cute, and more than a little bit clever, but Ian knew that Nadine was not his destiny, even had he believed in destiny.

Dream a Little Dream of Me ended, yet she still clung to him. Ian believed this to be more out of intoxication than affection: she had her head on his shoulder and for a second, he thought she might be asleep. When Keith Richards' blazing three-note guitar riff to *(I Can't Get No) Satisfaction* leapt forth from her aunt's radio, Nadine roused herself. She looked up at Ian and smiled. It was with fondness, he noted. The impish gleam had retreated. *Maybe she's sobering up,* he said to himself.

Nadine disengaged her arms from around his neck and returned to the bench. Bellona poured her a cup of cider. "He just doesn't know where to look," Bellona said, referring to the song.

Nadine shook her head at the proffered cup. "I think I've had enough to drink for tonight," she said. When Bellona looked crestfallen at her niece's refusal – it was her aunts' special harvest blend, after all, *an aphrodisiac,* a mixture that they hadn't concocted since before Daina's birth, and all that – Nadine relented. "All right. But just one." Bellona smiled happily again when Nadine took a large swallow. "It's delicious."

Ian asked Penny to direct him to the facilities, and while he was gone, Nadine took the opportunity to say, "I'm sorry I never mentioned him to you guys. But I figured that you'd be meeting him soon enough." She smiled gratefully. "Thanks for telling him about what will be. Thanks for showing him his path."

Bellona returned her smile. "It's our blessing and our curse."

But Penny didn't smile. "We have only *shown him* his path. He has yet to step onto it." She sighed, and stirred the cauldron with the

185

ladle. "This needs refreshing, Bell." Her sister nodded and went into the house.

Penny studied her niece. "And as it is *his path,* you must not resent the manner in which he follows it, 'Deen. This young man, who is so in your mind, will always be in your life.

"If we choose to be metaphysical, we can say that your souls are linked. You've been together before, as parent and child, brother and sister, even lovers, perhaps; and you'll be other things to each other in future lives. Friends. Enemies. Again, maybe even lovers. But both future and past are inconsequential. They've gone or have yet to come, and it's an utter waste of time to concern ourselves with them now." Penny waved her hand in dismissal. "Our only concern should ever really be with what happens in *this* life. And while Ian will be ever after *present* in your life, he –"

"That's good enough for me," Nadine said quickly, then added, "Don't jinx me, Aunt Penny."

It came out far harsher than Nadine had intended. She saw her aunt's chin go up; she was stung at the rebuke. "As you will," Penny said evenly. "But don't fail to remember that *your will* is not the only one at play here."

Nadine opened her mouth to reply, but at that moment Ian and Bellona reappeared. Ian carried a large, old-fashioned ceramic jug, and Bellona had a small, fat burlap sack, stained and spotted. They set each on the table beside the cauldron.

Nadine arose: it was her turn to use the facilities. A wave of dizziness assailed her, as she feared it might. She told herself that she would continue to drink Bellona's cider because it pleased her aunt, but she would make sure that she only sipped it from now on. She walked into the house, trying to control her stagger.

Bellona filled Ian's cup one last time from the existing batch, then she and Penny commenced to pouring in the golden liquid from the jug; they tossed in spices from the bag, stirred, tasted, repeated; they chirped comments, impressions, suggestions to each other all the while.

Ian wandered over to the other side of the deck and looked out into the night. His elevation was at just below the tree-tops; he couldn't really see anything, except the floodlit clearing and the trees themselves, but he could hear laughter and music filtering up from the party below. He didn't mind that he was missing it. *Ya been to one party, ya been to them all,* he thought. And up here, he was the very center of attention.

FIFTY-SIX

When Daina stepped onto her aunts' deck, the first thing to catch her eye was the gladiator. He was standing half turned away from her, gazing out into the darkness. All that black leather seemed to absorb and distill the moonlight; the red of his toga seemed to glimmer. If she followed the almanac as her aunts did, Daina would've known that the moon would reach its third quarter in two days, so it was bright tonight, on its way to full, and maybe that was why the Roman seemed to be so ethereally lit, like he'd been touched by some filmy fairy glamour. Or maybe it was just because it was Cousin Ian standing there, and he was *fine*.

She recognized him immediately from his picture, although Ian in the flesh, in his gladiator regalia, was so much more remarkable than he'd appeared in the little photo: it was the difference between reading a description of a symphony and hearing one played. Unbidden, Daina's feet took a few steps closer to him, then she stopped just to admire him again.

Damn! She shivered. He looked so *good* . . . Maybe she was only imagining him; maybe it was some trick of the light and her libido. Daina looked over her shoulder for confirmation that he was really there. Her aunts, costumed for the holiday, hovered around the iron cider pot, but returned her gaze. Daina's incredulous expression asked, *Are you* seeing *this?*

Bellona's smile was simpatico with Daina's mind – the Roman was gorgeous, sexy, *stunning*. Penny's appraisal was more circumspect, or perhaps she just preferred to keep her opinion to herself: he was okay.

Daina turned back, and now he was looking at her. She drank in details unobservable from Nadine's black and white picture: his eyes were dark blue; his hair, chocolate brown – there seemed to be little auburn tinge to it, Daina thought, maybe from the moonlight.

Ian had turned to remark to Bellona and Penny about the noise from the party, and was amazed to see a black-haired girl standing across the deck from him, looking over her shoulder. So shocked was he at her sudden appearance, it was as if he'd forgotten that there were other women in the world besides the witch, the fortuneteller, and the Indian princess. Who was she? Where had she come from? He answered the second question immediately: she had to have come from the party that still raged below, because she was costumed, wearing a somewhat awkward-looking, oversized playing card.

He remembered a similar get-up from some political movie that Will and Rob had insisted that he sit through once. The outfit was silly on the actress in the film, and it did not become this girl, either, Ian thought. The girl in the film had been a blonde, but the one who had materialized before him had black hair, as black as the Ace of Spades – he appraised her costume again, and this time noticed that she had great legs.

She turned and looked at him, and after a heartbeat, what she was wearing slipped from Ian's mind, forgotten. She had a small, red, bow mouth – her lips were parted slightly as if she was as surprised to see him as he was to see her. She had large, luminous, light-blue eyes. She was petite, lovely – Ian had seen more than his share of little, dark-haired, blue-eyed girls – but this one was arresting. More than merely beautiful, she was *beauteous.*

They stared solemnly at each other, both entranced. Then Ian did what he always did when he saw a pretty girl that struck his fancy. He smiled. It had never failed him before.

His smile broke Daina astonished trance. Sure, he was *amazing,* but he was no Greek statue come to life. He was just a guy. A flawless, blue-eyed, striking specimen of a guy, but just a guy nonetheless. She smiled in return and closed the distance between them. "You must be Cousin Ian."

Cousin Ian blinked. He couldn't have predicted what he would've expected her to say, but it wasn't this. Finally he stammered, "You know . . .?"

"And rather well, unfortunately. I used to date –"

The pieces clicked into place in Ian's mind. This was Nadine's friend. They lived together in the house at the bottom of the hill. Nadine used to go with Rob and this girl used to go with . . . *"You were Will's girlfriend?"*

If Ian had ever believed that Will was an ass, if he'd ever suspected it for even a second – which, of course, he frequently had – it was all confirmed for him now. Will might someday become the preeminent orthopedist on the planet, but he would never again be anything but dumber than a sack of wet hammers to his cousin. Will had dumped *this girl.* Such a thought was inconceivable, for any reason, but not only had Will dumped *this* girl, he'd dumped her *for Marta.* Christ, what a dumbass he was!

She smiled ruefully. "I guess you could put it that way. For a few weeks, earlier this summer. I was in Parker with him at the end of May. I heard you taught Nadine to ski."

188

Nadine's name failed to register in Ian's mind. He still couldn't believe that *this girl* had been Will's girlfriend, and that stupid Cousin Will – or *anybody,* for that matter – would dump a girl that looked as good as she did.

Ian realized that it was his turn to speak. "Rob mentioned you. He said he hadn't been skiing because Will had wanted to take his girlfriend for a boat ride. But we never met." *Because I would've remembered* you, Ian said to himself.

"No," Daina agreed, and precisely the same idea danced through her mind: *because I would've remembered* you.

There was a pause while they unknowingly shared the same sentiment. Finally, Daina said, "You have to stop referring to me as *Will's girlfriend.* Jesus! That was all quite momentary, and besides, it's ancient history."

She tittered contemptuously, and Ian had to agree with her derision. It never would've been anything but momentary, even if Will had not been so monumentally stupid as to choose that harpy Marta over this extraordinary beauty. Will didn't deserve, and never would've been able to hold on to a girl like this.

She extended her hand. "My name's Daina."

Ian clasped her hand. An unaccustomed warmth flowed through both of them, almost electric, out to the limits of all their nerve endings, and then languidly back. Surprised at its intensity, Daina's first reaction was to attempt to remove her hand from his. Equally surprised, Ian's reaction was to squeeze her hand a little more tightly; he didn't want to relinquish it just yet.

Impulsively, he said, *"Hear my soul speak: the very instant that I saw you, did my heart fly to your service; there resides, to make me slave to it."* With a start, Ian realized that he actually meant it, for the first time ever.

Daina sincerely didn't want to laugh at him. He was too incredibly sexy. She wanted to continue to hold his hand, she wanted to bury her other hand in his shaggy hair and pull his face to her, she wanted to kiss him . . .

Daina wanted to do any number of things, but laugh at him was not one of them. But his words were so silly, so . . . absurd! *A slave to her service.* How ludicrous was that?

She successfully suppressed the laughter that threatened, and said, "Why thank you, Prince Charming." Daina knew her amusement must show in her eyes; she most certainly didn't want to hurt his feelings, so she quickly added, "That was very poetic.

You . . ." She was going to say, *You must like Nadine. She's always bursting forth with the same kind of inane, incomprehensible gobbledygook.*

But Daina didn't want to mention Nadine, specifically didn't want to say anything about him *liking* Nadine, so instead she said, "My friend says stuff like that all the time." She stopped trying to withdraw her hand, relaxed it in his.

"A man in all the world's new fashion planted, that hath a mint of phrases in his brain," Ian said and smiled. "I've got a million of them."

"I can't say that I'll understand them," Daina said truthfully. "But you're more than welcome to recite them to me, anytime you'd like."

"You'll laugh," Ian said. He had caught the mirth in Daina's eyes, just as she'd known he would.

Daina squeezed his hand. "Like I say, I might not comprehend – I don't think I've got a poetic bone in my body. But I'd never laugh at you, Ian."

Again they looked solemnly at each other. Ian wanted to kiss her, and Daina wanted him to kiss her, and she thought that it was crazy, she'd just met him, just this second. But it didn't matter because he was unbelievable, he was perfect, and if he would just go ahead and kiss her, she wouldn't have to think anymore, she could just dissolve into his arms, like she felt she was dissolving into his eyes . . .

Ian touched Daina's shoulder. It was too soon, she would probably turn away, he'd never tried to kiss a girl so soon, he'd never *wanted* to try to kiss a girl so soon, guileless insouciance had always been his M.O., but she wasn't turning away; if anything, she was leaning in closer to him. *Where the hell is this coming from, I just met her, she's just a girl, but her mouth, I want to taste her mouth –*

"Daina?" Penny called. Her aunt's voice had never seemed shrill to her before, but now it seemed to enter Daina's ear like the sound of a brick thrown through a window. "Would you care for some cider?"

Daina dropped Ian's hand and he immediately removed his other hand from her shoulder and again looked out at the trees.

"I certainly would!" Daina replied a little too loudly, a shade too cheerfully.

Ian looked back at her and they shared a harmonic congruence, like telepathy; seamless, complete: the kiss that they'd missed would not be missed again. It would be accomplished at the first available opportunity. They smiled at each other in this certainty and crossed the deck to join the witch and the fortuneteller.

Bellona handed her a cup of the revitalized potion. "You look so cute!"

"Thanks." Daina sat on the bench. All propriety now, Ian sat across from her in one of the chairs.

"Sorry we haven't made it down to the party yet," Penny said, and handed Ian a fresh cup without looking at him. "But we've been entertaining this refugee from the *Ludus Magnus.* How's it going? Is everyone having fun?"

Daina sighed. "It's kind of a disaster. Everyone's falling down drunk. Steve made this punch . . ." In mentioning her stupefied party guests and Steve and his punch, Daina was reminded of her original reason for climbing the path to her aunts' house. "Where's Nadine?"

She'd gone into Nadine's room to check on her, and finding her absent, had come up here looking for her. But for some reason Daina had not thought again about her friend's whereabouts since she'd stepped onto the deck. Daina knew the reason. He smiled shyly at her.

"Nadine's resting," Bellona said. "She went inside for a moment and . . . sleep called out to her."

"I'll bet," Daina said. She told them the tale of how Nadine had inadvertently consumed a hopelessly large amount of ridiculously potent corn squeezin's in a pitifully short time. She told them about how Chuck, some guy that had been following her around at the party, had sympathetically advised that she sleep on her stomach. "He knew what was in it," Daina said angrily. "He could've stopped her. He's a creep."

"She'll be okay," Ian said. "She just needs to sleep it off."

But to Ian and Daina's surprise, the Indian princess came back out onto the deck a few minutes later. Nadine's reappearance was no surprise to her aunts. They kenned her resolve to spend time with Ian tonight. The feather in her hair was askew, and her stripes of war paint were a trifle smudged, but besides that, she seemed none the worse for her alcoholic misadventure.

"I just needed a little catnap," she said and winked at Daina.

"Shall we take our witches' brew down to the festivities, then?" Bellona asked.

"No!" Nadine and Daina cried in unison.

"I'm kind of embarrassed about drinking too much," Nadine explained, too quickly. "They all think I passed out. It's gonna be hard enough facing them at school."

"Demonstrate your resurrection then," Penny suggested, knowing that her idea would go nowhere. "Like the phoenix rising from the ashes, show them that a little alcohol cannot keep –"

"I'd rather just stay up here," Nadine said. She was now shifting the responsibility for the party onto Daina's shoulders, so Penny and Bellona looked expectantly at her.

Daina smiled. "I didn't know how bad off Nadine would be. I didn't know how long I'd have to stay up here with her, so I enlisted Steve's help, seeing as how it was his fault in the first place. I told him to run them all out at eleven o'clock. He's a bartender, so he's used to corralling drunks."

"Ian's a bartender," Nadine told her, demonstrating how well she already knew him.

Ian's amazing, Daina said to herself. "Is he?" she said aloud.

Nadine nodded and smiled at him.

Daina did not. She didn't even glance at him. It wasn't necessary. She knew that she would be kissing him soon enough, and anything and everything else that they were of a mind to do. She knew it as surely as she knew the sun would come up tomorrow, as surely as she knew that Nadine would have a fierce headache when it did come up.

Daina had never been so instantaneously and completely attracted to anyone in her life, not even Lawrence or Jeffrey, and surely not some random guy off the street. Yet it was a fact. Ian Wilde was stunning, and she knew that she must have him, come hell or high water, as soon as discretion allowed. And Daina knew he felt the same way about her. She'd seen the look in his eyes, and she'd let him know she was just as eager. Neither morality nor polite custom would stand in their way. It was a done deal. Daina didn't have to stare at him.

Nadine thought it would be proper for her to make introductions between her best friend and her soulmate, but apparently they'd already met. She would've done it anyway, under ordinary circumstances, but she was not as sober as she pretended to be, and in her present state of mind – the imp took control whenever a wave of dizziness hit her – Nadine didn't want Daina getting too chummy with him.

It was an irrational streak of jealousy – hell, Daina wouldn't even look at him, and Ian seemed to be ignoring her just as much. *He doesn't look like a movie star, that's why,* Nadine thought and grinned into her cider cup. *But I was never much one for movie stars* . . . Her jealousy evaporated. Though he had the body of a god, Ian wasn't pretty enough for Daina.

"So we're not going to the party?" Bellona asked.

"We'll have our own party," Nadine told her.

Ian grinned. *"A feast of friends, 'Alive!' she cried. Waitin' for me, outside."*

Daina returned his grin. *"We want the world and we want it now."* She might not know Shakespeare; she'd never heard of Aldous Huxley, of *The Doors of Perception,* but she knew The Doors from Los Angeles. They were one of her favorite bands.

"Fair enough." Penny looked expressionlessly at each of them in turn. "Let the games begin."

FIFTY-SEVEN

After a few minutes, the celebration below was forgotten. The five of them laughed and talked and drank as if they were the only attendees at the only Hallowe'en party going on anywhere that night.

Bellona frequently moved the dial on the radio, switching effortlessly through a half dozen styles of music. When *Fist City* came on, Nadine and Daina jumped up and taught Ian a sort of square dance they'd enjoyed on rainy days with their aunts as children. It was simple: everyone stood in a circle and clapped, and then two people would move into the center and join arms, swing around, then swing out to the other side, and then another pair would do the same thing, and so on. It was the perfect energetic dance to accompany Loretta Lynn's outrageous bluegrass threat to the other woman: *I'm not a sayin' my baby's a saint 'cause he ain't, and that he won't cat around with a kitty. I'm here to tell you, gal, to lay offa my man, if you don't wanna go to Fist City.* When the song ended, they all collapsed around the table, laughing and out of breath.

When a slow number came on, Ian's dance card was always full. Bellona chose him for Roy Orbison's fabulously overwrought *Only the Lonely.* She squeezed him to her, as if she were her nieces' age, but she didn't just hang on him as Nadine did; she insisted on proper hand placement and a brisk box-step. But it was undeniable that Bellona enjoyed touching Ian: she winked at Daina over his shoulder and grinned gleefully for the entire number.

Penny blushed just a little bit when Ian offered his hand to her as twangy guitars heralded Tammy Wynette's *D-I-V-O-R-C-E;* but after a moment's hesitation she agreed. Penny tested all of Ian's limited terpsichorean skills, because she actually wanted *to dance;* it was not just a chance to hold him, an excuse for an extended hug, as it was for Nadine and Bellona. Penny schooled him in the proper steps, and after a moment Ian was competently spinning the witch out to arm's length and twirling her back in. It was fun.

When the tinny piano and Russian folk strains of *Those Were The Days* began, Bellona stood, held up her hands for silence, bidding them pay heed as, like a teller of tales, she sang along: *Once upon a time there was a tavern, where we used to raise a glass or two. Remember how we laughed away the hours, and dreamed of all the great things we would do?*

Penny organized her nieces and Ian into kick-line for the chorus, then they would stop and give ear to Bellona again on the melancholy verses. She delivered the last one directly to Nadine, as if it was one of her prophecies: *Through the door there came familiar laughter, I saw your face and heard you call my name. Oh, my friend, we're older but no wiser, for in our hearts the dreams are still the same.*

But Nadine was too young, too gleeful, too drunk and too much in love to take any warning from the song. The five of them finished up the last long chorus with gusto.

With the unmistakable violins of *At Last,* Nadine smiled coyly, hopefully, at Ian. He stood without showing his reluctance, but if the truth were told, he was tired of dancing with Nadine. He didn't mind Penny and Bellona; they were fun, like at family get-togethers, when he had been known to cut a rug and attempt a jitterbug of even a Charleston with his mom or the twins' mom.

But Ian knew that dancing with a girl his own age was a horse of a different color; it was to a specific purpose. It was that public foreplay, it was the precursor to a more private dance, and Ian didn't want to dance with Nadine in that manner anymore, because now he wanted to dance with Daina that way. The purpose was no longer there for him with Nadine, if it had ever been – Ian was not any more moved by this pretty young woman swaying against him than he was by dancing with her aunts.

Holding Nadine for the three minutes and eight seconds of the timeless paean to true love long delayed but finally contented was interminable to Ian. It seemed like it would stretch out forever, like it would go on until the crack of doom. Nadine didn't hang on him as heavily as she had earlier – she had sobered up a little bit, it seemed, at least as far as standing up on her own was concerned – but still she just put her arms around his neck, molded herself against him, and rocked gently from side to side. It really wasn't dancing at all. Nadine again put her head on his shoulder, and murmured along with Etta: *At last, my love has come along . . .*

Don't you believe it, Ian thought, a trifle unkindly. *Cause it ain't necessarily so.*

At last (ha, ha) the song faded and Nadine released him. Bellona changed the station again, and the driving beat and keyboards to *Touch Me* began. Morrison yelped, and emboldened by Penny's lesson, Ian grabbed Daina's hand. He spun her out: *Come on, come on, come on now, touch me, babe* – then brought her back against him and actually sung Krieger's words to her, and earnestly: *"Can't you see that I am not afraid?"* Daina smiled at him and the promise of that kiss, of consummation, was again renewed between them.

And then the cycle would begin again with a square dance, and then a dance with the aunts, and then some slow old ballad with Nadine wrapped around him like a vine. Then Ian would eagerly welcome Daina into his arms and dance with her again.

As the evening progressed and the cider cauldron's contents waned and were refilled, Ian began to notice fewer and fewer details of what was going on around him. Snatches of tunes; Bellona's wink, Penny's smirk; Nadine's head on his shoulder, Daina's pale-blue eyes, so full of promise . . . Disjointed details all seemed to blend together after a while. Time seemed to slow down and speed up jerkily, as if his perception were a strip of celluloid stuck in a projector that possessed no governor to steady the frames as they passed.

Because of this folding and stretching of time, Ian became convinced that there was something spiking the cider, something considerably more exotic than commercially available corn liquor. Daina and Nadine were dancing together while Penny and Bellona mixed up another cauldron. Ian said, *"One pill makes you larger and one pill makes you small –"*

"And the ones that mother gives you don't do anything at all." Bellona winked and Ian smiled at her appreciation for modern music.

He asked, "What exactly is in this, anyway?"

"Snips and snails and puppy dog's tails," Penny said, with a rare playful smile.

"That's what little boys are made of," Ian replied, and Penny raised her eyebrows mildly. Her expression said, *Ya never know.* "No *sugar and spice and everything nice?"*

"That, too," Bellona said, mixing and measuring.

Ian glanced over his shoulder. Nadine and Daina were trying to execute some complicated dance move wherein they crossed their outstretched arms and then joined hands and swung together and back, but it didn't work as planned, and they dissolved into shrieks of laughter and hugged each other.

He looked back at the witch and the fortuneteller. "Seriously –"

"Nothing as potent as Everclear," Penny promised.

"There's not much that's as potent as Everclear," Ian conceded. "But if I get stopped on the way home, I'd like to be able to tell the cops what I've been drinking."

To his surprise, Penny barked a laugh and grinned craftily at him. "Do you really think you're going home tonight, Ian Wilde?" She nodded at Daina and Nadine. "What did I tell you? By the time the sun comes up –"

"Are we back to the two girls at one time thing?" Ian asked crudely.

"Don't count on it," Penny returned. "That was something you dreamt up all on your own, boy. I never said anything about that." She narrowed her eyes, grinned like the Cheshire Cat. "But perhaps it's not too late. Just like Bell said, maybe if you ask nicely . . . Look at them . . . Is that what you really want?"

Ian did as he was bid. They had given up trying to dance and were now attempting a rather involved patty-cake slide: *Miss Mary Mack, Mack, Mack, all dressed in black, black, black* . . . They giggled and smiled at each other, best friends, and Ian considered. Sure, Nadine was pretty enough, but Daina was *incomparable.* With them both standing right there, he didn't even see Nadine after a moment. His whole mind was full of Daina: he wanted to enfold her in his arms, and kiss her mouth, her neck; he wanted to feel her back arch, he wanted to hear her scream his name . . .

Ian turned back to find that Penny and Bellona were watching him. No, he didn't want them both. There *wasn't* enough of him to go around. He wanted to give his full concentration to Daina alone.

"That's what I thought." Again Penny grinned. "Have some more cider, Roman. This is the best batch yet. Trust me. *You may rely on it.* Your have chosen your path, and it will not disappoint."

FIFTY-EIGHT

Ian realized that he was awake, but he didn't open his eyes, because he was unsure of where he was. Such a thing hadn't happened to him in a while, but it had happened. The bed beneath him was unusually soft and he heard birds chirping – his mattress was firm, and he'd never heard bird one while in his room, so he knew he wasn't at home. In order to determine just where it was that he might be, and with whom, Ian started with the last thing he could recall . . . *Daina.*

He remembered dancing with her again, slowly this time. She stood up on her toes and wrapped her arms around his neck, as Nadine always did. Ian remembered putting his hands on her hips, squeezing gently, drawing her against him . . . Everything else was foggy after that. He thought he might've kissed her, but maybe that was just the memory of her pretty mouth, the memory of *wanting to kiss her.* He didn't think they would've done it in front of the Indian princess and the witch and the fortuneteller – if they'd started making out, it wouldn't have ended there. But had he kissed her, anyway? The vision in his mind seemed more real than just wishful thinking.

Keeping his eyes closed still, he thought he remembered other details, too, just jumbled pictures without coherence: her arms were very white, and slender; he saw her head thrown back in ecstasy, thought he could hear her cry out in pleasure . . . But was any of it real? Had any of it actually happened? Just what was in that cider?

There was really only one way to find out where he was, whom he was with, what he had done. Ian opened his eyes.

Daina was sitting in a chair a few feet away, her legs crossed under her. She was wearing blue pajamas and a pair of ratty bunny slippers; she sipped a cup of coffee, and stared at him. When she saw that he was awake, she immediately set the coffee down on a bookshelf. Ian barely had time to register that he was in a darkly paneled room, before Daina slid into the bed and wiggled up against him. She smiled expectantly.

Without hesitation, Ian kissed her. Slowly, tentatively . . . Was this the very first time, or had he kissed her already? He could not say for sure, but if he hadn't, this was just how he'd imagined it. Daina put her hand on his shoulder, said, "Mmm," against his mouth. Encouraged, Ian touched her cheek, tangled his hand in her hair and kissed her harder. Daina responded, pressing herself against him, kissing him back. Her scent was intoxicating; he pulled her closer . . .

But it was only for a moment. Before things could progress any further, Daina broke their kiss. Dark lust glowed in her eyes; she panted, grinned savagely. "You don't realize that we're not alone, do you?"

Ian glanced across the room. "The door's closed. I'm sure they'd knock . . ."

Daina shook her head. "Not them." She ran her fingers off his shoulder, down his side, then paused. "Whatever could this be?" To Ian's amazement, Daina picked up *someone else's hand*, draped limply over his hip, and dropped it. Ian looked over his shoulder. Nadine was curled up behind him, her face against his back, snoring softly.

Alarmed, he looked back at Daina. "I . . . didn't . . ." It was neither question nor statement, just a fervent hope. Ian didn't know how he'd wound up in bed with Nadine, but it surely wasn't what he wanted. Ian didn't ever do anything he didn't want to do, not even with an eager, pretty girl, and the impressions in his head – were they memories? – they were of Daina, not Nadine. He wanted to experience them again, or for the first time, and it was looking like Rob's cast-off was going to ruin it for him . . .

"No, you didn't." Daina rolled gracefully out of bed. She offered her hand. "But if you'd like to, we have to go somewhere else."

Ian scooted delicately away from Nadine. He didn't want to wake her, *Oh, God, please don't make me have to deal with* that *right now, not when Daina had just said,* If you'd like to . . .

There was a rough second when he was trapped: Nadine was lying on the cape part of his costume, preventing his escape. Ian thought about that mean old joke, when a girl was so ugly you'd rather gnaw your own arm off rather than risk waking her up. It wasn't that Nadine was ugly; Ian just didn't want her. Daina leaned over and released the gold clasp. The red material slid away, and Ian, half-naked now, was free.

He stood, took stock of his remaining attire. He was still wearing the knee high sandals, the skirt, the multi-buckled belt, even the armlets. Beneath the skirt, he detected that he was still wearing the somewhat constricting loin-cloth-underskirt affair that had come with the costume.

199

Ian realized that he was free of sin: no matter how much he'd had to drink, no matter how much he didn't remember, no matter which girl had wound up curled into his back, he hadn't done anything. Not with anybody. If he had, he would certainly be bereft of this complicated underwear – it would've been the very first thing to go – and he surely wouldn't't've wasted the time to put it back on afterwards.

But he was confused. If he was still fully clothed – well, more or less, now that his toga was gone – why did he seem to be able to remember flashes of Daina? Kissing her, holding her; a smoldering glance, a white wrist, a pink-nailed toe, a belly-button, a shapely thigh?

Eyes still twinkling darkly, Daina looked him up and down. Then she echoed Bellona's appraisal: "Mercy." She stepped closer to him, ran her hands over his chest, then up the sides of his neck, into his hair. She kissed him again, and again Ian saw those flashes in his mind, scenes of lovemaking that he could not say for sure had happened or not.

Daina broke the kiss and looked up at him. Ian felt silly, vulnerable; but he had to know. He whispered, "Did we . . . You and me . . . Did we . . . already?"

"No," she whispered back. "We only dreamt it." She took his hand and tugged him lightly toward the door.

Ian hesitated. "You dreamt it to?"

Daina nodded; her lip curled seductively and that dark sparkle continued to dance behind her eyes. Ian had never seen a woman as beautiful as Daina was at that very moment, steeped, *soaked* in unanswered desire for him. Ian had still been dreaming, but Daina, her own dream passed, had been awake already, waiting for him.

Who knows how long she's been sitting in that chair, waiting for me to wake up? How long she's been waiting for our dream to be reenacted in the flesh?

He would not make her wait a second longer.

FIFTY-NINE

Like Daina, Nadine also dreamed about Ian. Unlike Daina, it wasn't the first time. Nadine dreamt of Ian all the time, awake as well as asleep. In this one, she was all cuddled up with him, like when they danced, except they weren't dancing: they were in bed. The dream was so real that Nadine could smell him.

At last she opened her eyes. In her sleep, she'd gathered the toga that he'd left behind into a ball and hugged it to herself. She put the garment to her nose and breathed deeply. *Oh, God, he smelled so good!* Then the giddy idea assailed Nadine: maybe it *hadn't* been a dream this time!

She had only static bursts of images in her mind, like a slide show run too fast. His cheek, his knee, the curve of his bare shoulder; his incredible voice, whispering her name; his intoxicating scent. Nadine had dreamt of all these things before and sometimes more coherently, but there was something about *this time* that made it seem so much more real.

And she had his toga, more than half of what he'd been wearing the night before. Wasn't that proof that he'd been here in bed with her, just like it seemed in her mind? Wasn't it proof that they had, finally, *at last* . . . She buried her nose in the fabric again. She'd had way too much to drink – that was why the memories were sketchy and garbled – but the *quality* of them seemed so real. It had to have happened. She ached for it to happen again.

Nadine could smell bacon cooking and fresh coffee perking. These delicious, homey smells had no doubt roused Ian before her, and she expected to find him in the kitchen with her aunts. The room in which she found herself had been Daina's, right up until the time that Penny and Bellona had opened up the house below and given it to her. How thoughtful of Daina to lend it to Nadine and her soulmate for their first night together! There was a giant, overstuffed couch in the living room, covered in plush blue velvet. Daina had probably slept there, or maybe she'd just gone on back down the hill to her own bed.

Nadine hopped up. It was a little chilly in the room, and she was barefoot – where had she left her little beaded moccasins? Bellona had lent them to her, to go with her outfit, and she couldn't have lost them . . . Maybe they were still out on the deck. Yikes! It had been a doozy of a party! Nadine threw Ian's toga over her shoulders and left Daina's old room.

Bellona and Penny were eating, seated at the little counter that divided the kitchen from the living room. Penny turned at her niece's approach and asked expressionlessly, "Breakfast, 'Deen?"

"Yes, thank you." Nadine sat at the counter and helped herself to bacon and eggs, toast, a cup of coffee. She discovered that she was ravenously hungry, and stuffed her face for a few minutes without speaking or even thinking. It was only when she became aware that her aunts had stopped eating and were staring at her that she spoke, with her mouth still full, the first two words that came to her mind. "Where's Ian?"

Bellona looked away, almost guiltily, but Penny's expressionless gray eyes remained locked with Nadine's. "Ian's gone."

Something in Penny's tone chilled Nadine. She finished chewing, swallowed. "He'll be back."

"Sure he will, honey," Bellona said.

The assurance, the comfort, the *pity* in her aunt's voice frightened Nadine more than Penny's cold tonelessness. Penny shot her sister an annoyed glance, and Bellona looked away again.

"I told you that he'd remain in your life, 'Deen," Penny said evenly. "Christ, we'll never get rid of him now." She tried to catch her sister's eye, but Bellona got up hastily, went to the sink and started to wash her breakfast plate.

"But where is he?" The look on Penny's face made Nadine laugh nervously and quickly answer her own question. "I'm sure he went home to sleep it off. That cider you guys made . . . Wow!" Penny observed her silently, emotionlessly, as she prattled on. "I'm feeling a little groggy still, myself. I really should go home, too." Nadine stood abruptly, looked down at her empty plate.

"I'll get that for you, dear," Bellona told her. Her voice contained a certain sad wistfulness, which she tried unsuccessfully to hide. "You go on back to the house and get some rest. I'm sure you'll see Ian later. I'm sure everything will be –"

"Oh, you'll definitely see him later, 'Deen." Penny spoke the words softly, but there was a razor's edge to them. "But just like I tried to tell you, you might not like –"

"Okay, then!" Nadine said breathlessly. "I'll see you guys later this afternoon!" She turned and fled her aunt's house.

SIXTY

The dewy grass was cold on Nadine's bare feet as she picked her way down the path, concentrating on avoiding sharp rocks and pointy sticks. It was better to do that than think about Aunt Penny's words, Aunt Bellona's pitying expression.

But there couldn't be anything to worry about. Ian would be back. He'd taken off early this morning because he was embarrassed. It was not exactly acceptable or at least not very polite to be sleeping with a girl under her aunts' roof; under their very noses. They were from a generation where people were supposed to be married to do that, and he hadn't wanted to offend them, so he'd tiptoed out.

There was no way for him to know that Penny and Bellona were free thinkers before such a label had been invented. They viewed men as creatures put here for women's pleasure, and this was the attitude they had always communicated to their nieces, ever since they had grown mature enough to understand it. There had never been any moral treatises on what good girls and bad girls did, no discussions of nonsensical patriarchal rules.

Their only caution had been that the truths of nature could not be ignored. "Anatomy is not destiny, as Freud maintained, however," Aunt Penny said. "You fortunate young women nowadays no longer have to confront a calendar with trepidation, dig roots by the light of the moon . . ."

"You just have to take your pill every day," Bellona said happily.

A reminder to take their pill every day was the sum of their aunts' admonitions regarding interaction with the opposite sex, with an occasional, "Have fun!" thrown in.

But Ian couldn't know that. Her aunts' attitudes were unusual even for the times. He couldn't be blamed for feeling guilty. Nadine was unsure whether or not they had actually done anything that he would feel guilty about – but either way, she was sure that she would hear from him later in the day.

Her feet were covered with pine needles and dirt and other flotsam from her trek down the hill, but the Indian princess was too tired to bathe right at that moment. So she just ran her feet under the shower, without undressing, then retired to her room. The shades were drawn; only a small, stray beam of light snuck in here or there. It was almost as dark as if the sun hadn't been up. She threw Ian's toga onto her unmade bed, then stripped down to her slip.

Nadine was looking forward to a little nap; maybe she would more clearly dream of the night she'd spent with Ian. She slid into bed, and gathered his toga up; but when she squeezed it, it writhed and wriggled in her arms. Nadine shrieked a long note in surprise, leapt out of bed. Even as she flew to the light switch, she realized what must have possessed his gladiator's cape, what had brought it to unexpected, squirming life in her arms.

She flipped on the light and looked back. Sure, enough, there was Grimalkin, standing in the middle of the bed, looking ruffled and offended. Since she and Daina had moved in together, the wily old mama cat had adopted the same tactic that she'd used at Nadine's parents' house: anytime a door was left open, she snuck in to sleep on Nadine's bed. Nadine had thrown Ian's toga over her and it was still draped halfway across her flank. She gave her tail a twitch and the red material slid off.

"Oh, 'Malky, you scared the Bejesus out of me." The cat jumped down and darted under the bed. Nadine's squeezing had apparently scared whatever passed for the Bejesus in cats out of her, too.

There was a sharp rap at the door, a worried voice. "Nadine? Are you all right?"

It was Ian! Hope surged through Nadine like a Roman candle. He hadn't gone home – he must've decided to sleep it off on the couch. Nadine had walked right by and not noticed him there. The final piece was falling into place! What had or had not happened last night would soon happen again. She would open the door; Ian would embrace her . . .

"Yes!" Nadine cried. "I'm okay. It was just the cat! Would you like to come –" She flung the door open.

Ian was standing in the hall, a concerned expression on his face. He was half-naked, with the bottle-green colored sheet from Daina's bed wrapped around his waist. He grasped a wad of it at his hip, to keep it from falling off. Daina stood behind him, wearing only her long blue pajama top. She was hastily buttoning it.

The worry drained away from their features when Grimalkin saw her opportunity for escape and bolted out of the room, zigzagging dizzily past them, then making a hard left into the living room.

"You wouldn't think a cat that old could move that fast," Daina commented.

Ian smiled at her over his shoulder, then looked back at Nadine. "You're okay? That was a helluva scream."

Nadine pointed at Grimalkin's escape route. "Just the cat," she croaked.

"Okay. We'll see you later then." Without a backward glance, Ian turned around, as did Daina. He put his arm around her shoulder (the one that wasn't holding the sheet), and she put her arm around his waist. They entered Daina's room and shut the door.

Nadine stared, dumbstruck, at the blank, closed door to Daina's bedroom. They didn't care that she'd seen them; they didn't have the decency to even be ashamed.

Nadine had told Daina that she'd found a new man – she'd not revealed that it was Ian, true – yet how could Daina imagine that it could've been anyone else? Nadine had abandoned the party that had been her suggestion to be where he was; she'd spent the entire evening slow dancing with him. Who did Daina think she'd been talking about? *Chuck?*

But Daina didn't care that Nadine had chosen Ian. She had inveigled him somehow, enticed him right out of the bed they'd shared, while she slept on, unaware. Daina was a tramp, a whore. A lifetime of friendship seemed to slip, to tilt back and forth like a see-saw for a moment . . . Then it just slid away. Daina would pay for this. Somehow, Nadine would make her pay.

And Ian – *how can he do this to me?* Pain knifed through Nadine, and it was as if it was manifested physically. The hurt eddied through her in waves, as the liquor had done the night before. She thought she would pass out: this betrayal was more potent than all the Everclear ever distilled. Nadine grasped the door frame for support. Penny and Bellona had told him his future, and yet he'd gone right ahead and . . .

Doubt, mixed with a weird kind of hope, assailed Nadine. She had to hear the exact text of the prophecy that her aunts had revealed to Ian. Maybe they hadn't explained everything fully to him, maybe he hadn't grasped his fate. Maybe Ian just didn't understand what was destined to exist between them, and maybe that's why he'd just gone along at this whore's filthy suggestion.

Nadine understood how Daina could betray her – it had always been just a physical thing to Daina. She'd never felt love for any of them, and therefore, she didn't believe that Nadine could feel it either. And even if she had acknowledged that Nadine could be in love with Ian – Daina didn't mind walking all over Nadine's feelings.

Daina couldn't have been ignorant of the fact that Nadine wanted Ian for herself. She just didn't care. The way he looked had engendered an itch in Daina, just like it did in all the other girls, and Daina had just gone right ahead and let him scratch it for her. Nadine would punish her for that. Nadine vowed that she would make Daina understand the supreme agony that she felt at this moment, somehow, the utter devastation of the loss of someone she loved . . .

Nadine still stared at the closed door in wounded amazement, until she heard, muffled, Daina's high, delighted laughter; then there was that short drum roll, the inimitable keyboards, and Morrison sang, *Hello, I love you, won't you tell me your name* . . .

Nadine closed her door and flopped bonelessly onto her bed. She was too overwhelmed to even cry. She discovered that it was not sorrow that was so much in her mind, anyway – *Life being what it is, one dreams of revenge — and has to content oneself with dreaming.* Nadine would not be content with dreaming. This deep disgrace in sisterhood would not go unanswered.

When the music's over, she thought, *turn out the light, turn out the light, turn out the light* . . .

SIXTY-ONE

The sun blazed in the west, as the last All Hallow's Day of the decade faded inexorably toward night. Upon Penny and Bellona's deck, all traces of the little party from the night before were gone: the cider fixings were put up for the season, the wooden cups washed, the cauldron and tripod stored, the spent can of Sterno discarded.

Penny and Bellona liked to eat alfresco; that was why they lived in a house whose major architectural feature was a deck. Now they hastened to set the little wooden table before the sun went down. They quickly brought out plates, silverware, the food itself.

Her portion delivered, Bellona sat and waited for her sister.

Nadine said, "What did you say to him?"

Bellona jumped, startled, and spun halfway around in her chair. Her niece had moved the other chair away from the table and placed it near the center of the deck. There she sat, her legs stretched out in front of her, ankles crossed. Her arms were folded across her chest. She frowned dangerously.

Nadine was dead set on getting to the bottom of why Ian had suddenly decided that he couldn't resist Daina's whorishness. The one-time Indian princess had lain in bed all day, and between fitful naps, she'd reviewed the events of the night before, organized her thoughts. No matter how she sliced it, her mind kept coming back to one idea: things had gone awry, the train had jumped the tracks, Ian was even now back at the house, *still fucking Daina,* all as a result of whatever it was that Penny and Bellona had said to him.

There could be no other reason. The cards didn't lie. Nadine and Ian were *supposed to be together.* But there are no sure things in life. Just because something was meant to be, it didn't mean that human machinations couldn't put it asunder.

"For heaven' sake, 'Deen!" Bellona cried. "You nearly scared the life out of me! Why are you lurking all the way over there?"

Penny came outside then, and set down a pitcher of iced tea. She echoed her sister. "Why are you so far away? Here, come have some supper."

A lifetime of habit impelled Nadine to rise and cross the short distance. Not only were her aunts the best cooks she'd ever encountered, Nadine had also experienced more enjoyment here, at their table, than she'd ever known at her parents'. It wasn't that Sam and Irene were cruel, or even that they didn't love her. It was just that she'd been a shy and bookish child, and the three of them hadn't talked a lot. And after Nadine became entranced by, entrenched within, the realms of those forces unseen that her aunts had taught her, Nadine had even less to say to Mom and Dad.

So these two women, and Daina, had become Nadine's true family. At least they had been until this morning.

Nadine fought down the natural inclination to join them. "What did you say to him?" she repeated.

The sisters blinked expressionlessly at her for a heartbeat, and Nadine believed that if either of them said, "Who?" she might just start screaming and not stop.

But they knew. Penny, expressionless, said, "Why all this melodrama, 'Deen? Come, have some supper."

"What did you say to him?" Nadine's voice rose half an octave.

Bellona smiled kindly, gently. "We just told him what we'd seen. That he was at a crossroads, and that the choice he made last night would affect him for the rest of his life."

Penny sat down on the bench across from her sister, but didn't move to eat. "What exactly is it that you think *you saw,* Nadine?" she asked with a kind of annoyed curiosity. "What has made you attach such obsessive importance to this one young man?"

"He's adorable, Penn." Bellona's smile peeped out. "Why, if I was twenty years younger . . ."

"Twice twenty years, nay, *thrice,* and you'd still be too old," Penny replied, and smiled at her sister. Her smile faded when she looked again at Nadine. "He's just a marginally attractive young man, adrift in a sea of them. Why have you imprinted on him so utterly, 'Deen?" When Nadine didn't answer immediately, she continued. "He *is* adept at a turn of phrase, I'll give you that." Penny grinned shrewdly. "But just as with your Aunt Bellona, I doubt that it's *this* aspect that you appreciate the most about him."

"Actually, that's exactly what it is," Nadine replied snootily. "I think he has a brilliant mind, and that's what I love the most about him. Unlike Daina, who only wants him for his –"

"Clever, maybe." Bellona rocked her hand back and forth above the table. "I don't know about brilliant. But he is extremely nice to look at."

"If you love him only for his mind, then I don't understand what the problem is," Penny said slowly. "His mind, whether brilliant, clever, or perhaps only just quick –" Penny winked at her sister, "–

will henceforth be at your disposal, just like I told you. I don't see why you feel the need to cross-examine us –"

"He's my soulmate," Nadine said conversationally.

She'd rehearsed what she would say next, because the truth of it had suddenly struck her earlier in the day, whilst she'd been reviewing the facts. The folly of ever allowing Ian to step foot onto her aunts' property was driven home to her by this sudden unveiling of the truth. The thought had never crossed Nadine's mind before, but once she'd seen it, she could never *unsee* it. It was inescapable, it was the oft-mentioned elephant in the room, never acknowledged before, but always there, nonetheless.

"You knew he was fated to be mine, but you advised him to pick Daina. Because she's blood to you."

Bellona and Penny's expressions immediately, inexplicably reversed. Normally happy and cheerful, Bellona's face paled, sobered, went blank in incredulity. Penny, usually reserved, stern, imperious, hooted laughter and slapped her knee.

"Your *soulmate?* From what sibyl of Delphic skill did you learn *that* word?" Penny giggled.

"I read the cards. Right before I met him. And they said –"

"They said, 'Nadine is a victim of wishful thinking, of biased interpretation, of seeing in the cards just what she wants to see, and no more!'" Penny thundered. "Come!" She leapt up, her dinner forgotten. "Recreate for me this life-altering read! I'm sure that you remember how it dealt out. I'll show you the error in your transliteration!"

Nadine remained seated. "It wasn't wishful thinking. First, I asked how long Daina and Will would last, and the answer came back: *not much longer.* I asked how long Rob and I would last, and I was returned: *not much longer than that.* Then I asked what was in store for me, and the cards foretold that I would soon meet my soulmate. Not three minutes later, I met Ian."

"The next thing then she waking looks upon, be it on lion, bear, or wolf, or bull; on meddling monkey, or on busy ape, she shall pursue it with the soul of love." Again Penny cackled. *"This is the very coinage of your brain,* Nadine. Just because you *perceive* your soulmate in the cards, doesn't mean that the next attractive young man that plucks at your . . . *heartstrings,* is he."

"I didn't see him. I only heard his voice. Yet I knew he was the one. The cards never lie."

"Show me their tale, and I'll point out the lie that you've read into them, 'Deen. *Concentrate and ask again.* When we seek answers about ourselves, there's a reason that we have another read what is dealt. *For who so firm that cannot be seduced?* Who so emotionless that they aren't tempted to see only what they want to see? To avoid just this sort of misguided misinterpretation, we –"

Appalled, Bellona whispered, "I can't believe that you would suggest that we could ever –"

"Hush, Bell! You can show her your hurt feelings in a moment. This haughty witch must be schooled in the truths of the world! What did the Roman say? *You can't always get what you want.* The cards don't need to lie, if we lie to ourselves. Show me what was dealt, Nadine."

"No."

There was a pause, and the very air seemed to crackle, to grow hot and dry from the tension between them. Then Penny said, "All right." She sat back down on the bench. "Would you like to hear what *we* saw?"

"I'd like to hear what you told him, how you convinced him to pick Daina, your blood, *your niece,* over me –"

"Enough!" Bellona roared. She slammed her fist down on the table. The silverware rattled. "How dare you, Nadine? How dare you suggest that we, burdened with the gift of prophecy, would ever use it to further one over another, even if one is blood to us?

"We are not kept soothsayers, hired crystal-ball-gazers, paid to advise, to *convince.* We see *what will be;* we don't suggest how it should be accomplished. We told the boy that he stood at a crossroads," Bellona repeated, her light-blue eyes blazing. Nadine felt a moment of fear; she had never seen happy, powerful Aunt Bellona angry like this before. "We simply told him that there would be two girls here for him last night."

Penny smirked. "Your princely *soulmate* applied his own interpretation *to that –"*

"We told him that whichever one he chose – she would love him with her entire being."

Nadine barked laughter. "Daina doesn't love him with her entire being. She only loves him with her –"

"We mentioned no names –"

"Just yesterday, we saw this particular young man entering your lives, 'Deen, and there he will remain," Penny said.

"I've known him for months," Nadine said mockingly.

"But he just met Daina," Penny countered. "Like I told you, your souls are linked. Yours, his, Daina's –"

"We didn't see what choice he would make, Nadine. Only that a choice *would be made,*" Bellona continued, still angry. "We are above *giving advice;* it is a petty, foolish juvenile that attempts to *control* the future. What will be, will be. We can use what glimpses we are given as forewarnings; we can only attempt to prepare for the inevitable." She laughed harshly. "It is of absolutely no consequence to us which one of the two of you this young man has chosen. Long ago, when she was just a child, we saw that Daina's path would be –"

"Perhaps we should leave Daina's path to Daina," Penny suggested quickly.

"Indeed," Bellona agreed. She began again. "Once upon a time we saw where Daina's path would lead. Before last night, it was unclear, but we know now who will accompany her upon it."

"She stole him from me," Nadine whispered, mostly to herself.

Penny shook her head firmly. *"My sources say no.* That's simply not the case, 'Deen! At different points in our lives, we are the chooser or the chosen, the victor or the victim, the maker of the decision or the one who must abide by the decision that's been made. Last night, it was Ian's turn to be in the driver's seat. Nobody *convinced* him; not us, not Daina, not you. All we told him was that he would make a choice."

"If we hadn't been on hand to tell him, he still would've made it, 'Deen. It was an intersection in his life, a juncture; *two roads diverged in a yellow wood . . ."*

"But he's my soulmate." Again Nadine whispered; again mostly to herself.

"There's that unfortunate word again!" Penny cried in exasperation. "What exactly does it mean, Nadine? I can't intelligently discuss a concept whose meaning is unknown to me. It's a silly word. Perhaps he *is* your *soulmate;* I cannot tell. What I do know is that he has chosen Daina as *an help meet for him,* to be his lover, his bride . . ."

"Life is long, 'Deen," Bellona said, suddenly softening. "Perhaps you'll also find –"

"But you've never seen it, have you?" Nadine hissed. "No *helpmate* for Nadine, no true love –"

"Cannot predict now," Penny said with amused sternness. "No one sees everything, Nadine. You're not even twenty-two years old. I don't think you're a desperate old maid quite yet."

"Not like us!" Bellona said and at last giggled. "Men are like buses, 'Deen. If you miss one –"

"Yeah, I've heard that one." Nadine sighed. She seemed to arrive at her own crossroads. "This is all I ask: that you never tell Daina that I . . . That I once . . . *coveted* her man." She smiled now, grimly. "That sort of thing tends to displace the mirth around the dinner table."

"We would never –"

"I would ask, if you love me, that you swear it."

Penny and Bellona looked at each other, shrugged, did not hesitate. "We swear," they said in unison.

Penny narrowed her eyes and studied Nadine for another heartbeat. Her fiery umbrage had abated, now replaced by resignation. *Men are like buses, the only cure for a man is another man, there are plenty of fish in the sea, she was looking for a man when she found this one, so another one wouldn't be hard to find . . .* All the clichés poured through Penny's mind.

Penny allowed herself a moment of pity for her niece. Nadine's love for the clever Roman was like a living thing; it was a shame that Ian had not picked her. But such was the way of life: *you can't always get what you want.*

Penny reflected that Nadine had grown into a competent witch, maybe even a powerful one. Nadine had long been a *solitaire* – Penny knew that she reveled in petty curses and peeks into the near future gleaned from the cards. *But perhaps,* Penny decided, *I should now also regard her as a practitioner.*

Where before Penny had been able to see the depth of Nadine's desires, now Nadine's feelings were closed, walled off. That could mean that Nadine had accepted what had occurred; *what's done cannot be undone.* Ian had chosen Daina. Nadine was strong, beautiful – she would find another.

Or, Penny realized, her sudden inability to ken Nadine's thoughts could mean that the stubborn witch had simply buried them, hidden them from Penny's prying mind. Maybe Nadine had accepted reality – the boy had chosen her friend – or maybe Nadine still harbored the dark fallacy that she'd give voice to earlier: *she stole him from me.*

Nadine was stubborn. If she believed that she had been wronged, who could guess what course she might take to satisfaction? Penny knew that right and wrong, what had happened and what one only believed had happened, didn't matter at all, not in the end. Only perception mattered. *The truth that survives is simply the lie that is pleasantest to believe.*

And if Nadine insisted on cleaving to this insane fantasy, that Daina had stolen her *soulmate,* Penny didn't think that Nadine would just roll over and take it. *Madness in great ones must not unwatch'd go.*

But surely, Nadine could see how ridiculous it was? Daina hadn't stolen Ian from her, because Nadine had never possessed Ian. Surely, eventually, she would just let it all go?

"Come, 'Deen, have some supper," Penny said.

After another moment's hesitation, Nadine gave in and joined them.

SIXTY-TWO

The first time was anonymous, selfish, brutal: *mad as the sea and wind, when both contend which is the mightier.* Daina had encompassed no societal propriety from the first moment that she'd seen Ian washed in the moonlight, and she employed not a whisper of shyness once she had him behind closed, locked doors. She didn't care to discover what *he* liked the first time, and she surely didn't care what he thought; she simply unleashed the cloudburst of her desire until she was *become a deluge,* and Ian received it, without question, without hesitation, until he was *overflow'd and drown'd.*

But these were words of sorrow, and Ian was not sorrowful. *Who shall measure the heat and violence of the poet's heart when caught and tangled in a woman's body?*

Ian had seen women's hunger before, but never like this. Daina's desire transformed her, made her awesome, breathtaking, splendid. And because it was only for him – by some unnamable force outside of himself, Ian knew that *it was only for him* – he responded from the core of his being. This was not some eager girl that he'd just effortlessly picked up, someone who would be forgotten, replaced in a few days. Daina was beautiful, a wild, stirring being of nature, and she was unabashedly showing him all that she wanted, because she wanted only him. The power of her desire for him alone was new to his experience: Ian knew that he had not been merely eenie, meenie, miney, mo'ed this time.

When at last they collapsed together, panting in wonder, Ian tangled his hands into her hair, and looked into her still-surprised blue eyes and told her that he loved her.

"I know you do," she said and kissed him again.

Taking her words as a challenge, Ian aimed to show her just how much he loved her, bringing all of his not-unimpressive skills to bear. And at the end, amazed, breathless as she'd never been before – all others were irrevocably forgotten – Daina said the words back to him. *"Ian! I love you!"*

He replied in kind. "I know you do."

And it was not out of smugness, or superiority, but because it was the plain truth. It was just like that song, the one he'd heard every time he'd turned the radio on since the spring: *Golden living dreams of visions, mystic crystal revelation, and the mind's true liberation . . .* Ian laughed with joy unknown before, and gathered her up in his arms.

Moments later, as they were about to begin again, Nadine screamed.

Seeing Nadine standing there, with the look of shocked disbelief on her face, Ian realized that her aunts' prophecy had come true. There *had* been two girls for him, and he'd made his choice, and the one he chose loved him with her entire being, just as they'd told him she would. He looked over his shoulder and smiled at Daina. He'd never doubt the witch and the fortuneteller again. A woman had changed his life.

When they closed the door to Daina's room again, he drew her to him, whispered against her hair, *"What made me love thee? Let that persuade thee there's something extraordinary in thee. I cannot: but I love thee; none but thee; and thou deservest it."*

Daina whooped laughter. She pranced to her little hi-fi, switched it on, dropped the needle onto the vinyl. There was the familiar drumroll, the keyboards.

Hello, I love you, won't you tell me your name . . .

SIXTY-THREE

At sundown, Daina and Ian realized that they were hungry for something else besides just each other, and arose to go out for something to eat. They decided on the tiny mom and pop pizza place just down the road from the house. Daina knocked on Nadine's door to see if she'd like to join them, but she was absent. It was just as well, because they really weren't ready for other company just yet. They still had only eyes and thoughts and words for each other.

Ian darted out to the truck wrapped in Daina's sheet. He rummaged around behind the seat until he found a pair of flip-flops, his swim trunks and a crumpled shirt. Daina laughed out loud at him when he put them on, and suggested that he could probably still pull off the gladiator outfit, seeing as it was only one day after Hallowe'en.

"No shirt, no service," Ian said and grinned back at her.

He did look a little bit like a displaced person, but it was all he had with him. He hadn't brought a change of clothes, because he hadn't thought that he wouldn't be going home after the party. He'd never in his wildest dreams imagined that he'd ever know anyone like the fiery, black-haired beauty that he'd met at Rob's cast-off's stupid little costumed get together.

Ian felt a little silly, a little self-conscious, being so inappropriately dressed for the season, wrinkled and slovenly. But he wasn't ready to leave Daina yet. He had places to go, people to see tonight. He had to share his revelations with Rob, he had to laugh at Will.

But not quite yet. He wanted to hear Daina's voice some more, listen to her words, contemplate her thoughts. He wanted to take in the whole person, learn everything about this woman. He was sure now that Penny and Bellona's prophecy was truth – Daina had changed his life, and he just wanted to look at her and consider all the happy ramifications of it for a while longer.

Daina knew that now – after the very first passions had been spent – now usually came the time for doubt. So it had always been in the past. Who was this guy? What did he do, how did he think? How was he judging her, and how would that judgment manifest itself in his behavior?

Because she had believed that none of the men she had met in the past were going to be around for very long, Daina had never held back, never played coy, once she decided that she wanted to be with them, even if it was only for the night. She'd never given a thought to their perceptions of her lack of shyness, and so it had been with Ian.

Neither of them had been shy.

Daina had never wanted anyone so much, from the first moment she saw him, and she had sensed the exact same desire in him. She had only had to wait a few hours, but in retrospect, it had seemed like a lifetime. There were the circumstances of the little get-together with her aunts and Nadine; she and Ian couldn't just disappear into the night.

But then Ian had disappeared on his own. Daina had been listening to Penny hold forth on ancient Hallowe'en traditions, but when she took a breath and Daina looked around for Ian, he was gone. Nadine was gone, too. Curious to where the two of them had gotten to, but neither worried nor jealous – Daina had known his mind from the first glances they'd shared – she found the door to her old room open. Ian was passed out on her old bed and Nadine was curled up behind him.

Just as curious, wondering what had become of the young people, her aunts joined her in the doorway. It was not a scene of passionate embrace, by any means. "Two dead soldiers," Bellona said with a grin.

"Some people just can't hold their potions," Penny agreed.

Daina had smiled, kissed her beloved aunts goodnight. She'd gone back home, cleaned up the empty paper cups and beer bottles strewn throughout her house, emptied the ashtrays, washed out the punch bowl and put it away. Daina bathed, put on her pj's, tried to rest. She would see Ian sometime tomorrow, and then . . .

But the moment Daina closed her eyes, the memory of him filled her mind, a gorgeous Spartacus, standing there in the moonlight, that fire of yearning for her alive in his dark-blue eyes. Her bed seemed narrow and constricted, a chained coffin for a starving vampire. She couldn't sleep. Daina thought she might never sleep again, not until she had kissed him, until she had run her eager hands over his exquisite body. Awake, still she dreamed of him.

Daina put on her bunny slippers and went back up the hill. She snuck back into the silent house just as the sun was coming up. She made a pot of coffee, and with a steaming cup in hand, she went back into her childhood bedroom to watch Ian sleep. To wait for him.

He and Nadine were in exactly the same position. Her aunts' cider was soporific, narcotic – Ian and Nadine were not so much asleep as comatose, Daina thought with a grin. Yet the delicious, cinnamony concoction hadn't had the same effect on her. She was not even remotely sleepy: she felt alive, aware, tingly. Again Daina thought that she would never rest again, not until she had exhausted herself *with him*. She reached across and brushed the hair out of his eyes; Ian smiled in his sleep at her touch. Daina waited.

She considered Nadine curled up with him, her arm thrown possessively over his hip. It was obvious that Ian had passed out first, and Nadine had crawled in behind him. Daina wondered – was Ian the one that Nadine had been referring to as *her new man?* She'd told Daina that she hadn't approached him yet, out of fear of *jinxing it*. If Ian was indeed the object of Nadine's affection, he was ignorant of it; it remained a secret, unrequited crush.

He clearly didn't know; he'd shown not a scintilla of interest in Nadine the night before, had looked like an uncomfortable, whipped pup every time she'd made him dance with her. If it was Ian that Nadine had been considering – *outlook not so good,* Daina thought with a wry smile.

Daina recalled probably the only snippet of verse that she knew, something Aunt Bellona had recited to her once, when Daina was trying to decide whether or not she wanted to go to all the trouble of attending senior prom with the captain of the football team. He was cute, but Daina had been unsure that she wanted to jump through all the hoops of taffeta and wrist corsages involved with such an event.

"When love once pleas admission to our hearts, (in spite of all the virtue we can boast), the woman that deliberates is lost," Aunt Bellona said.

Those few fanciful words had decided Daina. The football player wasn't that cute. She'd skipped senior prom.

Daina didn't know the context of the quote, or who'd said it – *Ian would probably know,* she realized with a little grin – but it came back to her mind now. *Ya shoulda spoke up when ya had the chance, 'Deen,* she thought. *If Ian was the one you thought you wanted – que sera, sera. You lose. He wants* me. *Another one'll be along in a minute . . .*

SIXTY-FOUR

Now Daina watched him across their pepperoni-pizza-for-two, the house specialty. He was *so unbelievably sexy;* but life couldn't be spent only in bed. Although if it could be arranged somehow, Daina thought, she would give up a lot just to attempt such a thing with this one.

She hoped he wouldn't turn out to be a boring snore-fest outside the bedroom, like Will had been. She hoped that he wouldn't stare dreamily at her, like he was in love, as a few of them had done. She hoped that he wouldn't talk down to her like he was her lord and master, as if it had been his own magnetism, and not simply her momentary desire, that had made her agree to sleep with him. That had happened before – 'ol Will had shown a little bit of that misplaced conceit, before he had lapsed back to his normal, plain vanilla, unexciting self.

Daina discovered that she wanted to *like* Ian, outside the bedroom. She wanted to do more than just tolerate him, as she had Will and all the others, until eventually she wasn't able to stand them at all. She wanted to keep Ian around, enjoy his fabulous self, for as long as possible. And she had to at least *like* him to do that.

But Ian was just Ian. He smiled, dropped a line of verse here and there. He was friendly, clever; he was amused, happy.

And goddamn, he was sexy! Daina continued to marvel at it. She wasn't entirely oblivious to what he said – she kept up her end of the conversation – but mostly she just looked at him. Every smile, every gesture: the way he shook the hair out of his eyes sometimes, the way he would look over his shoulder for a moment, then turn back and grin at her; the play of the light through his dark hair, that adorable squint. There was not one single thing about Ian that didn't absolutely *compel* her attention.

Daina thought that she could just *look at him* forever. He wasn't delicate of feature like the actors she'd once coveted, but *hot damn,* she had never in her entire life been so attracted to anyone. And once she got him naked! Sitting here in this dim little pizzeria, Daina shivered, just remembering it. She wanted to hold his hand, run her fingers over his wrinkled sleeves, feel his muscled arms. She wanted to touch his back, she wanted to hug him, to kiss him . . .

Ian was fascinating, hypnotizing. Even if he sometimes said silly things, Daina reflected that it would be a long time before she would ever even begin to be bored with Ian. She discovered that she *did* like him.

She didn't love him – Daina had never felt anything for a man other than a momentary lust, a passing fondness – and telling him that she loved him last night had been a trifle over-the-top. But on the other hand, Daina thought, maybe it hadn't been. She certainly loved how he made her feel, just by being here in the world, just by being nearby for her to look at. And when he touched her, when he allowed her to touch him . . . It came to Daina suddenly that she had never in her life loved *anything* more than that.

SIXTY-FIVE

After their quick dinner, they drove back to Daina's house and Ian kissed her tenderly at the door. "I've gotta go to work," he told her. He consulted a non-existent watch on his wrist. "I'm gonna be late as it is. I'm on 'til midnight."

"What would you like for breakfast?" Daina was not being coy or sly. Like the sun, she already knew that he'd be here in the morning. She just wanted to know what to have on hand for him to eat.

Nor did Ian pause at the question. He'd known her less than twenty-four hours, but it seemed like he'd known her all his life, like he'd never *not* known her. Little details, like having to ask what he wanted for breakfast, kept pointing up the fact that this was not the case. They'd just met. It was incredible.

"Bacon and eggs is always good," he told her.

"Okay," Daina kissed his nose. "I'll see ya when I see ya."

SIXTY-SIX

When he got home, Ian found his parents in the den, watching the news. "TWA Flight 85, en route from Los Angeles to San Francisco was hijacked last night by nineteen-year old U.S. Marine Raffaele Minichiello," Jerry Dunphy told them. "Mrs. Winifred Chapman, the maid who discovered murder victim Sharon Tate on August 9th, is now living in seclusion."

The moving finger writes; and, having writ, moves on: nor all your piety nor wit shall lure it back to cancel half a line, nor all your tears wash out a word of it, Ian thought and grinned to himself. Commerce and industry, hijackings and the investigations of heinous crimes – none of it touched him tonight. He had met a girl, and she had changed his life.

Ian said hi to his dad, kissed his mom on the cheek. "Rough night, son?" she said with an indulgent smile, indicating his appearance. "Did you sleep in the truck?"

"Don't ask him where he slept, Marcia," his dad said, trying to be stern. "Not unless you really want to know."

Ian grinned. "Henceforth, I'll always be sleeping in the same place, Mom," he said, thinking, *It'll be with Daina.* "I'll tell you all about it soon. But not now. I gotta go earn my keep."

"And it's about time," his dad said, his grin breaking through to match his son's.

Ian bounded up the stairs to take a quick shower and change into something presentable for work. On his way back out the door, he called his royal cousin.

"Meet me at the bar. And bring Will. I've got news."

SIXTY-SEVEN

On the day after Hallowe'en, 1969, custom was slow at the little just-off-campus bar where blue-eyed Ian Wilde tended bar. He saw Rob and Will when they strolled in, before they saw him, as they paused to greet three girls sitting at a table by the door. Will smiled warmly at them and Rob mirrored his smile, and Ian reflected that, as Doctor Mengele had so fatally observed, it was fascinating how completely identical twins could be.

Ian had never had the slightest bit of difficulty telling them apart, at least not if they were looking at him. But if they hadn't seen him yet, like now, his perception was just like everyone else's: it was like seeing double. Sprung from a single egg's divide, they seemed to be the same person. But all they had to do was glance in Ian's direction and they would resolve immediately into individuals: Rob would always smile – Ian was his best friend. Will would never smile, because Will had never been able to hide the basic dislike he'd always harbored for his cousin.

Their small talk completed, the charming Wilde twins approached the bar. Will was on the left: Ian could tell because of his austere frown. But Ian grinned at him anyway and vaulted over the bar. He took Will's face in both hands, and kissed him directly on the mouth.

"How the hell are ya, Cuz, my best friend in the whole wide world? I just spent the night with your ex-girlfriend, and I've gotta tell you, you are just about the dumbest . . . Never mind. That's no way to show my gratitude." Ian slapped his shocked cousin playfully on the cheek and leaned back against the bar.

After a moment, when it appeared that his idiot cousin wasn't going to say anything further, Will recovered from the surprise of goddamned Ian kissing him in front of a bar full of people. He said, "Ex-girlfriend? You're gonna have to be a little more specific than that."

"They are legion," Rob said.

"I'd forgotten the breadth of his charisma." Ian grinned at Rob, then addressed Will again. "I'm talking about your last one. Daina." Ian shook his head. "I must say that your taste is definitely in your mouth, Will. The idea that you'd throw Daina over for Marta . . ." He shook his head again, the very picture of disbelief.

"Where did you meet . . .?"

Will didn't really care. He paused, shrugged, then said, "Have at her. She's all yours. She was a little . . . *down to earth* for my tastes. But if you like her . . . Different strokes for different folks, I guess." Will winked at his brother. "But if you'd like a little advice on what kind of *stroking* Daina likes, why . . . All ya gotta do is ask me. *Cuz.*"

Rob looked at Ian to see how his cousin would react to *that* little bon mot. He was surprised when a shadow crossed Ian's features; his eyes narrowed and they glittered dangerously. His smile turned sardonic, his voice soft, just the tiniest bit threatening.

"Just because I kissed you, don't think you can talk to me like I'm a whore, my brutha."

Rob's own smile evaporated in surprise at the change in Ian's tone.

"Now, once upon a time," Ian said to Will, "you liked Marta. You invited her all the way to Parker, just so you could chivalrously demonstrate just *how much* you liked her. But, alas . . ."

Ian's face resolved itself into pathos, and now Will's smug grin faltered.

"Marta discovered what she liked, and like it she did, right under your pining, puppy-dog nose. What Marta liked was *me*. And thoroughly."

Ian wiggled his eyebrows at Will, who wasn't smiling at all anymore. Rob's grin crept back, however. He'd heard all about how thoroughly Marta had *liked* Ian.

"But Marta, ambitious society girl that she is, has changed her mind, and not a day goes by that I don't thank her for it. She has her future to think about, after all. Where she'd like to end up on that social ladder. Married to a *doctor*, perhaps? These kind of things concern a girl like Marta. To someone like her, there are certainly other things in life than just spectacular sex with the local waterski bum, and she's willing to make compromises to achieve them."

Ian blinked slowly, arrogantly, then he flashed a quick grin at Rob. "Although she did frequently say that I was . . ." Ian shook his head, as if embarrassed at Marta's praise.

"But that's neither here nor there, now. Is it, Will? All water under the bridge, just memories for cold winter's nights. I hope to dance at your wedding, my most fortunate cousin. You have won Riverside's most eligible debutante, and she's all yours, regardless of what she ever thought of me.

"But while we're on the subject of what the ladies like . . . I'm sure that you believe, through your brief couple of weeks with her, that you figured out, all on your own, what Daina likes. But I doubt it sincerely, *Cuz,* because what Daina likes now is *me,* just like Marta once did."

Again, Ian grinned quickly at Rob. "And since we are gentlemen, a discussion of what these discerning ladies *like* . . . Why, such a discussion is beneath us, don't you agree? And therefore, I would *beseech* you not to bring it up again, Will, lest I have to summarily put the sword to such unsophisticated talk . . ."

Will blinked, startled at the menace in his cousin's eye, no longer veiled: If Will said anything off-color about Daina again, Ian would take great relish in shutting him up.

His point made, Ian laughed. "Let's just say, it's best to leave sleeping dogs lie, wouldn't you say? Rob?"

"Indubitably," Rob agreed immediately.

Speechless, Will just stood there. Another heartbeat passed, and Ian clapped him heavily on the shoulder, "But since I owe so much to your colossal lapse in judgment, please, do me the honor of allowing me to buy you a beer." The Blue-eyed Bartender again vaulted back over the bar and went to the taps. "Nay, allow me to buy you an entire pitcher." He nodded at the three girls at the table by the door. "Yon ladies appear to have a mean thirst. Allow me this small gesture to help you entertain them." Ian spun the filled pitcher in front of Rob.

"Why, thank you, Cuz!" Rob said. He took the pitcher and crossed the room to present it to the ladies. Ian gave a little nod of his head and winked at Will, who still stood there dumbfounded. "My treat. Enjoy." Ian then turned, effectively dismissing his cousin, and waited on another patron.

Will walked over to the table. "What the hell was that?" he said to his brother.

Rob, smiling, was pouring beer into the surprised girls' glasses. He shrugged. "Apparently, Cousin Ian *likes* your ex. I can't really blame him. She's cute." He winked at the blonde sitting closest to him. "But not as cute as you." The girl tittered.

"Where did he meet Daina?" Will asked.

Again Rob shrugged, and filled a glass for the freckled girl seated beside the blonde. "Maybe he ran into Nadine at school. She must've introduced them." Rob started to pour beer into the last girl's glass.

225

Now Will grinned. "If anybody was going to wind up with Ian, I would've guessed it would've been Nadine. You didn't catch how she looked at him in Parker. Just like Sissy."

Rob's smile faded. He looked over at his cousin, then back at his brother. He remembered that one weekend when he'd been sick, how Nadine had rather unceremoniously abandoned him to go skiing with Ian and Marta the next morning. And Nadine didn't even ski. Rob's normal eloquence left him. Nonplussed at the very idea, all he could say was, *"Really?"*

Will nodded. "I thought sure that we'd get back from Europe and find them all paired up. The minute he was single, it seemed like she was in a mighty big hurry to dump you."

"I dumped her," Rob protested.

"Did you?" Will looked over at Ian. He was talking to two frat boys, and completely ignoring a doe-eyed coed that was smiling winningly at him. He gave her the beer she ordered and took her money without so much as glancing at her.

Rob also looked at him again, then back at his brother. He shrugged a third time. "Who cares? Just like he said, it's all water under the bridge. Who cares who he's with? Daina, Nadine. Who? They're all ancient history." Rob smiled expansively at the three girls as they sipped their beers. "We have these lovelies to keep us company tonight."

SIXTY-EIGHT

After Ian went home, Daina reclined on the couch and turned on the television. A not-unpleasant feeling of weariness descended upon her. It was as if she was enveloped in a great pool of warm water, swirling gently around her suddenly heavy limbs. As Jerry Dunphy began his newscast – "From the desert to the sea, to all of Southern California, a good evening" – Daina felt herself drifting off. She had been awake for at least thirty-six hours; she had met and enjoyed the most spectacularly sexy man she'd ever known, and he wouldn't be off work until midnight. A little nap would do her good.

Daina lazily opened her eyes when she heard Nadine snap off the TV. She yawned, stretched her arms above her head, dropped them limply to her sides. She smiled at her friend.

Nadine smiled back blankly. "How was it?"

"Incredible." Daina smiled, stretched again. She hugged herself, remembering just how incredible it had been.

"I can imagine," Nadine said.

Her tone of voice was neutral, devoid of the usual prurient, *I wanna hear details* edge that habitually accompanied such a remark between them. This absence caused Daina to glance inquisitively at her friend. Nadine stared back at her steadily, expressionlessly.

The idea crossed Daina's mind again: "The guy you told me about . . . The one you like. It wasn't Ian, was it?"

What if it is, you conniving bitch? the imp screamed in Nadine's mind. *You didn't think about that when you dragged him out of the bed he was sharing with me, did you?*

Nadine didn't fail to notice Daina's egotistical use of the past tense, either, as if one night with her had erased all of Ian's romps with anyone else, past or future. As if he would never *like* anyone else again.

Nadine had always overlooked Ian's friendly proclivities in the past, because she believed he was fated to end up with her. Maybe it wasn't too late, after all; her aunts' prognostications be damned. Ian had just taken advantage of what had been so blatantly offered to him, like he usually did. He was just a man, after all, and Daina was a whore.

"Nah," Nadine said in answer to Daina's question, adding a broad, dismissive wave of her hand. "Ian's cute, but he's a little too much of a tomcat for me. I watched him pick up two girls at once when we were in Parker." Nadine watched for a sign of jealousy in Daina, but she was disappointed.

"I don't doubt it," Daina said appreciatively. "He's . . ." She shivered in delight.

"He was supposed to be going with this girl named Marta when he picked these two chicks up." Nadine's voice took on a sympathetic note which didn't reach her eyes. "I didn't tell you this before, Daina, because it didn't matter at the time. But – the girl that Will left you for? It was Ian's girlfriend, Marta."

The name rang a bell in Daina's mind. Rob had said it to his brother: *You're just jealous because he got to Marta before you did.*

And later, Will had said into the phone: *Just calm down, Marta, for Christ's sake!* Then: *My cousin's girlfriend thinks I'm Doctor Feelgood.*

Then Will had gone to take her some pain killers. Now that Nadine had said her name, Daina made the connection – *You're just jealous 'because he got to Marta before you did* – the old girlfriend that Will had to reconcile with? Daina had already heard of her before.

"Marta and Ian had been going together for more than a year, but then . . . I guess Marta got tired of Ian cheating on her," Nadine continued, still looking steadily at Daina. "Ian caught her and Will in the sack together. I overheard him tell Rob about it. Then Will came home and broke up with you."

That was when the pieces began to fall into place, Nadine thought. *Transitory relationships were being pushed aside, paving the way for Ian and me to be together. But the witches at the top of the hill interfered, attempted to change the course of true love. They told him half-truths, plied him with their* aphrodisiac *cider, pointed him toward her . . . But all that had worn off by now.*

Maybe he'll still see. Daina's just another tramp, just another girl like the two he picked up in Parker, just like the endless string that hand their phone numbers to him every night at the bar. Daina was nothing to him. Maybe he'll still see . . . Maybe it's not too late after all.

"Maybe Ian just took an interest in you because he wanted to get back at Will for nailing his girlfriend," Nadine opined.

Daina's eyebrows went up in surprise. What a cruel remark!

Daina knew that what Nadine was proposing was absurd. Ian hadn't chosen her out of some kind of petty revenge. The amazed expression in his eyes last night had said it all – he wasn't thinking of Will or Martha, or whatever her name was, when he looked at Daina. He wasn't thinking of backstabbing or vindication. He'd simply *wanted* Daina, and completely, in exactly the same way she'd wanted him.

Ian had harbored no ulterior motives last night; his only drive had been desire for Daina – distilled; undiluted by anything so common as thought. Diana knew this like she knew how to breathe. She reminded herself to bring it up to him – *you chose me because you wanted to get back at Will* – Daina knew they'd have a fine guffaw over that one. Ian had chosen her because she had chosen him; it was as simple, as inexplicable as that.

But even if Ian's motivation had been to somehow repay Will, Daina couldn't believe that Nadine would be so cruel as to point it out. The thought crossed Daina's mind that despite her denial, maybe Ian *was* the one that Nadine had been after. *Why else would she attempt to wound me like this?*

But you lost, sister, Daina thought with her own streak of cruelty. *All the mean insinuations in the world aren't going to change that. He's mine, for as long as I choose to keep him.*

Nadine was studying her, waiting for a reaction, so Daina said, "If Ian was just trying to get back at Will, it would've been a one off, wouldn't it? *Hey, Will, I fucked your ex-girlfriend, how 'bout them apples?"* Nadine blinked as if slapped at Daina's profanity. *"Now we're even!"*

Daina grinned salaciously. "But that's not how it is, 'Deen. He'll be back tonight, after his shift at the bar. Let's just say he's . . . We're . . ." The understanding surprised Daina, even as the words came out of her mouth. "Let's just say, we're a couple now."

Nadine was appalled at Daina's smugness, her confidence, after just one night with Ian, like she truly believed that she was something special to him. She was just an easy piece of ass, just like the hundreds of others that Ian had carelessly picked up. How could she possibly believe that she was any different to him?

Nadine smiled tightly, displaying a touch of pity. "I'd have him take a shower once he gets here. I've been to that bar, seen him . . . *at work.* You never know what kind of germs he might pick up there."

Again, Daina was surprised at Nadine's nastiness. She changed the subject back to her original question. "The guy you were talking about . . . Your *new man?* Was he here last night? Was it the blonde?" *The asshole that just stood by and watched while you drank enough Everclear to stun a moose?*

Nadine raised her chin defiantly. Why not? Why couldn't her new man be Chuck? She would rather voluntarily jump into a pit of Punji sticks than go out with Chuck, but Daina didn't know that. Daina didn't see past their looks – Chuck was tall and dimpled and blonde – he was certainly more attractive than dumpy, squinty Ian – or at least Nadine would lead Daina to believe that she thought so.

"Yeah. Big 'ol Chuck." Nadine looked at her feet sheepishly. "I didn't want him to see me after I got so drunk. That's why I hid out with you guys. I'm sure he took off after he thought I passed out. I'll make my apologies the next time I see him."

"I'm sure he'll understand," Daina commented sympathetically. She couldn't help adding, "Maybe the four of us can all go out together, like we used to do with the twins."

"Sure," Nadine said. *Right after I blow my brains out. But you first.* "That sounds like fun."

Nadine imagined the look on Chuck's face. She didn't know what would surprise him more: that Nadine was suddenly willing to go out with him, or that they were going to double with Daina and the Blue-eyed Bartender, the guy that was supposed to be *Nadine's* boyfriend. Regardless, Chuck would believe that it was his wit and inestimable charm that had led Nadine to throw Ian over and at last succumb to him. Oh, yeah. That would be just loads of laughs.

Nadine continued to look at Daina for another heartbeat of uncomfortable silence. Then she said, "Well!" a little breathlessly. "I'm bushed. I'm going to turn in early. I'm sure you want to get ready for your date."

There was that subtle nastiness again, when Nadine said *date,* as if there was something dirty about it. Her tone was inescapable, and Daina wondered if Nadine even realized it was there.

"I'll see you in the morning," Daina replied and Nadine flounced quickly out of the room.

You'd better get over it, sister. Daina stood and stretched again. *I would never have imagined that our friendship could ever be in jeopardy because of some man.* She grinned to herself. *But Ian is more than just some man. He's something* else. *And for as long as he's around . . . You're just gonna have to get over it, 'Deen.*

SIXTY-NINE

Ian chewed a limp strip of bacon and looked down at his soggy scrambled eggs. If this breakfast was any indication, he decided that Daina probably wasn't much of a cook. Not too many girls were, these days, he reflected, what with Women's Lib and all. Their men could starve, or fend for themselves – most young women were too busy *finding themselves,* to learn how to make crispy bacon and fluffy eggs at their mother's knee.

There had been that chubby one Will had dated for a second, however. What was her name? Katy? Candace? *Catherine.* That was it. Now she could cook. Ian recalled the whole summer of Catherine's good cooking in Parker last year. He thought that he might even have picked up a pound or two from it, if it hadn't been for skiing every day behind the *Ooh-La-La,* and entertaining all the ladies that the sleek wooden boat had helped him to meet.

But Ian could not possibly care less about Daina's culinary skills. He could tell that she was concerned about his reaction to them though, so when she looked worriedly at him, he smiled and quickly gobbled up his sodden breakfast. Her coffee wasn't too bad, and he smiled at Nadine over the rim of his cup when she came into the kitchen.

"Breakfast, 'Deen?" Daina chirped.

"I'll just have some toast," Nadine returned evenly. She already knew Daina couldn't cook. She flopped down into a chair beside Ian, took a piece of Daina's slightly burnt toast, grimaced at it. She regarded him coolly whilst she buttered it. She took a bite without speaking to him, then abruptly rose and left the room.

Ian considered Nadine's sudden unfriendliness; he believed that he knew its source. "I've been thinking that maybe we should get our own place," he said matter-of-factly to Daina, as if had been something he'd been mulling over for a long time. As if he had known her for more two than days; as if he knew what her favorite color was, or her middle name.

Daina was at the sink, gamely scrubbing the eggs out of the skillet. She set it down and turned to look at him. Deadpan, she asked, "And why is that?"

Ian manfully crunched into a nearly black slice of toast. How was it possible for anyone, in 1969, to burn toast?

"I was just thinking. I'm sure Nadine's aunts and her parents . . . I'm sure they know I'm here. I'm sure they saw the truck parked here overnight. I'm sure they're not too happy about a strange man staying at their girl's house."

Daina's couldn't hide her grin. "Whatever gave you the idea that this is *their girl's* house?"

Ian returned her grin. "It's all fate, you see. When I first met Miss Penny and Miss Bellona – it was because Nadine had dragged me up the hill from the party. And then she abandoned me in the woods. Like Hansel and Gretel, I happened upon the witch's gingerbread house . . . And they told me my future."

Daina's smile darkened a shade, faltered. Here was her legacy come home to roost once more, her aunts and their supernatural divinations, something that she'd tried to escape, or at least ignore, for most of her life. "What did they say?"

"They lured me up on the deck with the promise that I would meet two girls that night. I naturally assumed –"

"I bet you did."

Ian shrugged. Becoming, overnight, a one-woman man, had not dimmed his arrogance. "But Miss Penny disabused me of that notion. 'You mustn't be greedy, my sweet young friend,' she told me. 'You must choose between them.' She told me that one of the girls that I would meet that night would change my life. And she was right."

Damn them, Daina thought. *Why did they always have to be meddling?*

"But what does that have to do with . . . Why do you think that this is Nadine's house?"

"'Economics first,' Miss Penny said, then called me some nasty name in Latin. She said that one of the girls I would meet was poor, that I would have to support her. I was all right with that," Ian lied.

"They said that the other one was wealthy, *propertied.* Then Nadine showed up and introduced me to them as her aunts. It occurred to me then that these crafty old spinsters were trying to set me up with their niece. I thought that there was only one girl, not two, and they wanted to make Nadine seem more eligible. Her aunts lived there, her parents across the street; she had this nice house at the bottom of the hill. I figured that they just wanted me to know that Nadine stood to inherit it all.

"But I was mistaken. There *were* two girls. And Nadine's aunts' prophecy was true. I just didn't choose the one with the real estate. So I was just thinking that maybe, since I didn't choose their wealthy niece, they might be more happy if her friend and I moved somewhere else."

Daina laughed, her aunts' interferences forgotten. "You have misled yourself, Ian. You know what happens when you assume." He just looked blankly at her, waiting for her to enlighten him. "It's true that Nadine's parents own the house across the street. *They and the bank,* as Penny is fond of pointing out.

"My parents were killed in a car accident when I was seven, Ian. I was raised in this house; then, after Mom and Dad were gone, my mother's sisters raised me. We've been friends, Nadine and I, since she moved in across the street when we were nine. We've always been like family, so she's always referred to Penny and Bellona as her aunts, too. But the witches at the top of the hill aren't actually Nadine's kin.

"Just this summer, they decided that I was a grown up. 'You can't be cooped up with your old aunts anymore,' Bellona said. 'You need a place of your own.' So, while Nadine and I were . . . out of town, they opened this place up, had it painted, then presented it to me when we got back. I invited my best friend to move in with me. This isn't Nadine's house, Ian. It's mine. We don't have to move anywhere."

The revelation that Daina was the wealthy girl of which the witch and the fortuneteller had spoken, the *propertied* one, affected Ian not in the least. He was from money enough, and thereby he had never taken financial solvency in women into consideration – not in the slightest.

But he pretended that it mattered to him for Daina. "Maybe I should be nicer to you now that I know you're a rich girl. Mind my p's and q's."

Daina sat on his lap and wrapped her arms around his neck, kissed his nose. *"Can* you be nicer to me? I don't think so. Besides, I'm not a rich girl. This land has been in the family for a long time, and *our forefathers made sound investments,* as Bellona says. It's not like I can be buying Porsches and jetting off to Europe every summer, like your cousins."

"They said you weren't extravagant." *How accurate it all was!* Ian marveled.

Daina's mind clouded. "What else did they say?"

"That last night I stood at a crossroads. They said that the girl I chose –"

"Did you think Nadine liked you? When she invited you to the party?"

Ian shrugged. "Nadine's always just been Rob's ex-girlfriend to me." Then he smiled. "Your aunts said that you both liked me. With *your entire being.*"

Daina looked at him skeptically. "I'd never even seen you before." But that wasn't entirely true, was it? She'd seen that exquisite photograph of him . . .

"But it's true isn't it? Don't you love me with –"

"So Nadine *did* have a crush on you," Daina interrupted. She didn't want Ian to dwell on her unfortunate exclamation from their first moments together. She certainly loved what he *did,* what they did *together,* but as far as loving him . . . Daina had never loved anyone, except her parents and her aunts and her best friend. Certainly not any man.

Ian shrugged. "If Nadine had a crush on me, she never let me in on it. *Who could refrain that had a heart to love and in that heart courage to make love known? They do not love that do not show their love.* Regardless, it's way too late now. *My bounty is as boundless as the sea, my love as deep; the more I give to thee, the more I have, for both are infinite.*"

Daina was a little disconcerted at Ian's flowery declarations of how much he loved her, but she figured that it was just the way he was. She giggled and kissed him, and knowing that he wanted her to say something back, she said, "That's right. You're my man now." *Until you become tiresome, and I become bored with you, just like all the rest.* A thought struck Daina, and she wiggled her eyebrows at him. "I'm supposed to love you *with my entire being?*"

"That's what they said."

"Far be it for me to disagree with my aunts' predictions." Daina stood and took Ian's hand. "Come. Allow me to demonstrate." She tugged him toward the bedroom. She didn't know about her *entire being;* but Daina knew that she would never pass up an opportunity to love Ian with her *entire body.*

"Lay on, Macduff," Ian said softly. He embraced her, nuzzled her ear. *"And damn'd be him that first cries, 'Hold, enough!'"*

It didn't matter to Ian that Daina laughed at his verses, that she didn't care to comprehend the beauty and the depth and the meaning of the words. For the first time in his life, *he* felt them; in his heart, in his soul. The concepts had always existed in his mind, but before he met Daina, they'd resided there only as abstract ideals, divinely, timelessly rendered – but they were feelings and sentiments that belonged to someone else.

A well-timed *how do I love thee* had never failed to gain a girl's attention in the past. She would feel the words, make herself believe that Ian meant them especially for her. The knack had always been but a tool for Ian before. It was the same as when a shade-tree mechanic, someone who worked on cars for his own pleasure, discovered that he could get girls by fixing theirs. Ian had not learned poetry for the purpose of bewitching women; he had learned it before he had understood anything about women. The music of language had always fascinated Ian.

But his talent for a romantic turn of phrase had never failed to impress them, nonetheless. Except Daina wasn't impressed, not in the least.

It didn't matter to Ian. In fact, he found her lack of wonder amusing. When Ian spoke to Daina in verse, the words now meant something *to him,* for the first time in his life. It didn't matter that she only smiled indulgently, uncomprehendingly, in response. Ian felt these immortal truths in his soul, instead of just his mind, now, and that was almost as agreeable to him as the belief that he had actually discovered his own Juliet, his own Miranda, his own Cleopatra.

Daina loved Ian for himself, not because of the borrowed words of famous poets. That was refreshing, too. Ian knew that Daina wanted him, even if he was silent. Even if he recited limericks. The words didn't matter.

Daina laughed at him now, shook her head, paused to kiss him. "The things you say." She led him to the bedroom.

SEVENTY

Nadine visited her parents frequently now, anytime her melancholy over Daina's continued presence in Ian's life threatened to overwhelm her. On December 2nd, she walked across the street to have dinner with them.

Thanksgiving dinner had been a particular trial for Nadine. She hadn't had the meal with her parents in years. Her aunts always cooked, and since Nadine thought of them as family more than her own kin, Nadine's mom and dad had always gone to other relatives' homes without her. So now, she couldn't escape. The new, happy couple had decided to cook everything themselves, refusing all help from Nadine, and even from those chefs extraordinaire, Penny and Bellona, and Nadine had to sit by and witness it.

The turkey had been dry, the stuffing soggy. Cooking was just not Daina's thing. But it wasn't the mediocrity of the dinner that had irked Nadine. It was having to endure Ian and Daina's twittering, mindless domesticity all day, the *honeys* and the *babys* and the *sweeties;* the fond smiles, the cute, quick kisses.

Regardless of how happy they *seemed* to be, Nadine had decided on a course of action: she would just wait out this temporary thing between her soulmate and Daina. It had only been a little over a month, and so what if they still smiled and laughed and held hands like they'd just met that very day? So what if Nadine sometimes had to wrap her pillow around her ears so she couldn't hear them at night, *again,* still as noisy and exuberant as if it was their first time?

It didn't matter that Daina saw herself as *going with* Ian, that she thought of him as her one and only, her *boyfriend.* Marta had thought of him the same way, had she not? And that had lasted more than a year; but it had splintered into dust at last. Nadine was patient. This thing between Ian and Daina would run its course, too. Then she would make her move.

Nadine wouldn't have far to go. She knew that Ian had lived at home when he was dating Marta. Now, for all intents and purposes, he lived with Daina. Nadine thought it would be a little awkward when Ian finally saw the error in his choice – what would he do, just move his stuff down the hall to Nadine's room? Would Daina have to listen to him and Nadine then?

As much as Nadine would enjoy that, at least a couple of times, in the long run, it just wouldn't do.

Nadine figured that, once Ian saw his true path, they would just find a little place somewhere together. A sunny little apartment . . . Nadine would find a job to help with her share of the rent, and she would finally make a break with Daina. That chapter of her life would conclude.

That such a thing had to occur was sad, but it was past time. There were other people in the world, even other witches. Nadine thought she might strike up a deeper friendship with Aunt Lily from Mohini's, once she and Ian started their lives together. It was only a matter of time, of having a little patience . . .

Nadine's dad had gruffly accepted Ian's residence under the same roof as his daughter. Sam had overlooked those few overnight visits from the twins earlier in the summer – his daughter was not a child, after all, and was allowed to *express herself* with a young man occasionally – it was the way of the times.

He'd been glad when those importuning twins had disappeared, however. They hadn't been around for very long, and Sam believed that such brief relationships might be his daughter and her friend's lot: that's what they got for being so willing to *express themselves* overnight with young men. It was that whole buying the cow, getting the milk for free thing. But it wasn't for him to judge. They were old enough to make their own mistakes.

But Sam knew that the dark-haired kid had been there every single night since Hallowe'en. Such shacking up was disgraceful. He was glad that there weren't any other houses on their street, that there weren't any nosy neighbors around to witness Daina kissing and hugging on this guy in front of her house in broad daylight, when they weren't married.

But Sam was also secretly glad that the stocky kid was there with the girls, especially at night. The shame wasn't on his daughter, and he was less worried about her safety, if there was a man at the house. Times were scary. They still hadn't caught whatever monster it had been that had slain that pretty actress and her friends in LA.

Irene Germaine was just glad to see her baby girl tonight: the house had been a little lonely since Nadine had moved across the street, so anytime she dropped by, her mother made her feel more than welcome. She'd made spaghetti for dinner this evening, just because it was Nadine's favorite.

"Well, it's about time!" Sam exclaimed. With a flourish, he folded over the *LA Times* he'd been reading, and shared the news aloud with his girls. *"Band of Nomads charged in Sharon Tate*

Murder Case. *The three suspects in the brutal Sharon Tate murders belonged to a nomadic band which lived on the edge of the searing Death Valley and pillaged their way through California, police said Monday.*

"The group was broken up last October when sheriffs' deputies raided their camp and arrested twenty-six young men and women. Some of the women were nude when they were arrested. Others wore only bikini bottoms. Men in the group had shoulder-length hair and wore 'love beads.'"

Sam looked across the table at his daughter. She was wearing several strands of beads, large and small, brightly colored. *Love beads.* To hide his shock, he resumed reading the paper to them.

"The group had set up elaborate observation posts equipped with walkie-talkies surrounding its camp . . ." Sam skimmed. *"The group, described by Los Angeles police chief Edward Davis as a 'roving band of hippies,' migrated from Spawn Movie Ranch in the San Fernando Valley northwest of Los Angeles after the slayings. The suspects were also linked with the stabbing deaths of a middle-aged couple in Los Angeles two days after the five Tate killings."*

Sam folded the paper over and put it on the table. He studied his daughter. She looked blankly back at him, with her long straight hair, parted down the middle, and her tight sweater – she was obviously braless underneath – and her hip-hugging bell-bottoms. Her *love beads.* All that was missing were flowers in her hair. Sam recognized it for the first time, and was shaken: his proud, strong-minded daughter was a hippie.

He looked at his wife, obliviously scooping out pasta onto their plates, then back at Nadine. She was looking down at her plate now. Sam noticed that she had a kind of dreamy, distracted look on her face, as if her mind was somewhere else besides at the dinner table; she looked tired. Was his hippie daughter on drugs?

Sam suddenly feared the influence of modern times on his impressionable little girl – who knew what was going on over there, with her trampy friend and her boyfriend? That girl's aunts – they didn't care what a disgrace their niece had become. Now that he thought about it, they were really hippies themselves, living up there in the woods, making candles, not working.

Sam realized with a start that maybe he hadn't properly monitored his daughter's life, and look what Nadine had become! A hippie, just like these that had been arrested for *murder!*

"I think you should move back home, Nadine." Maybe it wasn't too late. If Sam could just get her away from the influence across the street . . .

"What?"

Sam knew he had to tread carefully. He didn't want to alienate her, make her defensive. He knew that some of his colleagues at work had become estranged from their children, just for objecting to some of the new values that they embraced. So Sam didn't directly attack the whole hippie issue, but went back to the one thing to which he had already taken exception. Not anything that Nadine herself was doing, but – "It's not proper for you to be living over there, with two people that aren't married."

"He's not *her* boyfriend, Sam," Irene reminded her husband, and the words sliced through Nadine like knives. "Our daughter's not doing anything wrong."

"Still, it's just not appropriate," Sam insisted.

"I can't just leave Daina," Nadine countered. *Unless it's with Ian. You're really gonna be pissed when that happens, Dad.*

"Of course not. Not just up and leave her." Sam seemed to agree. "I'm not trying to . . . *put a heavy parental trip on you,* Nadine." Sam smiled, proud of his grasp of the lingo. "I'd just like you to think about coming back home. Will you do that for your ol' Dad?"

"Besides, maybe they might like some privacy, 'Deen," Irene observed. Nadine wished her mother would just shut up. Every word out of her mouth was like a blow.

To close the discussion, so her mother would stop talking about *Daina's boyfriend,* and their *privacy,* Nadine nodded. "I'll think about it, Dad."

SEVENTY-ONE

Daina took a deep breath and studied her reflection in the mirror. It was December 13th, and while it was Saturday, and not Friday, she reflected that she felt unlucky anyway. She blinked at herself. Now she was sounding like Nadine. Jinxes and bad omens. *How am I,* Daina asked herself, *anything but lucky?* She lived with the sexiest man in town, and he had eyes only for her. Sometimes it amazed Daina just how lucky she was.

But today . . . Diana was wearing false eyelashes, a little light-colored eye-shadow. But not too much. A tame, almost girlish shade of pink lipstick. She'd gotten her hair done – the hairdresser had parted it on the side and gave it a little teased pouf on top, and curled the ends up gaily. Her bangs were plastered across her forehead. The whole thing was positively stiff with hairspray.

When she'd returned home from the salon, Ian had blinked at her in dismay. "Oh, my Christ. You look like Laura Petrie."

Daina smiled ruefully. "What 'til you see the dress." He went to embrace her, but she held up her hands. "Don't. You'll crumple the . . . the *upsweep.*"

Nadine was sitting on the couch, paging through the latest *Cosmo.* She looked up coolly. Ian was right – Dick Van Dyke might appear at any moment and trip over the ottoman.

"What's the occasion?" she asked.

Once upon a time, Nadine would've known why her friend was coiffed as if she was going to a meeting of The Daughters of the American Revolution. But not so much anymore. Daina and Nadine didn't talk like they used to. Ian was always there, and Daina was always talking to him. She and Nadine had become strangers.

"We're having dinner with my parents." Ian said. "It's not really a big deal –"

"It's a dinner *party,*" Daina countered. "I'm meeting them for the first time. And it *is* a big deal."

Ian shrugged. "They'll love you."

"I'm sure they will," Nadine agreed neutrally, and went back to her magazine.

Daina went into her bedroom and Ian again looked at the TV.

I'm sure his parents are just dying to meet the whore that their son's been shacked up with for the last month and a half. Nadine smiled grimly to herself. That was her father's term – *shacked up* – and Nadine liked it. It rolled off the tongue like a curse. It was an ugly-sounding expression, and it reflected the ugliness that Nadine saw in Ian and Daina's situation.

They weren't joyfully in love, like Ian would've been with Nadine. It was just an animal, sex thing with him and Daina. They weren't soulmates; they were *shacked up.*

And this fact annoyed the hell out of Nadine, and she grew impatient for the day when Ian would comprehend it all for what it really was. On that glorious day, his eyes would be opened, and he would at last see Nadine. He would realize it was she who really loved him, completely, for his mind, his wit. Not just because he had equipment opposite from hers.

Once in her room, Daina took a deep breath, exhaled nervously. She held the dress she had purchased for this seminal event in front of her and considered her look in the mirror. The thing was awful. It was long-sleeved, of a heavy knit fabric, a plaid of light and dark yellow, crisscrossed with thin black stripes. It had a high collar, and a placket down the front, accented with two rows of black buttons. The skirt fell demurely to just above Daina's knees; she'd tried to find something a little longer, a little more *modest,* but this was the best she could do. There was a little yellow hat to go with it. A *hat,* mind you, like something Holly Golightly might wear – it was not a beret, or anything hippie-ish like that.

The dress was as staid as something Pat Nixon would don, but Daina's sentiments unknowingly echoed Nadine's: *Will it make his parents see me as anything more than the shameful little chippie their son is living in sin with?* Daina shook her head and sighed. *Very doubtful,* she said to herself.

Daina couldn't say why she cared what Ian's parents thought of her. She didn't even really care what Ian thought of her, except that she knew that Ian thought the world of her. Ian loved her, whatever that was supposed to mean.

She had stayed at his parents' white-columned house with him one weekend when the professor and his wife were safely out of town, and it wasn't that Daina had been *impressed* with the big manse . . . It was just that she'd realized that Ian was from a different world than she was, the world of white gloves, hats that weren't berets, sororities and fraternities. Ian was from the same world of power and privilege that had spawned Will and Rob.

Daina had realized with a shock that when she was a freshman, she'd flunked an English class that Ian's dad taught. Surely, he wouldn't remember her? She guessed that she was willing to pretend to be a fine, upstanding coed, to pretend to be the kind of girl that Ian's parents would've picked out for him, just for his sake. She knew that he loved his parents, and she didn't want to be the cause of any discord between them. She didn't want to see the smile fade from his face – she *so* enjoyed Ian's smile – because of anything to do with her.

Daina hung the ugly dress on the door, next to Ian's suit. It was dark brown, the same color as his hair. She brushed a stray piece of lint off the wide lapel of the jacket, straightened the crease in one of the flared legs of the pants. He'd chosen a dotted tie of a matching brown shade, and a light blue shirt. It was a nice suit. Regardless of his nonchalance, Daina knew this dinner party at his parents' *was* important to Ian – hence the suit.

Daina searched in her closet for a suitable handbag. She only owned two. There was the brown suede one with the long strap and the equally long fringe, and the big bulky one which she used every day, sewn together out of scraps of myriad shades of blue denim. Neither matched her outfit, neither would correspond to the *I'm not a wild, hippie tramp* vibe that she was trying to broadcast.

Nadine might have something smaller, but Daina didn't feel like asking to borrow a bag from Nadine right now. They weren't really as close as they'd once been, and Daina didn't really want to stand around and make small talk about tonight's event while 'Deen searched in her closet for a more appropriate handbag. She probably didn't have anything smaller either.

Daina decided that she just wouldn't accessorize this evening. She didn't really need a bag anyway; the only thing that she couldn't leave behind for a few hours was her lipstick. She snatched it off the dresser and dropped it into the pocket of Ian's suit jacket. He was making her go to this thing; he could just carry her lipstick for her.

Daina turned to consult the mirror one last time before donning her prim threads. She picked at the rigid hairdo a little bit, then decided it was best to leave it alone. It wasn't like it was going to move around much on her head. She thought that her lips could use a touch more prissy pinkness, so she reached back into Ian's pocket. Her hand missed the lipstick tube and touched a small, hard square. Puzzled, she brought it out. It was a little velvet jewelry box. Without thinking, Daina popped it open. The diamond ring glittered.

Daina felt her knees go weak and she staggered to the bed to sit down. No. This just couldn't be. Ian was going to ask her to marry him. That was the true reason for this dinner party with his parents.

He probably planned to make a scene, to get down on one knee, probably between the hors d'oeuvre and the salad course – Daina didn't know much about rich people, but she and Nadine had played at tea parties with her aunts as a child, and they had instructed their nieces about the essentials of fine dining – but this just couldn't be.

Ian couldn't want to marry her – she didn't want to marry him. Why, the man Daina married . . . Their son . . . It couldn't be Ian. *I don't love him,* she told herself. *I've never loved anyone. He's just a guy. He's just someone to spend time with. Lazy Sunday mornings in bed, evenings curled up together on the couch. Warm and safe and wonderful . . . It's been the best time I've ever known. He's so much fun, but it's not meant to be like this forever. Sooner or later, I'll get tired of him. I don't love Ian . . .*

Daina stood up. She was still unsteady and it took a moment before she trusted her legs to propel her forward. She dropped the little box back into Ian's pocket.

This just couldn't be. It couldn't be Ian. She didn't love Ian. Her future was not to be with happy, carefree, affectionate Ian . . .

Daina had to figure out what was going on. There was only one thing to do.

She went back out into the living room, and when Ian and Nadine glanced up at her, Daina felt like a jail breaker pinned by the searchlight. The bloodhounds would be upon her at any moment. Why wasn't she dressed yet? Where was she going? Some explanation was necessary: the two of them would start giving her the third degree if she didn't speak up immediately.

"I'm gonna run up the hill. I want to . . . I want to borrow a pair of earrings from Aunt Bellona. I'll be right back." She darted out the door, slamming it too hard behind her.

Daina jogged up the trail, the words repeating over and over in her mind like a chant: *I don't love Ian; he's not the one. It's gotta be someone else. Not Ian. I don't love Ian. No. It can't be him. Not beautiful, sexy, blue-eyed Ian . . .*

Penny and Bellona were sitting at the dining room table. Penny was dealing the Tarot.

"Ian bought me a ring," Daina said without preface.

"And isn't it lovely!" Bellona replied with a smile.

"You . . . *You know?"*

Unemotional as always, Aunt Penny's eyes flickered up to Daina's. "Of course we know. We've known for quite a while, actually, from the day you first –"

"He came up here and asked us for your hand," Bellona said with a little giggle. "He was very formal. Very serious. It was adorable."

"And you said yes?" Daina was incredulous.

"Of course, dear." Bellona exchanged a glance with her sister. "Didn't you say yes?"

"He hasn't asked me yet!"

Bellona's smile faltered in confusion. "Then how do you know about the ring? We thought it was to be a surprise."

"It's a surprise, all right." Daina collapsed into a chair beside them. "I found it in his pocket. Just now. We're going to his parents' for dinner."

"He's going to ask you then," Penny said. "Don't be churlish, Daina. Don't spoil the boy's fun in popping the question."

"I can't marry Ian!"

Bellona blinked. "Why ever not, dear? He's –"

"He's not!" Daina bellowed. *"I don't love Ian!"*

Penny offered a rare smile. *"A lie gets halfway around the world before the truth has a chance to get its pants on."*

"It's not a lie! He's not the one! I don't love him!" Daina looked desperately at Bellona. "What you said, when I was a little girl! It's can't be Ian! I couldn't put him through –"

"She pined in thought, and with a green and yellow melancholy, she sat like Patience on a monument, smiling at grief. Was not this love indeed?" Penny grinned.

"No." Daina shook her head vigorously, perhaps a shade hysterically. "It's not Ian. I won't marry him."

Penny sighed. "You'd better marry somebody, dear, and quickly. This cohabitating trend might be all the rage these days, but people still tend to frown upon a baby born out of wedlock."

"A –?"

"My, my, *my*, Daina! How you *have* been deluding yourself!" Bellona clapped her hands together in glee. "You don't love Ian. You're not –"

"Count back, Daina," Penny advised. "When did the moonflow last visit you? Not since this man you don't love, but whom you love quite often indeed, has entered your life, I'll wager."

Daina concentrated, and her eyes widened when she realized that she hadn't had a period since the middle of October. Now she reckoned that it should've arrived a few days before Thanksgiving. But she'd been so excited, so caught up in the preparations for fixing the meal all by herself – just her and Ian – that she'd forgotten all about it. "Oh, my God! I'm nearly six weeks' –"

"Yes," Bellona said. "He's still just a tiny speck, but he's in there."

"Rejoice, therefore!" Penny smiled and patted her niece on the shoulder. "After Ian surprises you with his proposal, you'll have a little surprise of your own for him. But you must get rid of that stupefied expression, Daina. It's not very becoming." Penny chuckled. *"Your face, my thane, is as a book where men may read strange matters."*

"So it's all true, then. Ian is the love of my life. I guess I knew it all along. I can't live without him. I just wouldn't let myself see it. I didn't want it to be him." Tears welled up in Daina's eyes.

Alarmed, Bellona drew a handkerchief from her sleeve and held it out to her niece. "Here, child. You'll ruin your mascara."

Daina took the pro-offered handkerchief and daubed absently beneath her eyes. "But . . . Our son . . . You said . . . *a blot of tragedy . . ."*

"What else did I say, Daina?" Bellona asked, smiling. "I told you that I saw your love shining through. It will endure."

Daina recalled Bellona's words. *"Ever-after is a very long time, and we must take happily as it comes.* But my . . . Our son . . ."

Bellona waved her hand. "He will be bright, healthy, exceptional. You'll have a lifetime of joy with him. He'll reach his majority before –"

"Enough," Penny said gently. "You've cast enough shadows over her life, Bell. Seek to know no more, Daina. Live in joy today – you'll have decades of joy – and tomorrow will resolve itself."

SEVENTY-TWO

Nadine was still awake when Ian and Daina returned home. Snug in her flannel pj's, she was drinking a glass of warm milk, reading Regardie's *A Garden of Pomegranates,* and feeling like quite the old maid. She should be out on the town with a date, closing bars and having a good time. But she just didn't feel up for it these days.

She heard a key scrabbling in the lock, then Ian burst in, smiling gleefully, carrying Daina in that horrible dress, as if she was a new bride. Shock, as electric and painful as lightning, jolted through Nadine. She immediately grasped the reason for the hilarity, this premature enactment of an ancient tradition – she saw the diamond sparkling like some cursed idol's eye on Daina's left hand.

Ian set Daina down, then threw his arms wide. "Congratulate us, 'Deen! We're getting married!"

A door slammed in Nadine's mind, locking all hope away forever, irrevocably. She blinked as if the sound had happened outside of her head. *There was the door to which I found no key; there was the veil through which I might not see: some little talk awhile of me and thee there was – and then no more of thee and me . . . Farewell, fair cruelty.*

Penny and Bellona had won; they had diverted the path of destiny to serve their own flesh and blood. They had tricked lighthearted, spirited, free-loving Ian into yoking himself to this cold whore for the rest of his days. *Bigamy is having one wife too many. Monogamy is the same.* Nadine suddenly pitied Ian, almost as much as she pitied herself.

Nadine now discovered a consuming hatred for Daina: it seethed, like a vicious heartburn. *What an apt phrase,* Nadine thought bitterly. She noticed that Daina was watching her closely, carefully. *Well, I'm not gonna let this haughty bitch see my pain. I won't allow her the satisfaction of gloating.*

Nadine assumed an expression of delirious best wishes. She hopped up and gave Ian a big sisterly squeeze, then one for Daina.

"I'm so happy for you!"

SEVENTY-THREE

The following morning at the breakfast table, Sam Germaine opened the Sunday edition of *The Los Angeles Times,* and the headline leapt up at him: *Susan Atkins' Story of 2 Nights of Murder.*

He glanced across the table at Irene, who was reading a battered, dog-eared copy of *The Feminine Mystique.* He reflected that his wife always seemed to want to review traditional feminine roles *when Christmas was a' coming and the geese were getting fat.* Irene always seemed to *want something more than my husband and my children and my home* at this time of year. Sam thought it was mainly because she hated doing all the Christmas shopping.

He looked back at *The Times.*

The lengthy confession ran to nearly three pages. His eggs, toast, and coffee forgotten, Sam read it with the same appalled curiosity that gripped people across the entire country, maybe the entire world. Who would've known that such a monster could reside within a young woman? What was this country coming to?

But then a more personal horror began to grow in Sam. As he read the straightforward recitation of the deaths of all these people, he kept thinking of own daughter. He didn't believe that Nadine could ever become a murderer, never in his wildest dreams – but didn't Nadine use the same kind of jargon? Wasn't Nadine a hippie, too? She and the killer were the same age. They probably listened to the same kind of music . . .

Sam had always been baffled by his daughter's music. Some of it was all right, he supposed – Irene sometimes had the radio tuned to modern stuff when he came home from work, and he frequently heard it blasting out from the house across the street. But to Sam, most of what his daughter listened to seemed dark, incomprehensible. In the back of his mind, he believed that it was all actually about sex and drugs; that maybe it even somehow promoted just the kind of insanity that had occurred in LA in August. Hell, just last week a kid had been stabbed to death at a concert at some racetrack in Northern California.

Sam was suddenly fearful. By allowing his daughter to spend most of her life across the street with strangers, he realized that Nadine had become a stranger to him, too. She'd never been in any trouble, had always pulled down good grades in school. She wasn't even shacked up with the first available guy, like her friend. *But that girl* is *her friend. Her best friend. Her only friend.*

Sam's first inclination was to say to himself, *Yes, maybe I have allowed Nadine to become a stranger. But she's a nice, well-adjusted stranger.*

Yet the stories in *The Times* lately about murderous, maniac young people gave Sam pause. He admitted that Nadine was a stranger to him; what kind of evil might be lurking behind her brown eyes these days? And if it was already there, was it too late for him to save her, to get her away from the bad influences that had put it there? Was it too late to get his baby back?

Sam read the hippie murderer's confession again, and even though he tried to discount his fears as ridiculous – Nadine couldn't be like this girl, even though they were the same age – reading Atkins' words, he kept hearing expressions that he knew that Nadine would understand; he heard Nadine's turn of phrase. He heard Nadine's *voice.*

His alarm increased incrementally from the very first sentence: "One day a little man came in with a guitar and started singing for a group of us in that place where we were living, in Haight-Asbury in San Francisco." Sam had heard Nadine mention that very place to her mother, not six months earlier. Irene was originally from the Bay Area; she told Nadine that she knew the place well. Nadine said it was somewhere she and Daina longed to visit.

"He gave me nothing but love, complete love, gave me the answers to all the questions I've ever had in my mind." *All you need is love, love. Love is all you need.*

"This whole world and everybody and everything in it has been God's game, and that game is just about to come to an end. Judgment Day for every human being on the face of the earth is coming." *Cancel my subscription to the resurrection.*

"He just told me to do everything Tex said to do. Charlie had control over everybody. I never questioned what Charlie said. I just did it." What was it that that hophead college professor had told them? At the *Be In,* whatever the hell that was? *Turn on, tune in, drop out?* Wasn't that some kind of mind control, too?

"So Charlie wanted to put some fear into him, let him know that what Charlie said was the way it is." *We want the world and we want it . . . now.*

"When I saw the faces again—it blew my mind." How many time had Sam heard Nadine say that something had *blown her mind?*

"I knew they 'turned on,' just looking at the house. They hide it from society, by just looking at them, I knew they used narcotics."

Well, Nadine didn't use narcotics, Sam assured himself. But then he immediately frowned, not sure at all.

Would he be able to tell? Nadine always seemed to have a distracted look on her face, lately, ever since that dark-haired kid moved in with them over there. She always looked tired; was she . . . *strung out?* Maybe her hippie friend's boyfriend was giving drugs to Sam's only child . . .

Sam read on. The description of the slaughter was emotionless, matter-of-fact. He couldn't shake the idea that he could hear it all recited in Nadine's voice: "There wasn't much I could do because I couldn't find my knife."

"My lawyer is coming soon, and he's bringing me a dish of vanilla ice cream. Vanilla ice cream really blows my mind."

What is this world coming to? Sam asked himself desperately.

He arrived at a decision. He had to get Nadine away from the people she had fallen in with across the street. Who knew what kind of drug-taking, free-loving, *dangerous hippies* they might really be? He tossed the newspaper on the table, and without consulting his wife, he marched out of the kitchen. His worry caused him to gather momentum; he strode purposefully across the living room, threw open the front door, raced across the street.

He pounded on the door to this den of God-only-knew-what, where he had so foolishly allowed his daughter to reside. He was out of breath, and when Nadine opened the door, he panted harshly. "Pack your stuff. You're moving back home this instant!" Sam would brook no argument this time. He would drag her home by her long, straight, hippie hair if he had to.

Sam Germaine's daughter sighed. She looked worn, sad. He had arrived not a moment too soon. After a pause, she gave in immediately, with no argument at all. Sam believed that she must have seen the resolute determination in his eyes.

"All right, Daddy," Nadine said. "Daina and Ian are getting married. I don't want to live here anymore, anyway."

SEVENTY-FOUR

At sunrise on his wedding day, Ian stood on Daina's front porch and considered the geography of their odd little neighborhood, as if seeing it for the first time. The lay of the land of the corner of the world where he would that day become consort (if not king), worshipped figurehead (if not actually ruler), struck him like something out of a medieval tapestry, like a fairytale vision. Penny and Bellona's dwelling became the white castle on the hill and the houses below were the little feudal farms.

The old witches' place possessed no battlements, although anyone could look out from that great wooden deck and pour down boiling oil, if they had a mind . . . Yet the gingerbread house was hardly a castle. Ian smiled at the silliness of the thought. His imagination was always a lively companion – he saw things on a larger scale, a what-if scenario, like a writer. And if his fancies weren't really true, the untruth lived comfortably beside the reality in his mind. During his reign in this singular neighborhood, just as often as not, the fantasy would be the truth and the reality the untruth. Either way, they all lived together in Ian's mind without much conflict. He was an observer. He was not a questioner, not a terrier rooting out meaning. The sun rose in the east; gravity existed; to the victor went the spoils.

Ian would accept it all as part of the extraordinary life he had stumbled into. It would oft times be strange, but it would never be boring.

SEVENTY-FIVE

"Oh, for Christ's sake, Cuz, have a drink!" Rob extracted a thin metal flask from the breast pocket of his best man's finery. "You're making *me* nervous!"

Ian took a quick swallow. The liquor burned, made his eyes water. He considered himself in the mirror, splendiferous in his tuxedo. He smiled weakly. "How do I look?"

"Like a sucker," Rob said good-naturedly. He cocked an eyebrow. "It's not too late to run, you know. I'll keep 'em all busy while you just slip out the back door. I'll meet you in Parker. We'll go skiing."

"It's too cold to go skiing," Ian said. It was Saturday, January 24, 1970, and he was the first scion of the Wilde family to be getting hitched. His family couldn't believe it; Ian hardly believed it himself. "Besides . . . I'm no coward. I love her."

"I know. You've told me. Endlessly. *Let me count the ways.*"

"I'm just a little nervous."

"What kind of a best man would I be if I didn't make the offer to you help you escape?" Rob slapped his cousin on to back.

The groom smiled. *"Give me my robe, put on my crown; I have immortal longings in me."*

Rob shook his head. "Come on, Ian, you poor, love-sick sap. Let's do this thing."

SEVENTY-SIX

Though the past relationships of the wedding party might have been typical for young people in the first month of the forward-thinking new decade, their histories still would've made the minister blush. The groom had once known the auburn-haired bridesmaid, *in the biblical way.* Her fiancé had once been on the same kind of intimate terms with the bride. The best man and the maid of honor had also been an out-of-wedlock couple once, but no longer. He was now engaged to the other bridesmaid, a pretty girl that could've passed for the maid of honor's sister.

Nadine was the maid of honor – *Now, by this hand, I swear, I scorn the term* – she thought, whenever anyone referred to her by it. She'd had her choice of escorts for the nuptials. The world was her oyster, she was single, fancy-free. All the eligible men in town had been at her disposal.

Except by noon, the only man she had ever loved would no longer be eligible.

The wedding had been planned quickly. It was an open secret that Daina was pregnant, and any and all petty squabbles and past entanglements were forgotten by the young ladies in an effort to bring the ceremony to fruition at its earliest. Andrea giggled and laughed and tried to make conversation with Nadine, as if they hadn't shared the same man. Marta and Daina would never be bosom buddies, but they became friends enough, while planning the nuptials. There was really no reason that they shouldn't be friends: each believed that she had wound up with the better catch.

Marta, social butterfly that she was, was an old hand at event planning, so, in concert with Ian's Mom, she had taken the reins and made it all happen, seamlessly. She booked the minister and the band and the caterers; she made Will think it was his idea to secure the use of his father's estate for the ceremony.

Nadine assisted her aunts in creating and assembling Daina's gown. It was simple, flowing, lovely. It was also empire-waisted, just in case, even though Daina hadn't really started to show yet.

Throughout the hasty planning, Nadine kept putting off finding a date. The task held no joy for her. Whomever she picked to accompany her would have to rent a tux to round out the wedding party; that was a drag. Looking for a date to *Ian's wedding* also gave the whole thing a cold, concrete reality that Nadine still wasn't ready to accept yet. She shouldn't be looking for a date for Ian's wedding; she should be *the bride* at Ian's wedding.

As the day loomed, Marta detected a gaping hole in the way things were supposed to look. There was the bride and groom – check. The best man had a bridesmaid, as did Will, the second groomsman. But the maid of honor was lagging in naming an escort – the wedding party was lop-sided, uneven. That wouldn't do. Marta didn't know what Nadine's problem was: she was pretty enough, if maybe a little quiet and solemn. How hard was it to find a date for a wedding? At last, Marta suggested to Nadine that she pair up with her brother Sid for the ceremony; he owned his own tux.

Nadine agreed without argument, seeing as how she could not possibly care less – not about her date, or about any other aspect of Daina's wedding. Nadine didn't care too much about anything at all that Saturday. She'd already fought Sid off once; she didn't think she would have any trouble handling him again, should the need arise.

It didn't. Another one of the guests at the wedding was actually Sid's date. He'd just agreed to be in the wedding party because his sister had suggested it, and it gave him an excuse to wear his tux. After all the pictures were taken, Sid ignored Nadine in the same manner as he had that day at Lake Elsinore, after she'd spurned his advances.

Nadine considered herself positively stoic for undergoing the whole ordeal of Ian and Daina's wedding. She couldn't just sever her friendship with Daina, no matter how much that idea might appeal to her. Penny had said that Ian would always *be in her life,* so Nadine maintained the bones of her friendship with Daina. How could Ian be in her life if she wasn't around where he was?

Nadine's life had darkened from the moment she had seen Ian standing in front of her bedroom door wrapped in Daina's sheet, but like an oak, she had withstood it all. Their smiling glances, their cutesy conversations, their boisterous, marathon sex sessions. Nadine had agreed to be Daina's maid of honor; she had helped with all the preparations. She'd borne witness, heard the minister say, *What God has joined together, let no man put asunder. And so, by the power vested in me by the State of California and Almighty God, I now pronounce you man and wife – and may your days be good and long upon the earth. You may now kiss the bride.*

And Nadine had weathered every single one of these indignities with a plastic, happy-for-her-friends smile stapled onto her face. But when the newly christened Mr. and Mrs. Ian Wilde had their first dance, Nadine felt her joyful, congratulatory façade crack, like spackling plastered perfunctorily across the San Andreas Fault. The happy couple had chosen Etta James' immortal *At Last* for their first dance together as man and wife.

Nadine remembered dancing to it with Ian on Hallowe'en, when the future was still bright, when *she still had a chance.* Nadine had always considered it to be *their song.* She just couldn't stand by and watch that whore dance with him to *their song,* that loathsome witch who had used her body to trap him into marrying her. Nadine felt the sob well up in her throat, and she knew that she wasn't going to be able to just smile this one down. She backed away from the circle of happy relatives and smiling well-wishers and fled into the nearest bathroom.

She let loose one quiet wail, one ugly, wracking sob, and let the tears roll their black streaks down her face. Nadine watched herself cry in the mirror; she wept for the prospects that would now never be, for the destiny that had been beheaded by that treacherous bitch and her scheming kin. And again that desire for revenge cooled the blood in Nadine's veins, soothed her tears until they slowed, then rather abruptly stopped. Daina would someday stand before a mirror and sob like this; Nadine would see to it. Daina would weep over some truncated future, some purpose unrealized. Nadine vowed to be the root of her pain.

As she washed her face and touched up her make-up, Nadine promised herself that Daina would pay for her lifetime of deception. Not only would she rue the day that she had stolen Ian, but Nadine would see her sorry for every single other slight, also.

In the black days since Hallowe'en, Nadine had come to the conclusion that more than half of her life had been a lie. Daina had never truly been her friend. Penny and Bellona had never loved her, had never considered her one of their own. They had just pitied her as the lonely child from across the way; they had used her like a servant's child to keep their little black-haired princess company.

The sisters had thwarted destiny for their blood's sake: they couldn't have Prince Charming take up with the scullery maid instead of the heir to their sorceresses' dynasty, now could they? They had blindfolded Ian with their false prophecies, had spun him around and around with their drugged cider, as in a game of Pin-the-Tail-on-the-Donkey. And then they'd simply pushed him at Daina. And Daina had gone right ahead and caught him.

Daina stole him from me.

The fact that Daina had never, ever really cared about their friendship has been underlined for Nadine the day after she and Ian had burst gaily through the front door and announced their engagement. It was that Sunday when Sam Germaine had flown across the street, freaking out.

Nadine had told Daina that her dad had talked himself into the idea that drugged, cannibal, hippie mind-control was pouring out subliminally through the rock and roll on the radio, coming directly from Timothy Leary and Charles Manson. Or something like that. The upshot was, Dad wanted her to move back home immediately, so he could watch over her and forestall these influences from continuing, through his paternal love and All-American white-bread chutzpah. Or something like that.

Nadine had expected Daina to object: hadn't they been friends forever? Just because she'd stolen the love of Nadine's life, just because she and Ian never ceased to rub Nadine's nose in it with their constant kissy-face, pressy-bod affection, just because they were now going to get married – that was no reason for Daina to allow her best friend to bow under to her dad's ridiculous, *Los Angeles Times* fomented paranoia, was it?

But Daina couldn't even muster up an *Oh, 'Deen, you can't go!*

Instead, she'd just dropped the other bomb. Like the news coverage of the war, Nadine thought she could hear the whistle of artillery and the ensuing explosions in her mind, right after Daina said, "It's just as well, 'Deen. We're going to need your room. For a nursery. I'm pregnant."

"So that's why you're getting married!" Nadine exclaimed, the picture suddenly clear. "You have to!" If it wasn't so awful, it would've almost been funny. Not only had the deceitful, scheming whore stolen her soulmate, she had also trapped him. Ian didn't want to marry Daina. He didn't love her! He was being forced into it!

Daina laughed. "I don't have to do anything but die, 'Deen. Isn't that what Penny always says?"

"And live until you die," Nadine added darkly. And put up with the betrayals dealt so cavalierly to you by people that you trusted, that you had always believed loved you. "But Ian wouldn't let you . . . He has a sense of responsibility."

That's all it was, too: a sense of responsibility. He didn't love Daina. But still, her deviousness had paid off. Ian had agreed to marry her, to give his child a name. Penny and Bellona had probably supplied her with some kind of fertility charm to seal his fate.

Again Daina laughed. "Ian doesn't even know yet. He asked me to marry him all on his own. I'm going to tell him tonight. So we can set a date quickly . . . before I start to show." She'd had the nerve to giggle then.

Daina had taken her Aunt Penny's advice to heart – she would have decades of joy – so she'd allowed the joy to envelop her. Her life was wonderful: she was in love with the sexiest man in town, and he was utterly devoted to her. They were going to get married, going to have a baby. There was not a single dark cloud on the horizon, not one ominous blip on anyone's extra-natural radar.

Not now. Not yet.

Christ, how I hate you! Nadine thought at that moment. She said, "It *is* just as well, then, that this freak out happened now. If Ian will help, they can take my stuff across the street today. Dad's anxious to have me back." *Just as anxious as I am to get out of here.* "You can tell Ian the good news about your baby, after I'm gone, when you're all alone."

Nadine realized that she had best pretend to be happy about this. Marriages, children – they didn't guarantee happily-ever-after. Divorces happened. It was becoming more common every day. Despite a baby, Ian might still come to his senses, and it could occur at any time. So Nadine had to stick around.

She smiled and enthusiastically clapped her hands together. She couldn't quite bring herself to hug Daina, however. "A baby! How exciting!" *I'd like to thank the Academy,* Nadine thought grimly to herself. "Do you want a boy or a girl?"

"Oh, it's gonna be a boy," Daina replied with a sigh. She nodded over her shoulder, up the hill. "It's been foretold."

Daina experienced a moment of dark resignation: *a blot of tragedy – it's been foretold.* But the eclipse passed as quickly as it had appeared. *Decades,* she reminded herself, and her sunny happiness returned.

But Nadine had caught the shadow as it crossed Daina's smile, and reveled in her enemy's sadness, apparently engendered by some prediction from on high. Maybe her baby was going to have two heads. Or cloven hooves and a tail.

"Have you thought of what you're going to call –"

Ian came in the front door and when Nadine stopped speaking abruptly, he eyed her inquisitively. "Your dad just stopped me in the driveway, 'Deen. Something about helping him move your furniture?"

I'm sorry to leave you to your fate, my darling, since you have been so falsely pushed into it. But I'll be just down the road when you need me. They can't keep me away from you that easily.

"Yes. I thought that you guys might want some privacy, now that you're gonna . . ." Nadine winked at Daina. "Now that you're getting married."

SEVENTY-SEVEN

Nadine Germaine, not quite twenty-two, college graduate, was at odds and ends. *At sixes and sevens,* as her grandmother used to say.

She was bored, had no ambition, had no idea what she wanted to do with her life. What she *had* wanted, once upon a time, was to live that life with Ian. It had been fated to be, but in a very short time it had become apparent that fate was to be delayed. Barely five months had elapsed between the night Nadine read her destiny in Parker, and the heartbreaking moment when she'd beheld Ian wrapped in that bottle-green sheet.

That was the very day that her destiny had been detoured by Daina's deceit.

Then came their insanely hasty marriage; another nine months passed and their son's arrival was imminent. Such a very short span of time, yet it seemed to Nadine that she'd spent her entire life in anticipation of a future with Ian, and now all of that was gone. Nothing but emptiness and hatred and a vague, undefined, parched thirst for revenge remained.

But if Nadine was lonely, she wasn't alone.

Chuck had noticed Daina waltzing into the bar on several occasions and kissing Nadine's boyfriend; he asked around and was amazed to discover that they were now an item. He'd marveled at the news: *What back-stabbing bitches women can be!* Apparently, Daina had stolen this squinty guy right out from under Nadine's nose. Chuck definitely had to look her up and comfort her now.

Chuck told himself that God hated a coward and just showed up at Nadine's door one Saturday afternoon. He was surprised to discover that she and Daina still lived together after the affront of Daina's stealing Nadine's bartender; he was even more surprised to find out that the bartender lived there with them. Chuck thought it best not to bring any of it up to Nadine, and he thought he detected a little gratitude for that on her part.

Nadine was hesitant at first – she went out with him whenever he asked her, but wouldn't let him touch her past a little hand-holding and kissing, as if they were still in junior high. When Nadine abruptly moved back home – it was just across the street – Chuck realized that he'd been right all along about the tension between these "friends." If he mentioned Daina or her boyfriend, Nadine invariably frowned.

But not long after she moved back to her parents', Chuck's persistence paid off.

Nadine relented. Chuck had his own place, so she went back there with him and just gave in one Saturday night. Ian was unattainable – at least for the moment – but life was long. Once Nadine took a good, long look at him, she decided that tall, blonde, hale and hearty, dimpled Chuck wasn't so detestable after all, not a bad second choice. For the time being.

Like any other red-blooded American girl, Nadine had needs, and believed it would be unhealthy not to acquire an outlet for them. Brooding, carrying a torch, depriving herself of this simplest of all pleasures – *O, that way madness lies; let me shun that; no more of that.*

Nadine would not allow herself to fall into despondent celibacy, to become a bride of Christ to a dream of Ian that had never even once seen fruition; she'd never even kissed him. But the dream remained, and to keep it alive, Nadine needed a partner. As she had done with Rob, Nadine used Chuck to assuage her unrequitable desires. Whenever the fancy struck her, she just closed her eyes and imagined that Chuck was Ian.

After a while, Nadine discovered that Chuck was all right. The chauvinistic bluster that had so enraged her dissipated once he assumed that he'd won her. He became respectful and almost gentlemanly, and Nadine believed that Chuck genuinely cared for her, maybe even loved her. And her parents liked him. Nadine didn't love him, would never, *could never love him.* But he would do for the moment.

SEVENTY-EIGHT

Medical science had predicted that Ian and Daina's child would enter this vale of tears in the *middle* of July, and thereby, his parents thought it would be safe to visit friends in downtown Riverside on Independence Day. But Daina went into labor in the late afternoon, and while the fireworks went off on nearby Mt. Rubidoux, Adrian Robert Wilde decided that he would be a patriotic, all American boy and surprise them all: he arrived at 9:37 on July 4, 1970.

During their first months together, Ian had learned that while Daina looked uncomprehendingly at him when he recited the immortal words of bards and poets, she never failed to smile in appreciation when he would favor her with a snippet or two of rock and roll. He wasn't much of a singer, but he tried gamely, and his efforts never failed to delight his bride.

When they entered the hospital, Ian asked her if she was scared, and she nodded.

"What about me?" he asked, and hugged her to him, as closely as he could with the burden of their unborn child between them. "This'll be the first night we've ever spent apart." He sang softly into her ear. *"No sugar tonight in my coffee, no sugar tonight in my tea . . ."*

Daina giggled and squeezed him, her fear vanishing. She was in love with, married to, the most inviting man in the universe, and once the momentary inconvenience of bringing his son into the world was surmounted, she looked forward to once again providing him with all the *sugar* he could possibly desire.

Throughout her pregnancy, Daina had listened to her aunts debate the issue of her impending delivery. Bellona had been a midwife in her youth, and maintained that, "Obstetricians are arrogant, ham-fisted, incompetent quacks. You should have him right here at home."

"Community Hospital was good enough for Denise," Penny countered. "Daina can have him there, the same place where she was born. It's better to be in a modern hospital, Bell, in case there are complications."

It turned out that both aunts were partially correct. As Daina's delivery progressed, it was discovered that Adrian was in a breech position; a Caesarian-section was performed. It was touch and go for a time: the boy or even his mother might not have survived a home delivery. Thanks to modern obstetrical techniques, Adrian was delivered without injury; a bouncing, healthy, nine pound, five ounce baby boy.

But in the aftermath of the hasty procedure, the doctor told Daina that she would probably not conceive again.

SEVENTY-NINE

Nadine had managed to evade going downtown for the fireworks with the parents-to-be on the 4th of July. Instead, she'd stayed home with Sam and Irene and Chuck, and barbequed. When Ian called to tell them that Daina had gone into labor, Nadine stood listening over the answering machine, watching the cassette tapes whir, but she didn't pick up the phone. Ian asked if Nadine could run up the hill and tell her aunts that the baby was coming. Could she give them a ride to the hospital?

Nadine harrumphed. They were seers, were they not? Foilers of destiny? Surely they could anticipate something as commonplace as the birth of a baby, even if it was two weeks early? Or maybe they should just move into the twentieth century and get a phone installed. Nadine would not play messenger for Ian, nor taxi driver for the perfidious witches on top of the hill. They could hitchhike to the hospital for all she cared. As it turned out, they were at Mohini's when Daina's time came; they just walked across downtown Riverside to await the much-anticipated heir.

Nadine erased Ian's message as soon as the tone sounded. There was no reason to drive all the way downtown, fight the holiday traffic, just to sit around in a hospital waiting room. No reason to disrupt her pleasant little get-together with her boyfriend and her parents. Nadine couldn't possibly care less about Daina's baby.

She recalled that Daina already knew that it would be a boy – *it had been foretold* – and Nadine remembered that a shadow of melancholy had crossed Daina's face at the mention of the prophecy. Nadine sensed that there had been something else to the foretelling, more than just the baby's gender, and she once again hoped fervently that the sorceresses' divination had been about hooves and a tail or some other abnormality. Daina deserved as much for being a thieving whore.

Nadine knew that she would have to play the congratulatory friend soon enough, but there was no reason to wait around for the event ahead of time. *Tomorrow, and tomorrow, and tomorrow, creeps in this petty pace from day to day . . .* That was how Nadine looked at her life, anymore, just days lighting the way to a dusty death. A much-deserved future, the truth of the Tarot – *it is a tale told by an idiot, full of sound and fury, signifying nothing.* Fate could be turned aside by a couple of meddling old women, at least temporarily. Tomorrow would be soon enough to see Daina's whelp.

In the morning, Nadine pretended that she'd just received the call. Irene was thrilled that the little girl from across the way had at last delivered: she wanted to see the baby immediately. But Sam unknowingly echoed his daughter's secret sentiment – he would be seeing the child soon enough, since it would be living across the street – so there was no need for him to run all the way downtown to view it. He stayed at home and Nadine and her mother journeyed to Community Hospital.

There was a crowd outside of the tired mother's room: the proud papa, the ecstatic grandparents; Lily and Penny and Bellona, chirping of blessings. Rob was there; and Andrea, who insisted on hugging Nadine like they were friends or something.

Nadine wished at that moment that she had dragged Chuck along, because he was so much better looking than Rob. Will even had an uncharacteristic smile and a slap on the back for his cousin. Nadine thought that Will wouldn't be quite so friendly if he observed, like she did, that Marta seemed to stand entirely too close to Ian, gazing up wistfully at him. *Welcome to the club, sister,* Nadine said to Marta in her head. *At least you had your chance with him.*

Nadine deposited Irene among the smiling group of friends and relatives, each waiting for their chance to pop in and quickly congratulate the new mom. Nadine had no desire to interact with any of these people. She was in less than no hurry to visit with Daina.

But she was curious to see what the traitorous union of the man she loved and a scheming whore had produced, so she left the crowd to their gladness and went down the hall to the nursery.

Nadine asked a nurse to point out Mr. and Mrs. Wilde's first heir; once she saw him, Nadine realized that she would've had no trouble recognizing him on her own. Unlike most of the little fair children that surrounded him, Adrian wasn't bald – *born with a headful of hair, like the Dog-Faced Boy,* Nadine thought derisively. Adrian's hair was black, like his mother's. The only other baby with hair was a little red-headed girl a few cribs over, and Nadine though distantly of Steve Andre, concoctor of near-lethal fruit punches.

Nadine had never found newborn babies to be adorable. She thought they all resembled Winston Churchill, like wizened, toothless old men, looking quite tired and weak from the monumental effort that it took to be born. She thought that she would've had no trouble, had she lived in another era, drowning an unwanted one, or abandoning it on an ice floe for a polar bear to devour. It could be said that the maternal urge was absent in Nadine, especially when she gazed upon Adrian Wilde for the first time.

He was big and healthy, a little red-faced from his recent ordeal; Nadine thought he was ugly, like a little, black-haired monkey: he looked just like his mother. *Mama's baby, Daddy maybe,* Nadine thought uncharitably, and hoped that every single other person that beheld him would think the same thing.

But Nadine knew after a moment that it would not be so: when the little creature opened his eyes, Ian was unmistakable in him. It seemed like Adrian was staring right at her, like he was calmly considering her. He wasn't, of course. It was an illusion – he probably couldn't even focus that far away yet. Regardless, after a moment, Nadine had to look away. It was too much like gazing into his father's dark, cobalt-blue eyes.

Adrian would've been a much prettier baby had he been hers, Nadine thought; he would've had a nice shade of brown hair instead of that peasant black like his mother's. Like an icepick, the knowledge stabbed Nadine's mind: *Adrian should've been mine.* And because he wasn't, because he looked like his mother (despite his father's eyes) – Nadine hated him.

This tiny spark of humanity had been produced through Daina's treachery. In Nadine's mind, Ian's part in that production faded in importance, and she thought of the little boy no longer as *their* baby, but simply as *Daina's baby.* And because he was become only something that belonged to Daina, *something beloved of Daina alone,* Nadine found that it was easy for her to hate him.

EIGHTY

Within months of his son's birth, Ian finally knuckled down and achieved his teaching credential. It was a cakewalk for him. He'd been receiving a full-time, top-flight education since he was eighteen; he had a practically eidetic memory, at least for the classics. All he'd ever needed was the motivation to put it all to work. His loving wife, his darling son, had at last provided it.

When he went in for his interview, Ian had no preference for a grade level and was willing to take whatever was offered. While he qualified to start teaching high school English, the lady at the superintendent's office, with the cat's-eye glasses on a chain and the beehive hairdo, took one look at him and decided that young Mr. Wilde as a high school teacher just wouldn't do. He was certainly competent, at least on paper. But teenage girls these days were clever, demanding, curious, unafraid – and while she didn't think that the attractive applicant before her was an innocent in the world by any means – he was definitely a babe-in-the-woods to the teaching game.

These hippie tramps would leer at him, drop a few suggestions; and even if he didn't leer back or take them up on it, she didn't think a lot of grammar would get learned if she just plopped him down in high school for his first position. The junior high girls would develop crushes on squinty Mr. Wilde-with-the-nice-smile, too, she was sure. But they were still too young to proposition him. They were even young enough to believe, perhaps, that learning their verb tenses would be the best way to please him.

Ian was assigned a 8th Grade English class at Central Middle School. It was fine with him.

At the same time, Nadine felt rootless, adrift. She had no inclination to find a job of any kind, nor did she have a hankering to continue with her education. Since the baby had been born, Nadine simply couldn't stand to be in Daina's company: every second was monopolized by that stinky, squalling, worthless, little blue-eyed monkey. On the rare moments when he slept, still Daina's conversation revolved around him: *Adrian sneezed today and I was worried, Adrian rolled over today and I rejoiced.*

Nadine couldn't stand to be at home, either. Like some kind of contagion, it seemed that all her mother talked about was Daina's baby, too. Wasn't he adorable? When was Nadine gonna marry Chuck and have one of her own, so Irene could become a grandma?

Now there was a truly horrifying thought. The idea that Nadine would ever want to be tied in such a manner to Chuck, that she would allow her body to become bloated and distended in order to bring his screaming, snot-nosed issue into the world – it just proved to Nadine that Irene really didn't know her daughter at all.

More horrifying than the idea that her mother wished her to reproduce herself with Chuck or anyone else, was the evening when Nadine came home to find her father dandling Daina's eight-month-old rug-ape on his knee. There had been some scheduling mishap – Penny and Bellona had promised to meet Lily downtown at Mohini's and didn't want to miss the last bus, and neither Daina nor Ian had returned from wherever the hell they were – so the aunts had imposed on Nadine's parents to watch the little boy for a few minutes until his parents arrived back home.

Irene was joyful; even Sam was amused by the tyke. "You should think about getting one of these, 'Deen," quoth he.

Nadine had seen *A Clockwork Orange* not three nights before, and was reminded of the scene where Alex returns to his parents' home to discover that he has been replaced in their affections by Joe the Lodger. It was something of a shock, and even though Nadine didn't feel an overwhelming desire to *snuff it,* she did consider gathering up an armload of drycleaner bags for Adrian to play with.

Nadine decided at that moment that she had to escape. She had to get away from Daina and her detestable offspring. She could not understand why everyone insisted that he was so cute – he was an ugly child to Nadine, just as she thought it was meet that he should be, seeing as he was a product of *homemade sin.* She had to get away from her parents, who billed and cooed over Adrian as if he was blood to them. And Nadine also had to get away from Penny and Bellona. Adrian's very presence never failed to underline to Nadine that she was not blood to *them,* else *she* would be with Ian, and Adrian – who would then be cute indeed because he would look like *her* – would be Nadine's baby.

Chuck had once thrown out the suggestion that the two of them should join the Peace Corps. Nadine had laughed long and hard at the very idea – why would she ever want to leave the country, why would she ever want to so distance herself from the man she loved? But just as the Walrus said, Nadine now realized that *the time had come*. She had to get away from all of them, and that included Ian.

So just before Adrian's very first birthday, Nadine and Chuck signed the papers, got their shots and left to join other youthful ambassadors of the United States overseas.

EIGHTY-ONE

The Doctors Wilde were scheduled to begin their residencies in August of 1973, so over the 4th of July weekend they decided to go to Parker to make merry one last time before this next step in their medical careers, and celebrate their littlest cousin's third birthday, as well. The exigencies of life and love and school and marriage and childbirth had prevented the entire crew from assembling there all together since before Adrian was born, so it felt like an almost bittersweet reunion, because times had changed: Ian was deliriously happy with his lot, though he was no longer the libertine he had been before meeting Daina; the twins knew the carefree days of college were irretrievably over. They saw the holiday as the last hurrah of old times, before the grueling days and interminable nights of residency began.

Rob and Will were still with their college sweethearts: Rob's arrangement with Andrea remained informal: they were still *engaged to be engaged*, but as Ian had predicted, Marta was a social climber. She wasn't getting any younger, so she had demanded a ring and a five year plan from Will.

Andrea had been to Parker once or twice with Rob; it didn't hold many memories for her. But Rob and Will and Ian and Marta and Daina all thought briefly that while the little three-bedroom house on the water had not changed, their partners and alliances certainly had.

Nadine was somewhere in the wilds of Africa, as lost and incommunicado to Daina, her one-time best friend, and Rob, her one-time lover, as Livingstone was to the British Empire a century before. When the light was a certain way, or sometimes, if she would catch a glimpse of Andrea out of the corner of her eye, Daina would be startled by Rob's girlfriend's resemblance to Nadine. But she would not reminisce for long – her life was too full with her wonderful husband and her adorable baby to mourn Nadine's absence.

Rob was blithe; he lived in the moment, and memories of Nadine didn't cross his mind. Ian hadn't thought much about Nadine when she lived across the street from him; like Rob, she had not entered his thoughts once since she'd left the country.

Ian tolerated Marta, and made it a point to never find himself alone with her. Ian knew that Will didn't like to see them even speaking together, and although he didn't know it, Will had good reason to not want to come upon his fiancée *vis-à-vis* with his cousin. At the raucous, impromptu celebration that Rob had thrown on the night of Adrian's birth, while Daina was still in the hospital, Marta had consumed a mite too much champagne and had cornered Ian in a deserted hallway at the Wilde guest house and made a somewhat sloppy pass at him.

Ian had rather rudely turned her down: he'd laughed in her face. Marta had never made another attempt, and was thereafter aloof to him, except on the rare occasions when she was in her cups, and Ian would glance over to find her staring thoughtfully at him. He didn't think that anyone else noticed it, maybe not even Marta herself. But he remembered that look, remembered she'd adopted it whenever she'd referred to him as *her multi-talented whore.* So he made sure that the two of them were never alone together. Ian didn't want to have to fight Will over any kind of suspicion he might develop about something that was never, not in a thousand lifetimes, *ever* going to occur.

Daina was comfortable and easy-going around Will. She sometimes even kidded him about the way he was either silent and watchful or verbosely boring. Marta was a friendly person, so she was friendly to Daina, although she secretly thought of Ian's little woman as rather an unsophisticated rustic, devoid of the most rudimentary of social graces.

Marta knew that Will saw Daina in much the same light, so she felt no jealousy regarding her fiancé's brief history with Ian's wife, lo, these many years ago. If she entertained any envy at all for Daina, it was because the artless peasant had not only ensnared the one that Marta had let get away; she had also induced him to love her completely. So much so that Ian was not even amenable to a little, meaningless, I-won't-tell-if-you-won't quickie on a night when his wife wasn't even there. What a party-pooper he had become!

If Will ever caught his fiancée ogling his cousin, he just told himself that he was being paranoid, that he was imagining it. He despised *goddamned Ian* no more or no less than he always had, but he welcomed Daina's presence. In Will's mind, Daina kept Ian from looking at Marta, even if Daina didn't keep Marta from looking at Ian. Regardless, Daina being there definitely kept Marta from getting drunk and *touching* Ian, insisting that he dance with her, like she'd done the night his son was born. Will was grateful for that.

And Daina also kept Ian from launching *One Wilde Ride* upon the Colorado's hot waters and bringing back with him any extra girls that might prove a temptation to either of the soon-to-be orthopedic residents.

Will (and Rob, too) had frequently stepped out on Marta and Andrea in the early days of their relationships, but Ian had never cheated on Daina. From the moment that his cousin had thanked Will for dumping Daina – and threatened to shut him up if he ever said anything untoward about her again – unfailingly, unflaggingly unfaithful Ian had become the very epitome of loyalty. Rob had listened indulgently to his poetic paeans about his Juliet; Will had dismissed Ian's words as he always had, and instead had observed his actions. He was amazed when Ian did not so much as speak to, *did not so much as look at,* another girl since he'd met Daina.

So Will was glad that his ex-girlfriend was there. Lucky Cousin Ian didn't pick up pretty townies and tourists by the boatload anymore. And because he didn't, because of Daina, thereby, none of Ian's cast-offs wound up in Will's bed. Although he would be loath to admit it, that very thing had occurred more than once when they were in college.

And while Will was addicted to Marta and her incomparable mouth, she could be a stone-cold bitch sometimes . . . So, the fewer willing young ladies around, the better.

While the little house on the river was the same, the vacationers had grown up. No more wild, drunken, sleep-with-who-brung-ya-or-whomsoever-else-you-might-choose bacchanals. Rob and Will's runabout still sat six, but now there was an addition on Daina's lap in a little life-jacket, and they all went out together, as opposed to the Wilde boys trolling the river stag, to see what they could pick up.

Sissy still worked at her dad's ski shop. A perverse streak in Will made him insist that the court and their consorts (and one heir) stop in and pay the townie a visit, the moment they arrived in town, before they even went up to the house. Will wanted to witness the look on Sissy's face when she kenned Ian-in-love; he wanted to see Daina's reaction to the girl Rob had always referred to as *Cousin Ian's Parker Wife.*

To Will's surprise, Sissy had grown beautiful: Nadine would've noted that she had quite skillfully learned how to apply make-up. Will glanced quickly, guiltily at Marta to make sure that he hadn't allowed any ungoverned appreciation for the river rat to show on his face. If he had, Marta either hadn't noticed or didn't care.

Throughout their relationship, Marta had never failed to notice Will's froggy looks at other women, but she believed him too domesticated at this late date to even think about making a jump. She knew Will certainly wouldn't risk what they had for a go at this homespun desert townie, no matter how well she'd cleaned up.

Besides, Sissy had never cared overly for Will, anyway, and it was pitifully obvious to Marta that the girl had never stopped loving Ian. Sissy hid it a lot better than she had when she was sixteen, but it was still there, in the way her eyes grew big and round when she looked at him.

It occurred to Marta that Sissy was aware that maybe everyone could see her affection: to make herself cease staring at him, Sissy exclaimed over Adrian, snatching him unceremoniously from Daina and roughly tossing the surprised tot into the air. She gleefully asked Ian if he could ski yet.

"No, but he can already swim," Daina replied, glancing curiously at Ian. She had heard Rob's stories about the scrappy little high school girl who would stay out and ski all day with Ian, because she loved it as much as he did, and because she loved him most of all. And there was disapproving Dad right there, standing behind Sissy, still frowning at Ian. Daina was amused to see the discomfort that the girl's affection and her father's distrust still engendered in her husband. She and Rob shared a grin at Ian's expense.

After Daina spoke, Sissy blinked expressionlessly at her for a heartbeat. This was not some momentary pick-up of Ian's, who would be forgotten and replaced the next day by someone else, someone who had never been her. This was Ian's *wife,* the mother of his delightful little boy. Sissy was no longer a petulant child, and she accepted reality with genuine grace, far better than Nadine ever would.

Ian introduced his actual wife to the girl that his cousin had always termed his *Parker wife.*

"It's so nice to meet you!" Sissy said. She quickly handed Adrian to his dad and gave Daina a hug.

Rob smiled and hugged Sissy next, kissed her on the cheek. "Come skiing with us."

"I have to work," she replied, and Will immediately thought, *That's a lie, and an unadulterated one.* Marta would have agreed with him. Sissy didn't have to work if she didn't want to; her dad owned the store. Sissy didn't want to be around Ian and *his wife.*

"Barbeque tonight then," Rob said. "Watch the fireworks. Like the old days."

But the old days are gone forever, Will thought. *No more chasing Ian around the house, begging him to give her a little. No more gazing longingly at him while he skied all goddamned day. Not with his little family here.*

But to Will's surprise, Sissy said she'd be there, that she wouldn't miss it for the world.

Sissy had a little disclosure of her own for the Wilde boys when she arrived at the barbeque. Like Nadine, she hadn't carried a torch for Ian, forsaking all others for an impossible ideal. Sissy proudly introduced them all to her boyfriend, Jake, a young man of an age with her. It was obvious that they were quite fond of each other.

It came as a surprise to no one – least of all to Ian himself – that Jake had dark hair and blue eyes. Sissy had a type, just like Rob did. Her boyfriend bore more than a passing resemblance to a shaggy-haired, squinty-eyed water-skier upon whom she'd once had a hellacious crush.

EIGHTY-TWO

In the early afternoon of Sunday, July 8, 1973, Ian, Daina, and Adrian arrived back at their cozy little house; they were tired and glad to be home after the long drive. Daina stood in the driveway, carrying her sleeping son, and watched while Ian backed *One Wilde Ride* into the garage.

She reflected that before she'd met Ian, before Adrian had been born, she'd never imagined that such contentment could exist. Her boy was beautiful and clever, the very picture of a happy baby: he had not been a terrible two, just a playful, inquisitive toddler. There *had* been that one time, when he pulled Grimalkin's tail; but the ancient mama cat had just regarded him icily, flicked it out of his chubby hand, gave a little hiss, and ran off. Adrian had given his mommy a big, round-eyed look of amazement at his soft old friend's sudden coldness, and Daina had told him that cats didn't like to have their tails pulled. He had chased 'Malky down and apologized with a big squeeze; the cat had tolerated it. She had had feisty babies of her own.

And Ian – Ian's capacity for love never ceased to amaze Daina. He greeted his boy each day with joy and gratitude; he played with him, fed and bathed him, read him a bedtime story, sang him a lullaby. And after Adrian was down for the night, Ian never failed to show his affection for his wife as if it was their first night together, even after almost four years.

Through the windshield of his old truck, Ian saw his wife smiling at him. He smiled back, jumped out of the cab and quickly finished unhooking the boat. He would cover it up later, bring in their luggage, *later*. The baby had shared their bed with them in Parker, and thereby had their marital activities been curtailed. But Daina was smiling at him now – *O for a Muse of fire, that would ascend the brightest heaven of invention!* – Ian could never hope to put into words just what his wife's smile did to him.

He would swim the Hellespont, cross the burning sands of Egypt – he would do damn near anything for Daina's come-hither smile. Its subtle passion and unspoken promise invariably made him forget whatever else he might be doing at the moment and concentrate his entire attention upon her, as he had wanted to do from the first moment he saw her. But Herculean labors weren't necessary to get Daina to smile at him, to crook her finger, or nod her head toward somewhere where they could be alone: sometimes he just had to smile at her first.

There was a note from Aunt Bellona thumbtacked to the front door: *Come up as soon as you get home! We have a surprise!*

"Whatever it is, it can wait for a little while," Daina said as Ian unlocked the door. She handed Adrian to him and smiled again. Ian quickly deposited his still-sleeping son in the nursery and then joined his wife in their bedroom.

Adrian enjoyed a little nap, although his parents didn't sleep. When he awakened, the family walked up the path to be surprised. The trek took several minutes because Ian would stop and look at bugs and leaves and blades of grass with his son, marveling over them with him, and making sure he didn't try to eat any of them.

When they reached the top of the path, Ian pointed out a lizard on a tree trunk to Adrian. He then caught it, so the child could examine it up close. Daina went on the rest of the way to her aunts' house alone. She didn't like surprises in general, and throughout her life, she had always been a tiny bit fearful of any surprise that Penny and Bellona might have for her.

Daina slowly climbed the staircase to the deck. There was a gate at the top now, to keep Adrian from tumbling down the steps. Wooden lattice had also been installed between the deck and the top of the railing to corral him from falling over that way. Daina swung the spring-loaded gate open. Her aunts were sitting at the table, and a willowy, brown-haired young woman was standing with her back to Daina, by the railing. She was looking out at the trees, in the same place where Ian had been standing on that long ago All Hallow's Eve.

The girl turned, and Daina was amazed to see that it was Nadine, amazed at the changes that two years abroad had wrought in her. She looked thinner, older than her years. How old was Nadine now? Her birthday was in November – she was almost twenty-five. Even at a glance, Daina thought that Nadine seemed thoroughly worldly now, maybe even a little bit jaded.

Nadine smiled; Daina didn't fail to notice that her smile didn't quite reach her eyes. *Maybe she saw bad things in Africa,* Daina thought, as she ran across the short distance and enthusiastically hugged her oldest friend. Nadine allowed herself to be hugged, and returned Daina's long-lost-pals-reunited exuberance with a polite squeeze.

Daina took her hands, said, "I've missed you so much, 'Deen!" and hugged her again. It wasn't entirely true: Daina's life was full with her aunts and her husband and her son. But if she had given thought to anything that she was missing, it would've been her childhood buddy.

"I've missed you, too. All of you," Nadine replied, and it was, of course, a bald-faced lie. She hadn't missed any of them, not in the least. Her traitorous "best" friend and her interfering aunts? Nadine wouldn't miss them if they were all dead. She could not possibly care less about any of them.

Except, of course, for Ian. It had been her inescapable memories of Ian that had drawn her back home. That and a need to see a good ol' smoggy California sunset, and eat some good ol' American food and regain the health and vitality she had left behind in a Togo village.

"Where's Chuck?" Daina asked, mostly for something to say, as she found herself rather at a loss for words. Nadine's return was her aunts' surprise; she had not known what to expect, but it hadn't been this.

"Who?" Nadine chortled. "Ah, yes. Chuck. I'll tell you all about it later." She sighed. "For the moment, suffice it to say that Chuck and I didn't last too long, I'm afraid."

Nadine and Chuck hadn't lasted very long because within a week of touching down on the Dark Continent, Nadine had taken up with another volunteer, and when he traveled to another village, Nadine had gone with him, leaving a bewildered, angry, and possibly heartbroken Chuck behind without so much as an *It's been fun.*

Charlie was about the same age Ian had been the last time Nadine saw him. He was a photographer, like she was, and Chuck would later believe that this was what had initially attracted his worthless girlfriend to the guy. Nadine would learn a lot about photography from Charlie: he would show her how to hone her skills, teach her how to take care of her equipment in the steamy climate, teach her how to set-up a quick and dirty darkroom in the field. But it hadn't been the camera around his neck that had first attracted the new arrival to the more seasoned volunteer.

Charlie hailed from Nashville, Tennessee, and all the education in the world couldn't erase the hint of a southern twang from his voice. It was dark, mellifluous; Charlie called her *honey* and *darlin'* from the moment they met, and Nadine believed immediately that she could listen to Charlie talk forever. Not another person would ever have seen a resemblance between Ian and Charlie; he had sandy-colored hair, and brown-eyes. He was thin and spare; he wore glasses. He'd never waterskied in his life. But in Nadine's mind, he had Ian's voice, magnified in its excellence by that trace of an accent.

The first thing he said to her was, "Welcome to your home away from home, darlin'," and Nadine heard Ian.

Pretending that Chuck was Ian had grown stale; they were dissimilar in every way. But now she could hear Ian's voice. She wanted to hear Charlie whisper her name; she wanted to hear him call her *darlin'* in a more intimate manner than in just anonymous greeting. By this means, Nadine could imagine anew that she was with Ian.

Charlie was quite surprised when she slid in under the mosquito netting with him late one night, that first week. Chuck was quite surprised when Nadine packed her stuff and went up-river with him the next week.

Charlie and Nadine worked and loved and laughed and lived together for the entire two years of her stint with the Peace Corps. He was the only thing that made the sojourn tolerable to her. The living conditions were appalling, the food horrible, the dirt and the bugs and the climate dreadful. Nadine somehow managed not to contract malaria, but she did have bouts of stomach sicknesses and various fevers. She lost weight.

Throughout it all, Charlie's incomparable voice kept Ian's memory alive in Nadine's mind; she even taught him the words to Browning's *Sonnet 43*. Charlie discovered that counting the ways never failed to induce Nadine to show her appreciation.

When her two years concluded, Nadine promised that she would re-up and return to him. But it was doubtful. Nadine didn't love Charlie any more than she had loved Chuck, and she sincerely didn't love living like a native in Africa. And she missed home. She missed Ian.

Now Nadine heard a tread on the stair and knew it must be her soulmate. At last, after two years! How would he look? What would he say?

Ian looked exactly the same, muscular and squinty-eyed and beautiful. He was carrying Daina's ugly little brat. He opened the gate and set the kid down; the pint-sized monkey ran to his mother.

Ian smiled at Nadine and her heart stopped, as it always would, whenever he smiled at her. He said, *"Soft you now! The fair*

276

Ophelia! Nymph, in thy orisons be all my sins remember'd." He crossed the deck and gently enfolded her in his arms.

All the memories rushed back on Nadine with Ian's scent: how much she had always loved him, pined for him! How he had been so cruelly deceived by these evil witches, snatched from his true destiny, *stolen from her!* She squeezed him for an impossibly short moment, just to feel his body against hers again, like when they'd danced together, so long ago. Nadine didn't care if it was inappropriate, if it was too intimate. She pretended that she didn't feel Ian stiffen and try to back out of her clinging clinch.

It's not your *sins I remember, my darling. It's theirs. You were duped. It's their sins that I'll punish someday.* She squeezed him for another heartbeat, then released him.

Daina was holding her son's hand. Round-eyed and solemn, the boy stared fixedly at Nadine. Here was a stranger, and he didn't know what to make of her.

"You remember Adrian, Nadine?" At the sound of his name, the toddler looked up at his mother questioningly. She dropped down to her knees beside him and gave him a reassuring hug. "This is your Aunt Nadine, Adrian. Say hello to her."

Adrian noted the smile on his mother's face; he looked at his dad and his aunts. They were all smiling at him. This stranger must be okay. He toddled over to her. "AnTeen!"

Nadine looked down at the homely little creature. He was holding his arms out to her. She realized after a moment that he wanted her to pick him up. *Well, people in Hell want ice water . . .* But from the expressions on everyone's faces, Nadine understood that they all expected her to pick him up, that they believed that she should *want* to pick him up. The idea couldn't have been further from her mind, but since it was apparently the thing to do, the thing that was done, just picking up strange children because they demanded it, she did it.

She said, "Hello, Adrian. You look just like your mommy." But he still had his father's dark blue eyes, and his hair was straight and shaggy like Ian's, even if it was black like his mother's.

"AnTeen!" he said again, and threw his germy little arms around her neck, pressed his face against hers. Nadine felt as if Daina's son hugged her for a millennia; she felt uncomfortable, unsure of exactly what to do. Dropping him, *flinging* him away, occurred to her. But she knew that was just not done.

At last, the baby abruptly let go of Nadine's neck, then turned and looked to his mother again. Nadine felt that she might never have been more grateful for anything in her life than when Daina removed her loathsome offspring from her arms.

Daina set Adrian down and he ran off across the deck after Holt, the white tomcat, who waited until the boy was almost upon him before scampering up on the railing out of reach.

Ian and Daina and Nadine sat on the bench. It annoyed Nadine to note that they immediately held hands like high school kids. Penny and Bellona sat across the table from them, and Nadine was struck with how the scene was almost identical to that Hallowe'en so long ago. She wondered fleetingly if Ian still had that gladiator get-up, and she was wounded anew by how she had been betrayed by all the women present, these sisters and their niece. The starkness of their treachery had fogged over somewhat in Nadine's mind whilst she'd been away, but here it was again, as plain as black and white. If the purpose of the universe had not been thwarted by their machinations, then she would be sitting here holding hands with Ian, and Adrian would be her son.

Adrian climbed up on the end of the bench, then clambered uninvited into Nadine's lap. "See my ducky, AnTeen," he said, and presented her with a slightly grimy rubber ducky. "You can have him."

Again, Nadine felt all their eyes upon her, as if this was some kind of test she had to pass. "Thank you, Adrian." She took the toy and set it on the table in front of her.

"Squeeze him, AnTeen," Adrian instructed. "He squeaks."

Nadine squeezed the ducky, and he did indeed squeak. She waited for the child to climb back down from her lap now – she dearly wanted for that to happen – but Adrian was perfectly happy where he was. He picked up the ducky and squeezed him so that he squeaked close to Nadine's ear, then the boy giggled. Nadine was appalled. When was Daina going to remove this thing from her again?

But Adrian was like one of those house cats that always settles in the lap of the one guest that loathes cats. For no reason that Nadine could fathom, Daina's little boy had imprinted on her. She was his new best friend.

They chatted for a while. Ian told Nadine about his teaching job; she told them upbeat, generic stories about the Peace Corps. Penny and Bellona were mostly silent and watchful, as was the boy, who never left Nadine's lap. Eventually, the conversation faltered. These people realized that they had become strangers. If they were ever to become friends, become family again, they would have to talk about new things, current events; even the future. The two years that separated the past they had once shared from today was a yawning gap.

Nadine said that she should go back down the hill and see her parents. Her arrival was indeed a surprise: apparently she hadn't told anyone that she was coming home. They all trooped down the deck steps to see her on her way up the path. Ian carried Adrian, then set him down at the foot of the stairs. He immediately hugged Nadine around the legs for a quick moment, then scooted away, as if he would run up the path. The adults followed after him several paces, then he came back, and loitered behind his mother, looking up at the grown-ups.

Bellona attempted to make conversation again, with an utterly non-sequitur remark about horseracing. "Lily won a hundred and fifty dollars last month," she concluded.

"On a horserace?" Daina said.

Bellona nodded. "The horse is called Secretariat. Lily said he won all three of the big races – something that hadn't been done for a long time. And she had a tip from a reliable source . . ."

Nadine thought she might fall asleep standing up from boredom. Where did Bellona come up with this stuff? Why did she think anyone wanted to talk about racehorses? To keep herself awake, Nadine observed Adrian. He was climbing back up the deck steps, by sitting on one riser and then rolling himself over into a crouch and then pulling himself up onto the next one. Again Nadine marveled how like a little chimpanzee he was.

Daina said, "I never would've pegged Aunt Lily as someone who would play the ponies."

Ian nodded. "Me, either."

He had met the proprietress of Mohini's House of Magic not long after his wedding, when he and his new bride had dropped off an order of candles. Daina had noticed that the green-eyed witch had smiled admiringly at her new husband, looked him up and down for a long moment. Later, when he was out of earshot, Aunt Lily had been quite congratulatory. "Good job, my child! He's stunning."

Daina had said thanks. Aunt Lily's acknowledgment of Ian's looks didn't come as a surprise to her, because she had grown up listening to all her aunts' appreciative comments about attractive men. They had taught Daina that men were here for her pleasure, hadn't they? And none of them had ever been even remotely as pleasurable to her as Ian.

"Lily's from the South," Penny was saying. "They appreciate good horseflesh there. And she's always been a gambler."

"You forget that little old ladies had lives, pasts, *histories,* before we became little old ladies," Bellona said and winked at Ian.

"Duly noted, Miss Bellona," he replied and Nadine was amazed by how he could still remain charming in the face of the old biddy's senseless prattling, even after all these years. Horseracing, yet! "I think that –"

"Look at me, AnTeen!" Adrian called. He had made it up four steps, and turned to call attention to his feat. He tottered on the edge of the riser.

"Adrian!" Daina took a step towards her son. *"Hold on to the banister!"*

But the littlest Wilde was too little. Still smiling, not looking where he reached, he leaned over to do as he was told, to grab onto the hand rail that was a good five inches out of his grasp. He promptly fell off the side of the staircase.

Daina shrieked and closed the distance between them. Adrian was already sitting up on the ground, his mouth forming a silent *O* while he gathered the breath to wail in pain and surprise. As his mother scooped him up, he let the cry loose.

"Oh, my God, Adrian!" Daina screamed as if he had fallen from the top of the stairs, as if he had bloody gashes and broken bones. Nadine gaped at her overreaction.

Adrian had a little scuff on his forehead, above his right eye; it couldn't even be called an abrasion. Yet Daina was behaving as if he was dying. She clutched him to her. His mother's panicked reaction made the boy cry harder: if Mom was freaking out like this, there must be something seriously amiss. Daina was scaring him far worse than had the fall and the little bump on his head.

Ian almost had to pry him away from her. "Let me see him, Daina!" She relinquished her death-grip on the child, and once in his father's calm arms, Adrian stopped crying almost immediately. "Are you okay, buddy?"

"I fall down, Daddy," Adrian said.

Ian ruffled the hair from his brow and looked at the faint scrape. "Does your head hurt, son?"

"No, Daddy." The fall, as well as the tears, still wet on his cheeks, were already forgotten. "Where's my ducky?"

"Let's go get him," Penny said, and took the boy from his father. "I'll take a look at his head."

"He's fine," Ian said.

Penny nodded, and whisked Adrian up the stairs. She moved with surprising speed for a woman of her years, indeterminate though they might be, Nadine noted. She thought that Penny hurried not so much out of fear for the little monkey's injury – it was truly only a scratch – but to get him away from his hysterical mother.

Ian turned his attention to his wife, who still sobbed uncontrollably in Bellona's arms. "Daina, baby, he's all right!" She threw herself at him, seized him as tightly as she had Adrian. Ian looked over his shoulder at Bellona in confusion, then back at Daina. "Honey, what's wrong?"

"It's the prophecy, Ian," Bellona said softly. "Daina, child!" She laid a gentle hand on her niece's back. "It's not now! Adrian is fine! He has *years* –"

"What are you talking about?" Ian asked. Nadine wondered the same thing.

"Adrian's gonna die!" Daina wailed. Wild-eyed, she looked at her aunt. "That's what it is, isn't it? *The tragic blot?* My baby's gonna die!"

"What are you talking about?" Ian repeated, mystified. Nadine stood by in silence. It was as if they'd forgotten that she was there, as if she had become invisible.

"Everybody has to die, Daina." Penny, also unnoticed, had descended the stairs, carrying Adrian. She set him down, and he ran over to his mother, who snatched him up once more, as if she'd thought that she would never set eyes on him again.

"Look, Mommy," he said. "Ducky." He squeezed it so it squeaked.

"I see, baby," Daina replied, and laughed shakily. She realized that Adrian was unhurt.

Whatever this dire prediction is, Nadine thought, *this* tragic blot, *she recognizes that it's not going to come to pass today. I wonder what's been foretold?*

And now a word, in uncouth rhyme, of what shall be in future time . . .

Nadine looked at Ian. *Get to the bottom of this, Daddy. Your lady-wife can't be having conniptions every time her clumsy kid takes a little tumble.*

"Adrian just wanted to show Mommy that he's okay," Penny continued. "Now I bet he'd like a cookie." Her normally dour expression fled, replaced by the sweetest grandmotherly smile Nadine had ever seen. She blinked in amazement at the change. "Do you want a cookie, Capo?"

Adrian nodded, then looked at his mother, touched the tears on her face. "Don't cry, Mommy. I just fell down."

The tears threatened again, so Daina just nodded. She handed the three-year-old to Bellona this time, and she carried him back up the stairs to get his cookie.

Ian looked to Penny for explanation. Her serious expression returned, and she sighed. "When Daina was a little girl, it was prophesied that she would find that one true love, the kind for which all women long. And this love would endure." Penny smiled faintly.

Understanding dawned in Nadine's mind at that moment, as clear as a spring sunrise. She had never heard of a prophecy concerning an everlasting love for Daina, but if they had seen such a thing for their niece . . .

That's why you and Bellona had to steal my *true love, the one fated for* me! *It all makes sense now. You stole Ian for Daina to fulfill your own prophecy! And she just naturally went along with it!*

Penny sighed again, and her smile faded. "But it was also foretold that her son, the product of this great love – *your son*, Ian – would suffer tragedy."

All the pieces slid into place; there was a resounding clang in Nadine's mind, like the stereotypical prison door. Daina had never been one for trying to make her relationships last, because she had always been a coward, had always been afraid of this looming misfortune.

Ian still held his wife, and she whispered, "Adrian's gonna die," against his chest.

"We all have to die," Penny repeated.

"But that's what it is, isn't it?" Daina said. "The tragic blot? It's death, isn't it?"

Penny shrugged. *"Most likely."*

This simple admission struck Nadine as an unspeakable cruelty. She flinched as if she'd been back-handed.

"Adrian is not fated for a long life. And yet . . ." Penny trailed off, sighed again. *"Cannot predict now. He's exceptional."*

"Of course," Ian said with a smile.

Penny flashed a smile back. "I mean, besides just because he's your son. How exceptional he is remains to be seen; he's only a baby. He may not live for very long, but he *will live*. Just like we've told you, Daina, whatever his tragedy will be – it's not from a slip down the steps when he's three."

"When?" Ian said softly.

You always believe them, Nadine said silently to him. *When they told you that you were at a crossroads, that you had a choice between us, you just let them pick for you. It was all a joke to you then. They pointed you toward her, and why wouldn't you choose the whore that just immediately gave it all to you, the second you met? If you had listened to fate with your heart, instead listening to the old beldames' words and Daina's sluttiness, then you would've seen that I was the correct choice.*

Again you choose to believe what they tell you, but it's not funny anymore, is it, Ian? Now you hear the relentless footsteps. Would you had listened earlier, you would not be doomed now.

Nadine considered Daina and her aunts and thought self-righteously, *It seems that what goes around comes around, does it not? Your boy is condemned? That's what happens when you thwart fate's true path.*

Nadine smiled to herself as another idea struck her. Perhaps these witches of her unfortunate acquaintance weren't the only ones that could guide fate. *Come, you spirits that tend on mortal thoughts . . . You murdering ministers, wherever in your sightless substances you wait on nature's mischief! Perhaps I can have a hand in the boy's undoing!*

Penny said, "Does anyone know when they're going to die?"

Ian hugged his wife closer to him. "Apparently you do."

"The prediction always comes out the same. He will live past his majority. Whether that's eighteen, twenty-one, twenty-five, thirty . . . Regardless, there's no reason to get hysterical every time he takes a spill, Daina. Like I told you, he has decades. Any of us would be grateful to be as fortunate as Adrian Wilde will be."

"Listen to your aunt, baby," Ian said gently to Daina.

You always do, don't you, Ian? Nadine thought, hating him just a little bit.

"If something's going to happen to Adrian . . . Hell, something can happen to anybody's kid, Daina. You're gonna drive yourself crazy if you dwell on it now. When it's time to get his driver's license, maybe your aunts can . . .?"

"Scry," Penny supplied.

"Maybe they can read his future again then. For now . . . Just let it go, Daina." She nodded against Ian's chest, put her arms around his neck, soaked up his comfort.

Sick of the connubial bliss – she hadn't traveled halfway around the globe to come back and witness this all over again – Nadine spoke up. "I'm sure everything will be fine." The happy couple (though not so happy at the moment) looked at her as if seeing her for the first time. They *had* forgotten that she was there. "I'm going to go see my mom and dad. I'll call you later, Daina."

EIGHTY-THREE

Nadine moved back in with her parents; they were delighted to have her. Sam had never been quite sure about the Peace Corps – he always believed that there was too much of a hippie element to it for it to be in any way beneficial to his daughter. But she had wanted to see the world. Irene was just glad to have her baby back home.

Nadine knew that she wouldn't stay forever. She just needed to rest for a while, to feel healthy and American again. She wanted to look at Ian; she wanted to watch him, listen to him, love him in her mind, as she had from the first moment that she'd heard his voice.

She also was curious about this dire prophecy that had been saddled upon Daina and her son. While Penny had reassured Adrian's parents that he would reach his majority, Nadine wondered vaguely if the seeds of his doom could somehow be planted now. She didn't actively seek out methods by which to harm the child; she didn't really consciously think of *hurting* him. But she did ponder what kind of outside influences might be brought to bear – not by *herself*, of course – that might shorten his life. It was really just an intellectual exercise on her part.

Penny had said that Adrian was, *would be*, exceptional. Nadine couldn't see it: he seemed like any other snot-nosed brat to her. She had a hard time fathoming how anyone made it to adulthood – Adrian, at three years old, had to be watched constantly, lest he wander out into the middle of the street and get run over, lest he decide to sample the cat's food, lest he fall down the steps. Were all children so self-destructive?

Nadine pretended to enjoy Daina's son; she volunteered to babysit whenever Penny and Bellona were unavailable. This wasn't very often: the old crows doted on Adrian. They called him *Capo Dei Capi*, or just *Capo* for short. It was a Mafioso term meaning *the boss of all bosses*. Although they claimed to be *children of the world*, Nadine had always suspected that her aunts were simply of run-of-the-mill Italian extraction, and this ridiculous nickname for Daina's offspring proved it to her.

But sometimes Ian would be busy grading papers, and Daina would need to dash to the store for something, and instead of running Adrian up the hill to her aunts, Daina would just drop him across the street with Nadine. Adrian was always glad to see his *AnTeen,* and Nadine pretended to be glad to see him. Her affection was a façade. Nadine hated Daina, and she saw Adrian perennially as *Daina's child,* something, someone who was precious only to Daina. Adrian was her enemy's vulnerability.

The day that Nadine had discovered that Ian had chosen the wrong woman, the day he had been concerned when he'd heard her surprised shriek at the cat, the day she had inadvertently interrupted their first lovemaking session: Nadine had vowed on that day that she would make Daina understand the supreme agony that she'd felt, the utter devastation of the loss of someone she loved. And Nadine had renewed the vow to herself on their wedding day. Daina would someday stand before a mirror and sob at the loss of the future, over a *to be* that would henceforth *not be.* Nadine would see to it.

She had long considered cobbling together a curse to cast upon Daina. Nadine had considered it from the first moment when she realized that the three witches had colluded to steal Ian from her. She had studied evil spells, both foreign and domestic, but could never quite decide on an apt form for her justice to take. Should she attempt to mar Daina's beauty? Should she render Ian impotent, and therefore kill the only thing that truly mattered between them?

That was out of the question. Ian was her soulmate. Nadine could never harm him, never, not in the slightest. He was innocent, as much a victim as she was.

After hearing the tale of her aunts' divination, Nadine forgot all about concocting curses. It was unnecessary. Daina was already cursed; her loss had been foretold: the *tragic blot* in her life concerned Adrian. The eternal powers would exact Nadine's revenge *for* her, without her assistance. Daina had stolen Ian from Nadine, and for that she would pay with her son's life. No jinx from Nadine was needed to precipitate Adrian's doom. Nadine would just have to sit back and watch fate take its course.

Adrian would bring sorrow to his mother, later if not sooner, and all that was just fine with Nadine.

Also by LM Foster

A Passing Resemblance
Contrariwise – A Tale of Twins
Corvino
Crypsis
Duck Feet
Peter's Sisters

Two Green Keys:
Two Green Keys
Adapted for the Screen

One Wilde Ride Trilogy:
Part One: It Might Have Been
Part Two: An Exceptional Boy
Part Three: What Should Never Be

Stars and Guitars:
Talk To a Movie Star
Where The Guitars Play

Tom and Wiley:
This Carnival of Strange
Wiley Royce
Generally Recognized as Safe
Wiley Royce Versus The Martians